PRAISE FOR THE BEAST HUNTERS SERIES

"*Beast Hunter* sweeps you up in a rousing tale that twists the fairy tale world on its head. Quick to read, but sticks with you and makes you eager for more."

—H.L. Burke, award-winning and bestselling author of over twenty eclectic fantasy novels

"Clever and fresh, with a compelling, relatable heroine, *Beast Hunter* is a fitting prequel to the Beauty and the Beast story, *Kill the Beast*. A potent little novella that will leave you eager for more!"

—Janeen Ippolito, author of the Star-Crossed Fairy Tales, including the award-winning Cinderella retelling *Met By Midnight*

"*Beast Hunter* is an absolute must-read for those who love twisted fairy tales with strong female leads. Family drama, mystery, shadowy characters, and a heroine you can't help but root for, what's not to love? I was hooked immediately and now can't wait for the rest of Ro's story to unfold."

—Dawn Ford, award-winning fantasy author

THE LOST SLIPPER:

"*The Lost Slipper* is a retelling of two fairy tales that could have easily been enough to carry the story on their own, but the addition of 'Diamonds and Toads' to the Cinderella narrative brilliantly escalates the tension and increases our poor heroine's suffering. A thrilling, emotional tale for anyone who ever thought, 'Cinderella had it too easy.'"
   —C.O. Bonham, author of *Runaway Lyrics*

"*The Lost Slipper* is a short but satisfying read about grace and kindness when beset with cruelty, creatively combining two beloved fairy tales into a new, complex fable."
   —H.L. Burke, award-winning and bestselling author of over twenty eclectic fantasy novels

"As someone who enjoys every Cinderella iteration I've ever come across, *The Lost Slipper* blends my favorite familiar elements of the story with unique twists—such as who the Fairy Godmother really is and the behavior of the stepsisters. With allusions that bring to mind *Ever After*, *Ella Enchanted*, and *Into the Woods*, readers will enjoy how Harper weaves this story and will be left wanting more!"
   —Alicia Grumley, poet, Cinderella aficionado, and cohostess of Diversity Is Lit Book Club

KILL THE BEAST:

"A wonderfully complex, beautiful retelling of the classic story *Beauty and the Beast*. Better than Disney!"
—Anna Tan, author of *Amok*, *Coexist*, and *Dongeng*

"Michele wrote an amazingly flawed beauty. Rosette is angry and hot tempered and believes rumors and judges the beast on his fierceness. I can relate to a beauty who makes mistakes and who isn't some unattainable example of what women should be. And yes, she still likes books. Finally, a retelling of *Beauty and the Beast* that makes me feel for both Beast and Beauty."
—C.O. Bonham, author of *Runaway Lyrics*

"An enjoyable retelling of the ORIGINAL *Beauty and the Beast*! Forget Disney—this is French inspired with delicious food, disappearing castles, and fairies. The lead character is tough, feisty, and not your traditional beauty. I stayed up (too late) reading this one. If you like fairy tale retellings, check out *Kill the Beast*!"
—J.M. Hackman, award-winning author of the Firebrand Chronicles

"The premise immediately captured my attention, and the story did not disappoint! Who wouldn't be intrigued by the idea of Red Riding Hood hired to hunt and kill the beast from *Beauty and the Beast*? The setting is so vivid that I felt like I was walking through the dilapidated castle and grounds alongside Ro. If you enjoy retelling mashups, you won't want to miss *Kill the Beast* and the rest of the series!"
—Savannah J. Goins, author of *Whisper of Weapons*

SILENCE THE SIREN:

"Ro is back, and I am here for it. Battered from her previous adventures, she launches headfirst into a new one full of excitement, betrayal, and numerous twists. I absolutely loved the tie-ins from various fairy tales and Harper's unique spins on classic stories. If you want a story full of blooming romance, friendship, and sacrificial love, you'll want to dive head-first into this book."

—Hope Bolinger, author of the Blaze trilogy and the Dear Hero duology

Silence the Siren is a fresh take on a classic fairy tale that I did not see coming! Michele Israel Harper weaves a wildly creative tale that will have your heart beating fast with excitement one moment and then breaking the next. Ro is the heroine we've all been waiting for. You'll be rooting for her as she takes on man and sea in this odyssey-esque adventure. Can't wait to see what Harper does with the rest of the series!"

—Julie Hall, USA Today Bestselling author of the multiple award-winning Life After series

"*Silence the Siren* takes readers on a high seas adventure that sets personalities from all over the fairy tale spectrum on a crash course with peril and betrayal. Michele Israel Harper offers a delightful cast of characters who struggle with complex emotions, tight dilemmas, the very real frustrations of their own limitations. The story's deft weaving of resonant retelling and original twists will keep readers enthralled to the last page."

—Rebecca P. Minor, fantasy author, artist, and Realm Makers founder

"*Silence the Siren* does not fall into the fairy tale trap of simple good and evil, but features a protagonist who insists there are two sides to a story—and then is frustrated when neither is as honorable and noble as pretended. Perseverance and honesty are as important as strength and ferocity (although we get those, too!). And it's all in a fascinating world where multiple fairy tales mingle and tangle."

—Laura VanArendonk Baugh, award-winning author of *The Songweaver's Vow* and the Shard of Elan series

"Michele Israel Harper continues her unique spin on fairy tales well-loved. While the Huntress dives into waters unknown, there is enough familiar and new to keep readers invested in this intricate and expanding world that feels almost as real as our own history."

—Derrick Elchers, author of *The Battle for Art*

"Michele Harper creates a marvelous world in *Silence the Siren*, where French fairy tales are spun into something new, their golden story-threads woven into lavish, compelling tapestries. From pirates to princesses to sirens, things are never quite what they seem. Enemies become friends and vice versa, magic turns up in the most unexpected places, and the promise of true love hovers on the horizon."

—Merrie Destefano, award-winning author of *Shade: The Complete Trilogy*

QUELL THE NIGHTINGALE:

"Such a fun fairy tale mash-up! I loved seeing all the unexpected connections and characters. There are also deeper themes woven into the story—silence, secrets, and stuffing your feelings only gives pain more power. *Quell the Nightingale* is definitely an adventure worth taking!"
     —C.E. White, author of *Vincent in Wonderland*

"Prepare to be enchanted by this tale of a fiery huntress much better at facing magic beasts and evil spells than romance! Swoony heroes, a grouchy granny, and fun-loving family will warm your heart and keep you smiling. Ro's quest through dark forests and fairy tale kingdoms will have you turning page after page!"
     —Savannah J. Goins, author of *Whisper of Weapons*

"The fairy tale medley I didn't know I needed! *Quell the Nightingale* introduces beloved characters at every corner in a new and fresh way. It balances high stakes and romance with a quirky and humorous—but strong—female lead at the helm. It's a tale that will keep you guessing until the satisfying end."
     —E. A. Hendryx, author of the Xerus Galaxy Saga

ALSO BY MICHELE ISRAEL HARPER

Beast Hunters Series:

Beast Hunter: A Prequel Novella

The Lost Slipper: Cosette's Story

Kill the Beast

Silence the Siren

Quell the Nightingale

Slay the Wolf

(Coming Soon)

Stop the Snow Queen

End the Fey

Restore the Realm

Candace Marshall Chronicles:

Ghostly Vendetta

Zombie Takeover

Vampire Feud

(Coming Soon)

Mummy Resurrection

Standalones:

Wisdom & Folly Sisters:

Part One

Part Two

Wisdom & Folly Sisters:

The Complete Story

Slay the Wolf

BOOKS COMING SOON FROM
MICHELE ISRAEL HARPER

Elvish Duology:

The Elvish Queen

The Mortal King

Standalones:

Queen of the Moon

Dreamworld

Stars Collide

The Ravens

Altered Time Saga:

The Lady Bodyguard

The Lady Spy

The Lady Assassin

Altered Time Novellas:

Lady in Hiding

Making of a Lady

Lady Out of Time

Tales of the Cousin Kingdoms:

Ruby Dragon Kingdom

Diamond Unicorn Kingdom

Sapphire Griffin Kingdom

Emerald Pegasus Kingdom

Time of the Dragons

Slay the Wolf

Book Four of the Beast Hunters

Michele Israel Harper

Love2ReadLove2Write Publishing, LLC
Indianapolis, Indiana

Copyright © 2025 Michele Israel Harper

Published by Love2ReadLove2Write Publishing, LLC

Indianapolis, Indiana

www.love2readlove2writepublishing.com

ISBN: 978-1-943788-81-1 (Ebook)

ISBN: 978-1-943788-79-8 (Paperback)

ISBN: 978-1-943788-80-4 (Hardback)

LCCN: 2024949989

Library of Congress Cataloging-in-Publication Data is on file at the Library of Congress, Washington, DC.

Quotes from all fairy tales are in the public domain and manually translated from English into French by Michele Israel Harper.

This is a work of fiction. Names, characters, incidents, and dialogues are products of the author's imagination and are not to be construed as real. Any resemblance to actual events or persons, living or dead, is entirely coincidental.

Hardcover and character art "Snow White" and "Pirate Captain Rose Red" by Laura Hollingsworth

Character art "Ro and Olt," "Ro and Wolf Pup," and "Ro and Olt and Kip" by Jenelle Hovde

Paperback cover design by Sara Helwe (www.sara-helwe.com)

To Jasmine,

*Who loves Ro and Olt as much as I do.
Thank you for squealing in excitement
with me over these characters!*

To Jenelle,

*For the loveliest art in the entire world.
Thank you for bringing Ro and Olt to life!*

PART I

"Little Red Cap"
Le Petit Chaperon Rouge
—Jacob Grimm and Wilhelm Grimm—

The wolf thought to himself: "What a tender young creature!
What a nice plump mouthful—she will be better to eat than
the old woman. I must act craftily, to catch both."

Le loup se pensa : « Quelle tendre jeune créature ! Quelle belle
bouchée bien dodue ! Elle sera meilleure à manger que la
vieille femme. Je dois me montrer rusé pour les attraper
toutes les deux. »

1

Ro stared into the full-length oval mirror, stunned by what she saw.

The baby-blue dress, the height of fashion, made her eyes look like chips of ice. Hard, cold, cruel chips of ice. That belonged to a frost queen ready to slay everyone in sight.

Her décolletage was in danger of unseating itself from the high shelf it had been placed upon, jutting at an unnatural angle. She hadn't even been aware she had this much . . . well, there was just *so much*. In plain view of others. As it should not be.

Stays dug into her ribs so that she couldn't take a full breath. Her dress was so tight it itched. And there was so much material! How could she move through the ballroom for an entire evening like this?

Not to mention, her masquerade masque had enough feathers sticking out of it to either make her sneeze all night, or to make anyone who stood too close join her in her misery. It was monstrous. Heavy. She could barely see out of it.

She quickly put it back on its stand and tried not to look at it.

Knowing her, she'd spend the full evening tripping in

her uncomfortable heeled shoes, shoving her unmention-ables in strangers' faces from her towering height, and sending everyone in her vicinity into sneezing fits when she dared glance down at herself yet again to ensure she was decent.

She couldn't go downstairs like *this*.

Someone made a strangled noise, and Ro thought it was her until she glanced up to find Cosette staring at her reflection in horror.

"Oh. Oh my *chère*."

"I *know*," wailed Ro in the most un-huntress-like manner ever.

The queen of France covered her mouth and came closer, and Ro blinked against tears . . . until she noticed her sister was covering a smile.

Her head whipped around with a LeFèvre-worthy scowl. "It's not funny!"

Cosette smothered a laugh. "Of course not, dear. I told the seamstress to make it in the latest fashion, but I had *no idea*. Shall I — ?"

Ro tried to cross her arms, but the tight material across her shoulders wouldn't let her. She settled for propping her fists on her hips. "I refuse to go to my own party like this." She raised hopeful eyes to Cosette's. "Perhaps I can stay here? Read a book instead?"

"And not attend the ball that I, your favorite and most beloved sister, am throwing in your honor? For waking my very own daughter from a sleeping curse? So all the realm can celebrate you?" Cosette's eyebrows lifted higher with every word, and Ro couldn't tell if she was mock-offended or truly offended.

Ro sighed and turned back to the mirror. Cosette hadn't let her forget any of those details for even a moment, no matter how many times Ro had protested she didn't need a ball. She loved to dance, oui, but there would be others present, and she avoided other people as much as humanly possible.

"But, well, look at it, Cosette. I can barely walk, let alone breathe. It's awful."

And Ro was close to tears again. Over a stupid dress. She sniffled and hated herself for it.

A radiant smile shone on Cosette's face. "Then let me fix it for you."

Ro groaned. "It's already too much dress and not enough hunting leathers."

Cosette firmly said, "Let me do this for you," and began adjusting the material, remaking Ro's dress. While she was wearing it.

First, the color bled from ice blue to the deepest, loveliest red, just a shade darker than the cloak Ro wore on her hunts. The color set off her crème complexion and deep-brown hair to perfection. Then her shoes went soft and flat, cushioning her toes instead of pinching them.

Now she wouldn't feel like a giant looming over the other guests.

The fit of the dress relaxed until Ro could move freely, and she twisted and bent and touched her toes to make sure she could fight if called upon. Also to peek at the lovely dance shoes she now wore, more ballet slippers than the currently fashionable low-heeled dance shoes. And in the same rose-red shade of her dress, too.

She straightened to find Cosette piercing her with a cool stare.

"Oh." Ro fiddled with her thumbs. "Je suis désolé. I am sorry. For moving."

Cosette accepted her apology with a regal nod and returned to her task.

Ro stared into the mirror as the dress changed around her figure. The fabric went from scratchy to soft, her stays melted away—praise Dieu—and instead of stiff, wide material that stuck out on either side of her like a cheese wedge, now the dress fell in soft waves all around her. Almost like rose petals.

"Oh, Cosette," she breathed. "It's absolutely beautiful. I love it. Merci. Merci beaucoup."

Cosette flicked her fingers dismissively. "De rien. It is nothing."

Ro shook her head. "Non, it is not nothing. It is magnifique. Mon Dieu, it's amazing that you can do such things!"

Cosette had had far too much fun honing the fairy powers inherited from her mother, the Queen of the Fairies, though she tried not to use them often, or in others' company.

Again, Cosette was dismissive. "It's just silly things, like clothes or hair or shoes."

"But you just . . ."

"It's of no consequence."

"Non," said Ro fiercely. "Do not do that. Do not trivialize it."

Cosette turned to her with a frown.

Ro softened her expression, trying to wrangle her feelings into words. "You love it. You've always loved such things. How you look. Helping others look their best."

Her sister shrugged. "It's nothing like freeing the people of France and Prussia and Angleterre of their pesky curses."

"Arrête. Stop. I will not allow you to speak of my sister that way." At Cosette's startled look, Ro smiled. "You love fashion. You're good at it. There's no shame in either of those things."

Cosette suddenly blinked back tears, then crushed Ro in a hug. "Merci," she whispered.

Then she pulled back, regained her composure with a sniff, and smoothed Ro's dress. Added some embellishments. Curled Ro's straight hair over one shoulder in a gentle wave.

Finally satisfied, Cosette kissed Ro's cheek and turned her to face the mirror. "There you are, dearest."

Ro's mouth fell open. It was even lovelier, the fabric silky and smooth and shining in a subtle sheen, red crystals now edging her bodice and each unfurling rose petal of the skirt. She'd never seen anything like it.

Simply put, Cosette had outdone herself. Ro actually liked the dress. And once Olt saw it . . .

Ro's cheeks burned as she thought of stolen kisses and of how much she *knew* Olt would like this dress.

And now she had a whole new set of concerns.

She couldn't go downstairs looking like *that*. What would Olt say? He'd probably turn all mushy and do something ridiculous like propose.

Ugh. Non, thank you. They were nowhere near that stage of their relationship.

Worse, what would Liam do? Probably corner her in some remote region of the palace and try to convince her all over again they were meant to be together. Not that he was speaking to her right now, not after she'd rejected him.

Again, non, merci.

On second thought, she'd changed her mind.

Ro started shaking her head as panic suffused her. "Never mind. I can't wear this. Choose another. Right now. I am not walking in there looking like this, this . . ."

"Vision? Loveliness? Beauty?" Cosette beamed at Ro's reflection.

"Ugh! Exactly!" Ro threw her hands into the air. "I am none of those things. Help me out of this gown this instant! I'll wear something more . . . sensible."

She caught another glimpse of herself in the mirror, and her traitorous self felt a pang at the thought of taking off the dress. Maybe just this once . . .

Non, non, non. She would not, *could* not, go down looking like this.

Her heart fluttered like a falcon trying to escape its

handler. She'd be the center of attention in an instant! It would be an absolute nightmare, her worst nightmare —

Her eyes slid down the silken bodice and traced the curve of material that enhanced her figure to something magnificent. Her hunting leathers were designed to be comfortable, useful. To protect her from the elements, from a rogue blade. They weren't crafted to enhance her . . . she glanced down . . . feminine aspects.

She tugged at the heart-shaped bodice, trying to get it to cover a little more. What had been perfection only moments before now made her sweat with nerves.

Glancing over her shoulder, Ro presented her back to her sister. "Help me out of this, s'il vous plaît."

Cosette tapped her chin. "Hmm, I wouldn't even begin to know how. Getting out of a peasant dress is quite different than one with all these laces and bows and buttons, and I'm afraid I have servants to do these kinds of things for me now."

She shrugged in a helpless manner.

Oh, so now that Ro was panicking, Cosette suddenly didn't know how clothing worked?

Ro growled a little. "Then ask a servant to help me! Where did they all go, anyway?"

Before Cosette had come in, Chantie, Margot, and Arletta had been bustling around, trussing Ro up in that ridiculous ice-blue dress, painting her face with powder and rouge, and smearing goop in her hair to make it stay in one place all night.

All things Cosette had reversed as well, thank Dieu.

At least she wasn't wearing the towering light-pink wig Cosette wore, nor the frothy pink monstrosity whose lace had to weigh more than Cosette soaking wet. Of course, it was of little comfort. Cosette looked like the queen she was in such clothing, clothing Ro would never be able to pull off.

Her sister let off a musical laugh and flounced toward the door, each step an exaggeration of how much she didn't care about her own sister's discomfort. She kissed her fingertips and wiggled them in Ro's direction right before she disappeared around the corner.

Ro stared after her with her mouth hanging open. Of all the — "Cosette! Get back here this instant, or I swear I'll . . ."

Her voice trailed off as she darted out of her dressing room, across the sitting room, and rounded the doorframe to find the hallway completely empty.

The long hallway. With no more than a handful of doors to hide behind.

Cosette was wearing twice as many layers in her frothy, frilly pink gown, plus the wig that gave most people headaches, which made gliding movement and mincing steps necessary, if impractical. How had Cosette vanished so quickly?

"Magic, probably," she grumbled to herself.

Cosette was having *way* too much fun discovering her latent fairy powers.

She groaned. Why had Cosette thrown this stupid fête in the first place? So Ro had awakened the princess from a sleeping curse, then helped free an entire royal family from Germany, Olt's family, from the same enchantress's curse. (They had declared they were throwing their own ball in her honor as soon as she and Olt returned — Ro was planning on that taking years.) So what?

A hefty book of pirate adventures, a plate of macarons in a rainbow of flavors, a carafe of café with a side of crème and sucre, and a quiet evening to herself were thanks enough.

Perhaps she should've insisted harder that was all she wanted?

Ro sighed and went back to the mirror. She hadn't meant to let her panic run free, but the dress was just so eye-catching. She didn't want to be the center of anyone's attention.

Then she remembered the masque, still on its stand. She

spoke before remembering her sister couldn't hear. "Oh, Cosette! But the masque . . ."

Her eyes fell on it, and she sucked in a breath.

Now curling rose vines and lacy black thorns, eye holes large enough to see out of in case she were attacked—or needed to escape small talk—it was delicate, elegant, and stitched from black lace.

Lifting it carefully from its stand, she tied it on and sighed in happiness. A single rose blossom caressed one cheek, but it was so light and airy, it appeared to have been painted on.

She smiled. Perhaps she could go down like this. Just this once. And unless she wanted to hide in her room all night—tempting—she'd best get it over with.

Decision made, Ro set off down the hall, trying to pretend she wasn't trembling from brow to heel.

She'd just go downstairs, endure Trêve's announcement, boon, and enduring thanks, mingle for a few hours, dance with whomever Cosette threw her way, then grab Olt and escape.

Olt. A smile curved her lips. Who knew she would fall for someone so perfect for her—

Before the thought had fully formed, she'd been yanked into a curtained alcove and was being thoroughly kissed.

2

A familiar scent enveloped Ro, and she wrapped her arms around Olt's neck and leaned into the kiss. His warm lips moved against hers, and she couldn't help her smile.

This was exactly where she wanted to be. In his arms.

Well, tucked against him, his single arm holding her tight, as his other had been lost to the curse. But it didn't make her love him one livre less. Something she reminded him of every time he needed reminding.

After a moment, Olt pulled back slightly. His eyes widened, and he moved back further so he could take her in. "You look amazing!"

Warm green eyes flecked with gold, light-brown hair tied back in a queue, and a chiseled jaw with the exact right amount of scruff—Ro could say the same thing about him. Her Prussian prince.

Though he much preferred to be known as a sailor.

Ro grinned and went in for another kiss. "You're just lucky I could tell it was you pulling me in here, or you'd be curled up in the corner in pain."

"Kissing you is worth any potential bodily injury."

Ro laughed and leaned her head against his firm chest, sighing happily.

At the sound of footsteps rushing by, he tugged her deeper into the nook hidden behind a heavy tapestry, backed himself into the wall right next to the window, and pulled her close. Then, as if they were magnets unable to help being drawn to the other, he lifted her chin with one finger and drew her lips to his.

Ro didn't mind. Well, not anymore. She leaned into him and lost herself in his scent, his touch.

She hadn't thought it possible, but she'd finally gotten used to kissing Olt. And she wasn't as terrible at it as she thought she'd be. Also, he was quite imaginative, finding so many hidden-away spots to enjoy themselves in.

Thank goodness he never tried to kiss her in front of anyone else, though. It had taken her long enough to get used to the idea of her and him. She couldn't imagine enduring the teasing her brothers or Cosette would send her way.

As he often did after kissing her, Olt pulled her close and began playing with her hair. Ro relaxed against him, her safe haven.

"Cosette's going to kill you if you mess up her creation."

He kissed her forehead. "I'll be careful, promise."

She snuggled closer. "Mm. I don't mind."

He was welcome to hold her, play with her hair, or kiss her as much as he liked. As long as it was just the two of them.

"What are you thinking about?" he asked tenderly.

"Oh, I was just thinking of Captain Red."

"What?"

Ro hid a smile against his chest. "Well, more accurately, I was thinking of Madame LaChance."

He pulled back and looked down at her, brow furrowed. "I kiss you like that and you're thinking of, of . . . *them*?"

Ro couldn't hold back her laughter any longer.

"Oh. You're teasing me." He peeked above her head and frowned. "You are teasing me, right?"

Ro sighed. He'd been so serious lately. Struggling like he wanted to say something but couldn't find the words. Staring into her eyes like she was his whole world and he couldn't live without her. Declaring out of nowhere how good they were together.

It made Ro distinctly uncomfortable.

She'd gotten used to the kissing, *oui*, but his gazing at her like that? She didn't deserve such looks of longing or passion or devotion or whatever they were.

A part of her still worried he'd tire of her as he got to know her better. That he'd move on to someone else as soon as her grumpy, no-nonsense self wore at his sunshine personality.

She jerked herself away from such thoughts.

"I am teasing you," she said, "but something about them has been bothering me. I just can't remember what." Ro shrugged. "It'll come to me eventually."

Reaching into her pocket, she fingered the compass Captain Red had given her, but as always, the moment she no longer touched it, its existence was snuffed out of her mind.

Gnawing on his lip, Olt stared down at her like he was trying with all his might not to blurt something he'd regret. Apparently his intense dislike for pirate captain Rose Red and businesswoman Madame LaChance was still in full swing.

Ro sighed. "You might as well just tell me whatever you're thinking. You know I'm not any good at guessing."

"You aren't planning on . . . going to see them or anything, are you?"

She wished she could erase the concern in his eyes. He had nothing to worry about when it came to the two women. So why did he? "Captain Red is in the Caribbean with her stolen ship and crew, remember? I couldn't see her if I tried. Well, not easily, anyway."

His shoulders sagged in relief.

"And Madame LaChance . . ."

He stiffened.

Ro chose her words carefully so she wouldn't send him into a panic. "Something is nagging at me, that I've forgotten something rather important regarding her, but for the life of me, I cannot figure out what."

Now Ro was the one gnawing on her lip. She smoothed away her worry so it wouldn't feed Olt's.

"Ro." He took her hand in his and stared intently into her eyes. "This is very important. I beg of you to hear me. Captain Red was Madame LaChance's enforcer. It was a blow to her pride that the captain you hired and who used to work for her stole her ship and disappeared."

"So far you're not telling me anything I don't already know."

"I'm getting to that." He rubbed her knuckles with his thumb. "Madame LaChance likely holds that against you, and I promise you, she is not one to be crossed. Please, stay far away from her."

Ro frowned. "I work for her on occasion. She has contacts I couldn't begin to access on my own. I'd hate to lose a working relationship with her."

Such distaste spread across Olt's face, Ro struggled not to laugh. If he curled his lip any further, she could accuse him of snobbery. Not that Olt thought himself better than anyone else. His years as a hardworking sailor had cured him of that, if he'd ever felt that way.

"Believe me, that isn't a relationship you want to continue," he said with all the disdain a haughty prince could muster.

Ro rested her hand against his face, smoothing away his expression, thrilling at the stubble under her fingertips. Was she ridiculous or what? "Olt, the day I sail a ship better than you is the day you can tell me how to do my job."

He blinked at her, startled. Blast. That hadn't come out at all as she'd meant it to.

She tried again. "What I mean to say is, well, sometimes I need those distasteful contacts. When someone is in danger, when I'm racing to save a life or stop a creature from rampaging and killing the innocent, I need as clear a path as possible to my goal. I can't afford to burn bridges."

He still wore a slightly shocked expression.

Ro grimaced. "That really came out awful, didn't it?"

"I just . . . yeah." Then he took a deep breath and let it go. She truly didn't deserve him. "But I understand. Just, maybe, I don't know. Limit your contact with her? If possible?"

Relieved she hadn't once again ruined everything by her brusque manner, Ro lifted up on her tiptoes and gently kissed him. "I'll do my best."

But it bothered her all the same. She hated feeling like she was forgetting something. A feeling that had become all too common lately.

That and she didn't do well sitting around, playing at French courtier. She needed some kind of hunt to occupy her.

She tried to keep her thoughts off her face, but of course, with Olt, that didn't matter one whit. He could read her emotions in the colors that danced above her head like a mini Aurora Borealis.

His ability wasn't even a little bit fair.

Casting a quick glance above her head, he tried to read Ro while she attempted to wave the colors away, as if that would make a difference. What were her emotions telling him?

A ghost of a smile appeared on his lips. "I can see you're plotting, you know. Please don't do it. Don't return to England and speak to Madame LaChance."

"You could always come with me."

"And leave behind my duties to your sister and the crown?" he said in mock-outrage. "My family would have my head. As would yours."

She laughed. "Are you enjoying them? Your duties."

He began to trace whorling patterns in the lightest touch over her face and neck. "I am, actually."

"You sound surprised." Her voice came out far too breathless.

He shrugged. "Olov was trained for diplomacy, not me. My brother thought I should stay home, help rebuild the kingdom after the destruction the empress wrought, and that I was foolish for riding headlong into the forest after you."

Blinking rapidly, Ro tried not to let his words affect her, but as always, Olt didn't miss a thing. He was quick to catch her change in mood, no matter how hard she tried to hide the flash of hurt.

"I swear to you I had no idea they'd asked you to stay away. I—"

She placed her finger over his lips. "Shh. I know, Olt. You don't have to keep apologizing. They were only doing what was best"—she spoke right over his attempted interruption—"for *you*. You were healing. After so long without you, they needed you. I don't bear a grudge."

Even if it did feel like a fresh wound every time she was reminded his family didn't want her near him.

Though there was likely a completely rational explanation. Probably.

Olt gave her a devilish grin and pulled her closer. "I think I know of a way to drive such thoughts from your mind."

Ro grinned right back. "I'd like to see you try."

Olt took to her challenge with zeal, and then, all too soon, he was pulling away. Ro reached for him, but he rested his forehead against hers, breathing heavily.

Ro was having just as much trouble catching her breath. How on earth did he *do* that to her?

"I love you, Ro. You know that, don't you?"

"Uh-huh." She was more interested in kissing him right now, but he kept talking. For some reason.

"You know I would never hurt you. That I would protect you with my life."

"Oui." Of course she knew that. She just wanted to get back to the kissing.

"We have to stop."

"What? Why? We were just getting started." Ro went in for another kiss.

With a laugh, Olt pressed his fingers to her lips in a half-hearted attempt to stop her, but she kissed them anyway. He groaned. "I have to go. I don't want to."

"Then don't."

"I have to get ready."

"That'll take roughly five minutes." She gave him a quick once-over. Shirt, trousers, shoes. "Besides, you look ready to me."

His neck went dusky red. "I mean, I have an errand to run."

Ro pulled back, eyes wide. "An errand? Aren't you coming out there with me?"

He tugged at his collar. "Ah, non, not exactly. The king . . . your brothers . . . I have something to do before I . . . meet you there."

She started to panic. "You're going to make me be presented all by myself? You do realize I'd planned to survive the evening by hiding behind you the whole night. And how do you have an errand right before the ball? Couldn't you have done this earlier?"

Olt eyed her. "You know the fête doesn't start for several hours yet, don't you?"

Ro's mouth fell open. "Hours? It isn't starting right now?"

"These French fêtes always begin late and last till the wee hours of the morn." He kissed her quickly, taking advantage of her being too stunned to reply. "I have to go. I'm so sorry. I'll see you there."

"Don't go," she said as she tried to taste him once more.

He didn't let her. With a roguish wink and a gentle brush of his lips on her knuckles, he was gone.

Ro sighed, crossed her arms, and leaned against the wall. "But I was so hoping we could just stay here," she said to the curtain.

A chuckle was his only response before his footsteps took him away from her. To whatever errand he had to run, instead of being her human shield while Trêve paraded her in front of all the nobles.

She stayed behind the tapestry for a while, half-hoping he would return, half-hoping she could hide from any guards, Mesdemoiselles-in-waiting, or, most of all, the queen of France.

But he didn't come back, and she was fairly certain Cosette would find her and drag her out anyway, so she reluctantly went to discover why she'd been made to get ready so early.

❧

At the end of the hallway, Ro leaned her elbows on the cool stone of the banister and watched the chaos below.

Sure enough, servants bustled through the halls, preparing for the grand fête. Then why had Cosette wanted her down right away—

Her eyes caught on a familiar figure. She froze.

Her père. Here. With his horrid new wife and two step-daughters in tow.

Well, she was new to Ro, anyway. They'd been married for quite a few years, and Ro had yet to meet her. But it didn't matter. She didn't want to be introduced to Madame Béatrice or her daughters. Ever.

They'd made Cosette's life a living hell, treating her more like a servant than a daughter, yet she'd forgiven them anyway.

Ro's nostrils flared. Her fists clenched. And her chest rose and fell rapidly as it got harder to breathe. She did *not* need this right now, not when she was already stressed about being the center of attention for over a thousand guests.

Her père was speaking to a servant. He was dressed for tonight's fête, but wealthy clothes couldn't hide what age and years under France's curse had done to him.

And years of drinking and gambling. She couldn't forget those, even if she tried.

Stooped, pale, and shriveled, he leaned heavily on a cane as every part of him trembled.

Ro strained to hear what he was saying, to hear if he was berating the servant, but she only caught snatches of directions on how he wanted his place setting laid out and his food prepared.

As if the hostess and cook didn't intimately know their jobs. Typical.

But he was still shaking, just a little. Perhaps it was an ailment she didn't yet know of? At a noise, he glanced upward and stilled, his eyes homing in on her.

Ro felt as if the balcony had tilted and she was in danger of tipping right off its edge and down the three stories below to land at her père's feet.

There was a flurry of activity as the three women saw where he was looking and held a hurried discussion, their eyes flicking to Ro as they spoke. Her père's gaze never wavered.

After an eternity of Ro being unable to breathe, his eyes lit up, and he made as if coming right for her. Though she wasn't sure how he'd navigate all these stairs.

With a cool look, she turned away, and the moment she was out of sight, she ran, all the way to Trêve's library, the first place she could think of to hide.

She heaved the massive door shut and rested her forehead against it.

Non, she couldn't see her père. The look on his face—did he actually think she'd be glad to see him?

As if it had happened yesterday, she could picture his fist slamming into her jaw when she'd refused to be given like chattel to a beast, right before he'd thrown her out of his home and told her never to return. His spittle-flecked words were as clear as the day he'd said them: "Then you are dead to me. Get out. And don't *ever* come back."

That after years of neglect and absence and drunken stupors while his children fended for themselves.

Ro's nails bit into her palms. She wasn't about to go out there and pretend the last twenty-plus years he'd mistreated them had never happened.

Spinning on her heel, she seized the first book she saw, settled on a chaise longue, and tried to concentrate. But no matter how many times she read the first paragraph, its meaning escaped her.

What was her père even *doing* here?

❧

Cosette found her some time later. "Rosette, why, wherever did you go? I expected you downstairs hours ago."

Her sister's full lips pouted, as if Ro had spoiled some great plan of hers. Ro just bet she had. Still, she was too raw to address it.

Ro raised her book, her smile as feeble as her charade. "Where else?"

Cosette lifted the book from her fingers and read the title aloud. *"Suitors and what to do with them."*

Ro snatched back the book, face aflame. *That's* the book she'd grabbed from the shelf? What on earth?

Cosette's laugh rang out like musical silver bells, and Ro's face grew hotter.

Her sister wiped one eye at a time with dainty gloved

fingers. "Oh, Ro, that title is apt, considering the situation, but I can't see even you picking up that particular book." Still laughing, she leaned forward and kissed Ro's cheek. "Might I suggest you actually read it, dearest?" She lowered her voice. "You might want to learn more in that particular area, if I may give some friendly sisterly advice."

She winked, then made her way out of the great library, her laughter trailing behind her.

Ro was two seconds from hurling the book across the room, but paused. She cracked it open and read a few lines. What lay within horrified her.

Dress in what pleases him? Mince and giggle and primp and act demure, just to get his attention? Learn fan signals to flirt in secret code while others pretended not to notice? Laugh at whatever he says and never, not ever, make your opinion known unless called upon—and then agree with whatever he said?

She slammed the book shut. If that wasn't the worst advice she'd ever read!

Cosette popped her head back in, making Ro jump. "Oh! I forgot why I came in here. Trêve is ready to make his announcement and is requesting your presence." She winked. "No more hiding, dearest."

And then, with another brilliant smile, she was gone.

Great. It was time to be the center of attention.

Ro marched over to one of the shelves, stuffed the book behind the other tomes, and stomped from the room. Flirt? Laugh at everything he said? Bat her eyelashes?

She'd rather die.

3

As soon as Ro rounded the corner and came upon the masses teeming in the hallway, she ducked into a curtained nook and held her stomach, just trying to breathe. She couldn't do this! What was Cosette thinking, throwing her a ball when that was the opposite of anything she'd ever wanted in her whole life?

Only once the buzz of hundreds of arrivals faded into the ballroom and music swelled did she have the courage to leave the safety of her hiding place. She made her way to the entrance Cosette had directed her to use and stood there, willing her hands to stop trembling.

A guard dressed in vibrant sunflower-yellow and royal-blue livery hurried off to let the king know she was present, and then two more gripped the handles to the balcony doors and waited for the signal to open them for her.

Ro fingered the petals of her dress as she dreaded her announcement to the entire French court.

She could do this. Just walk in there, tilt her head regally, and at the first opportunity, slink to the side of the ballroom and hide behind any available potted plants.

She reminded herself that she looked good. She had

nothing to be ashamed of. Olt was waiting for her. Hopefully. If his errand hadn't kept him away.

And if she were mobbed for the story of how she'd awakened the princess from her sleeping curse, all she had to do was hide behind Olt or Cosette and they would be the life of the party for her.

Why had she agreed to this again?

Ro wiped her palms on her dress. The current song ended in a flourish, then there was an expectant pause.

"And now our honored guest of the evening, Huntress Ro LeFèvre, Defender of the Realm . . ." The announcer droned on, throwing out titles Ro's pounding heart muffled as rushing blood roared in her ears. She sincerely hoped she wasn't about to pass out and make an even bigger spectacle of herself.

The doors opened to a blaze of candlelight.

Ro forced a wide smile to stretch over her lips. Lips that had been painted to match her dress. Lifting her chin, she swept forward. Time to face the French court. And quite possibly hide from her père the entire evening.

The ballroom was stuffed to the brim. So many people, dressed in a riot of colors. So many faces, staring straight at her. It was all she could do not to turn and flee.

She caught Cosette's eye, and her sister made a motion for Ro to smile. She thought she was. Her lips stretched wider, Cosette's admonishment not to bare her teeth and growl at the guests echoing in her memory.

Her cheeks trembled from the effort.

Too much. Everything was too—

Her eyes caught and held on Olt. Dressed in a smart black frock coat trimmed in silver, a shimmery red vest that matched her ballgown, and dark gray breeches with white hosiery, he waited for her at the bottom of the steps, as handsome as ever as he smiled up at her.

Her whole being lit up, and her smile turned genuine.

Everyone and everything else turned into background

noise, a tapestry against which Olt stood out in sharp relief, and she kept her eyes on him as she glided down the stairs. He held out his hand, she took it, and he brought hers to his lips.

"May I have this dance, Mademoiselle?" His eyes sparked with appreciation and mischief, as if he *knew* he'd taken the worst part of the night and made it a thousand times better.

Ro said simply, "Of course you may."

His arm came around her waist, and she held out her skirt to make up for not being able to hold his other hand.

He gave her a melting smile, the music swelled, and he swept her away.

§

As one does when more information is available, Ro reflected later that the ball was rather lavish that night, more so than usual. Guests watched her and Olt closely, whispering behind their fans, abruptly stopping conversation whenever she or Olt veered too close.

Trêve's announcement not only held thanks for waking the sleeping princess, but he emphasized how much they both meant to the country at large and the royal family in particular.

She wished she would've noticed something was out of the ordinary much sooner. But she had eyes only for Olt.

Who was soaking up her attention and giving far too much in return.

In fact, Olt was being downright devilish. Dancing with her almost exclusively—not that she minded one bit—winking at her, catching her off guard at the worst times, such as when she was twirling under the chandeliers.

Then he'd steal kisses, not at all trying to be discreet.

Ro's face flamed more than once, she tripped whenever she caught one of his winks, and his furtive kisses muddled her mind and made it impossible to think. What was he doing, acting this way in front of so many people?

This sent her to the champagne fountain more than once, which didn't help clear her head. That and spinning away to avoid her père every time she saw him hobbling toward her from across the room.

Couldn't Cosette have warned her that he would be here?

But then Olt would sweep her into another dance, full of teasing and winking and heated looks.

Too much more of Olt's teasing, and she was going to drag him out to the garden to a secluded spot and kiss him for hours. Ha! Teach him to tease her into a frenzy all night long.

After a particularly rousing dance set, she was holding a champagne flute, gulping more than daintily sipping, as she should've been if she didn't want to grow intoxicated, when Olt called the ballroom to silence.

She only half paid attention. The warm air was stifling, and Olt looked far too handsome in his frock coat, one sleeve sewn closed at the shoulder, tailored to fit his form to perfection.

Why on earth was he flirting so much, for heaven's sake? It was as if he were taking their secret meetings and displaying them for all the world to see. She knew how he felt about her, but did everyone else have to as well?

"And that is why I must proclaim my love before all of you, Dieu as my witness."

Ro barely heard him, her glass raised, a warm buzz filling her head and ears. She just wanted this night to be over. Could she escape yet? Maybe after Olt's speech?

Then he was taking her hand, staring down into her eyes; she was gulping her last sip, a servant was taking her empty flute of champagne.

She immediately wished she had another.

"Rosette Jacqueline LeFèvre. You would make me the

happiest man in all the realms if you would consent to being my bride."

A few gasps and rustling skirts, as people pressed closer, were the only sounds as the room grew still. It felt as if guests collectively held their breath, waiting, excited, thrilled to witness the queen's beloved sister become engaged.

Ro could only stare. Olt didn't falter, just gazed at her with so much love and hope in his eyes. Her eyes drifted to his hand, which had released hers at some point and was now held out to her, a ring lying in his palm.

She gulped as she took in the intricately carved, rose-shaped ruby. He was serious. His words hadn't been a champagne-induced fantasy. And the updated color of her dress made that much more sense.

The pressure was almost crushing, and Ro thought she would explode under its weight. She blinked rapidly. Did he have to ask her *here*? In front of all these people?

"Oui," she whispered, for what else could she say?

With a whoop, he fisted the ring, wrapped his arm around her, and kissed her deeply, soundly, and quite openly in front of the king and queen and every subject who could fit themselves into the ballroom.

The French nobles cheered and jostled forward to add their congratulations, but Trêve and Cosette pushed their way to the front, joined by her brothers Claude and Pascal and their wives. A bevy of sisters and their husbands followed, clamoring to be noticed offering the most profuse congratulations.

It gave Ro a profound headache, and it was all she could do to stand there and smile with all her might, instead of running off into the night and galloping away on Fairweather, never to be seen again.

At least until the fête was over and every guest had gone home.

The more she smiled, the more dread pulled her stomach straight down. This was a disaster.

She and Olt needed to talk.

⁂

Once congratulations and well-wishes had blurred into background noise and Ro couldn't focus on anything else said to her, Ro dragged Olt to the refreshment table to get something in her other than champagne. And to give herself a break from the crush.

Olt stopped her from serving herself in a chivalrous manner she decided not to refuse, and as he chatted with someone also grabbing a light snack, Ro studied the ring on her finger.

Translucent red, it glowed with an inner light. It shouldn't have been possible, but the red gem was cut into the shape of an unfurling rose—with a small ruby at its center—and the band was made of the same red stone, which also shouldn't have been possible.

If she looked closely enough, little notches hooked the band together, as if made of several pieces, but nothing shifted, the entire thing solid ruby.

Olt handed her a plate and pulled her close so they could speak over the clamor. "Do you like it?"

Ro stared at the ring, astounded he'd even found such a piece of jewelry. "Olt, it's . . ."

"Extravagant? Perfect? Completely you?" Olt grinned, obviously pleased with himself. "Though blasted difficult to create, according to the jeweler."

A touch scary how perfect it is for me, Ro did not say.

Was it . . . glowing? All by itself? Ro squinted at it, but non, it must've caught the light from the chandeliers.

"It's real, I assure you." Olt chuckled, though it had a strained quality to it.

Ro didn't bother stopping her scowl. "I don't care about that. You know I don't."

"Oh. Huh." He tugged at his cravat, tied in an ornate knot high on his neck, in a way that looked distinctly uncomfortable. Like it was strangling him. "That's . . . I didn't realize. I should have. I apologize."

Ro tilted her head. Why was that his first assumption? She could tell he was valiantly attempting not to glance above her head. Not only had he trained himself not to in public, since it was distracting in conversation—and he'd learned the hard way to keep that part of him a secret from others—crowds messed with his synesthesia. The riot of colors above multiple people's heads made it difficult to read an individual.

Thank goodness.

"Actually, I'm more concerned I might lose it in a hunt." Ro flicked the rose, thankfully molded so it didn't have sharp edges. Still . . . "It might catch on something and fling off into the underbrush. Or break."

He kissed the back of her hand, right above the ring, and raised sparkling eyes to hers. "That is, if you even want to keep hunting."

Ro's mouth fell open, but Olt didn't see as another pair of well-wishers assaulted them. Er, interrupted. Ro plastered on a smile and tried to pretend she was incandescently happy.

Because she was. She *was*.

4

Congratulations turned to talk of their wedding, and someone asked when they were getting married. Spring? Next fall?

Ro stared at the stranger in horror and couldn't bring herself to answer, even under the expectant stares of Olt, Cosette, and what felt like thousands of others.

One insane life-changing event at a time, merci beaucoup.

But people wanted to know, and guests kept asking, until Ro was eyeing nearest exits.

It didn't help that Olt deferred to her. Likely he thought he was giving her a choice, but it just added pressure to an already-tense situation.

Thankfully, excited chatter of the engagement turned into a celebratory dance, full of spirit. The French didn't need a reason to celebrate, but they would certainly use this opportunity to do so.

Just as Ro used the opportunity to escape, the moment Olt's back was turned.

Now she sat in her bed, in her nightclothes—a pair of breeches worn soft and an off-white shirt where the buttons had fallen off the wrists and neck, leaving a gaping ruffled neckline—her knees to her chin while she gazed at the ring.

It was lovely. Somehow, Olt had commissioned it to be both simple and exquisite. How did one cut a ruby so that each individual petal looked so lifelike? That the ruby itself made up the band? And how long until Ro's huntress lifestyle broke off each petal one by one?

No matter how much she admired the ring, she couldn't get away from the question that circled in her mind like a swarm of buzzards.

Did she want to marry Olt?

She loved him. Had opened her heart enough to accept his touch, his kisses, his love. She didn't cringe now when he said nice things about or to her, even if she silently disagreed. She was just happy *he* thought those things.

But did she want to marry him? She honestly had no idea.

Ro flopped back onto the pillows and stared at the ceiling. She didn't want to tell him *non* either. Would he take "not yet" well?

What if she lost him because of it? What if she told him she wasn't ready and then he left and she woke up one day and figured out she was ready and he was no longer in the picture?

Yet what if she went along with it, let him marry her, let her sister choose a date and throw together a lavish wedding, and the opposite happened. What if she woke up one day and discovered she'd made a huge mistake and shouldn't have gone through with it?

She didn't *know* what she wanted.

This was a nightmare in the making. She had to get away from her thoughts.

She grabbed the book on the nightstand, turned to the page she'd last been reading, and stared at the paper, her swirling thoughts leaving the text incomprehensible.

Someone lightly tapped on her bedroom door.

Ro's head came up. Who on earth would disturb her at this hour?

Without giving Ro a chance to respond, Cosette came bounding into the room and sprang onto the bed. She was dressed in a nightgown and a wrap, her face scrubbed free of makeup and her light-pink wig missing, but her hair was still elaborately coiled, as if she'd run out before her servants could finish preparing her for bed.

"I knew you'd still be up!" Cosette said with far too much excitement.

Ro groaned and replaced the book on her stand. "Cosette. Not now, all right? I just need to . . . process."

"Nuh-uh. You don't get to keep me from enjoying this. Besides, if Olt has any say in the matter, the two of you shall be wed within a fortnight."

Ro sat straight up. "A fortnight?"

That was too soon. *Too soon.*

Cosette laughed merrily. "You know what that means, don't you?"

Ro most certainly did not.

"That means we must have *the talk.*" Although her eyes gleamed, Cosette shrugged prettily, pretending nonchalance. "Since Mère isn't here to do it for you, and I wouldn't trust a single one of our sisters with such information."

A slow-emerging horror had begun to dawn on Ro's already addled mind. "The talk? You don't mean . . ."

Cosette gave her a shrewd look. "Unless you know what I'm about to say? A few of my Mesdemoiselles-in-waiting are far less . . . virtuous . . . than I'd come to expect of unmarried ladies, what with our upbringing."

"Non. Non, non, non. Do not do this, I beg of you."

Whatever was on Ro's face made Cosette giggle and clap her hands. "Good! I can be the first to explain it to you."

"Explain . . . what exactly?"

"What happens"—Cosette paused dramatically—"on the *wedding night*."

Ro flung off her blankets to make her escape, but before she could hurtle from the bed, Cosette grasped her arm and hauled her back. When had her sister gotten so strong? Ro was a huntress, for pity's sake!

Cosette giggled some more and arranged pillows so they would both be comfortable.

Ro sat there, fists clenched, stiff as a plank, trying to reconcile herself to the fact that she was just going to have to endure this. Once Cosette made up her mind, she could not be stopped.

"All right. So!" Cosette said. "You've kissed Olt—don't deny you haven't. I know what the two of you are doing every time you disappear behind another curtain in the palace—"

Ro covered her face with her hands. This could not be happening.

Cosette tugged her hands away. "You know that feeling after you've been kissing a while? Or! Even when you start. That feeling like your skin is on fire, like you can't get close enough, that there's something . . . *more* . . . you want to do, but you aren't quite sure what?"

"Fine. It's not like this night could get any worse. What about it?"

Cosette went on as if Ro's words hadn't been dripping in sarcasm. "Once you're married, that *more* becomes perfectly clear." She paused and tilted her head. "You know that verse in your precious Scriptures, something along the lines of, 'There is something too wonderful for me: the way of a man with a maid' or some such?"

Never mind. She couldn't do it. Ro needed to stop this right now.

"Cosette, Father had horses. He bred horses, raised horses. If I wasn't reading, I was *with* those horses. They had foals. I helped birth those foals. I have an idea how this works—"

Ro stopped suddenly. Not that she'd thought of that in conjunction with Olt. Dear Dieu in heaven, she wasn't ready for this relationship, was she? She just wanted to hide even *thinking* of Olt in that way.

See? She was in no way ready for this. Marriage. Children. *More than kissing.*

Children . . . something teased her mind about that, then was gone in a flash.

Taking advantage of Ro's pause, Cosette outlined in great detail what went on between a husband and a wife on their wedding night, and Ro was certain her face had gone up in flames. By the end of it, Cosette was fanning herself.

Her sister leaped off the bed much in the same manner she'd entered. "Oh my, look at the time! I must go see my husband . . . for reasons . . ."

And she fled without another word.

Ro stared after her, mouth ajar, before flopping on the bed and burying her face under a pillow. *Non.* She was *not* thinking about why Cosette had run out of her room so suddenly. She was *not* thinking about doing such things with Olt.

Though if she had to be honest with herself, even a teeny-tiny bit, it was rather encouraging that Cosette enjoyed it so much.

Non! She was just . . . going to forget this conversation had ever happened.

Ro slipped off her ring, placed it on her nightstand, and rolled over, tugging her blankets up under her chin. But no matter how hard she tried to coax it to her, sleep could not be found.

All through the long, sleepless night, the glittering ring sat on her nightstand and mocked her, shimmering in the firelight and taunting her with Olt's hopes and happiness and dreams and expectations of her.

What were they, exactly? Would she be brave enough to ask? Or would she simply ignore it until after the wedding, when such things should've been discussed earlier?

More than once, the ring seemed to flare with light, but when she would look at it, the ruby simply reflected the glowing embers from the fireplace.

It was so extravagant. So exquisite. So unlike what a huntress should wear. She didn't want to lose it on a hunt. Maybe she could wear it around her neck?

She sat up, remembering what he'd said at the ball. Olt didn't expect her to stop hunting, did he? What exactly had he meant by that comment?

She wasn't the homemaker type. She was more than happy to turn over a brace of hares she'd trapped in exchange for their being turned into an edible meal, with the pelts sold for some livres besides.

He remembered these things about her, didn't he? He wasn't expecting her to suddenly become something she wasn't, was he?

She plopped back on her pillows, exhausted from her spinning thoughts, and stubbornly tried every trick she knew to fall asleep, determined to at least catch a few hours before she had to face people once more. But still it eluded her.

Then, in the deepest part of the night, before dawn started brightening the sky in preparation for the sun's blazing, glorious entrance, snatches of dreams intruded on her wakefulness.

In them, her grandmère, through Ro's eyes, roamed the forest, hunting something large. Whatever it was, it made Ro's heart beat faster and eyes fly open what felt like seconds after she'd shut them.

And those strange wolves, the hairless ones that had bitten her the last time she'd been in the Black Forest, kept jumping out at her. Ro silenced each one with an arrow to the eye, not wanting the big one to hear her. To find her.

Ro rolled over again, putting her back to the ring. She'd just be facing it again in a few seconds, but for now, she was at least going to pretend to ignore it.

She eased her eyes closed again, just wanting *sleep*.

Ro rounded a dense patch of trees into a glen with a protruding rock formation. At its base, a darkened area of brush hid a recessed cave, something Ro knew without investigating.

Ro and her grandmère gasped at the same time as a clawed hand came out of the cave, almost as big as one of the other wolves. A snout emerged next, one so monstrous Ro couldn't even begin to fathom how large the creature must be.

With a roar, it sprang at her grandmère.

Ro's instinct was to run, which was exactly what her grandmère did.

Clenching the bedclothes in her fists, Ro started to sweat.

The thing chased her grandmère, crashed after her through the forest, shook the ground as it bore down on her.

As Ro ran, one moment as her grandmère, the next as herself, a thought occurred to her. The creature was toying with her, letting her think she could escape, only to leap forward and scare her into running all the harder in a new direction.

Ro cheered on her grandmère to run faster, even as she put in just as much effort to get away herself.

Grandmère was so close to her cottage—she was going to make it. Surely her own land would keep her safe.

And then the thing was upon her.

Her grandmère whirled in time to be raked across the stomach with enormous claws.

Ro jerked upright in bed, breathing heavily, sweat dampening her brow.

Waiting to see more, she sat there, but the narrative snuffed out each time she woke, and nothing new presented itself as her heart tried to pound itself right out of her chest.

She felt her abdomen, but she hadn't been sliced open. There was no blood.

Ro sagged against the headboard. It was just a dream. She was fine. Her grandmère was fine. Truly.

But her panic didn't lessen. The whole thing felt so *real*.

Scared to fall back asleep, Ro stared at the ring as it hastily tried to snuff itself out and hide the fact that it had most certainly been glowing. The dream swirled through her mind, and the sun rose and lightened her room by degrees, until it was time to go down to breakfast.

Trembling, Ro stumbled out of bed, dressed, and went in desperate search of café and crème and sucre.

5

$\mathcal{R}$o hurried down the hall toward the family breakfast room, anxious to get away from her horrible dreams.

When she entered, she glanced around to see who else had gotten up this early. Liam, Cosette, and Olt sat at one end of the table, while her brothers were settled partway down toward the other end.

Ro had to admit she was surprised to see them here, especially her brothers. Breakfast was often served around noon after a late-night fête, and she'd been hoping to eat alone.

Well, to guzzle café, rather.

At least no other guests were allowed to intrude.

Relief swept over her like a wave. Ro had refused to allow nobles to mill about and watch her eat, as was custom for royals, so Cosette had set aside this room for their immediate family. Even better? Her annoying sisters had their own breakfast area, after Cosette had gotten exasperated with them one too many times.

Ro paused. Why hadn't that struck her as odd before? Cosette may have been short with them a time or two, but banishing them . . . that was something Ro would do, not Cosette.

She brushed away her unease as the Messieurs stood for her, smiling their greetings before resuming their seats. Except for Liam, who, stone-faced, gave a short bow and immediately left, not meeting her eyes.

Ro's heart gave a pang at that. Was he still upset with her? Over their disagreement? He hadn't been at the ball last night, either.

A servant stood along the wall, right next to the ornate silver café station. The carafe's glistening silverwork winked at her in the slanted sunlight and drew her in like a beacon.

Ro's eyes lit up. Exactly what she was looking for.

Before she could beeline for it, Olt hurried over to kiss Ro. She didn't know what to do with that, so she let him.

He looked down after he squeezed her hand in greeting. And frowned. "Where's your ring?"

Her heart dropped as she stared at her naked fingers. "Oh, ah, désolé. I must've left it on my nightstand." She turned toward the door. "I can go get it . . ."

Casting a quick glance above her head, he laughed and pulled her toward the breakfast buffet. "Non, non, stay and eat." He kissed her fingertips, and Ro flushed. "I just wanted to show it off a little. But please, eat first, then we'll go get it."

Just being this close to Olt brought to mind the incredibly awkward conversation with Cosette last night, and it was all she could do not to hide under the table. Or flee.

Ro offered a smile she hoped wasn't as brittle as it felt—it was hard to pretend ease after being awake for most of the night—and went straight for the ornate silver coffee pitcher and tried to pour herself a cup.

But nothing came out.

Maybe if she poured harder . . .

She stood there with her empty cup, still trying to make

liquid magically appear from the spout. Maybe if she tapped it she would loosen whatever blockage was keeping her from the life-giving brew.

Snickering broke into her rather violent tapping, and she shot her brothers a dirty look. And set the carafe back on its base.

It wasn't one that was meant to be picked up when poured.

François, the palace's maître d'hôtel, in charge of making sure the household ran smoothly, came through the door from the kitchens, looking unruffled, but she could've sworn rushing footsteps had preceded his appearance. He came to her side at a sedate pace. "May I fetch you anything in particular, Mademoiselle?"

Ro offered him a quick, relieved smile. "Just café, s'il vous plaît."

He bowed at the waist, and Ro caught herself from asking him to stop doing that. Again. It would be a waste of breath.

"My deepest apologies, Mademoiselle. We are at a . . . shortage. A runner has been sent to fetch more with all haste."

Ro stared at him, his words circling her skull in a buzzing echo and still not making sense. "There is a . . . shortage?"

He bowed again. "To my deepest shame and regret."

"Of café?"

"As I have said. Shall there be nothing else, Mademoiselle? A poached egg, or a slice of brioche, perhaps? I do believe the kitchens have received fresh baskets of apples and pears as well, as they are in season."

"Non, merci. I'll just"—she pointed to the mounds of berries, arranged so that they looked like living art, grown in palace greenhouses year-round—"I'll eat this. Merci."

"Very good, Mademoiselle." Ro received her third bow of the morning. If François didn't take such pride in treating his betters in the way he believed they deserved to be treated, she'd almost think he was trying to annoy her.

She'd come back later, then. When there was café.

Catching her mournful glance at the empty carafe, François said, "My apologies, Mademoiselle. I shall bring you a cup the moment more is brewed."

Ro smiled her gratitude and turned away so she could mourn in peace.

In her periphery, François directed servants to replace anything that had been even slightly diminished with a mere flick of his fingers. Except the café.

Dejected, she set down the still-empty cup and filled her plate with a few pastries and several helpings of fresh fruit. The moment she sat next to Olt she tucked into her food, keeping her head down while conversation flowed around her.

"So how many children do you want? Will you start trying right away?" Cosette's voice was far too chipper.

Ro froze. And slowly raised her eyes.

Olt was beaming right back at her sister. "Oh, we want lots of children. Maybe not right away, but soon. I would love a huge household. Children running through, playing, bringing joy and noise and laughter. It's a good thing we both come from big families."

Ro's stomach clenched. Olt wanted children? Lots of children?

Why hadn't they talked about this?

Although Ro had determined no one would ever be thrown out of her own family over a disagreement, as her père had done to her, she hadn't given a family of her own much thought. She'd been too busy chasing down fairy-tale creatures that liked to gnaw on humans.

Didn't they need to discuss these things before declaring they wanted a passel of children? Or throwing out a wedding date?

Seriously, how many times had she been asked that last night?

She didn't *know* when she wanted to get married. She didn't know *if* she wanted to get married. And now she had to decide how many children she wanted?

Ro studied Olt's smiling face and sparkling eyes. He was clearly still drifting on a high note from last night. Although, he was always upbeat, ridiculously lighthearted, making jokes and teasing smiles from her or anyone else who needed their spirits lifted.

Even losing an arm to the swan curse he and his brothers had been placed under hadn't kept him down for long. In fact, he may have bounced back even more boisterous than before.

Ro frowned. He'd hidden pain behind smiles and laughter in the past . . .

Yet Olt loved being surrounded by people. Ripped from his family for so long—no wonder he wanted to make his own. She could picture him with children. Laughing, chasing them, patiently teaching them—he'd make a great father.

But would she make a good mother?

And, more importantly, did they want the same things?

She'd have to think about that.

Just then, one of her brothers said, "Grandmère," and her head whipped around.

Claude and Pascal snickered over whatever they'd said.

As casually as she could manage, Ro asked, "Have either of you heard from Grandmère? I thought she would've attended last night's soirée."

Especially had she known Ro was getting engaged, which everyone else seemed to know ahead of time. Except Ro.

Even if that was how this was supposed to happen—not that she had any experience whatsoever in being engaged— she would've preferred *some* warning before the question was sprung upon her in front of the entire French court.

Claude and Pascal exchanged a glance that made Ro wonder what she'd missed.

Claude sighed. "You're not going to like it."

Ro raised an eyebrow.

"She was supposed to come, said she would even, but she never showed."

"Because *someone* forgot to go meet her," Pascal muttered.

"I didn't forget," Claude replied hotly. "It just, well, slipped my mind."

"That seems to happen quite often with you," Pascal said unforgivingly.

At Ro's horrified look, Claude hastened to explain. "But don't worry! We got a note saying she couldn't make it after all."

Ro wondered why she was just now hearing about this.

"Because we didn't want to distract you," Pascal said promptly, so she must've muttered it aloud. "You had enough going on, so we thought we'd take care of that for you."

And they'd done a fantastic job. That she managed to keep to herself.

"Did she say anything was . . . wrong?" Ro asked carefully, trying not to give away her concern.

"Non, nothing wrong," answered Claude, then took a sip of café. "Just busy."

Ro stared longingly after the magic brew of wakefulness as her brothers devolved into talking of other matters — mostly of who had made the biggest fools of themselves during the soirée — but Ro couldn't dismiss the nagging feeling that something was terribly wrong with her grandmère.

It was just a dream. Wasn't it?

Yet that feeling gnawed on her like a dog enjoying a particularly delectable bone. She needed to check on her grandmère. Make sure she was all right.

Ro glanced at Olt, who was happily chatting with Cosette, more light and joy on his face than she'd seen in an age.

Leaving right now was a terrible idea. Not only would the timing be suspect, but should she really run off? Over a dream?

So she took a deep breath and let it go. If there was a problem, a real problem instead of an imagined one, Ro would deal with it when the time came.

After breakfast, she followed Olt and her brothers out while Cosette stayed behind to talk to a servant. Ro peeked behind her as they left. The café still hadn't been refilled.

Surprising her because she was looking the other way, Olt pulled Ro close and kissed her cheek. "Meet me in the garden maze. I have a surprise for you."

She attempted a smile. "Oh, um, oui. Yes. I will. After I grab my ring."

He squeezed her hand, eyes twinkling. "Good plan. See you there."

He kissed her cheek again and turned to talk to her brothers as all three walked away down the hallway, leaving Ro blushing and unsure of herself.

She'd gotten used to being kissed, oui, but not in *front* of people. Kissing was private. For the two of them. Not the entire palace.

With a sigh, she went to retrieve her ring.

Just then, Cosette came out of nowhere and looped her arm through Ro's. "May I have a moment of your time?"

Ro bit back another sigh and turned a smile on Cosette. Just because she was out of sorts didn't mean she should take it out on her sweet sister. "You need never ask. I always have time for you."

"Bon. Because I have something to show you." Cosette looked around. "Is Olt not with you? I thought you left at the same time."

"He and Pascal and Claude went elsewhere. But I can go find them . . ."

Cosette gave her a brilliant smile, though it appeared

forced, or perhaps strained, before she set off for another part of the palace far away from Ro's room. "No need. Trêve would like to speak to you regarding a matter of some importance."

Ro fidgeted as her room moved farther away with every step. "I am meeting Olt in the gardens soon . . ."

"No trouble," Cosette said matter-of-factly. "This concerns him too, though it's probably best to ask you first."

Ro grumbled, but there was no redirecting Cosette once she was set on a course. Before Ro could ask for more details, Cosette pulled her into Trêve's private office, the one he hid in when avoiding his courtiers or certain heads of state. He was not to be disturbed in this office.

Yet Cosette waltzed in as if she owned the place. Which she pretty much did.

"Trêve, my love. I've brought her."

His head came up from the large sheets of paper he was perusing. His eyes lit, and a wide smile stretched his lips. "Ah, there she is! Thank you, my dear."

Light-blond hair, crystal-blue eyes, and a dark-blond beard, with a tall and muscular frame, Beau Alexandre Trêve was a good king. He was currently rebuilding the city and reestablishing his power base after the curse had shattered so much.

Cosette had soothed the beast he'd once been, and he was perfect for Ro's sister. She couldn't be happier they'd found each other.

Cosette hurried over and gave him a kiss, and Ro glanced around, wishing for café more than anything. Maybe Trêve had some? But non, no café service was present. He'd probably had some earlier than either of them at breakfast.

As had everyone else. Except her.

She was just the slightest bit salty about that. She wasn't handling this all-nighter particularly well.

The moment they were done kissing, Trêve smiled and

waved Ro forward. "Come! I was hoping to speak to you about le Château des Roses Noires."

Ro leaned over the desk to find blueprints of the old château splayed over its surface. The one she'd been trapped in for three years. Seeing it reduced to lines on a page diminished its power somewhat, but she couldn't help thinking of all the time she'd spent trying to escape it.

"You see, I am assigning properties to my most loyal nobles, helping them restore the old, great houses, and I wanted to speak to you before I assign this one to someone else."

Ro straightened. "Assign it to someone else?"

Surely she hadn't heard correctly.

Trêve looked somewhat apologetic. "Oui. It pains me to return there. Besides"—he pulled out another map and pointed to an area just outside of Paris—"I am building a new summer château here." Low-key excitement, as if he were restraining himself, lit in his eyes. "I plan on calling it Mont-parnasse."

"Versailles would be better," Cosette grumbled under her breath.

Ro bent to look.

He said, "It's only a few hours' carriage ride from Paris instead of days. If the need arises, I can return right away."

"But—give it, the other château, to someone else?" Something in Ro revolted at the idea. Though she couldn't imagine why.

He looked at her, completely serious. "I did not want to do so without first speaking to you."

Ro blinked. "Why me?"

"To see if you wanted it, of course. A title would come with its ownership, and the land would need to be worked . . . it would employ a great many people." He smiled. "The château grounds would need to stay with the château, of course, but you are welcome to dole out the surrounding land as you see fit. Assign it to friends or family, sell parcels, or reward your workers with ownership, if you so wish."

Ro's mouth fell open. As much as she appreciated his efforts to empower his people after being helpless so long under a curse, should she be in charge of such a thing, really?

Trêve held up both hands. "You do not have to, of course. I merely wanted to ask before I offered it to another. And, well, with the announcement last night . . . who better to give it to than a soon-to-be-wed couple?"

He offered her a sheepish grin, as if simultaneously pleased and embarrassed to speak of her recent engagement.

Ro felt the exact same way.

But to receive a title! It had been so long since her family had held noble status—since she was a child, really—and to be offered a château! That . . . meant a lot.

It was secluded. It was a three-day horseback ride from Paris and her family. And it would be all hers, no court or gaggle of people to pester her, only a few servants to keep it running. And whoever she hired to work the land, of course, land she'd hunted on for most of her life.

A château of her own. To disappear to anytime she wanted.

Though tempted, she couldn't agree. For some reason.

Least of all, she needed to speak to Olt. Grandmère had also offered them her cabin in the woods, and Ro hadn't even told him. Mostly because she didn't want to rush their relationship, but, well, it was too late for that, wasn't it?

And could she live in a place where she'd been trapped? Where Allura had been placed to rest while Ro broke her sleeping curse? Would she be able to walk its halls without the ghosts of her past following her at every step?

"I'll—I'll have to think about it."

He bowed slightly at the waist. "But of course."

"How long do I have to decide?"

He gave her a gentle smile. "No rush, huntress. Not if

you're considering it. Let me know what you and Monsieur Olt decide, and we'll go from there."

Ro nodded, then grinned. "Show me your plans for your new château?"

His eyes danced. "But of course."

Ro and Trêve bent their heads over detailed blueprints and maps, and Trêve pointed out extensive grounds, gardens, château wings, and all three levels, a monstrous feat, its sheer size blowing her away.

Ro couldn't help but notice how different it was from his other summer château, the one he'd been trapped in. It was so much more open and spread out, as if allowing sunlight to reach as many surfaces as possible.

"Why did you choose this location?" she asked.

There was no mistaking the enthusiasm in Trêve's voice. "It is on the outskirts of a charming little village with a good-sized chapel that serves the surrounding area, perfect for mingling and showing our people we care for them and will take good care of them. And for getting away from the constant demands in Paris, of course."

Someone pushed in a café cart, and Trêve and Ro spoke at the same time, neither looking up. "Merci, François."

Cosette gave off a trill of a laugh, one that hinted at unease. "Goodness me, how do the two of you do that?" Again that laugh. "You can tell which servant comes into the room without their saying a word or your having to see them."

Ro startled. She'd forgotten Cosette was in here.

She glanced up to find Cosette tapping her fingers on her crossed arms while shooting Trêve an annoyed stare.

Trêve didn't look up as he answered. "If you'd been trapped in a château for nearly twenty years as I had—or for three years, as your sister had—I guarantee you'd be able to name a servant by their tread or scent or, nay, their very presence."

Ro didn't miss the tightening of Cosette's jaw at the

mention of Ro's time spent at the château. She couldn't help but wonder: What had changed in her sister? She'd thought they were past that.

François finished laying out the items on the cart just so, then looked straight at Ro. "Your café, Mademoiselle."

Ro gave him a grateful smile.

François beat a calm retreat at one flick of Trêve's wrist.

Giving herself time to think, Ro went straight to the carafe François had left and poured herself a cup of the deep-brown liquid, breathing in its rich nutty scent. She stirred in a liberal spoonful of sucre and added enough crème to turn its color a light tan.

Then she drank it straight down.

Sipping her second cup, Ro stayed on the opposite side of the room and kept sneaking glances at her sister.

They'd been at ease with each other when it was just the two of them, and although Ro avoided the courtiers that followed her sister like peacocks, Cosette's tone had sharpened, she'd lost some of her angelic patience, and she wasn't as much . . . herself . . . as before her daughter had fallen into her enchanted sleep.

She'd thought Cosette would bounce back stronger, but perhaps the hurt was too deep. Or was there more going on?

Was she . . . not happy with her life? Did the thought that had once plagued Ro—that they weren't truly sisters—now plague Cosette?

Although she'd raised them both, Ro's mère was mortal, and Cosette's was the Fairy Queen. Ro hadn't thought it would come between them, but perhaps she was wrong.

And the thought that hurt most of all . . .

Was it time for Ro to move on? Away from life at the palace? For good?

Ro blinked back tears and studied the textured blue wallpaper unseeing. Perhaps Olt's proposal had come at the perfect time. Perhaps she needed distance from her sister.

Or her sister needed distance from her.

Ro brushed invisible lint from her sleeve. "I . . . should join Olt now. He'll be waiting for me."

Trêve glanced up with a hopeful look in his eyes. "You'll tell him? About my offer?"

Ro smiled, though it wobbled. "I'll tell him."

Snatching one last glimpse of Cosette, who was pouting in Trêve's direction, Ro fled.

Ro was halfway to her room when something she could only describe as a feeling slammed into her, knocking her into the wall.

Her grandmère lay in a clearing deep in the forest, gripping her axe, reaching out with one hand. Bloody cuts covered her face and arms, and a red patch swelled on her stomach. A grimace twisted her features, as if she were in a great deal of pain.

"Rosette. I need you. Please . . . hurry . . ."

The vision snuffed out, leaving Ro clutching the wainscoting, panting, hardly able to stay upright.

The dreams—those had been easier to ignore. This? She couldn't. She had to go to her grandmère. She had to go right now!

Pushing herself off the wall, Ro ran straight to her room, ripped off her light-blue day dress, and threw on her hunting leathers and red cape. Then she grabbed the already-packed bag she kept ready for emergencies and stuck as many weapons to her person as would fit while still able to ride comfortably.

Her crossbow was the last thing she slid into its holster across her back.

At the last moment, she skidded to a halt next to her stationery and scratched out a note.

Cosette:

Grandmère needs me.

Ro

Then she was off to the stables to saddle Fairweather, urgency pushing her forward as if a hand were at her back.

No matter that it was a nine-day journey on horseback, she hoped she would be in time. Though she couldn't imagine how.

6

Ro couldn't push Fairweather as fast as she'd like through the city. Roads were crowded, and a festive air hovered over Paris in the wake of Allura's sleeping curse having been broken.

And then there were all the building projects Trêve had commissioned to replace rotting wooden structures with sturdy stone, as well as restoring the many stone buildings that had fallen into disrepair during the curse.

The city was practically glowing under the shine of its restoration.

At any other time, Ro would've enjoyed it, would've taken her time to view the structures going up around her, tasting delectable treats the street vendors had to offer, weaving through the thoroughfare at a steady pace.

But today she pressed her horse through the crowd as fast as she dared, just trying to get *out*.

The sun beat down on her, and sweat trickled between her shoulder blades.

When she reached the edge of the city, the encroaching countryside beckoned to her, just out of reach on the other side of the city wall. Wagons and carriages and lines of people waited to get through the crowded gate.

Chest tight, Ro weaved her way through the mass and unashamedly used Trêve's name and her status as the royal huntress to bypass the long wait. For once she didn't feel even a little guilty using the reputation she'd earned for herself.

She'd just passed the gates when pounding hoofbeats raced up behind her.

Ro nudged Fairweather to the side of the road to let the rider pass. She planned to pull out after the rider and use whatever path they forged to get through the traffic spilling in and out of Paris.

The rider grabbed her horse's reins.

Ro spun around, and her eyes went wide. "Olt!"

He did not look pleased. Perhaps a little angry, even. She was certain guilt was splashed all over her face, and based on his thunderous expression, she wasn't hiding it so well. She shrank back. She'd never seen Olt this upset.

"You're leaving." His eyes flicked down to where her hands clutched the reins, where an engagement ring should be. The ring on her bedside table at the palace.

Her skintight leather riding gloves made it obvious a ring wasn't hidden under them.

Hurt bled onto his face, which he quickly hid away, but it didn't matter. Ro had seen it, and by the time he lifted cool eyes to hers, she was aching deep in her heart.

She hadn't wanted to hurt him, but she'd done exactly that.

"Olt, I . . ." She didn't know how to finish.

He took several deep breaths, as if he'd been the one running instead of his horse, and spoke calmly. "Where are you going? I saw you tear out of the stables . . ."

His eyes drifted over the stuffed saddlebags, her crossbow, and the bag of provisions she'd snatched from the kitchens, her loaded-down horse making it painfully clear she wasn't going for a quick ride.

Ro pointed toward the palace. "I left a note . . ."

Which he'd apparently not gotten. Not that it had been full of details. And it *had* been addressed to Cosette . . .

Ro's words spilled out in a muddle. "Grandmère . . . the dream . . . it felt so real . . . I have to help her . . ."

A cart rumbled their way, so Olt, still holding her reins, urged both horses onto the grass. A cool breeze tried to whip Ro's hair out of her hastily tied-back queue, offering some relief from the searing heat of the sun. Autumn was on its way, and the cooler weather couldn't get here fast enough.

They dismounted and faced each other.

Ro twisted her hands and bit her lip. This looked so horrible in every way. Why hadn't she left Olt a note too? If she'd stopped to think for one second instead of racing off headlong . . .

"Slow down," he said, looping the reins so the horses would stand still, and faced her. "Tell me everything."

So she did, explaining her dream, and then that *thing* she'd experienced in the hallway, whatever it was.

She'd tell him about the offered château later. It wasn't important right now.

Olt looked thoughtful, but there was a wariness to his eyes, something that said, well, not that he *didn't* believe her. More that he was trying to convince himself that she was telling him everything.

Ro tried to relax her hands, but she couldn't stop clenching them.

"We could send a messenger," Olt said cautiously.

"Then we'd have to wait for a response. Non, I need to go right now. Something's wrong, I can feel it. I might be too late already."

"And that's it? Nothing else?" Olt asked.

"Of course not," Ro said hotly. And perhaps a tad defensively. After a brief pause, she adjusted her pack. She'd said everything she needed to say, and the urgency hadn't lessened. "I need to go."

"I want to go with you."

"Olt, you can't. You're the new ambassador for Prussia, and you have your job to learn, meetings to attend, and a people's heart to win. If you leave now, they'll wonder how committed you are."

When he looked like he was about to argue, Ro stretched up on her tiptoes and kissed him full on the mouth, making it a good one. She didn't know when she'd see him again.

He clutched at her, but she pulled back. If she didn't leave now, she wouldn't be able to.

Olt said, with a frustrated growl, "I still don't like it."

She caressed his jaw with her gloved hand. "I know you don't. I don't like it either. But I must check on her. I feel it in my bones. That dream . . ."

Ro shook her head, unable to put it into words.

He glanced down, his jaw flexing. When he looked back up, she startled and pulled away at the underlying anger there. "Are you sure you aren't leaving because I asked you to marry me?"

Hurt, Ro could only stare at him, brow furrowed. "Is that what you think? Honestly?"

"You won't wear your ring, you won't talk about the wedding or plan our future together, and you won't set a date. Oui, that's what I think."

Ro's throat burned, but she didn't deny it. She realized with a sinking heart that she couldn't. She couldn't deny it.

Tears filled her eyes, but she lifted her chin. "If you want the ring back, it's on my nightstand. Next to my bed." Where she'd left it in her haste. "Cosette will get it for you if you need her to."

"Ro, wait." He caught her arm as she tried to mount. "What is it? What are you so afraid of?"

She recoiled, the words like a slap. "Afraid of? Nothing! If you don't want to wait here for me, that's your choice."

Her chin quivered without her permission, and Ro clamped her teeth to stop it.

Gazing deep into her eyes with a frown, then glancing overhead, Olt softened at whatever he saw there. "Oh, Ro." He leaned his forehead against hers, and she went perfectly still. "Don't you know I'm not going to hurt you?"

Ro jerked back. "Yes, you will. You will. You don't know it, but you'll leave, just like everyone else, and I'll be alone again."

She stemmed the flow of words that had come from absolutely nowhere. Good grief. Might as well bare every other insecurity while she was at it.

She hadn't even realized she felt that way.

His eyes held the deepest understanding, and a little fissure cracked in the wall that held back pain inside Ro's chest. She gasped at the intense trickle of feelings it released and spun away, blindly groping to pull the reins over Fairweather's head to get out of there before anything else came pouring out.

But Olt was there, blocking her way, gently pulling her to face him. "Ro, you need to hear this. I love you. I'm not going anywhere. You're a part of me now, and I'm going to spend every day proving to you that I can be trusted. Hopefully you'll let me prove it to you for the rest of our lives."

At Ro's widening eyes, he gave her a gentle smile.

"I'm a patient man, huntress, but I know what I want. And I want you."

She was already shaking her head. "You can't know that. No one likes me when they get to know me better."

Although she was trying to back away, Olt wasn't letting go. "Ro, listen to me. I understand it'll take time for you to trust me, and I'll wait. I won't push. But *you* have to decide this is what you want. I've pursued you and I've chased you and I've waited for you, but if this isn't what you want—if *I'm* not what you want"—he swallowed hard, his voice thick—"then I'll respect that. Go. See to your grandmère. And then come back and tell me. I'm not going to force you into anything. You're worth it."

Worth it? She'd never been worth anything. Not to her père . . . not to Gautier . . . not to the English king . . . not even to Trêve. She was just a huntress, available for their use, to be discarded when she was no longer useful or wouldn't do as she was told.

"You *are* worth it, Ro. And I'll prove it to you. Even if it takes the rest of my life."

She shook her head again. Even he didn't have that much patience.

His voice was husky. "You aren't getting rid of me that easily, huntress."

Humiliated beyond compare to be so exposed, for him to read her so easily, hating the warm glow that would surely turn to despair when someone better came along or he tired of her prickly nature, Ro stuffed everything down deep.

And backed up, right into her horse. "You don't mean that."

He gently—so gently, she wanted to weep—cupped her face. "You're wrong, Ro. I love you, and I mean every word." His thumb brushed her lips. "I'm here to stay. And I'll love you the only way I know how. By never giving up on you. On us."

Ro couldn't even respond. Just stared at him, lips parted and tingling from his brief touch.

He gave her a tender smile and kissed her again. "I'll wait here for you."

The weight of his words slammed into her all at once, and fear crushed her like a wave. "Don't."

He dropped his hand in surprise.

"Just don't, s'il vous plaît. Take the ring. You deserve

better, and I need time. I need, I need"—she didn't know what she needed—"I need to go."

He glanced above her head, as he'd been doing throughout their conversation, trying to get a read on her, and at whatever he saw there, his face drained of color.

His stunned expression haunted her as she swung up onto Fairweather's back. She jerked Fairweather's head around—he shook it in protest—and kicked his sides. "Yah!"

Her horse galloped down the road that would lead to Prussia and her grandmère's cabin in the Black Forest. She thought she heard Olt call her name over the pounding hoofbeats, but he didn't come after her. Not that she blamed him.

She didn't want to lose Olt—she didn't—but she couldn't give him what he wanted, either. She wasn't ready to get married. To make a family that could be broken as her père had broken theirs.

She wasn't good enough for him, and it was past time she set him free.

But, Dieu, she didn't want to.

Tears streamed down her face as she raced away from Paris.

7

Reaching the Black Forest seven excruciating days later, instead of the expected nine, Ro directed Fairweather onto one of the paths her grandmère had shown her, and the woods allowed them passage.

It was better than being lost for days on end, such as the first time she'd come to this forest. The path opened before her, not quite a fairy path, but similar, leading her straight to her grandmère's house.

Focused on her goal, Ro rode at a steady yet relentless pace, urgency her constant companion, letting Fairweather guide her on how much the aging horse could take.

The last time she'd been here, it was smack in the middle of summer, and the trees were a drab green, the air warm and heavy. Now yellow leaves bled through the greenery, and the air was cooler than it had been in Paris.

The trees fell away to reveal a familiar opening, and Ro yanked on Fairweather's reins to halt his progress. He shook his head in protest. She rubbed his neck, an apology for her unintentional rough treatment.

Her fingers tightened in his mane, holding tight to keep herself steady. She could do this.

Fairweather stilled as if he could sense his mistress's mood and the potential danger before them.

Ro slipped from his back and guided him forward. She was at the back of the property, behind the cabin where Grandmère kept the woodpile, and she couldn't see much from here. Staying within the tree line, she circled the property. The moment the clearing in front of the cabin came into view, she stopped, gazing in horror.

The circular clearing was trashed. Uprooted trees lay everywhere, some speared into the ground, as if they'd been torn from the surrounding woods and thrown like javelins into the clearing. Long gouges carved deep in the earth churned up dirt in furrows, as if for spring planting. Splintered boards littered the ground. And the cabin . . .

The cabin had been smashed straight down, as if something large had . . . stepped on it?

Shortening Fairweather's reins so they wouldn't get caught on any branches if he had to escape, she dropped them and said, "Stay. Watch for wolves. Flee if you must."

Ro drew her crossbow from its saddle holster, loaded it, and made sure her bolt quivers were full. Easing toward the pile of kindling that used to be the cabin, Ro sneaked around it, crossbow raised.

A spot of red cloth lay on the far side of the clearing, near the woods on the opposite side. Exactly where it had been in Ro's dream.

"Grandmère!"

Taking off running, Ro slid to her grandmère's side. She took a moment to quarter the field, but seeing nothing, she moved the red cloak off Darya's face and lifted her grandmère with one arm, clutching her crossbow in the other.

"Grandmère! Where are you hurt?"

Her grandmère made a strangled noise as Ro lifted her, and Ro cradled her gently, not daring to move her further. Wishing she hadn't moved her at all.

As she took in her grandmère's features, certainty settled in Ro's gut. It was *just* like her dream. Only this hadn't happened that long ago. Not even an hour, judging by the freshness of her wounds.

"You came. I knew you would." Gasping for breath, Grandmère lifted a bloodied hand and placed it on Ro's cheek, her other hand clutching an axe to her chest. "I-I . . . want you to have it."

Ro shook her head. "I don't understand. What happened? Who did this?"

Tears streamed down Ro's face, making it hard to see.

"My cabin. My axe. The land. It's all yours." Grandmère barked a laugh, her spittle flecked with blood. "Granted, 'tisn't much, not after . . ."

"You don't have to speak. We'll get help. We'll—"

Darya interrupted her. "The wolf . . ." The old woman wheezed. "You must . . . you must get rid of it."

Ro blinked. Surely she wasn't speaking of the same wolf as in her dream. He was monstrous. As tall as the trees. Maybe she meant the strange hairless wolves from last time?

The old woman twitched. "My axe. Use it."

"It will . . . kill it?"

She seemed to rally at that. "*Nein.* You must not kill it. Do you hear me? Do not kill it! You must drive it out, make it leave, but you must never, ever kill it. Not in this world."

"That will be . . . tricky."

"*Ja,* it will," the old woman rasped. "But you are a protectress. Only you can make it leave. Only by . . . your hand, now."

"But—"

Grandmère tightened her grip on Ro's hand. "A box . . . the heart . . . in the forest."

Ro recoiled. "You buried a heart in the forest?"

As if frustrated she couldn't make herself clear, the old

woman gave a single shake of her head, gasping for air. "*Nein* . . . the box . . . the heart . . . you must find it."

"Oui. I will." If she could figure out what Darya was talking about.

Ro held her grandmère tighter as she struggled to take another breath. It sounded as though her lungs were filling, like she wouldn't be able to take many more. Ro didn't want to leave her, but . . .

"Don't talk. I'll get help. I'll—"

"Chut, ma chère. I haven't much . . . time. It's yours. It's all yours. Rebuild. Start your life anew. Protect this forest . . ."

Grandmère's apple-red cloak slowly leeched of color, turning a silvery gray that somewhat matched the old woman's skin under all the blood.

Ro stared between it and her grandmère.

Darya gave her a tired smile. "I knew . . . if I hung on . . . a little longer . . . you would come . . ."

Even as she spoke, the cloak drained of color, the life faded from her eyes, and Darya's chest went still.

Ro cried out, dropped her crossbow, and tried to shake Darya awake—but she couldn't. Her grandmère had passed from this world into the next.

"Grandmère? Non! Grandmère!" Ro clutched the old woman close, her heart breaking.

It wasn't supposed to end like this. It wasn't. Ro was supposed to have years more to listen to her snide remarks, to learn everything she needed to know, to marvel over her cantankerous attitude and deny how similar she and Ro actually were.

And Ro had barely scratched the surface of all Darya knew, of all the woman could teach her. She hadn't come back and trained with her, as she'd meant to.

She thought they'd have more time, and now it was too late. Ro dropped her head on the motionless chest and sobbed.

The skin on the back of her neck prickled. The forest stilled, and Ro slowly raised her head, tears forgotten.

Birds ceased their song, small creatures skittering through the underbrush went silent, and rustling leaves became unnaturally still, as if the wind were holding its breath.

Something was stalking her.

Sudden movement was out of the question, but on instinct, she spread the hem of her cloak over her grandmère's body, made sure the red hood covered her own head, and stretched out a hand for her crossbow. Miraculously, it hadn't misfired when she'd dropped it, but it had fallen out of reach.

Her eyes caught on the axe the old woman still clutched in one hand, though it had slipped down on her stomach.

If she could just slip the axe out of Darya's tight grasp . . .

As Ro slowly reached for the axe, she scanned the trees. Seeing nothing, she glanced at the treetops. Every muscle in her body locked up.

There, glowing golden eyes. Watching the clearing. Gazing just past Ro and her grandmère.

A being as tall as the trees swept the treetops to either side and began to push through into the clearing. A long snout emerged, thickly furred in wiry black hair.

The wolf. From her dream. The one as tall as the forest.

It was *real*?

Ro couldn't imagine the axe—or a crossbow bolt, for that matter—would do anything against a creature this enormous. A hide so thick. It hadn't worked for her grandmère, so why would it work for her?

But she had to try.

Ro continued to reach for the axe, slowly, trying not to draw attention. Thankfully, the wolf was focused just past her, sniffing the clearing, as if the size of its giant shaggy head alone made it impossible to see Ro, tucked there below its chin. All it had to do was glance down . . .

Her fingers closed around the axe's handle, and a glowing ripple shot away from Ro and into the trees, riffling leaves and swaying branches.

The enormous creature spun as trees crackled behind it. Letting out an ear-splitting howl—one that had Ro hunkering low to the ground in a primal fear reaction she couldn't control—the wolf took off into the trees, bolting away faster than her eyes could track. Suddenly, Ro could no longer feel its presence.

After an eternity, Ro came to herself in the same position, still shielding her grandmère with her body, the birds having resumed their song and flight, the scurrying in the forest and rustling leaves relaying its normal orchestra.

She sat up slowly, shaking, unable to do more than breathe and thank the Creator that she was still alive. What *was* that thing?

Not wanting to leave her grandmère, knowing she had to, Ro gently laid her body on the forest floor, leaving the axe clutched in Darya's fingers. Ro grabbed her crossbow, the weapon she knew best, and went after the beast. But the trail went cold.

It had pushed trees aside, leaving snapped limbs and crushed undergrowth in its wake, including long black hairs that resembled rope dangling from branches, until the trail just . . . stopped.

And she couldn't pick it up again.

Reluctantly, Ro returned to the clearing. She didn't like leaving such a creature alive. Yet she couldn't begin to know how to hunt or follow it back to wherever it came from, either. She needed more information.

Grief struck her heart as she stared down at the lifeless shell that no longer contained her grandmère's spirit, and Ro closed Darya's eyes and covered her face with the now-silver hood of her cloak.

Her first thought was she needed to get a message to Cendre—now a daughter of the sea—if she didn't already know through whatever means sirens kept up on news from the above-water world.

Ro's little sister may have had a difficult relationship with their grandmère, fraught with tension and culminating in Cendre running away, but Darya had raised Cendre. Surely she would want to know. If any part of her human nature remained.

Her second thought was she needed to go after that wolf. Find its lair and drive it out. Before it killed anyone else.

And third . . . she would not be seeing Olt again for a very long time. If ever. Regret at the way she'd fled overwhelmed her.

Her throat burned, and she took a moment to suppress tears. She could grieve later. After she took out this great wolf and its minions, of which there had been plenty the last time she'd been in the Black Forest.

One had bitten her shoulder, in fact. Phantom pain twinged in memory.

Ro's eyes fell on the axe resting on her grandmère's body, clutched within her grasp. This was not how she'd wanted Darya's story to end. She took a deep breath. But she would honor her grandmère's last request to the best of her ability.

She reached for the axe.

"Don't."

Ro stilled, her fingers inches from the handle.

"Do not touch it unless you are willing to wield its power."

She frowned at the disembodied voice that came from heavy foliage only now hinting at colors other than green. "Show yourself."

A grizzled old man emerged. His movements were as spry as a man half his age, just as her grandmère's had been when she thought no one was watching, but he appeared ancient. Gray hair and beard, wrinkled and deeply tanned skin, shaded by a weathered tricorn hat. His boots had seen better days, his clothes were worn, and his frock coat looked like it had been military issue once upon a time.

When their eyes met, he fisted his own axe in strong hands and dipped his head.

"Fräulein." His voice sounded like he chewed gravel, and he glanced between the axe and Ro, as if unsure which concern to address first.

Darya had mentioned someone by the name of . . . "Gustave? The woodsman who works with my grandmère? I mean"—she glanced down at the old woman—"*worked* with her?"

Ro wiped a hand down her face, wrestling her emotions back under control.

Once she could meet his eyes, she found him studying her. "Aye, *Fräulein.*"

"I've already touched the axe." Ro eyed it. "Something . . . happened. When I did."

His eyebrows arched, and he took a moment to smooth away the expression. "I see. And was she able to . . . explain the consequences?"

Ro shook her head.

He grunted. "Help me bury the body. Before the wolves come back."

"I brought a horse. I'll go get him. To help move her."

He nodded his agreement, and Ro hurried away and soon came back with Fairweather. Without another word, Ro slid the crossbow into its holster, placed Darya's axe in a belt loop, and helped Gustave lift her grandmère onto Fairweather's back, thankful she didn't have to do this alone.

8

After they'd gone farther than Ro expected, they reverently set Darya at the base of a gnarled tree and wrapped her now-silver cloak around her body.

Ro assumed they were leaving her there long enough to retrieve shovels and dig a hole, but as she stepped back, tree roots crept around the old woman and pulled her tight into their embrace. Dirt churned as roots writhed in a roiling, snakelike mass.

Fairweather took off into the trees, the coward.

In a swift move, she swiped her grandmère's axe from her belt and raised it above her head.

"Stop!" The woodsman blocked her. "Don't use that axe upon the forest unless you're prepared for it to fight back."

She stared at him with wide eyes. He'd clearly lived too long alone in these woods. Fight back? Was he not concerned about the tree currently eating her grandmère?

The roots tightened their grasp.

Never mind. She had to stop this.

She skirted around him and heaved the axe down upon the closest root, but Gustave crossed her axe with his before it could bite into the tree.

66

"The tree's just doing what your *Oma* asked of it. Leave it be."

Ro strained to reach her as the tree wrapped its roots around her grandmère and pulled her deep underground, but Gustave was solid, immovable. The dirt settled, and Darya was no more.

"Where is it taking her?" she asked in a hoarse whisper, still not convinced she shouldn't go in there after her. Somehow.

"The terms of her agreement for being guardian of this land was that she would return to the Realm of the Fey and to her sisters who have gone on before her."

Sirens. Gustave was talking about Darya's siren sisters.

Ro's eyes widened. She didn't know such a thing was possible.

"Wait." Ro glanced between the tree and the old woodsman. "Is this the tree where Grandmère found Cendre?"

After the Fairy Queen had stolen Cendre and replaced her with her own daughter, Cosette, the tree had held on to Cendre's life long enough for Grandmère to find her, resuscitate her, and then raise her.

Surely this couldn't be the same tree.

His eyebrows lifted in surprise. "She told you the story? Aye. This be the tree."

Ro dropped her head, grief sweeping her afresh. No wonder her grandmère had built her cabin here, so close to the fairy tree that had kept Cendre alive.

From what she understood, fairy trees were how fey creatures traveled to and from their realm. Well, the creatures that were supposed to be here, anyway. And the trees existed in both places—the human realm and the fey realm.

Thinking of how the fey realm worked made her brain hurt.

Or, at least, that was how it had worked the time she'd

helped a fey creature get home who'd been trapped in an inn, making the owners think it was haunted.

She briefly wondered how the pixie was doing—and if he'd gotten himself into any more scrapes—before movement from Gustave reclaimed her attention.

The old woodsman removed his tricorn, held it tight to his chest, and stepped forward. Placing his hand on the trunk, he dropped his head and stood motionless.

Ro stood there awkwardly and let him have his moment. Should she look away? Walk off? Let him say goodbye in peace?

Before she could decide how best to react, he patted the tree twice, shoved the worn tricorn on his head, and strode away.

The moment he was out of view, she stepped closer to the tree, but not too close. She was wary of its roots, and she couldn't make herself touch its trunk.

The last time she'd touched such a tree, her hand had stuck fast, and . . . something else had happened. She frowned as she struggled to remember, but the memory just wasn't there.

One more thing to worry over later.

"Goodbye, Grandmère," she whispered. "Hug your sisters for me."

Ro bowed her head, then peeked at the foliage and gnawed on her bottom lip.

Just as she was wondering if she should go after Gustave, or if he needed more time to himself, he returned and eyed her. "You coming?"

"Oh, um. Oui." She hurried after him, not wanting to be alone should the giant wolf attack. Or should the tree try to eat her, too.

❧

When they'd traipsed through the woods a goodly distance, they came upon another cabin. One similar to her grand-mère's. Well, before the wolf had decimated it.

Fairweather waited for them, munching on the nearest shrub. He'd nearly stripped it bare of leaves.

Uncanny how he just showed up like that. Of course, she'd tell anyone who'd listen that her horse was smarter than he let on.

Gustave nodded to a building in the distance. "Barn's out back."

She grasped the reins, and Gustave showed her where he kept feed, hay, and the well for fresh water. Ro unpacked her horse, brushed him down, and followed Gustave to the cabin, saddlebags slung over her shoulder.

"This your place?" Ro asked, more to make conversation than anything. Ugh. Where else would they be? This was why she shouldn't open her mouth without thinking it through first.

He opened the door and walked inside—without responding or inviting her in. Ro frowned but followed him in anyway. He grunted when she crossed the threshold, but she had no idea what that meant.

Again the setup was very much like her grandmère's cabin, only more masculine and rugged. And slightly bigger.

He dug around in a box and produced a leather strap for her axe that included a wrap for its sharp edge. He handed it to her. "You'll need this. Carry your axe at all times."

Ro took it and nodded. Her grandmère had insisted on that very thing, before. Ro placed her bags in the corner, then set about fitting her new axe to its strap. She practiced drawing it quickly.

He prepared a swift meal of sliced salted ham and wedges of cheese. After brewing strong coffee for them both, he set an apple in front of Ro, then one in front of himself. They ate in silence.

After they were finished, Ro turned to the old woodsman. "Tell me everything."

He lifted weary eyes to hers, the pain of losing Darya within. "That might take a while, *Fräulein*."

"I know. But I need to know what I'm up against."

The old man grunted as he got to his feet. He led her to his fireplace and settled in a rocking chair. Ro eased into the matching rocking chair across from him and wondered how often her grandmère had done the same.

He may have been the only one who knew what was happening, but she wished with her entire being that Olt was here. That she hadn't taken his heart when he'd offered it to her and thrown it in his face, just because she was feeling vulnerable.

Best not think about such things or she'd be a blubbering mess. In front of someone else. Who looked like he'd never cried a day in his life.

To distract herself, Ro asked, "Are you a guardian of the forest, too?"

He got comfortable, lit his pipe, and began to speak. Ro settled deeper in her chair opposite the fireplace and began to listen.

"Your *Großmutter* was the guardian of this forest. I just assisted where help was needed," he said, his voice setting a steady pace.

Ro wanted to urge him to talk faster, to get on with it so she could find and slay the wolf that had killed her grand-mère. But she forced herself to speak in an even, reasonable tone. "Where did the giant wolf come from? And are those other wolves still here? The ones that attacked us last time? The hairless ones that stand on two legs and don't look like real wolves at all?"

"All in good time, *Fräulein*, all in good time. Although your *Großmutter* was tasked with guarding this forest, she never spoke of the details to me. All I know is one day I came upon her attempting to put up a lean-to while caring for a wee one, and I was no longer the sole caretaker of this forest. I helped her build a small cabin for her and her girl, and the rest, as they say, is history."

He rocked a few beats before musing, "Strange things had been happening, strange creatures trying to overrun the forest, but your *Großmutter* was there to combat them all." He glanced at her quickly, as if something had occurred to him. "Or did you call her *Oma*?"

Ro blinked at his sudden change of subject. *Großmutter* was formal German for grandmère, and *Oma* was informal.

She and her grandmère had not had that kind of relationship, easy and lighthearted.

"*Großmutter*, I suppose," she said. "Though I called her Grandmère, or Darya."

He nodded, absently. "She was a good woman, your *Großmutter*."

"I know," Ro said quietly. "I know."

Lost in thought, he puffed on his pipe and stared into the fireplace, his rocking chair creaking beneath him.

Ro tried to be patient, she did, but questions built up in her like a volcano ready to blow, and then they came spewing out.

"Why did you warn me away from the axe? What does it mean that I touched it? And what kinds of wolves *are* these? The hairless ones. I've never seen anything like them. And what of the giant one? How did she—why did she face the creature alone?"

She didn't want to outright accuse him, especially since she didn't know their relationship or how often they worked together, but a part of her wanted to know why he hadn't been there for Darya. To help her. To . . . save her.

Besides, Ro was angry at herself for not arriving sooner.

"How long has she been fighting the creatures, and why can't we kill them? How do we get rid of them?" Ro rubbed her face, weary from the long ride and overwhelming grief and unanswerable questions. "Where do we go from here?"

"Taking up the axe means you are the new protectress of this forest. That you agreed to take Darya's place and protect the Black Forest—and this world in turn—from the fey creatures that prey on humans."

Ro shot to her feet. "I most certainly did not! I'll stay and help get rid of the wolves, oui, but I did not agree to *live* here."

He just regarded her with somber eyes and puffed away until she slowly sank back into her chair.

"My apologies. Pray continue."

He gave her a solemn nod and went on. "Your *Großmutter* has been watching over this forest since she first came here, when Cendrillon was but a wee babe, but these creatures are new. She called these wolves *loups-garous*, if there are many, and a *loup-garou*, if there's just the one, though I believe the big one is something else entirely—"

Ro shot to her feet again. "Werewolves? The creatures are werewolves? Shapeshifters? Those who walk with wolf skins?"

She'd only ever heard of them in fairy tales, never in real life. Never in any of her travels. As far as she knew, men, or perhaps some kind of fey creature, could put on the skins of wolves and transform into brutal and wicked-fast wolves, much bigger and stronger than the regular wolves she was used to fighting.

She'd thought the beast was one, long ago, before she found out he was a cursed prince.

Ro realized Gustave was watching her. He once again waited until she was seated to resume his tale. "Although they are fairly new to this area, we've at least fought them and found what doesn't work. The giant one, the Wolf King—"

"The Wolf *King*?"

"—only just showed up, which is why your *Großmutter* came back early instead of spending more time with her family. And these loups-garous do not wear other skins. They enter our realm looking like wolves." He cocked his head. "Or perhaps what they think wolves look like."

Words fled Ro, and she just sat there, staring at the old woodsman.

He waited a moment, as if giving her time to interrupt, before continuing. "The Wolf King has been prowling the forest, searching for something. We've only caught glimpses of him, yet he has never engaged either of us until today. Your *Großmutter* was alone, *Fräulein*, because I did not know he would attack, neither of us did, or I would have been there. I can sense the others, but not the great one."

Ro nodded, her throat thick. She would've been there too, had she left sooner. Had she listened to the dream instead of waiting for Darya's call for help to drive her to action.

Something that was sure to haunt her for the rest of her life.

"We cannot kill the creatures, because it allows them to spawn anew, then come through with more besides, overrunning the forest. Darya figured if they're trapped and sent back, they cannot come through again. As if their entry to our world has been revoked." He shrugged. "It is a guess, truly, but it seems at least somewhat accurate, through much trial and error."

Ro rubbed her temples. "Come through *what*? And how did she trap them?"

"Through the rift between our world and the Realm of the Fey. It is weakest here, in the Black Forest, and many fey who have spread to other lands have come through here first. And . . . I do not know how to trap them. That is something Darya figured out. Through her protectress mantle."

"Great. That's just great." Ro pinched the bridge of her nose, hoping it would help relieve her forming headache.

"The mantle you have now taken up."

She jumped up and started to pace. "It's not that I object

to the idea of being the new protectress. I've done just that for most of my life. But I wasn't asked. I simply picked up her axe, and now I'm expected to stay and just . . . do what she did. But I have a family. A life! In Paris. That I need to get back to."

He eyed her. "Didn't she offer you her cabin?"

Ro faltered. "Well, oui, she did. But I hadn't accepted her offer."

"Yet you came when she called, and you picked up the axe when she put it down. Seems like you accepted her bargain to me."

Before Ro could throw out another objection, the old woodsman spoke in a quiet, powerful voice.

"Be careful what you say next, dearie. Whether you knew you were accepting it or not, bargains are sacrosanct here so close to the Land of the Fey. Should you deny, refuse, or appear to lie about taking up her mantle, it will not go well for you. You may lose whatever small powers you already have."

Ro snapped her mouth closed, her jaw ticking. She would just see about *that*.

"What exactly does this bargain entail?" she finally managed to ask.

"You are tasked with keeping the human realm safe. With denying passage to fey who try to sneak in through the veil. Those who enter through fairy trees to travel, buy, sell, or trade have permission from their queen to be here, and we don't bother them."

She reeled from his words. Once again, everything was *too much*. What had she gotten herself into?

His expression was unreadable as he studied her. "You picked up the axe. It will show you the way. You agreed to guard this forest, and so you'll do it, and you'll do it well."

Ro shook her head. "I'm telling you, I never agreed to that."

"You did when you picked up the axe," he insisted. "It

asked you if you would guard the forest, and you agreed. It could not have happened any other way. All that is left is for the forest to accept you."

Ro wanted to scream. What did that mean for her life in Paris? Her career as a huntress? What did that mean for her and Olt?

If there even was a "her and Olt" anymore.

"Now, it's a lot to take in, so I suggest you sleep on it." Gustave nodded to an open door that led to a room off the main cabin. "You may have my room this night. I'll sleep with the animals." At her concerned look, he amended, "In the barn. Don't worry about me, *Fräulein*. There's plenty of warm hay and a good, strong door. I'll be safe enough."

Ro checked the closest window. It was already dark out. No way was she traipsing through the woods to find someplace to camp with such creatures about.

Unsure what else to do, she gave a stiff jerk of her chin, and he gathered what he needed and left.

Unable to sleep in a strange man's bed, even if that man was her grandmère's friend and trustworthy enough, she hoped, Ro curled up in her cape in front of the fireplace and stared at the dancing flames, her mind spinning with all they'd discussed.

Mostly she just wished for Olt.

And her grandmère.

Both things she could no longer have.

A grunt woke Ro. Gustave stood just inside the front door, a full milk pail clutched in his work-thickened hands.

"Didn't care for the bed?"

Ro sat up and stretched. "I—suppose I fell asleep here last night. Truly, this is more than what I'm used to. I don't mind sleeping in the barn, if you'd like your bed back."

Gustave just grunted again and went to the stove, soon bringing a pot of coffee and some gruel to the small table. Ro, after seeing to Fairweather and pumping water from the well to wash her face and hands, joined him.

They ate in silence, and although the food was nothing spectacular, it was hearty and filling. Ro enjoyed eating in silence, not expected to talk (much) until she had a few cups of strong black café in her.

It was what she drank when she hunted, oui, but she missed crème and sucre.

She cleared away the dishes to wash, since he'd cooked the meal, and asked, "Where are we going first to hunt the wolves? I mean, the loups-garous?"

He opened the front door and sat next to it before lighting his pipe, apparently having noticed that Ro hadn't cared for the smell last night, even though she'd tried not to let her reaction show. Especially since this was his home, not hers.

It didn't take Ro long to clean the mismatched bowls, clay mugs, and small pot he'd cooked in, and that was about the time it took him to answer.

"The loups-garous come and go, and right now my senses tell me they don't wish to be found, so we wouldn't. I think our time would best be served by rebuilding your *Großmutter*'s cottage, *Fräulein*."

Ro's hands stilled in gathering her hunting items. Because even though she had no intention of staying past hunting the loups-garous, nor of taking up her grandmère's mantle, whatever that entailed, he didn't see it that way.

"I see."

Although, truth be told, if it was a fey bargain she'd stumbled into, then she had no choice but to follow through until she found a way to fulfill it or make a new bargain.

But who had she made it with? The fey? The axe? The forest itself?

There were so many things she needed to learn, and she needed to do so before the Wolf King attacked again.

He rose to his feet, emptied his pipe of ash, and shoved his tricorn on his head. "Bring your weapons. And don't you worry. The wolves will come to us, and we'd best stay ready for them. But until then, might as well do something useful."

"Should I not learn more about this supposed . . . bargain I've made?"

"That will come in time," he said cryptically, and quite unhelpfully.

Of course it will, she thought with a great deal of sarcasm.

So Ro finished gathering her weapons, swirled on her red hunting cape, and followed him into the Black Forest.

It was beautiful here. Quiet, peaceful—when creatures of myth and legend weren't attacking—and one could make a good life living off the bounty the forest had to offer, according to Gustave.

It also wasn't that far from Olt's family—a fact that now stung. Even so, she wanted a choice in the matter.

But since that choice had been taken away, what else could she do? She apparently was going to rebuild her grand-mère's cabin, move in, and fight some loups-garous in the meantime. Perhaps for the rest of her life.

She sighed. And wondered where she might find a messenger to send a missive to Cosette.

And what she'd write if she could find one.

9

either said a word as they made their way to the cabin ruins on foot.

First they prowled the property and took stock. Not much was salvageable, but the well had an intact covering and hadn't been contaminated. The herb garden behind the cabin had survived, and the shed Darya had stored supplies and dried herbs in had missed the battle.

Huge ruts torn into the earth would have to be raked out before rain came, mainly so Ro wouldn't trip over them every time she walked by. Although the back wall had seemed fine yesterday, today she could tell it was propped against the woodpile and would come down at the next stiff wind.

The porch and foundation were perhaps the only part of the cabin they could rebuild upon, and they were sound.

But the walls were destroyed. The roof was gone. And the wolf's foot had gone right through the floorboards into a space beneath.

The opening surprised Ro, so she took a closer look.

A splintered trapdoor lay at the bottom, a rug shredded through the wood, and Ro told Gustave she was replacing that. It was brilliant if she needed to hide or escape a fire. Which were both likely in Ro's experience.

A tunnel had been dug all the way out into the trees, an escape route should her grandmère have needed it.

Ro sincerely wished Darya would've used it instead of facing the wolf.

Ro found the door—the glorious, beautifully carved door—in the yard, half-buried under a splintered wall. Besides a few scratches, they should be able to sand down the edges and reuse it.

Grief struck Ro's heart that Darya would never again use this gorgeous door she'd commissioned. Ro quickly got back to work.

Grandmère's giant stove that Ro had been impressed could even be carted this deep in the forest was tipped on its back, the oven door dented, but it, too, might be salvageable with some new piping and the dents banged out.

Gustave merely grunted with each discovery. Granted, there wasn't much. But at least they had a place to start.

Digging through the splintered chest that held the family Bible and hand-drawn portraits of Ro's family, Ro picked up a crushed portrait—one of her mère and père. She cradled it to her chest, her throat burning, and the back of another portrait peeked out of the rubble.

Ro picked it up and flipped it over. This one was of a young Cendre, gaze already hard and defiant. Her sister. The girl who had been lost at sea, before Ro had even known who she was.

All drawn or painted by her grandpère before he'd died.

She only had vague recollections of Grandpère. Although he wasn't actually related—as she'd later found out her real grandpère was a prince in a seaside palace who'd married someone else—he'd been a wealthy artist with many patrons and had fallen madly in love with her grandmère, who had a lovely singing voice and used it to support her and her daughter. He'd taken her daughter in as his own and loved her too, so much so that Ro had never realized they weren't related—not until Grandmère had told her.

One day, she would search for her real grandpère—if he were still alive.

Not important right now.

She needed to focus on her task or she would be a blubbering mess.

They cleared away anything they couldn't reuse—personal items to the side to go through more carefully at Gustave's cabin—and piled the rest in the middle of the clearing. Gustave lit it on fire, and soon the pleasant smell of wood burning complemented the crisp autumn air.

Ro half expected him to just start hammering boards together, but to her surprise, he pulled out a clutch of papers and began sketching a new cabin, this one a little bigger, with a loft. One that might hold a family, or at least a newly married couple, Ro couldn't help but note. And it made her ache for Olt that much more.

What had she been thinking? Why had she run off like that? Olt deserved so much better than how she'd treated him, and now she was stuck here. She couldn't make it right if she wanted to.

Gustave would sketch a few options and then ask what she thought, and although Ro tried not to, she was soon swept away in choosing what she wanted. As the sun started to set, she held plans to a perfect little cabin, beyond pleased with how they'd turned out.

The main room used the same footprint as the original cabin, then there was a loft for extra places to sleep or store items, with the potential for two more rooms to be added to the back should she want to do so later.

Not bad. Not bad at all.

With the sun on its descent and the burn pile smoldering, Ro and Gustave gathered Grandmère's personal items, then set off for his cabin to clean up, eat, and fall into bed exhausted.

Ro was planning on doing that last one, anyway.

Apparently tomorrow they would fell trees and use Gustave's oxen to pull them into the clearing to start seasoning them—whatever that meant. At this rate, Ro wasn't going to have a spare moment to worry about Olt, the loups-garous, or whether or not she wanted to stay.

Gustave was going to work her to death, and she'd probably wake up at the end of it all and wonder how a whole cabin had been built around her.

After cleaning up and eating dinner, Gustave sat at his table and turned his sketches into detailed blueprints for her new cabin, and before Ro knew it, she was fast asleep before the fire.

The next day, Ro slowly got ready, not wanting to face another day without Olt. Without her grandmère. Without avenging her death.

She jumped as a knock on the cabin door startled her. "Come in," she called.

The woodsman entered and gave her an intense look. "First rule: Don't invite anyone in. Ever."

Ro barked a laugh. What was she supposed to say to his knock? "Does that mean I'm going to be a grumpy old woman just like my grandmère?"

He gave her a sharp look. "I'll have no disrespecting of your *Großmutter* in this house, *Fräulein*."

Ro's grin left her face. "I beg your pardon. I meant no disrespect. I, ah, my sense of humor falls flat. Often."

He nodded, accepting her apology and moving on. "Most fey can only come into your home if you invite them, and inviting the wrong ones can mean sudden death. Instead, say,

'If you can enter, you are welcome as my guest.' Then if they mean you harm, they cannot enter, and if they choose to accept your hospitality, they cannot trick you or stay overly long. I know a family who once hosted a fey lord for five years, and they couldn't leave the house or sleep in all that time, and when the fey finally got bored and left, they could only walk upon the ceiling. They fled the Black Forest."

Ro would have, too.

He was a wealth of information, truly. Now for him to help her find that Wolf King.

"Now, eat hearty. We'll be putting that axe of yours to good use."

"Does that mean you'll be training me? Picking up where Grandmère left off?" Ro sat at the table and took a bite of her gruel, filled with dried berries, hazelnuts, and fresh milk.

He shook his head, his eyes sad. "*Nein*, I cannot do what your *Großmutter* did. What she wielded was powerful magic. She held the fates of two realms in her hands, and she balanced them perfectly."

Ro's eyes widened with every syllable. How on earth could she learn what her grandmère did? How could she even *do* what her grandmère did? It seemed impossible.

"I can only teach you what I know about the forest itself. I wish with all my heart she could've trained you. You have a heavy task on your shoulders, *Fräulein*, and I do not envy you. But who knows? Perhaps once the forest has accepted you, it will show you what I cannot." He heaved his axe over his shoulder. "Now come. Daylight's a-wasting."

Sure, if he meant the sun had barely come up yet.

One thing pounded through Ro as the old man took her deep into the forest and taught her everything he knew about choosing and felling trees with every swing of their axes, to then be dragged into the clearing and left there. What would Olt think of this kind of life? Would he want to live here with her?

She didn't know. She had no way of knowing. She'd left him standing outside Paris as she'd run away as fast as she could, after telling him to take her ring back. No way would he want to marry her now.

Thankfully, hard work drove such thoughts from Ro's mind, and it was all she could do to survive the day and collapse on her pallet before the fire, exhausted, that evening.

Not looking forward to even more hard labor when every muscle screamed at her to soak in a long warm bath and not move for a few days, Ro walked into the clearing and ground to a halt. "What in all the realms?"

There, right where they'd left a pile of felled trees last night, lay evenly cut lumber, stacked neatly and glistening in light-fawn-colored beauty.

She turned to Gustave. "How on earth—"

"Do *not*," he hissed. Then in a low voice that barely reached her ears, "We do not acknowledge, and we do not give thanks. We go on as if nothing happened, and we do not say another word. Understood?"

Ro blinked, trying to decide if she should be affronted.

He sighed. "Perhaps I shall leave a book out for you to read after supper?"

Like that even made sense. She just stood there, waiting for him to expound, and he just stared back, not expounding upon anything.

Well if he was going to be mysterious about it . . .

Disgruntled, Ro marched away to inspect the lumber.

He moved to her elbow and cleared his throat. "We can begin by redoing the floorboards and the trapdoor. Then setting the frame, one for each wall. Then completing the walls and raising them with levers. Thatching for the roof should be easy enough—"

"Non, no thatching," Ro said. "Too easy to burn." She grumbled in a lower voice, "Whether by malicious intent or accident."

He didn't argue. He'd seen her attempt at cooking. Which was why he kept that particular duty and let her wash up after instead.

"Shall we begin?" he asked.

Ro nodded and ran her fingers over the smooth planks, not a splinter in sight. She took a deep breath, and the fresh scent of cut wood filled her senses. "Exquisite."

"It is that," he said appreciatively.

A pleased sound came from the trees, a high-pitched chatter that had Ro's head whipping around.

Gustave immediately shoved the cabin plans in front of her face in a desperate move. "Shall we start on the south wall or the west wall? After the flooring, that is."

She eyed him. "I'm just the muscle here. You tell me."

He grunted, and his eyes sparkled, which was the closest to a smile she'd gotten from him. "West wall it is."

They got to work, and Ro tried very hard not to think about how felled trees had transformed into a pile of lumber overnight.

❧

The book Gustave left out for Ro that evening, after he bid her goodnight and headed for the barn, was *very* interesting.

There was a section on brownies, fey creatures who would clean one's home and do other chores after the family had gone to bed, and the only way to thank them was to leave out bread and milk each night.

Which was not a suggestion.

Apparently it was deeply offensive to acknowledge their work, or to offer any verbal thanks, but leaving out the only human food they ate—and treasured—and then ignoring them was the height of manners.

If they were thanked aloud, or mentioned in conversation, they would vanish and never return. Yet you could praise your clean house or repaired shoes or newly made furniture as long as there was no direct thanks. It was a thin line, and some brownies were more sensitive than others, so it was usually better to say nothing at all.

And if you forgot the bread and milk—the only food they accepted, it seemed, except for red wine on special occasions—for even one night, they would also vanish.

Fascinating.

Ro flipped to the title page, but the only thing it said, in perfect handwriting, was *Stories by a Friend*. Except it was in German. Something she hadn't realized.

Although she knew the language well enough to converse now, reading was another matter. Yet she could read this book, which meant it was fey written. Or perhaps her protectress powers were doing strange things again.

Sometimes objects lit at night as if outlined in candlelight, especially if she were hunting. Sometimes distance would fall away, and she could take incredible shots with her recurve bow or crossbow. And sometimes time skipped, and she could see events mere seconds before they happened so that she could make better choices.

Or, as in the case of her grandmère, attempt a rescue.

But it never happened at the same time, and never when she wanted it to, and it always took her by surprise. Or epically failed, as in this latest instance.

If only she had a manual on how all this worked instead of—she flipped through the book—fairy stories. Handwritten fairy stories, at that. Then again, these sounded more like firsthand accounts than fiction.

But it wasn't until she came to the final entry in the book that cold fear washed over her.

"The Wolf King," she whispered.

Sure enough, she'd read this exact tale before a hunt, where she'd killed a dire wolf with a white pelt that now lined the inside of her red cape when it was cold.

She hadn't thought of that particular hunt in ages.

The white wolf had been killing people for fun, playing with them instead of eating them, making their deaths torturous and lengthy. It had been wrong, unnatural, evil—and she'd ended its reign of terror.

But not before she'd seen the Wolf King himself while she was trying to trap the white dire wolf.

Yet as surely as if her memory had been erased, she hadn't remembered it until this exact moment, not even when faced with the creature after it had struck down her grandmère.

Her jaw tightened. Grandmère was right. Someone or something had messed with her head, had erased important memories, and she was going to get them back. Somehow.

She flipped through the book again, then did a double take. She could've sworn there hadn't been blank pages in the back earlier.

Before she could talk herself out of it, she grabbed a quill and inkpot from Gustave's small writing desk and started scribbling as fast as she could.

It wasn't a story this time, as she liked to write, but it was everything she could remember about that hunt. She described the Wolf King, inscribing her memories in ink in case they deserted her again.

She'd conquer whatever had been done to her, but for now, she'd make a record, just in case.

And surprisingly, there were just as many pages as she needed and no more.

10

They made steady progress on the cabin each day, surprising since it was just the two of them. Clearly Gustave was used to building entire structures by himself.

She really did nothing more than hold and lift and hammer things as Gustave did the precision work. Still, it was back-breaking.

The wooden skeleton was in place; now they would use saplings to raise the completed walls and secure them. Saplings that, as with the trees they'd felled, they only cut after they'd asked permission, which was just bizarre to Ro.

Yet they moved on if he said the tree did not give it.

Next they would complete the roof, to be shingled in tree bark. After that they'd whitewash the walls and paint the trim dark brown, in the typical German style.

If anyone had told Ro a month ago that she'd be rebuilding a cabin she still wasn't certain she'd be living in, she would've laughed. Now they were raising walls and about to work on the *roof*.

Sweat slicked her brow, her sleeves were rolled up, and her cape hung on a nearby branch. Her muscles burned with that satisfying feeling of being put to good use, and she

87

readied herself to help Gustave fit the next piece of the house together.

Just as they were lifting a wall into place, Gustave tensed. "Set her down, nice and easy now. But quickly."

Ro did as directed, brushing her hands off once they were free. "What—" Then she noticed his face, and her whole body went on alert. "What is it?"

"Wolves. Loups-garous. Many of them. Headed this way."

Ro immediately slipped her cape over her sweaty tunic and trousers and reached for her crossbow.

"*Nein*. The axe."

Her hand changed direction, and she clutched the axe in both hands.

He grabbed his own axe and took off for the trees. "It's better to be surrounded by forest!"

Ro grumbled and hurried to catch up. Better for him, maybe. She preferred wide-open spaces that left plenty of room to fight.

They tore through underbrush turning as golden as the leaves overhead, and it wasn't long until they heard things—many things—crashing through the forest, straight toward them. They stopped, back to back, waiting.

"Now would be a great time to tell me what to do instead of killing them," Ro said, strangling the handle of her grand-mère's axe.

Gustave made a growling noise in the back of his throat. "I don't know what she did. She somehow used the trees." He eyed her. "You still can't hear them? The trees?"

Ro shook her head, frustrated. She had no idea what he was talking about.

He sighed. "Just . . . try not to kill the loups-garous. They do tire after a while, and they spook easily, so we'll just have to hold out. Wound as many as possible."

And then there was no more time for talking, for the wolves were upon them.

At the last moment, Ro turned her axe-head to the side and used it as a battering ram to fling creatures aside.

They swarmed her and Gustave, and both moved in a dance that came with years of honing their skills, of fighting for their lives. It wasn't easy, but they somehow kept themselves away from snapping teeth and tearing claws. Just barely.

The wolves were rangy, nearly hairless. Lean muscle roiled under skin with barely any fat to their cadaverous bodies. Their skin was a dark-brown color, easily seen past the scraggly black hair that sprouted in sparse patches all over.

This close, Ro could see what Gustave meant about their trying to look like wolves, but somehow getting it horribly wrong. She *hated* fey creatures that preyed on humans.

The loups-garous easily went between running on all fours to springing upright before flinging themselves at Ro or Gustave. Their arm span was ridiculous. Their knuckles brushed the ground as they ran hunched over on back legs. They were wild in their frenzy to get at fresh meat, and it was all Ro could do to keep them off her.

And then one wolf sprang off a tree and tried to drop on Ro from above.

On instinct, she swung her axe straight up and split open its skull. The metal bit into the creature as if it were happy to oblige, almost as if it wanted to join the fight.

As Ro rolled away, the loup-garou crumpled where she'd been standing, lifeless.

The other wolves howled and redoubled their efforts, and Gustave made a strangled noise, one that Ro could tell in the brief time she'd known him meant he wanted to berate her but was too busy to do so.

Ro lifted her chin and kept fighting. It was an accident. Besides, if he wasn't going to give her an alternative . . .

Suddenly, the wolves moved away as one, on all fours, and began to pant and howl and prance as if they were excited.

"Back away, slowly now," Gustave cautioned.

They shifted once more back to back, and Ro glanced around frantically. "Where? We're surrounded."

"Toward the weakest ones. There. We'll beat 'em both aside at the same time and make a run for it."

"I don't think we can outrun these wolves . . ." Still, Ro edged toward the weak pair he'd pointed out, matching his pace.

Sure, those two loups-garous were slightly smaller than their brethren, but that wasn't saying much. Each fey creature easily outweighed any wolf Ro had fought in her lifetime. Even the mad white dire wolf.

And then something caught Ro's eyes that she couldn't look away from.

The last time she'd been in the Black Forest, she'd defeated a sorceress called the Nightingale Empress who'd trapped Ro's niece in a sleeping curse.

The empress had kept hunters from finding her pagoda by erecting an invisible barrier. The structure could be seen from far away, but up close, anyone seeking the empress would wander round the pagoda and never find it.

Yet when Ro had cut the barrier, granting her access, it fell away like a limp skin.

This reminded her of that.

Something with claws and a muzzle with jagged teeth pushed out what looked like translucent skin in the middle of —nothing. Just air. It snapped at Ro, grinning its doggy grin that said it wanted to eat her face, and clawed at the milky skin-like barrier with a desperation that said it *was* getting through and it *was* going straight for Ro.

Hardly daring to look away, but needing to, she glanced to where the creature she'd killed lay. Where it should have lain.

But the spot was empty, and the one tearing through the

barrier—that Ro was guessing kept the fey realm from bleeding into the human realm—had a jagged scar on its skull where her axe had bit deep.

Just then, a single claw punctured, and the loup-garou stabbed the small tear with both paws and slowly, slowly tore a bigger seam, muscles bulging as if it took incredible strength to do so. "Um . . . Gustave . . ."

A teeming mass of loups-garous boiled behind the creature forcing its way through, and howls spilled out that sent chills right up Ro's spine.

Then Gustave was shoving her. "Go! Now!"

Ro didn't have to be told twice.

They batted aside the two smaller loups-garous as if the move had been choreographed, then took off into the trees.

They hadn't been running long when Gustave called, "This way! Climb that tree."

Now, although some of the trees in this section of the Black Forest were conifers, green year-round, most looked like matchsticks stabbed straight down into the soil, with greenery or fall colors starting two-thirds to the top. But every once in a while a giant, sprawling tree spread its heavy limbs wide, and it was to one of these Gustave led her.

The moment he reached the trunk, he slammed the axe into his belt and cupped his hands. Ro shoved away her axe and leaped, springing off his interlaced fingers into the lower branches.

"Can't wolves climb?" she asked breathlessly as she did just that. "These ones, anyway?"

Their front paws were more like grotesque human hands instead of wolf paws, with thick black claws jutting out of the tips, and their back paws somewhat resembled human feet. If those feet were gnarled and twisted and had the same thick claws. Grotesque, oui, but it also made Ro think they'd be able to climb and pick up things, like a human.

He grunted as he followed her up. "As high as you can go" was all he spared breath for.

They'd climbed halfway when the loups-garous reached them. They spilled out of the forest, their eerie howls raising the hair on Ro's neck and arms.

Gustave placed one hand against the trunk. "Help us, please."

The tree came alive. Heaving its limbs like battering rams, it swatted away wolves, not letting any near its trunk.

"Higher!" Gustave called, a bit desperately. "We're not high enough!"

Ro knew he was right, but she also wasn't letting go. The limb she was on swung madly, smacking away wolves with satisfying thumps, making her dizzy.

Making her question whether this was really happening.

She squeaked when another branch plucked her off the limb and boosted her high in the tree, where she could see what was going on but wasn't in danger of being flung off.

With each swing, yellow leaves fluttered to the ground alongside a few green, baring parts of the tree well before the coming fall weather could have a go at it.

Not a single loup-garou was getting anywhere near it.

A breathless Gustave eventually made it closer to the top, though he didn't dare go as high as Ro. She wouldn't have climbed this high either, given a choice, but the tree had made a basket seat for her, interlocking its smaller branches, keeping her secure and, strangely, comfortable.

Ro started counting wolves. "Weren't there about fifteen or so before?"

Gustave hooked an arm around the closest limb so he could lean against the tree and just breathe. "Only a dozen."

Ro shook her head. Unless she was mistaken—and it was possible with how the loups-garous kept picking themselves up and flinging themselves back at the tree—"There are over thirty wolves down there."

He grunted. "Forty-eight."

"Surely not."

At Ro's incredulous look, he expounded. "There are twelve to a pack. You killed one. A wolf, not a pack. It, in turn, was able to bring three more packs along with itself when it broke back through. Forty-eight."

Ro felt sick. She counted again, but although their movements were slowing as the wolves took damage, they were still too fast to get an accurate count. She'd have to take his word for it. "I'm sorry," she said quietly.

He just watched the fight play out below, letting her take in the consequences of her actions.

"How do I find out how to send them back?" She thought of the book he'd lent her. "Did Grandmère write it down somewhere?"

Maybe if she had, Ro could find out what heart was buried in a box in the forest at the same time. Or whatever Darya meant by that.

He shook his head. "Your *Großmutter* didn't put much stock in the written word. Learned it late enough in life that it was difficult for her, and I think she was embarrassed, so she didn't push herself to learn more."

Well there went that. Although . . . "Cendre said something about enchanted maps?"

Grief struck the old man's face, and he dropped his head as if he didn't want Ro to see. But she already had. "Aye," he said in a gruff voice. "She did make those. But she drew the maps, imbued them with magic, then Cendre wrote the words."

"Wait a moment. I didn't see any in the wreckage."

"Aye," the old man said, his composure back as he coolly surveyed the diminishing mêlée below. "Darya mostly made 'em for hire, but the girl took the last few with her when she ran away. Said she was going to see the world and Darya couldn't stop her." He chuckled. "A spitfire, that one, just like her *Oma*. Of course, Darya didn't think she meant it that time either, not till she found the girl gone with her maps." His voice quieted. "She didn't have the heart to make more after that."

Ro didn't know what to say, so she remained silent.

She'd give anything to see Cendre again, to get to know the sister she hadn't known she had, the sister who was now a siren at the bottom of the sea in Ro's place.

Before she could get too melancholy about that, or their grandmère, or Olt, Gustave patted the tree twice.

With a yip, a loup-garou held its paw and fled. As if it had set off an avalanche, wolves scattered in all directions, yipping in terror and whining, as if just now realizing how dangerous the tree was. It wasn't long until Ro could no longer feel their presence in the forest.

Wait. When had she started feeling their presence?

Gustave broke into her thoughts. "I thank ye, dear maple, for giving us aid in our time of need."

It is our honor to give succor to the new Daughter of the Forest. May her branches grow wide and full, and may her roots grow deep, as did her predecessor's.

Ro startled at the whisper-soft voice, but the branches tilted slightly, not letting her fall.

Gustave chuckled at her reaction, sounding pleased, and started climbing down.

She tried to follow, but in a reverse move, the tree swooped her down and settled her on the springy forest floor with all the grace it had used to pick her up.

Ro stumbled anyway, because it was her. And it was slightly terrifying that a tree was picking her up and setting her down and, and . . . *speaking* to her. Though its voice didn't seem to be spoken aloud, just in her head.

A limb reached out, as if a Monsieur were crooking his elbow, and Ro used it to steady herself. "Merci beaucoup," she said, feeling absolutely ridiculous.

It made a motion, somewhat like a curtsy or tipping a hat, and she glanced up to see Gustave still a long way off in the branches above her.

"Can you not help him as well?"

He would not appreciate our efforts.

She could see that. And then, as if a match had been struck, an idea flared to life. "Oh! Perhaps you can help me. How do I send the loups-garous back to where they belong without allowing more through?"

A branch reached out and caressed her face with its leaves, a gentle touch. *The trees will aid you, if you but ask. But beware, for the time comes when we must sleep, and it is dangerous to keep us from our slumber for too long a time.*

And with those words, the sprawling maple settled and became once more . . . a tree.

Gustave landed next to her, making Ro jump. "Shall we return to building your cabin?" At her sharp look, he said, "The loups-garous be at their rest for now. I don't foresee another attack this day."

"Actually, can we return to your cabin instead, s'il vous plaît?" Ro couldn't quite hold back her shudder. "I think I'm done for today."

Also, she wanted to read more of that book. She had a feeling she'd need to know much more if she wanted to survive this forest. Besides, she wanted to write down every detail of the fight before she forgot.

Ro yawned and didn't even have to pretend to be exhausted.

"Early to bed doesn't sound half bad tonight," he said, though he gazed longingly in the direction of the cabin they were building.

Ignoring the fact that he just wanted to go back to work like nothing happened, she said, "I couldn't agree more."

He gave her a long look before saying, "The loups-garous ran in the direction of your *Großmutter's* cabin. I don't think they can get past the protections, and I can check on it alone if you like, but . . ."

Grandmère's cabin! All their hard work. Better check on it with him, just in case.

Her grandmère had died the last time she'd been there alone, after all.

Changing direction, she took off, Gustave close behind. Far away, a wolf howled, and Ro spun toward the noise, axe immediately at the ready.

"They aren't too pleased that their quarry got away," the old woodsman mused.

"I'm not too pleased they *think* I'm their quarry," Ro grumbled.

The old man chuckled, dropped the axe he'd drawn over his shoulder, and set off at an easy stride that ate up distance but Ro could easily match.

A branch snapped behind her, and a prickle at her nape said she was being watched. She whirled toward the noise, axe held before her. Nothing. So she waited for her eyesight to do that thing where it lit everything slightly, allowing her to see prey or what hunted her, but her vision remained as normal as ever.

"*Fräulein*? What is it?" Gustave asked.

Ro shook her head, her unease not dissipating, even though she didn't see anything out of the ordinary. "I don't know."

After a slight pause, Gustave headed back her way.

She gave him a brief smile. "Just jumpy, I guess."

He too scanned the forest, then turned to her, a question in his eyes.

In answer, she headed toward her grandmère's cabin, her shoulders tense, ready for more loups-garous to leap out at any moment.

Matchsticks. Everything. All their hard work. Turned into kindling.

Apparently the wolves had swarmed straight here and torn everything to shreds.

Ro couldn't help but feel she was to blame, that if she hadn't allowed so many to come back through the veil with her unintentional kill, the loups-garous might not have destroyed everything.

She rubbed her eyes, gritty from a long, hard day.

"I don't understand." Gustave paced madly. "They shouldn't have been able to get inside the clearing! Darya had protections."

Some protections if first the Wolf King then his minions were able to breach it, Ro did not say. Gustave was aggravated enough.

He glanced at the shattered mess and stalked away from Ro, frustration in every line from his clenched fists to his stomping boots.

"Je suis désolé. I am sorry," Ro said. Although he'd been building it for her, he'd put in a lot of work. So had she, for that matter.

He swiped his hand through his hair, then shoved his hat back on. "I would leave some bread and milk out tonight if I were you."

Ro raised an eyebrow. She was pretty sure any brownies around here were his, and if she went back to see Olt, which she absolutely was going to do, someday, she'd lose their services anyway.

Besides, she didn't know if she trusted fey creatures. Any fey creatures.

"I'll think on it" was her only reply.

"Do that," he said tersely. "Then get those protections up so this doesn't keep happening."

Ro threw her hands to either side, her frustration surfacing. "And how exactly would I do that?"

"You have to claim this land as your own." At her blank, bewildered look, he gave a deep sigh and surveyed the splintered walls they hadn't been able to raise, and then the clawed and bitten piles of boards. "We might as well get started."

So Ro spent the rest of the day helping Gustave separate what was usable from what was not. Looked like they'd be felling trees again tomorrow.

When all Ro wanted to do was hunt down these creatures and end them all.

Ro sat crunching on an apple in Gustave's cabin, once more reading the handwritten book on fey creatures. Apples grew in abundance in the Black Forest in the fall, and she had to admit, they rivaled most of what she'd eaten to this point in her life.

She'd balked at leaving out milk and bread, so with a sigh, Gustave had gone back to do it. But she had a feeling his patience was wearing thin.

She'd have to make a decision, and she'd have to do it soon.

Picking up the axe was one thing, but if she needed to bond with the land, claim it as her own, agree to live here in order to defeat these loups-garous—she had to find out exactly how to do that. And he'd given her the morning to herself to decide what she wanted.

Sweet flavor flooded over her tongue as she flipped a page.

She'd read every entry on wolves, yet not a single one had any similarities to the loups-garous. Nothing told her how to become a protectress. Nothing explained anything of value.

What good was leaving out milk and bread for brownies if you couldn't keep the house standing long enough for them to clean it?

Ro slammed the book closed and set it and her apple aside.

If only there was a manual on how to be the forest's protectress! This book was an excellent source of information, just not what she needed right now. She'd asked several trees on the long march back yesterday, feeling absolutely ridiculous doing so, but not a one had stirred, and not a one had answered.

She dropped her head into her hands. "What am I going to do now?"

Surely someone had taught Grandmère? But who, and how could Ro find them?

And where was the giant wolf? It could spring from the forest, attack her, tear her to shreds, and with as little as she knew, she wouldn't have a better chance of defending herself than her grandmère.

No one else knew how she worked, and the one other person who did—well, as surely as she'd picked up her grandmère's axe, Ro had lost him, too.

A few tears tracked down her face.

Her grandmère was dead. Life bleeding out in front of Ro,

and there was nothing she could've done to stop it. Even if she'd gotten there in time, she wouldn't have been able to fight such a monster. And she missed Olt.

Was this what she wanted? To be alone? To cry alone? To die alone?

With all her heart, non.

She wanted Olt. She wanted a chance at life with him. And more than that, she wanted her grandmère not to be dead.

Ro had had enough. She was tired of waiting. Of worrying about Olt. Of twitching at every noise, fearful of an attack.

She had to focus. Take care of the tasks in front of her, right here, right now. Think of the future later. Figure out the next right step.

Whatever in the name of heaven that could be.

Gustave burst into the room without warning. "The loups-garous are back."

Ro bolted to her feet, swung her red cape around her shoulders, and grabbed her axe. She followed him out. "Give me as much information as you can. Where?"

He grunted, which Ro chose to take as agreement. "Not sure. But I felt them just now."

She sent him a sharp glance.

"Believe me, they'll find us."

"How do I send them back? Without killing them? You must know *something*."

He eyed her. "I don't know how Darya did it. I just . . . aimed the wolves in her direction, and she sent them back to the Land of the Fey."

Ro wanted to howl her frustration like a wolf. "Then what good will our fighting them do?" she demanded.

He whirled on her, clutching his axe, glaring in a way that made Ro step back. "What *good* it will do is keep the loups-garous' attack focused on *us*, instead of on the surrounding villages."

"Oh," Ro said in a small voice.

He nodded once, then was off like an arrow.

She shook her head and followed him into the woods, every sense alert. "But you must've seen *something* of what Darya did."

"We did not discuss it. We should have." He sighed. "In the heat of battle, I could not see what she was doing, but she used her axe, and she used her magic, I know that much." The tips of his ears turned a dusky red. "To me, it looked like she, I don't know, waved her hands or axe around and they just . . . disappeared. But it took great effort."

Well that was just lovely.

Ro needed to do *something* different. She couldn't just fight them off with nothing to show for it. One wrong move—one—and she wouldn't be around to protect anyone.

She needed to find out what her grandmère did and fast.

The wolves were upon them before Ro even knew what was happening. One moment, they were racing toward the howls; the next, the battle had found them.

She and Gustave immediately fell into fighting stances, flinging wolves aside and generally fighting a pointless battle.

It would be one thing if Ro were accomplishing something here. But non, she fought the loups-garous because they were there, because it was expected of her. Yet she couldn't kill them, she couldn't drive them out, she couldn't stop them.

With angry heaves, she batted wolves aside, wounding as many as she could, taking out her frustration on every target.

Too focused on the wolves, she got separated from Gustave. So of course everything that could go wrong happened at once. Ro was knocked off her feet. Her axe went flying. And loups-garous surrounded her on every side.

"Such a delectable treat."

"I can't wait to sink my teeth into flesh."

"And rend flesh from bone."

"And drink hot, hot, fresh blood."

Ro blinked as voices came at her from every side. Was it the . . . loups-garous? But their mouths hadn't moved. In fact, they were still growling, snarling, snapping at her with teeth bared.

But they weren't attacking yet, as if savoring the kill to come.

Her shoulder ached in a sudden flare-up, and she pressed it tight, attempting to drive away the phantom pain with her fingertips.

It only lasted seconds, but the memory of the wolf flying at her, sinking its teeth into her shoulder, and shaking her like a rag doll, came back in blinding clarity.

Ro gritted her teeth. She was *not* letting that happen again.

"Aren't you in position yet to distract her?" one of them snapped. Granted, the creature only snapped its teeth, but it let Ro know which one had spoken. In her head.

"Coming!" one yelped from far off.

"We don't need the distraction."

"We can take it."

"It is only a measly human, after all."

"Kill, kill, kill . . ." said one with what sounded like a giggle.

Ro surged to her feet and jumped toward them in a sudden, aggressive move. To jump away, in a prey move, would've made them instantly attack. "You are not killing anyone today!" she shouted, turning her terror into rage.

Well, she was still terrified. But she hoped it sounded like rage, at least.

A few jumped or shied away. The others froze, as if unsure.

"Did it just . . . speak to us?"

"Did it hear us?"

"Of course not. It is *human*."

"This *human*," Ro said, "isn't falling to a pack of loups-garous. Go back from whence you came!"

She jumped toward them again, which put her uncomfortably close, and waved her cape at them like a Spanish bullfighter, while her eyes darted every which way for her axe. Or if she could reach the knife in her boot . . .

A few more wolves shied away, and the leader, the alpha, growled, "As you were," in a low, dangerous voice.

One of the smaller wolves snapped its teeth. "It's mine!"

"Wait. I smell something . . ." the alpha said.

"Do you smell that?" another echoed.

One sneezed. "Poison."

As one, the other loups-garous perked their ears and peered into the trees, some standing upright. Ro was certain it was the only reason they didn't swarm her at once.

Oblivious, the lone giggling wolf crouched on its haunches and flung itself at Ro in a positively giddy manner.

As the loup-garou sprang at her, the flailing tree that aided her and Gustave popped into Ro's mind, and she glanced at the closest tree and gave a wordless cry of *Help me!*

She narrowly avoided its teeth, spun with the wolf's momentum, and heaved the loup-garou at the trunk. And the creature . . . stuck fast to the leafy deciduous tree.

Wasting a few precious seconds in which her throat could've been ripped out, she stared open-mouthed as sap ran down the bark and began to coat the creature. The others whined, pranced, and shuffled in nervous steps as they shifted their focus between her and whatever poison they smelled.

Before Ro could wonder what was happening with the tree sap, a thick black arrow came out of nowhere and impaled the loup-garou, leaving it sagging lifeless as it dangled from the tree.

Another arrow speared the alpha through the throat.

Calling them arrows was a misnomer. Made of heavy

twisted metal about the length of her leg, the bolt killed the alpha instantly and left it hanging midway between the ground and where it had been struck. Both dead wolves shimmered and started to fade.

Ro spun around, but more arrows flew out of the forest and impaled loups-garous all around her.

She dove for the ground and covered her head—not that it would do much good—and sincerely hoped she wasn't about to be stuck fast to the forest floor herself.

But whoever was shooting had incredible aim, and not one arrow touched Ro.

Taking advantage of the distraction, Ro scrambled for cover as more monstrous metal arrows came flying out of the forest, killing any loup-garou they touched. Even scratched. Smoke billowed from each wound.

She had to get herself some of those.

"What are you doing?" bellowed an outraged voice that could only belong to Gustave. "You can't *kill* them."

But the arrows kept coming until the giant, hairless creatures scattered and ran.

A light ashwood handle and metal wedge painted bright red peeked out of the underbrush, and Ro scrambled for her axe. But as her hand closed around it, something heavy slammed into her back. Ro pitched forward.

She tried to lift the axe, to defend herself, but something smashed into the back of her head, and she went down, hard.

Gustave might've called her name, but the buzzing in her head drowned out all else.

Her cheek found the forest floor, the carpet of pine needles and leaves jabbed her skin, and her eyes closed all on their own.

12

Ro stared at the canopy of leaves overhead and frowned. How had they gotten up there? She tried to remember. One moment, leaves were crunching underfoot, and the next, she sprawled in them. But face-first.

Now her head hurt, her entire body was bone-tired, and her mind remained fuzzy.

Hadn't she been fighting loups-garous?

A ringing noise intruded on her thoughts, and she sought the metallic sound, scraping over and over. Her eyes snagged on a sight far more horrendous than wolves, and she instantly came wide awake as adrenaline flooded her.

Gustave, crumpled in the middle of a clearing, out cold. Blood trickled down his temple, and he was trussed up in ropes and gagged.

Her eyes flew to the man sitting on a log not far from Gustave, a burly man dressed in tan hunting leathers, sharpening a wicked-looking battle-axe, twin blades curved in a deadly work of art.

Her and Gustave's single-bladed woodcutting axes were nowhere to be seen.

She tried to reach for the single small blade in her boot but found she couldn't move. She was tied up as tightly as Gustave, and her hands were tingling and starting to go numb. The gag in her mouth tasted foul.

Her movement caught his attention, and he looked up.

He stilled when their eyes met. His face remained stoic, but a pleased expression took residence in his eyes while she stared at him in cold fury.

Oh, he was going to pay for what he'd done to Gustave. Especially if he'd killed the old woodsman.

This man was older than she, perhaps in his late forties or early fifties. Though his hair hadn't started to gray, it was scraggly and unwashed, and his tan leathers, though they'd probably cost a small fortune at one time, were now cracked, stained, and peeling.

She tried harder to get to her knife, but he'd done an excellent job ensuring she couldn't move.

The hulking, thickly padded man simply looked amused as she struggled.

Which made him seem even more dangerous to Ro. She'd learned throughout her time as a huntress to listen to her gut, and something about him set her on edge. Well, more than the fact he'd laid them both out flat, and Gustave wasn't stirring.

"Huntress." His deep baritone rumbled out of his barrel chest and sent a spray of frightened birds into the air.

Ro couldn't answer, so she glared back, a demand to explain himself.

"Where are the combs?"

She blinked. What combs? Oh. The combs Madame LaChance had hired her to retrieve from the sirens. The ones she no longer had, because she'd given them to Odette to break the swans' curse. To break Olt's curse. She swallowed hard.

That's what she'd been forgetting.

He took it all in. "I see you know what I'm talking about.

You would be dead right now if not for the fact that I did not find them on you. On either of you."

Her eyes flew to Gustave, and she struggled to get to him.

"He's alive. For now."

She stilled at the obvious threat.

"Though I suggest if you want to keep him that way, you tell me where they are so I might fetch them for my mistress."

Ro went cold all over. Madame LaChance had sent a bounty hunter when she'd failed to deliver the combs? Ro gritted her teeth on the cloth in her mouth. She hadn't known it at the time, but she'd needed them more than Madame LaChance.

But that meant she owed a debt to a woman who terrified Olt, one he'd said not to cross. And Ro had dismissed his warnings because she'd never seen the woman's cruel side. It appeared she just had.

"Now, I'm going to remove the gag. No screaming, you hear? Or your friend over here will regret it." He set down the battle-axe and loomed over her.

She stiffened and did not cringe when he untied the gag, ripping out a clump of hair in the knot. She waited until he moved away to speak.

Ro tried to swallow but couldn't. "Water?"

He stepped out of her line of sight. She tried to move, to get away, but any movement caused incredible pain. She *hated* to be trapped, more than anything.

A faint nicker came from a horse before the man returned. He helped her sit up, propping her back against a tree. He crouched before her, tilted her chin up with one meaty, dirt-encrusted, and greasy finger—hopefully because he'd been oiling the axe wrapping and not because he'd never washed them—and poured water all down her face and neck, nearly drowning her.

She spluttered and coughed, and he pulled the waterskin

back and waited, his wrists dangling between his thighs, appearing pleased with himself.

Ro made a mental note: He liked to cause pain. She should not underestimate him. Or provoke him. Not until she could fight back.

As cold water dribbled down her chin and dripped off her jerkin, she made herself take a deep breath and let it go.

Escape was more important than fighting him right now.

He tried again, and even though Ro attempted to jerk away, he held her chin in place and poured much slower this time. He gave her just enough to whet her thirst and pulled away before she was done. His eyes were light brown and dead looking.

"I suggest you start talking, huntress."

"Will you let him go?" she rasped, nodding to Gustave.

He studied her. "I might."

Ro didn't break their shared gaze. "Promise me. Promise me that no matter what happens here, you will let him go."

"And you? I suppose you want me to let you go as well?" He smirked, the expression chilling. He had no intention of letting her go.

Her eyes slid closed for a brief second, accepting her fate. Just until Gustave was safe. "Whatever business you and I have has nothing to do with him."

"I have to be honest, huntress. That doesn't sound promising. For you."

She gave him a fierce glare.

After an eternity, he nodded. "You have my word."

Make him vow on the Fairy Queen's good name.

Ro blinked, startled. It had been so long since she'd heard that voice! Warmth filled her that her Creator was watching out for her. She was getting out of this. Probably.

"Vow on the Fairy Queen's name."

He tottered back and almost fell on his rump. "Excuse me?"

"You heard me." Ro's voice was as sharp as the crack of a whip.

He took so long to consider, Ro almost repeated it, but she told herself to wait. She shouldn't rush him.

He blew out a frustrated breath. "All right, I vow."

"Say it. Say it all."

He raised one hand, more than a little disgruntled. "I vow on the Fairy Queen's good name that no harm shall come to your companion. Not by my hand."

That made Ro wonder if someone else was here, someone who could harm Gustave.

"No one else in your employ or Madame LaChance's shall harm him either."

His disgruntled look sank in deeper. "He shall not come to harm because of me, but I cannot speak for Madame LaChance. Good enough yet?"

Ro's head hurt too much to think through all the twisty ways someone could get around the vow, so she nodded. "The combs your mistress seeks were destroyed."

He went perfectly still, as if startled but trying not to show it.

She kept talking. "I used them to save a life, well, many lives, but I never meant to keep them from her. I left Angleterre with them unknowingly in my possession, and I had every intention to return them to Madame LaChance once my mission was over. Then they ended up being vital to breaking a curse, and well, they no longer exist." Ro sucked in a deep breath and dropped her voice an octave. "I truly am sorry I failed in my mission to her, and I'm willing to do what it takes to make it right."

He nodded, accepting her words as fact.

As he should, Ro grumbled to herself. *A hunter does not lie to another hunter.* Though it would be dangerous to assume this man held to any of her standards.

"Then we are off." He started to move away.

"Not yet."

He turned to regard her.

"S'il vous plaît. Those . . . creatures. I must stop them. Or they will spread and kill many who live in and near this forest."

His grin was cocky. "I don't know that you noticed, out cold as you were, but I took care of 'em for you."

Ro glared. "You just made it worse, you cretin! They'll come flooding back, and bring many more with them, any moment now. I have to take care of it—"

The other hunter, though one of bounties, shrugged and moved away. "Then you may see to that whenever you're done with Madame LaChance." He spoke more to himself than Ro. "If she lets you go."

"Unacceptable."

The debt collector led his horse into the clearing. He rifled through a saddlebag, blocking Ro's view of whatever he was doing. "I don't think you're in a position to demand anything, huntress."

"But if I give you my word, I will keep it. Always. Let me finish my task, then I will come to Madame LaChance myself. Within a fortnight, if possible."

He was already shaking his head as he came over and squatted down in front of her. "I appreciate your honesty, huntress, but you are coming with me."

Too late she saw the handkerchief he held as he smothered her face with it. A sickly sweet odor that made her stomach heave dampened her senses, and although she tried to dodge it, darkness claimed her for its own.

PART II

“Snowdrop” or “Snow White”
Perce Neige / Blanche Neige
—Jacob Grimm and Wilhelm Grimm—

Snowdrop did not dream of any mischief; so she stood before
the old woman; but she set to work so nimbly, and pulled the
lace of her stays so tight, that Snowdrop's breath was stopped,
and she fell down as if she were dead. “There's an end to all
thy beauty,” said the spiteful queen, and went away home.

Perce Neige ne rêvait pas d'un tel méfait ; elle se présenta
donc devant la vieille femme ; mais celle-ci se mit au travail
avec tant d'agilité, et serra si fort la dentelle de son corset, que
Perce Neige en perdit le souffle, et tomba comme si elle était
morte. « Il y a une fin à toute ta beauté, » dit la méchante reine
pleine de rancune, et elle rentra chez elle.

Laurel
Hollingsworth

13

R̶o was jolted awake by the carriage coming to a jarring halt.

She sat up as her captor shifted next to her. She sent him a LeFèvre-worthy scowl, then belatedly remembered he couldn't see it. Not with the stinky burlap sack over her head, nor with the gag he'd kept firmly in place every time she woke.

Not that that had happened often.

He'd kept her unconscious for most of their journey, first while he tied her to his horse and flung her across its rump like a pair of saddlebags, then on the boat ride across the English Channel from France to Angleterre, or England.

It didn't seem to matter if she pretended to sleep or not. He'd dribble water all over her face in an attempt to get some down her throat, feed her a few bites of stale bread, then send her to oblivion the moment she swallowed. She'd tried to hold her breath, but he wouldn't let up on the handkerchief until she was forced to suck down a breath—and with it that horrifying odor that made her fall asleep against her will.

She never wanted to smell that scent again.

Now she was lightheaded, sick to her stomach, and

considering hugging the carriage driver for insisting she be allowed to wake up on the ride from the coast to the city of Londres, or London. In order for her to be fit to talk to Madame LaChance, but still.

Now if only the driver would help her escape this odious man. Plus he smelled horrendous, which did not help her nausea in the enclosed carriage.

Ro wasn't certain she'd be able to untaste the filthy cloth in her mouth for the rest of her life. Which she hoped extended past her meeting with Madame LaChance.

The carriage rocked as her captor opened the door and got out.

Then he helped her out of the carriage and onto a cobbled roadway. Though "helped" could easily be replaced by "yanked," nearly sending her headfirst into the pavement. She brought her tied hands up to catch herself, bracing against how much she knew it was going to hurt.

He caught her just in time.

Thanks to her almost-fall, the burlap gaped open enough that she could see just past the tips of her boots, letting her know it was dark out.

He took her arm and led her away from the carriage. She tripped after him, quite literally. Ro thought about fighting and attempting escape, then decided against it. If he was truly taking her to Madame LaChance, best to get it over with.

But all those loups-garous he'd killed . . . so many more would be coming back . . . and Gustave would face them alone. Had the bounty collector even untied the old woodsman before they'd left?

She made a strangled sound past her gag, but he shushed her and about pulled her arm out of its socket to keep her moving.

Oui, best to get this over with as quickly as possible.

Not that she'd be able to do anything about Gustave *now*, after however long they'd been traveling. A week, possibly?

Please, Dieu, she silently prayed. *May Gustave still be alive. Help me get out of this. And may Madame LaChance be . . . reasonable? Forgiving? Well, may she at least* listen *to me.*

She was hustled up some steps, then into a building, the labyrinth he pulled her through suggesting how large a structure it was.

They came to a stop. "Stay here," his rough voice demanded.

Then his arm was gone.

Ro raised an eyebrow. Did he truly think she would? Her hands had been tied in front of her for the carriage ride, so she immediately started to push off the covering.

His large hand pulled the cloth right back down, and she let out a growl.

A deep chuckle was his only response. Thankfully the gap remained, slightly skewed to one side. Perhaps she could start running blind and hope she didn't fall down those stairs or over a balustrade?

A brush of footsteps, soft whispers, then someone hurrying away.

Ro picked a direction at random and started to move, but she ran right into the hulking man who'd captured her, letting up a waft of his particular . . . stench.

She recoiled, desperately hoping she didn't smell like him now.

Then again, she hadn't been allowed to bathe since being plucked from the Black Forest, and she was almost certain he hadn't bathed either. Long before that, even. By choice.

Not that she'd *wanted* to bathe with such a captor watching over her. Hopefully Madame LaChance would let her before she returned to France?

His bark of laughter held amusement. "You don't give up, do you?"

"Never," Ro tried to spit out past the gag, her throat dry

for want of water, but the word came out more like "Neh-wah."

If that didn't add humiliation on top of everything else.

"Right this way, please," said a low, soft, feminine voice.

The debt collector pulled Ro in his wake as he followed whoever had spoken.

Soon they came to a gently lit room, and unlike the wooden parquet floor in the hallway, now Ro's feet sank into the plushest of carpets. She peeked through the slit.

Rose-pink carpet.

She sighed. Apparently they were in Madame LaChance's office.

Relief that he hadn't been lying flooded her, followed by blinding rage. How *dare* Madame LaChance send someone to truss her up and drag her away from her duties? Especially when her absence could cause the Black Forest to overflow with creatures only heard of in nightmares that would destroy everything in their path!

"Monsieur Grant, please, the huntress is my guest."

The bounty hunter grunted and yanked the musty burlap sack from Ro's head in one swift, deft move. Ro blinked against the onslaught of light, blinding in its intensity after being so long in the dark.

Madame LaChance's expression stole Ro's attention. She'd never seen such an *angry* smile before. "Ah, there she is. The huntress who doesn't keep her word, doesn't deliver on her promises, and cannot be trusted."

Ro tried to protest but couldn't, not with the gag in her mouth.

Madame LaChance jerked her head for the debt collector to finish untying her.

Just as before, the woman was dressed in exquisite French fashion, even at this hour. Her hair was perfectly coiffed and towered above her head in ash-blonde curls, a single curling strand lying over her shoulder. A beauty mark rested above full lips that had been painted a light pink to match the outer layer of her dress. Baby-blue ruffles clung to her elbows, hem, and underbodice. Her delicate appearance was deceiving, for a tiger lay underneath.

As the man cut into Ro's bonds, Madame LaChance took Ro in from head to foot. And frowned. "Monsieur Grant, I said she was not to be harmed."

He froze, and although his face didn't betray it, no more than a slight widening of his eyes, fear swept him. Gooseflesh trailed as the emotion brushed against Ro's skin, and she shivered, a motion Madame LaChance did not miss.

He tried for a cocky grin. "Ain't nothing worse than a bump on the head. How else was I to get her to come with me when she didn't want to?"

"You were not to lay a hand on her."

He shot Ro a nervous glance and licked his lips. "Aside from heaving her onto and off my horse, the boat, and the carriage, I ain't touched nothing."

After an eternity of no one daring to move, Madame LaChance nodded. "Very well. Continue. But should I find out otherwise . . ."

She nodded to Ro's bonds as if to remind him of his duty. He hastily finished cutting them. Ro rubbed the raw skin around her wrists.

As he reached for her gag, he scoffed. "Ya sure you want me to remove the gag?" He leered at Ro. "She's got quite the mouth on her. Couldn't get a moment's peace ta myself till I made her be quiet."

His grin did it. Without thinking it through, Ro punched him straight in the temple. It wasn't the knockout punch she'd intended, but he staggered back a step and shook his head, dazed. Ro felt in control for the first time since he'd knocked her out, and a warm glow filled her right before his face turned red and he was returning the strike.

Ro dodged it and kicked his side.

Suddenly, light flared, and she couldn't move. She tried to see where his next blow would come from, but she couldn't move her head, or any other part of her, and she could barely make out his outline.

He was arched away from her kick, holding his side, not moving either.

"That's quite enough of that, both of you," said Madame LaChance briskly.

Ro started to panic. She was just standing there, foot in the air, forearms raised to protect her face, and she couldn't *move*.

She squinted against the bright light, urging her eyesight to adjust, growling when it wouldn't—she'd been kept in the dark for a week, after all. Intense relief swept her when the light dimmed and the room came into focus.

Ro's eyes flew wide, and she took in as much as she could.

Madame LaChance stood next to her desk, an oil lamp the only source of light. Was that where the blaze had come from? For some reason, Ro didn't think so.

Her lavish office was just as Ro remembered. From what she could tell, no one else was in the room, and blood trickled from her captor's temple. Ro smirked. Grant saw it and scowled.

"Now away from each other, both of you." With a flick of Madame LaChance's wrist, Ro dropped her foot and stumbled away, and Grant stumbled in the other direction.

Ro yanked the gag from her mouth and gasped for air like she'd been drowning. "What in all the realms were you thinking? How *dare* you hire someone to kidnap me over a . . . a misunderstanding!"

She shot a glare at the burly, smelly man who'd carted her across Europe and a nausea-inducing boat ride in the most uncomfortable positions possible.

"You couldn't have asked to meet like a civilized person? You couldn't have asked *why* I couldn't see you after defeating the sirènes? You had to send someone to kidnap me at the worst possible moment? While my forest was being invaded by fey creatures that eat people?"

With a shout, Ro lifted a boot and slammed it into Madame LaChance's desk. It juddered, but the heavy furniture didn't move a centimètre.

"You couldn't have waited two *weeks*?"

The bounty hunter took a few steps away from Ro, as if distancing himself from whatever punishment was about to occur. It did not boost Ro's confidence. But she wasn't about to let either of them get away with this, not for one blessed minute.

Madame LaChance eyed Ro's tirade mildly. "Monsieur Grant, leave us."

"Ya sure bout that? She's a feisty one, ain't she? I'd be happy to put her down a peg or two. Hundred." He grinned with all his browning teeth, his dialect slipping to a much lower-class one around Madame LaChance. Ro wondered why.

"I'm sure. I will call when I have need of you again. Stay close."

He shrugged. "Iffen you say so."

He ambled out as if he had all the time in the world. Ro glowered at his back until the door clicked firmly shut behind him, then spun on Madame LaChance.

She raised one hand and spoke calmly. "I am not an unreasonable woman, huntress. I've waited far more patiently than I should have for an explanation. A letter. Anything. Yet you take my money, the protection of my name, and my bloody ship, and leave me without information for months? How else was I supposed to get your attention?"

All that Ro had been prepared to say fled her tongue, and she glared at her former benefactor. "Perhaps by not kidnapping me? Sending your own note, perhaps? *Reminding* me?"

"Would you have come to see me?"

Ro threw both hands in the air. "After I figured out where the wolves were coming from and got rid of them, oui!"

"Really. And another hunt wouldn't have intruded?"

Ro opened her mouth. And closed it. She couldn't deny that was a possibility.

"You did, after all, say you would return here immediately after your voyage, yet you did not."

Ro had a feeling saying she'd forgotten wouldn't go over so well. She'd been focused on calamity after calamity. A forgotten debt wasn't foremost on her mind.

Yet it was just so darn aggravating that she'd forgotten at all.

"So you decide it's perfectly fine to kidnap me and drag me here like some common"—Ro was so upset, she flailed for the right word—"person fleeing a debt!"

Madame LaChance raised one pristine eyebrow. "Is that what you were doing, huntress? Fleeing a debt?"

Ro scowled, but she could feel her face growing warm. "Of course not."

"Well then, I am very interested to hear what you've been doing all this time. Did you free your niece from her sleeping curse?"

Ro blinked. Did Madame LaChance know everything? She started to respond, but Madame LaChance flicked her fingers, and it felt like a fist was squeezing her throat.

Ro swallowed against it, certain it was just nerves.

Without missing a beat, Madame LaChance picked up several letters from her desk and began to read.

"My dearest Rosette,

"Please, come at once! I am begging you. My daughter is but three years old, and the dearest thing of my heart. Trêve and I adore her."

Madame LaChance switched letters.

"But what is so urgent—what I can scarcely believe has happened—our daughter—your niece—has fallen into an enchanted sleep, and we cannot wake her. Mon Dieu, we cannot wake her!"

Madame LaChance picked up a third letter.

"We don't know what to do! Please help us, dearest Rosette, please. If anyone knows what to do, it's you.

"With all my heart, I await your return.

"Your Cosette."

Ro's jaw dropped. How on earth—? She'd *burned* those letters! The whole stack of them, after waking Allura. Ro hadn't wanted them falling into the wrong hands.

Like Madame LaChance's.

When Ro was off hunting sirens, Cosette had written her letter after letter, all in the same vein, trying to reach Ro when her one-year voyage had somehow turned into three.

Something she had yet to figure out. It was as if time had just . . . vanished.

She let out a growl. Those were *her* letters. Madame LaChance had *no right*.

Yet there they were, whole again, clutched in Madame LaChance's elegant fingers. How?

Madame LaChance lifted her eyes to meet Ro's, far too interested, far too intense, all of a sudden. "So tell me. Did you wake her?"

Ro tried to speak, but nothing came out. Her eyes went wide.

"Oh, that's right. I forgot." With a snap of her fingers and a small smile on her lips, Madame LaChance somehow released Ro to talk.

"Of course I did!" Ro rubbed her throat, staring at the letters as if they might come alive and bite her.

Madame LaChance leaned forward and snarled, "Then why didn't you return here straightaway?"

Ro blinked rapidly, unused to the calm, self-assured businesswoman losing her temper. "Because it was up to me to save everyone from curses and enchantresses and fey creatures that keep trying to kill humans wherever they go! What else was I supposed to do? Let them all die?"

Ro could barely get the words out, she was spluttering so hard with rage. And fear. How had the woman kept her from talking?

Madame LaChance tisked. "I see you are the same uncouth, ungracious huntress as always."

Ro glared harder than she had in her life. "What am I doing here?" she demanded. "Surely I could have paid you in some other way than being brought here."

Madame LaChance smiled wide, but the expression didn't reach her eyes. "On the contrary. Do you recall our agreement?"

Ro flushed. "Of course I do."

"Of course you do. Three combs in exchange for a ship and crew to help you with your mission to defeat the sirènes. A very expensive ship and crew." She spread her hands. "And yet, the moment you return to England and I ask to see you, you flee, back to France and back to your sister. When I try to reach you there, where do you go? To the Black Forest. My debt collector followed you all over the map, but he could never reach you." Her fine eyebrows climbed her forehead. "One would almost think you were avoiding me."

"It wasn't like that—"

Madame LaChance snapped her fingers, and once again, Ro couldn't speak. "And then when my huntsman catches up to you, what does he find? The swan-ruler combs, missing. The power of the sea, not on you but for a fading scent. You, completely clueless to their import. To me. To the world."

Ro struggled to speak. To breathe. She clawed at her throat, but nothing was there. No massive hand crushed her windpipe with the force of a wolf's jaws, even though it felt exactly like that.

"You have not yet upheld your end of the bargain, Mademoiselle, and unless you do, there will be dire consequences. I will hear your explanation now." Madame LaChance held up one hand, then paused. "I should warn you. Excuses shall only warrant a quick death. Choose your words wisely."

Then she waved her hand, and the release washed over Ro's entire body. She gasped a breath, shivering from the feel of being held captive with no visible bonds, mind whirling with what to say.

She took several deep breaths to calm her racing heart, blinked back tears until she was certain they wouldn't spill over, and made herself *think* before words came pouring out of her mouth.

As soon as she could trust herself to speak, she said as respectfully as possible, "I have no excuses, Madame, but if you will permit me, I will share my side of the tale."

Madame LaChance didn't move a muscle, staring her down.

Ro swallowed hard. "The Sirène Queen gave me the pearl swan-wing combs when I asked, but she said the power of the sea—the coral comb—was not for the above world."

Madame LaChance's jaw tightened.

Ro rushed on. "I gave them to a messenger in case I did not return, and then went to the Sirène Queen's underwater kingdom and took the coral crown from her."

It was much more convoluted than that, but best to keep it simple and straightforward.

"The messenger . . . died . . . drowned, actually"—Ro had to swallow back her grief, but she wasn't about to tell Madame LaChance she'd given the swan combs to Cendre, whom she thought had died in the battle with the sirens, but whom her grandmère had said might still be alive, albeit as a siren under the ocean—see? convoluted—"but before we set sail, I discovered the coral comb had been replaced with the pair of swan combs. It is my belief that the sirènes took back the coral crown, but as with most fey exchanges, they had to replace it with something equal in value. Though that is only a theory."

Ro hesitated briefly, and Madame LaChance nodded for her to continue.

"When I returned to Angleterre, I found that several years had passed—years I could not account for—and urgent letters from my sister detailed a sleeping curse placed on my niece. She hadn't long to live, as you know from her letters."

Madame LaChance didn't so much as twitch.

Ro spread her hands. "What else could I do? I barely lifted the curse in time, and it took giving the swan-wing combs to the rightful ruler of Prussia to do so, who then became the Swan Queen. And I assume the coral crown, the power of the sea, can only belong to the Sirène Queen. Then I found out my grandmère is the protectress of the Black Forest, and her mantle passed to me when she died."

Madame LaChance went perfectly still at that.

Ro pressed her advantage. "And then I found creatures not of our world—great, hulking loups-garous that deal death with powerful jaws and massive swipes of their claws—are pouring in, and I am the only one who can stop them. And I am *not there* to do it." She shot a glare at the door the bounty hunter had exited through. "It is imperative I return to the Black Forest immediately, before this world is lost."

Madame LaChance's eyes widened briefly, enough to let Ro know she hadn't known what was happening in the forest, which made her feel slightly better. But only slightly.

"But you still have a debt to pay. I fear if you do not, this mantle you speak of will unravel most horribly."

Ro opened her mouth, then closed it. She tilted her head. "Truly?"

"Truly. Any broken promises turn fey-given mantles to rot and putrid decay."

Ro took a step back. Exactly like what had happened to the empress. The sirens. Marie, the sorceress known as Magic, who had cursed the beast.

Heart sinking like a stone in the ocean, Ro thought furiously. "All right. I see. Well then, allow me to finish my quest, then I will return and make it up to you."

Madame LaChance's smile was positively indulgent. "I'm afraid it doesn't work that way, my pet. Make it up to me, *then* I will release you to return to the Black Forest."

"And if the forest collapses while I am away? It may have already done so! This *bounty* hunter of yours killed a great number of the creatures, which means many more can return. They kill anything human, they spread fast, and I have to stop them!"

Ro clamped her mouth closed, surprised by how much she was telling Madame LaChance. She had nothing to hide, truly, but she didn't usually blurt out every detail like this.

Madame LaChance moved to her desk and sat, her back ramrod straight. "As I said, I am not unreasonable. I'd like to return you to your task as soon as possible, but first, let's talk about this trinket found on your person, shall we?"

Ro stared in growing horror as Madame LaChance placed a golden compass on the desk between them, an exquisite rose engraved on the cover.

The compass Captain Rose Red had given her, to call on her if Ro needed help, right before the pirate had stolen Madame LaChance's exquisite galleon and decided to stay in the Caribbean and plunder to her heart's content in a warm and beautiful environment.

Its twin was in Captain Red's possession, only silver with a snowflake encrusted upon it.

The pair of compasses had belonged to sisters Rose Red and Snow White. Each could call to the other by opening it and pressing on the clear cover over the compass rose.

A compass she'd forgotten she carried. Just as the swan-wing combs lay deep in her trouser pocket, forgotten until their magic called to her and requested she give them to the Swan Queen, their rightful owner.

It made Ro wonder why Madame LaChance wanted them so badly.

"I paid quite dearly for my combs, huntress, as you know."

When Ro didn't reply—Rose Red wanted to stay far away from Madame LaChance, yet Ro had just handed her a way to the pirate captain, even if unknowingly—the woman continued. "I would take this in exchange, but it cannot begin to compare with the combs' value. I truly do need those combs, and I'm interested in any thoughts you may have on getting them back. S'il vous plaît, sit. I'm listening."

Suddenly weary, Ro dropped into the chair opposite the desk. And told her every detail she could think of. Leaving nothing out.

How she'd hunted the Nightingale Empress, as the woman had called herself, to set Ro's niece free.

When she came to the part about the jade necklace, where the Nightingale had stored her power, Madame LaChance leaned forward eagerly. "Have you this jade necklace in your possession?"

Ro shook her head. "It was destroyed when we defeated the empress."

Madame LaChance deflated and sat back, looking somewhat disgusted with Ro.

A bit surprised she was talking so much—not that she had anything to hide—Ro was thankful when a servant twice refilled her water glass.

"So you see," she finished, "I don't think you *can* get them back. Not only did the swan-wing combs melt into some kind of crown, but if these crowns are linked to the queens' power, then it is a part of them until the next queen is crowned. It seems if they are taken away, they return to their owners." Ro fell silent.

At the end of the telling, Madame LaChance sat staring at the far wall, trilling her fingertips on the desk's surface.

Wiped out from so much talking, Ro leaned back in her

chair and was surprised to find a café service laid out for her. Petite crustless sandwiches cut into bite-size squares and a few small clusters of purple grapes waited next to a steaming cup of café. Unsure if she should eat without invitation, she shot her host a questioning glance.

At Madame LaChance's distracted nod, Ro fell to them with just about the grace of the wolves she hunted.

"Interesting," Madame LaChance mused. "Oui, once a queen takes on the power of the combs, you cannot steal it from her unless you kill her or she gives it to you willingly. And such queens are almost impossible to kill."

"Um, what?" Ro said around a bite of food.

"Though I do wish you'd kept the jade necklace."

"Destroying it was the only way we could defeat her. But what do you mean by—?"

Madame LaChance struck the desk with her palms in a graceful move that commandeered Ro's attention. "There's only one thing for it, then. You will have to do something else for me. Or, for someone I owe a favor, rather."

Ro's eyes widened. "But . . . didn't you hear me? I have to get back! Your man took me in the middle of an attack and left my companion to fend for himself. Tied up. If I don't figure out how to close that rift and stop those creatures from pouring through . . ."

"You are not going anywhere till I say so, huntress. You owe *me* first." She shrugged, the move delicate and French, but her eyes blazed with barely contained fury. "Once you have fulfilled the terms of our agreement to my satisfaction, you may go and do whatever you like. So I suggest you hurry if there's somewhere else you'd like to be."

"You don't understan—"

Madame LaChance shot to her feet. "Non, Mademoiselle, *you* do not! I have been patient, I have extended every courtesy, and you didn't even have the decency to explain yourself to me until you were tied up and dragged in here!"

A bite of food lay in an unappetizing lump in her mouth, and Ro was terrified that if she swallowed, whatever had happened to her earlier would make her choke and die. Ro's eyes couldn't possibly get any bigger. She'd never heard Madame LaChance raise her voice. Not once. And it was absolutely terrifying.

And she was right. Ro hadn't considered the consequences of her actions. She'd run off every time someone needed her help, and the fact she'd honestly forgotten that she owed Madame LaChance wasn't a reasonable excuse.

After a moment of not feeling that vicelike grip around her throat, Ro swallowed with difficulty. "But if I don't get back right away, what will happen to the forest?"

Madame LaChance brushed aside the words as if she couldn't be bothered by them. "Then I suggest you hurry."

Ro gritted her teeth. "What do I need to do?"

Madame LaChance told her.

And Ro's stomach dropped right down to her toes.

Captain Rose Red was going to kill her.

14

Ro stared at Madame LaChance in horror. The businesswoman stared right back without blinking.

"You can't be serious."

"I assure you, I am. Deadly."

Ro didn't doubt that for one moment. "I won't do it."

"And I say you will."

Ro tightened her jaw and lifted her chin. She wasn't about to do what Madame LaChance asked. She couldn't do that to her friend. *Wouldn't* do that to her friend. The pirate captain had been through enough.

"Do it. Do it right now. Call her," Madame LaChance said.

Ro snatched up the compass that lay on the desk between them, flipped it open, and pressed on the clear cover over the compass rose.

In a silent wave, a ripple of light shot out from the compass and kept going, past the walls, on its way to find Captain Red and the twin compass she held, the one that had belonged to her sister, Snow White.

Activating a call for help the pirate captain would know came from Ro.

One that she'd promised to answer immediately.

Ro stared at her hand, stunned, wondering why on earth she'd picked up the compass and pressed it when Madame LaChance told her to. Against her will.

Madame LaChance raised an eyebrow. "Well? Did the signal go out?"

Ro blinked. She hadn't seen it? Reluctantly, Ro nodded, and satisfaction filled the elegant French woman's face.

"Bon." She held out her hand, palm upright, and Ro placed the compass there without hesitation.

Madame LaChance set it on the desk, pulled out a slim, sharp dagger Ro had seen before, its golden hilt encrusted with rubies, and brought the tip down upon the compass.

Ro tried to scream "Non!" but it stayed trapped inside, where no one could hear it but Ro.

With an audible screech that wasn't hers, one that filled the room and made Ro's ears hurt, something in the compass struggled, fought, and went out.

Dead. Whatever it had been, whatever had made it pulse with life, was now dead.

Ro stared between the compass and Madame LaChance. How could she do such a thing? Destroy something that meant so much to the captain? That had been a gift to Ro. And what had she just killed?

Olt's warnings about the woman came back in blinding clarity, and she wished for the chance to tell him he was right. That she should've listened.

Although Madame LaChance tended to keep her emotions in check, the rage on her face was so startling, Ro would've taken a step back had she been able to do so.

But she sat in the chair, terrified to move. Possibly, unable to move? She was too scared to test it. Her throat had that tight feeling again, but she wasn't sure if it was from her billowing emotions or from whatever control this woman held over her.

Captain Red had treasured that compass above all else, a matched set to her sister's. And Ro had handed it over, hadn't even fought to keep it from being destroyed.

"You wanted to say something, huntress?"

"Why?" Ro whispered, tears thick in her voice, if unable to spill down her cheeks.

Madame LaChance curled her lips back, showing teeth that, just for an instant, were sharp and pointy, quite unlike her real teeth. But then they were gone, and the image slipped from Ro's mind as if it had never been.

"You shall see, huntress. You shall see. It may take time, and it may not happen right away, thanks to your ineptitude, but it *will* happen, and you *will* help me. Because you are bound to me."

"How?" Ro whispered with the greatest urgency, clinging to that meager permission to speak.

Madame LaChance's expression was so full of gloating, Ro wanted to smack it off her face. But Ro just sat there, all emotion trapped inside, unable to get out.

"Didn't anyone ever tell you not to eat anything offered by the fey?" She flicked a glance to the light meal Ro had consumed, nothing left but a few crumbs. And even those Ro had considered snatching up.

Suddenly, Ro remembered the first time she'd met Madame LaChance, when she'd hired her to hunt down the sirens and retrieve the swan combs and siren crown for her. She'd offered Ro macarons and café. And Ro had gobbled them up.

Just like she'd done now, with those finger sandwiches and grapes and café.

Had she truly been bound to Madame LaChance by eating something the woman had offered? And now Ro had to do whatever she said?

Well if that didn't give her a whole new fear for the rest of her life.

And did that mean Madame LaChance was fey herself?

The moment that thought came to her, it tried to vanish as if it had never been. But this time Ro struggled to hold on to it until it won the fight and evaporated.

Madame LaChance leaned across her desk, pinning Ro with a glare. "Let me be abundantly clear: You have two options. Go with Monsieur Grant quietly, remain untied, and be set free the moment the task is complete. Or go trussed up as my prisoner, and should you attempt escape, you will complete my task—with your legs broken."

Heart pounding, Ro waited for a laugh, for Madame LaChance to smile, to tell her it had all been a great joke, but her furious expression didn't shift in the slightest.

She was deadly serious.

"I assure you, you do not need your legs for this particular task. You can be carried. Or dragged. Or go willingly. Your choice."

Ro cleared her throat and licked dry lips. "That one. Willingly. No broken legs. S'il vous plaît."

She snapped her mouth closed before any more fear came spilling past her lips.

Madame LaChance's intense expression didn't relent. "Wise choice. Monsieur Grant?" The door opened immediately, and his greasy head popped in. "Deliver the huntress to her next destination." Then she spoke to Ro. "Do not fail me, huntress, or you shall regret it."

Before Ro could respond, protest, or devolve into a shivering mess, Grant hauled her to her feet and roughly pulled her from the room. Trapped under Madame LaChance's glare the entire way.

And Ro went with the bounty hunter, numb, heart breaking for what she would force the pirate captain to endure.

The whole reason Captain Red had fled the country in the first place.

Grant sat across from her in the carriage, studying Ro's face a little too closely for her liking. Ro rubbed her chapped and bleeding wrists, willing them to heal faster. Should her healing ability choose to work, that was. As with all of her fey-given huntress powers, they had a mind of their own.

At least her hands were left untied.

Her mind spun after her conversation with Madame LaChance. Another tremor rocked her. Non. Ro refused to go into this situation cowering like some weakling.

So she lifted her chin and glared back.

He grinned. "I hear I get to break your legs, both of 'em, if you run." He popped open the carriage door as the carriage rumbled down empty early-morning streets. "Go on. I really like breaking legs."

Ro turned her face away, but there was nowhere else to look. Curtains were drawn tight against letting Ro know where in Londres they were headed.

As if she had any question.

He laughed and slammed the door. "I'll leave it unlocked in case you change your mind. Even give ya a head start, iffen you want."

Ro ignored him, scared and trying not to show it. She just needed non-magically binding food and water, a full night's rest, and her head clear long enough to make a real plan. Such as deciding whether escape was worth attempting.

With how angry Madame LaChance was . . . Ro took a deep breath. No use scaring herself more than she already was. Information first. Panic second.

The carriage rattled to a halt after an eternity and all too soon. Then she was hustled out and marched into the palace through a back and secret way, to meet with King Wilhelm and to wake his dead wife, Queen Snow White.

Grant hauled Ro after a servant. She tried to wrench her arm back, but he kept a firm grip on it as the servant led them to a small, dark room that was practically a cupboard. They were left waiting without a word, and it didn't take long for Grant's stench to fill the tiny space.

Ro gave her arm one more tug, he let go, and she took a step away from him.

It was as far as she could go in the little room.

She was already wishing for the servant to return from informing the king of their arrival. Not that the king would be in a hurry to see Ro. In fact, the king had done nothing *but* make her wait the last time she'd been here. Wait to see him, wait to set sail, wait to return to France.

To say they had not gotten along well was an understatement.

Ro couldn't wait to see how King Wilhelm would respond to her presence. Or her assigned duty from Madame LaChance.

That was complete sarcasm, she would like to point out. To no one.

"So how exactly did you manage to summon the pirate captain, huntress?"

Ro startled, not expecting Grant to speak just then. She couldn't get over how deep his voice was or how it rumbled through his chest and hers when he spoke.

"None of your business," she snapped.

He raised a hand in a "be at peace" gesture—or perhaps "calm down"—then fell silent, in a ridiculously good mood after being told he could break her legs.

Ro chewed her lip. The compass had been offered as a gift of friendship. A one-time offer of aid in a time of need. And Madame LaChance had forced her to abuse it. And then destroyed it.

Ro's heart stuttered at that. The rage on the woman's face. The way she'd gritted her teeth — more like gnashed them — as she drove the dagger down upon the compass.

Was she that furious at Captain Red's betrayal? And how would Captain Red react when she found out the compass had been destroyed?

Now Ro was being forced into the one thing Captain Red had begged her never to do. The thing Ro had promised she wouldn't. And she'd just asked Captain Red to come watch it all up close.

Thank goodness the Caribbean was a three-month journey away. Hopefully Ro's task would be over before then and she could send someone to intercept the pirate captain before she made it to these shores and the trap surely waiting for her.

Ro needed to get back to the Black Forest.

Was Gustave even still alive?

She bit her lip as sweat beaded on her forehead. Dear Dieu, she hoped so.

Wait a moment. If broken promises unraveled fey-given mantles, what did that mean for her promise not to attempt this? Or did her previous agreement with Madame LaChance supersede that?

Thinking about how fey bargains worked made her head hurt.

Surprisingly, they were not left waiting long. Good thing, or Ro might've thrown up all over Grant's shoes. From nerves and his ripening stench.

He probably would've just wiped them on her red cape.

The servant came hurrying in and curtsied. "The king will see you now."

Ro's eyebrows climbed her forehead. Truly? King Wilhelm had barely acknowledged her for hunting the sirens. In fact, he'd given the credit to another hunter, one who hadn't even gone on the voyage. Not that the king had been able to control the wildfire spread of news after her successful return.

An imperious voice boomed, "Wot? I can't meet them in there. Bring them into a bigger room!"

The servant flushed and ducked out.

After a few whispered words—from the servant, not the king—King Wilhelm said, "Secrecy? I'll decide what's secret and what's not!"

As heavy footsteps stormed away, the flustered servant moved them into a bigger room, and there the king of Angleterre stood, imperious, rotund, and impatient.

"Yes, yes, there she is. Off with you now! I will handle this."

The servant scurried away, but Grant stayed right by Ro's side.

"Wot? What's this? I said off with you!"

Grant sketched a slight bow. "With all due respect, Your Majesty, I am ta be the huntress's bodyguard. She's a bit of a —how do I say this—in danger of running away? Not staying here? Taking the first ship out to sea?"

He grinned at Ro, and she sent him a cold look.

"Ha!" the king barked. "As if she'd run away from *me*. You may go. Take a bath or something in the meantime." He pulled a perfumed handkerchief from his sleeve and lifted it to his nose.

Not that the king smelled much better. But at least he tried to cover it up with what smelled like a perfume bath. Which kind of made it worse.

Grant gave him a mutinous look but pretended a respectful bow while he backed away. Right before he closed the door, his eyes met Ro's, and he made a breaking motion with both hands before shutting himself out.

Ro swallowed and turned to see the king positively beaming at her.

"Well, well, well. The infamous huntress, back in my grasp. How does it feel, knowing you haven't escaped me entirely?"

Ro sighed, too weary to engage with his inflated ego. "Why am I here, votre Majesté? A problem with the treaty?" she asked cautiously.

She knew why she was here, what Madame LaChance had asked her to do, but did the king?

He sniffed and put his handkerchief away. "No. Unfortunately, the sirens have kept their side of the agreement, trade has resumed, and the only reports of sinking ships have been from storms or other natural disasters." His eyes narrowed. "Unless they're using the storms as cover . . ."

Ro shook her head, weary of explaining this again, even if it had been some time since she'd last had to. "Not possible. They physically cannot break the treaty, votre Majesté. It is something to do with how the fey make bargains."

Which had come back to bite her, but he didn't need to know that.

At his doubtful look, she continued. "They would die if they betrayed their word." She narrowed her eyes. "Unless you broke it first, of course."

He sniffed again. "As if *I* should do such a thing." Then he clapped twice and spun toward a door on the opposite side of the room. "Come, huntress! You have much to accomplish for me."

After a beat, Ro followed him warily. If he tried to lay one meaty paw on her, she'd stab him with the closest fire poker, and hang the consequences.

But at least he was leading her in the opposite direction as Grant.

Small blessing, but she'd take it.

15

The king was huffing and puffing by the time they arrived.

Ro wondered more than once why he was escorting her instead of making a servant do it, but after traversing enough corridors and back stairways to make even Ro a little out of breath, they climbed a final stairway to a sizeable room.

Soldiers guarded a chained door at the far end of the vast stone chamber. There was no furniture in sight.

The king bent over his knees and sucked in wheezing breaths—she'd had to stop and wait on him so many times—until he finally stumbled over to the guards and flapped his hands.

Ro bit her lip to keep a laugh inside, but from a cold look one of the guards sent her, she hadn't covered her reaction quickly enough.

The soldiers rushed to unlock multiple chains across the door, then no less than twenty bolts all the way down the door—on both sides.

Even with this, the king railed at them. "Can't you see I'm in need of a sit? Move faster, imbeciles!"

Ro rolled her eyes, which the king did not see, but one of

138

the guards did. His entire body went rigid. She raised an eyebrow, and he turned away and went back to fitting keys to the right locks. Each key was stored in separate locked chests in cubbies all over the walls. There were hundreds. But the guards knew which ones to grab, unlock, and use next.

Ro watched them closely, trying to make sense of the madness. To commit as much as she could to memory, though that might not be any help at all.

After what felt like an eternity but was likely only ten minutes or so, the door swung open, and the guards turned away, one hand raised to block their eyes, their backs to the door.

King Wilhelm strode forward. Ro followed cautiously. He marched right up to a . . . casket? Covered in glass? And demanded, "Open it."

Two serving women, who were just finishing replacing burned-down candles with new in lumps of melted wax, hurried to retrieve keys from around their necks. They stood at either end of the coffin.

Ro stopped in her tracks. They weren't going to open it, were they?

The women unlocked the bubbled glass covering at the same time and heaved it open. It rose on soundless hinges and rested against the wall behind it.

"There you are, my darling wife! Have you had a good rest?" King Wilhelm leaned down and kissed his wife, right on the mouth, and kept on talking. "Is that a new dress? My but it looks lovely on you. I see you're wearing the pendant I sent you. That diamond is the largest in the world, and flawless, my dear. Flawless. Just like you. Only the best for my love! And if they've lied to me, I'll have their heads!"

Ro's eyebrows couldn't possibly climb any higher, and although she knew exactly what this was, seeing it was far worse than simply knowing such a thing existed.

This was the reason she was here.

Why Captain Rose Red had fled this mad country and mad king.

What Madame LaChance was forcing her to do.

What the king had demanded of Madame LaChance.

Wake Queen Snow White, the queen of Angleterre, King Wilhelm's wife and Captain Rose Red's sister, or else lose herself to the madness of an unraveled huntress mantle.

What lovely impossible choices.

"I have someone I want you to meet, my darling." Wilhelm held out one arm, and when Ro didn't move, he waved her forward, not taking his eyes off his wife.

Ro edged toward the coffin, not wanting to look, but also unable to help herself. Would she be a skeleton? Moldering? Ro didn't smell decay or rot. But if she weren't magically preserved . . .

Her beauty took Ro's breath away.

Hair so midnight black it had a deep-blue sheen, skin creamy and pale and flawless, thick lashes resting against cheeks with the faintest blush, lips a vibrant apple red.

She appeared healthy, alive—it made Ro's skin crawl.

Caught in an eternal sleep, kept in a glass coffin by the king's decree, her dead body was cleansed and dressed daily, the king's greatest known secret that he pretended didn't exist half the time. It was the whole reason Captain Red wanted nothing to do with anything or anyone at the palace.

The queen was surrounded by pristine white roses, and Ro wondered if they were changed as often as her dresses or if they were as preserved as she.

Her features were strong if delicate, and although her coloring was nothing like Captain Red's, Ro could see simi-larities.

They could almost be . . . twins . . . but Snow White's features were more elfin, while Rose Red was healthy and robust and as ready to sword fight someone as steal a pirate ship and crew to get as far away as possible from the mad king who dressed up her dead sister and pretended she was still alive.

Ro's mind spun with everything she knew of the queen.

Rumor had it that she'd been poisoned by a gift from her mother-in-law, though no one knew what had poisoned her.

First the woman had sent magical stay laces to strangle the girl with her corset, a haircomb to scratch and infect the girl with some horrendous disease, and then, when all else failed, an assassin to cut out her heart. The assassin had been swayed by her beauty and pledged his devotion instead, so poison was the next in a long list of assassination attempts.

The queen mother apparently couldn't handle her son marrying a commoner he'd found and wooed in the forest. Or her throne sat upon by another.

And the king couldn't handle things he wanted taken away from him.

The dowager queen had been beheaded once King Wilhelm found out what she'd done, something that would've never happened had she not gloated after Snow White fell into her enchanted death.

Ro most definitely needed to proceed with caution.

The king flung his hand toward wide bookshelves on either side of the coffin that encircled the rest of the tower room, not a window in sight. "The information you need is there. Well, what *not* to do, rather."

Ro spared them a quick glance. Then did a double take.

Not bookshelves. Cubbies. Filled with hundreds upon hundreds of scrolls.

Crammed in every square nook, sticking up out of wooden boxes everywhere, rolled-up scrolls also covered a large table between melting candles, several corner weights scattered over its surface.

Ro was stunned.

Palaces had massive libraries, oui, but those were filled

with leatherbound books. These held nothing but *scrolls*. It was like she'd stepped back into the Dark Ages.

"You will update me weekly on your progress."

Ro's head came around at his booming voice.

With that, he heaved himself out of the room, and Ro realized belatedly he meant to lock her in here with the two maidservants. She darted after him, but soldiers closed the heavy door, all the locks around the door engaged at once, and chains started to clink as they were fastened into place on the other side.

She pounded on the door. "You cannot keep me locked up in here, you, you, horrid *beast*!"

After a shocked silence, the chains clanked again, and Ro kept up a tirade of French curses until all fell silent. No one responded, and no one unlocked the door.

She spun around. "Is there no way out?" At no answer, Ro inspected every inch of the door before she noticed one of the women held out a piece of parchment. Ro read it aloud. "'The door cannot open for twenty-four hours after the locks engage.' Great," Ro muttered. "Just great."

The women stood on either side of the coffin, heads bowed, and waited for her to do . . . something.

Ro tried not to panic, but tears welled, and all she could think of was the look on Olt's face as she told him where she'd put the ring, wheeled her horse around, and left him standing there.

She'd made a horrible mistake. One she would take back this instant if she could.

And now she would never see him again. No one knew where she was, not even Gustave. She had no way of calling for help.

She was going to die in here.

A second later, she realized her exhaustion was making her spiral into despair, and she lifted her chin and marched with bold steps to the coffin.

She would solve this, and she would return to the Black Forest with all haste. And then she would find Olt and make things right if it was the last thing she ever did.

The women kept their heads bowed, but as she moved closer, they turned their bodies toward her.

Ro reached out with her senses hesitantly, but she couldn't feel anything fey from them. Nor did they seem to be able to wield magic. They were merely human.

Unless they were shielded somehow, of course. Like the swans who'd ended up being princes. They seemed normal until they were within their protective barrier, then the magic used to transform them was so thick, it was almost a taste on her tongue.

So. Proceed with caution.

Ro stopped in front of the coffin. "Has anyone come close to waking her?"

Neither woman responded, nor lifted her head.

"Can you tell me anything?"

In synchronized motion, as if they'd practiced, both women opened their mouths and showed her their tongues—or where their tongues should've been. Gaping holes ended in jagged gray skin, and Ro cursed. Then said, "Mon Dieu. That monster."

They closed their mouths and bowed their heads once more.

Shoring herself up with a deep breath, Ro laid her hand on Snow White's cheek, as the rest of her was covered in clothing.

She closed her eyes and concentrated as her grandmère had taught her, first seeking the feel of the magic—whether it was sticky, icy, volcanic, tarlike, etc.

Each fey clan wielded a different kind, and once Ro had enough experience, she'd be able to tell who'd placed the curse or what kind of fey creature had bled a human's soul within an inch of her life. But this one wasn't familiar. Maybe she could ask—

With a crash of grief, she remembered her grandmère would no longer be teaching her anything. Unable to hold them back, tears spilled down her cheeks.

Olt's stricken face, when he realized she was leaving, no matter what he said. Grandmère's broken body. The helplessness of waking, blindfolded, not knowing where she was, where she was being taken.

If she'd cost the woodsman his life for disappearing right then . . .

She'd never forgive herself.

The magic responded to Ro's tears. It climbed her arm in tendrils undulating like ocean waves, coming closer with each sweep, and finally, after a slight hesitation, reached out and touched Ro's cheek.

Eyes still closed, Ro pictured it, whatever it was, as it lifted the tear, eyed it, smelled it, tasted it, and drew it inside itself . . . somehow. It gently retreated in the same wavelike motion and went back into Snow White's body.

Ro let out the breath she'd been holding and opened her eyes.

Did that mean it was siren magic? Another fey creature from the sea she hadn't yet met? Or something else entirely?

Snow White lay still and silent, stunningly beautiful, yet Ro couldn't sense anything while the magic lay dormant. She needed it to come out again.

Yet no matter how much she reached for it, it no longer responded to her touch, her call. It had done whatever it wanted and had gone back to sleep.

Was the magic the only part of Snow White still alive?

Suddenly curious, Ro turned to the scrolls and snatched up the closest one. She unfurled it to find cramped writing—that would be *lovely* reading by candlelight—and found a doctor's name and a date at the top.

Journal-like entries marched down the page, separated by small swirls, and she held it close to a candle and read one in the middle of the page.

Dr. Edward Simon, in the year of our Lord, 1742.

I have attempted to appease the spirits and purge the bad humors from her body through incense and chanting by the Franciscan order of monks.

It should be noted that no food or drink can enter her mouth or nose due to a blockage, nor can said blockage be removed from the patient's throat. All attempts to do so have failed.

Although I see great improvement, she has yet to wake or open her eyes. However, I did observe, and my assistant agrees, that she has responded to our ministrations by small movements or noises that have not yet been replicable.

Ro frowned and grabbed another.

We have chafed the patient's skin with ice water and have placed a poultice of mustard greens, snail paste, and wild garlic on her chest to ward off evil spirits.

She snatched up another. More of the same.

Bleeding the patient with leeches has produced desirable results, paling her skin further and enhancing her beauty, though we have yet to observe her awakening. We are certain such a blessed event shall occur soon, once the bad blood has been purged from her body.

Insane treatments that had nothing to do with logic, true medicine, or fey magic, and all things that, if they did not harm their patient, would certainly be ineffectual.

She'd seen for herself how bloodletting had hastened her mère's demise.

Ro started scanning scroll after scroll, annoyed at the curling edges, discarding them just as quickly. All supposed physicians, healers, or priests. All trying ineffectual treatments to wake Snow White, to figure out what could be wrong with her.

Not a lick of sense in any of them.

Apparently one had tried a scalpel to the throat, but her

skin was impenetrable. Ro didn't know whether to be relieved that one of these charlatans hadn't slit the queen's throat or insanely curious why her skin could not be pierced. Both?

She huffed and threw a scroll back where she'd found it. "That's just ridiculous."

No wonder Captain Red had been so upset. The "treatments" the scrolls described were inhumane at best and downright torture at worst.

Ro laid one hand on the queen's forehead. "I'm so sorry for what has been done to you." She hoped the queen hadn't felt any of it. "I will do everything in my power to help you, if it's not too late."

At a flicker of movement from the women, Ro caught the tail end of their sharing a hopeful look. Ro jerked her hand back, self-conscious, but they schooled their expressions into placid blankness just as quickly.

Then they moved as one and laid out new clothing for the queen, bringing out jewelry, haircombs, and bottles of powders and potions. Next they began bathing the queen.

"You do this every day?"

The women nodded in unison and kept up their steady ministrations.

"Very well. Show me what to do."

Under their gentle direction, Ro helped bathe the queen, dress her for the night, and move her arms back over her chest, which were surprisingly still pliable, if cold. Not a mark marred her body, so thankfully the physicians hadn't done lasting damage.

As soon as they were done, the women locked the glass covering in tandem and tucked away the keys around their necks. They led Ro to the large table, showed her blank scrolls and supplies, and waited patiently while Ro set weights at each corner, added her name and the date, and recounted the magic in short, punctual details.

She sprinkled the scroll with pounce to dry the ink, then left it open to come back to later.

Blessedly, the women set up a curtain and gave Ro privacy for her own bath. After setting out a change of clothes, they took Ro's clothing, cleaned them, and hung them to dry.

Ro kept hold of and washed her red cape, not letting it out of her sight.

They shared a simple meal with Ro, then she was shown to a pallet hidden behind another curtain. Ro pulled it out, accepted the blanket and pillow handed her—both soft and luxurious—and lay down in full view of the dead queen across the room. Each lady-in-waiting bedded down on either end of the queen's coffin, on their own pallets.

As much as she hated to stop searching, to sleep in here with a coffin, to have accomplished nothing, Ro was exhausted, heartsore, and just wanted this day to be *over*.

She'd think clearer in the morning.

16

They fell into a routine that didn't distinguish night from day inside the horrid room with no windows and the queen's coffin. Ro could only tell days were passing by when candles were replaced, as well as when the queen was cleaned and changed once a day, which Ro did not help with, not after that first day.

Oh, she'd tried. But the servants shoved scrolls in her hands, and they were right. Her time was better spent trying to wake the queen.

So she read and read and read, absorbing as much information as possible, trying to find something useful. She used the massive bookshelves of cubbies to return parchment rolls she couldn't use, and the boxes to either side of the desk to hold scrolls that might be useful.

So far, she'd found three.

The circular tower room had a level above for storing the queen's gowns, jewelry, and bedding, and a level below for preparing food, accessing water, and holding cleaning supplies.

Although the women had allowed Ro to search both rooms —the only exit was across from the queen's coffin, and there

148

were no windows on any level—they had made it clear Ro was not to spend time in them. Her place was in the chamber with the queen.

Still, even with all distractions taken away, Ro felt guilty about getting no further in her research. She'd done nothing of value other than reading ridiculous entries by charlatans pretending to be doctors, and reaching out for whatever had responded to each of them the first time, though no one else had described it as wavelike magic.

Nothing seemed to work. For any of them.

There was never any kind of movement or response from the queen, such as was described in the scrolls. Likely they were pretending to make progress to keep their heads. Something Ro didn't like to think about, considering how Wilhelm's mère had lost *her* head. Even if she'd deserved it.

The women provided her with cut lengths of parchment and numerous quills and pots of ink and a shaker full of pounce to keep her own daily entries, and they wouldn't let her rest until each day's had been completed.

Not that there was anything worth writing.

On the seventh day, after the queen had been cleansed, changed, and put back to rest, flowers tucked around her once more, the chains at the door began clanking. Ro's head came up from her scroll, held open at the corners by weights shaped like snowflakes, and her heart started pounding.

Dear Dieu in heaven, she wasn't ready! She hadn't found anything yet. What would King Wilhelm do to her? What would Madame LaChance do to her?

Her legs ached in phantom pain at the very thought of being broken, and she rubbed her neck at the terror of being beheaded.

Should she try to run? To fight? Could she get past all those soldiers?

Taking deep breaths to calm her panic, Ro stood and stepped toward the door.

The women, who'd exploded into a flurry of motion the moment the first chain rattled, rolled up her scroll and shoved it into her hands. Each entry was still on the same parchment, mostly because there wasn't much of anything to report.

Ro worried her lip at how little she'd written.

She'd made quick notes, mostly lamenting how ridiculous the so-called doctors were and how she almost hoped they'd lost their heads after performing so many brutal experiments on the queen. She never knew if King Wilhelm beheaded all those he threatened, or if it was something he simply rattled on about, as he liked to do.

And since she didn't know who would be reading the scrolls, she hadn't wanted to add much about fey magic, especially with magically strangling laces and a diseased comb as the first attempts on the queen's life.

Captain Red was right. Although the body hadn't decayed in the slightest, Snow White wasn't sleeping. But how could someone dead be so perfectly preserved after so many years?

The women positioned Ro directly in front of the door, stood at her back, and waited for the door to open. And waited. And waited.

Eventually, the final lock pulled away, and the door swung open.

Ro blinked against the bright light spilling into the darkened chamber.

A page stood with his back to her, hands up and shielding his eyes on either side, as if he were a horse wearing blinders, and spoke in a loud voice. "Mademoiselle Ro LeFèvre, huntress of France, the king of England requests you attend him immediately!"

Once again, soldiers surrounded the page, their backs to Ro, one hand held up in their own attempt at a blinder, the other on the sword at their side.

Ro stood there, scroll clutched in her fingers, crinkling where she strangled it, and found she couldn't move.

This was it. She was through. She had nothing of value to report to the king.

How long had the others lasted? How long had they been allowed to experiment on the queen? Weeks, months, a few days?

Belatedly she realized she'd been so focused on the content of the scrolls, she hadn't thought once of how long each supposed healer had been trapped within.

Had the past week been her only chance?

The women at her back none-too-gently shoved her forward, and the page moved the moment Ro's foot struck stone outside the queen's chamber.

As soon as she was three steps out, the door at her back slammed closed, all the locks engaging at once.

Ro spun around. Fastened tight, the door was impenetrable, chains hanging from it and waiting to be meticulously put back in place. The guards started doing exactly that, locking them in a crisscross pattern they seemed to know well.

"Lady Rosette, if you please?"

Ro hurried after the page, thankful to be outside that chamber, wondering if the servants locked within ever got a break. And how did they get more supplies?

More importantly, she needed to escape. She did not want to go back in there. As far as she could tell, there was nothing she could do for the poor queen, just as Captain Red had said.

Would two broken legs really be all that bad? She'd have to get caught first, right?

※

As if her thoughts of escape had summoned them, more soldiers surrounded Ro on all sides the moment she stepped into the corridor.

Someone peeled themselves away from the stone wall and joined their group. She glanced back in time to receive a full grin from Grant the bounty hunter. Ro rolled her eyes and faced forward.

Parfait. Just when she thought she was rid of him.

Ro spent the journey through numerous palace hallways, steadily marching toward King Wilhelm, dreaming of different ways to escape.

She could trip, slide right through that gap those two soldiers kept leaving, come up on her feet, dart into one of the rooms they were passing, bar the door, and be out the window in ten seconds flat.

Or she could jump up, grab the next chandelier they passed under, swing over their heads, and bolt down the corridor behind them and out of the palace.

If Grant wasn't blocking the way, that was.

As they marched down a grand staircase, she eyed the banister, thinking of sliding down it, outpacing the soldiers, and disappearing down the servant corridor.

But then how easy would it be to blend in on the streets of Londres, really? Madame LaChance surely had others watching the palace.

When they reached the bottom of the staircase, Ro recognized where she was. Finally some familiar territory. She headed straight for the main audience hall, but the guards veered in another direction.

The page led them into a spacious room, one Ro had never been to before, where the king's advisors, inner-circle courtiers, and other important heads of state clustered around a giant banquet table—where no one was seated except King Wilhelm.

Apparently "stand and watch him eat" was on today's agenda.

Grant immediately sidled closer to her as if he'd been waiting for this moment with glee. Ro studiously ignored him, to which he grinned.

At least the soldiers to either side of her remained in place and kept him and his particular stench about an arm's length away. Still, Ro took shallow breaths.

She'd forgotten how potent he was. How could Madame LaChance stand him? She was fastidious in every other aspect, even requiring her female pirate crew to be clean and comport themselves in a professional manner.

Then again, those could've been Captain Red's requirements.

No matter. She needed to stop getting so distracted.

A flock of lords and ladies surrounded the food-laden table. King Wilhelm sat in the center, stuffing his face as if it were a competition and he wasn't about to let anyone else win.

Ro eyed him and the courtiers in turn, most of them whispering behind their hands as they took in her hunting leathers and the red cape she never went anywhere without. The king didn't even look up.

The page announced Ro, then withdrew at a flap of the king's hand. It looked like an injured, dying bird.

Ro stood before King Wilhelm, crumpled scroll in hand, and watched in horrified fascination as he demolished most of the food within reach. No manners whatsoever, food flying past him as he shoveled it in as quickly as possible—she couldn't look away.

"What?" she whispered, when he picked up a good-sized fish of some kind, bit right into the soft belly, and tore out a bite, as if he were some kind of animal.

Ro almost gagged. She sincerely hoped that thing was cooked.

"What was that, huntress?" the king bellowed around white fish flesh that sprayed as he talked.

She blinked rapidly and hoped she'd covered her disgust in time. "I said, um, I said—you called me, votre Majesté?"

Food fell out of his mouth and onto his clothing as he chewed and talked with his mouth wide open. "Let's see it, huntress! Show me your progress!"

Ro could almost forgive him for shouting every sentence if she didn't also have to watch him eat.

She tore her eyes away as the page appeared at her elbow, hand outstretched. She blinked at him, and the young garçon gave a significant look to the crushed scroll in her hand. "Oh!" She quickly handed it over.

As he walked away, she tried not to look at the king again, but her eyes went back to the carnage without her permission, and she wondered what kind of wild creature he'd been raised with or by.

King Wilhelm finished his plate and half of another before he sat back with a sigh and drained his wine goblet. He waved for a refill as his eyes drifted over Ro.

Ro stiffened at the perusal. It wasn't inappropriate by any means, just haughty and pretentious and made her feel like she was a bug under his shoe.

Like most of their interactions, really.

The page rounded the enormous table and came to stand at the king's shoulder, Ro's scroll in hand. The king wiped his hands, perched spectacles on his blotchy nose, which was bulbous and covered in broken blood vessels, and read each entry as the young boy unfurled the scroll for him.

"Why, you've done nothing but criticize others' methods!" He looked up at her. "Have you done no experiments on your own?"

Ro scrambled for a reply. "The . . . experiments, as you call them, were ghastly. I can't believe you let them do such things to your wife."

The soldier at her right stiffened, but Ro's gaze went right past him to Grant. He was glowering at her. Slowly, he shook his head, just slightly. Whatever that meant.

"You dare to criticize—" the king blustered.

Ro's gaze snapped back to him. "Although your wife isn't responsive, I have no way of telling what she can feel and what she can't. So oui, votre Majesté. I highly question what those charlatans and torturers have done to your wife, especially if there's even the slightest chance she can feel what's happening to her."

King Wilhelm's face drained of its ruddy color, leaving behind a greenish hue.

Ro's sense caught up with her temper.

Oops. Maybe she should've taken Grant's warning to heart.

But time pressed upon Ro's shoulders, every moment gone a moment lost to her enemies, to those creatures in the Black Forest. She didn't have time to play games.

The king struggled to his feet, and once again Ro was surprised at the weight he'd added to his sturdy frame since the last time she'd seen him.

"Everyone out! Out! Get out!" he shouted, his skin adding shades of bright red and torrid purple to the sickly green color. It was fascinating.

Ro stood firm, as did the debt collector and two guards at her sides, as palace soldiers ushered everyone else in the room out.

The moment they were gone, the king sank down heavily, suddenly appearing drained. "Bah! I don't have the energy to waste on verbal sparring. Or your temper."

Ro, who'd been preparing to argue, deflated. She wholeheartedly agreed. She'd forgotten how absolutely wearisome it was to be around the English king, and she was relieved not to argue with him further.

If only such a thing could last.

He waved a meaty hand in Ro's direction. "She cannot feel anything, and nothing caused lasting marks. Charlatans you may call them, but they were the only ones willing to do anything for her. Besides, they know better than to permanently harm her. Have you found nothing on your own? Nothing that has not been tried before?"

Ro worried her lip. "There is . . . something . . . I cannot describe. It reached out to me once, but it has lain dormant ever since."

"These . . . wave tendrils you mentioned?" The king scanned the scroll, then looked up at her expectantly.

She nodded.

When she said nothing more, he prodded, "And?"

"And . . . I have yet to get them to react to me again. I don't know why."

He sighed and waved at the servant to return Ro's scroll, then rubbed a hand down his face, smearing more grease than was already there. "All have said something similar. A reaction of some kind, then never again. In truth, I am close to having her buried and washing my hands of the matter."

The soldier at her side definitely reacted to that. Though it was more a complete stillness than any kind of movement, it caught Ro's attention nonetheless.

The page returned her scroll, and she took the grease-smeared parchment with two fingers. *Magnifique.*

As the silence stretched on, Ro casually glanced to her right.

Though a little pale, the soldier winked at her before returning her gaze to the king.

Ro blinked. That face . . . almost a replica of the one upstairs.

But this one was ruddy, healthy, and full of life, with piles of red hair most likely shoved up into that helmet.

Captain Rose Red had come to rescue her.

Captain Red was here to rescue her!

Grant's presence seemed to loom larger on the other side of the captain. Ro jerked her head away and concentrated on the king, her senses alert to action, to movement, to any type of signal.

She was getting out of here. *Without* broken legs.

King Wilhelm speared her with a sudden glare. "Well? Can you wake her? I heard what you did for your niece."

Ro spread her hands, wrinkled scroll crinkling with the movement. "In all honesty, votre Majesté, I do not see how. This is nothing like a sleeping curse. The magic reacted to me once, then lost interest. Nothing in these scrolls makes sense. I do not recognize the magic, and unless I can access it, I cannot begin to root it out."

At his darkening look, Ro talked faster.

"I *want* to help her. Believe me, I do. But, votre Majesté, I cannot stay locked within and have any hope of waking her. I must seek outside information if I'm to have any chance of undoing the curse. Have you no books on the fey? On other curses placed throughout your history? I want to interview some of these so-called physicians. Perhaps visit where the poison itself was brewed and study any of the recipes the, um, poisoner used—"

He picked up his goblet and slammed it down. Then swept a platter from the table, scattering a roasted pheasant carcass, celery-chestnut stuffing, and garnish all over the floor.

Ro jumped.

"This has nothing to do with fey magic! Nothing is wrong! She is fine! Now you . . . you . . . go be with her! See to her every whim! And do not come back here until she comes with you!"

He heaved himself to his feet and started throwing more food, and the soldiers on either side of Ro clamped down on her arms, backed away quickly, and marched her out of the room.

Ro's breath came in short gasps at the sudden change in the king's temperament, and she feared for her life. What had happened to all the other physicians who'd tried to wake Snow White?

In what had to be the most impressive timing in the world, they passed a door closing behind a servant, and Ro got a clear view of a gallows set up in an inner courtyard with a darkened chopping block in front of it before she was hustled past.

Ro swallowed. Oh.

She sincerely hoped Captain Red had a plan, here.

The other soldiers waiting for them outside the dining hall fell into place behind them, once again pushing Grant to the back. He growled, but they would not budge.

At least *one* thing was working in her favor.

The two soldiers who escorted her outpaced the others, and Ro's heart sped up to match their pace. Those falling behind hurried to catch up.

At the top of the stairs, the moment they stepped through the open double doorway, the two soldiers pushed Ro out of the way, grabbed pikes leaning against the wall, as if they'd been placed there on purpose, and shoved the soldiers coming up the stairs.

All in shining decorative armor, those at the top lost their footing and toppled down the stairs with shouts, taking down everyone else on the stairs, no matter how hard they hung on to the balustrade.

The bounty hunter went down under a pile of bodies. He let out a roar, but he was tangled in armored limbs and couldn't get out from under them fast enough.

"Switch!"

The soldiers with pikes fell back, then two more came out of nowhere and heaved the massive hallway doors. They closed far too slowly for Ro's liking.

The last thing she saw was Grant, pinned under a pile of soldiers and perfectly framed by silver armor, his murderous glare morphing into a delighted grin. Then the doors slammed shut.

A chill snaked its way down Ro's spine.

All four pirates placed the pikes in an X over the doors and hammered impressive curved nails into the wall to hold them in place.

At the same moment, someone grabbed Ro and shoved her into an adjacent room. Ro swirled out of the soldier's grasp and was in the midst of a counterstrike when the person double-tapped her shoulder. Ro stilled, and the soldier pushed up the helm covering her face.

One of Captain Red's pirates flashed white teeth at her as the other pirates pushed into the room with them.

Oh, thank Dieu. Ro thought a real soldier had grabbed her.

Now if only her heart would stop trying to beat itself right out of her chest.

Helmets came off to reveal more pirates Ro had worked with in the Caribbean to hunt the sirens, whose names she couldn't remember for the life of her.

Captain Red's crew were already stripping off their armor to reveal servant clothing underneath. They untied skirts from around their waists and shook them out, then stuffed their armor into an armoire.

"Go," Captain Red told them. "Mislead anyone coming this way. Make sure other corridors the guards can easily access are shut off. Then blend in and meet back at the ship."

"Aye, Cap'ain."

Ro beamed at them, and they grinned back before hurrying away to their tasks. Ro turned to Captain Red. "Am I glad to see you."

She tossed a smirk over her shoulder. "Thank me later, huntress. For now, escape."

Captain Red and her first mate, Merja, pitched their own armor into the closet as banging began at the doors they'd nailed shut.

Merja paused right before shutting the armoire. "Sure would be nice to have some of that new armor."

Captain Red waved them both to follow her out of the room. "Can't risk being caught with that right now." She winked at Merja, who followed close on her heels with Ro. "We can snag a lost shipment later, down at the docks."

"Promise?" Merja teased.

"Now when have I ever been known to tease about such a thing as armor?" At Merja's grin, the captain amended, "Though I've heard rumor that a shipment of leathers be coming in the next few weeks."

"Oh, aye," Merja practically purred. "Now *that* I can wait for." At Ro's questioning look, Merja elaborated. "Bit lighter, not as dangerous on the open seas. Fits better, too. And boiled and hardened just right? Deflects weapons like a dream."

"Ah." Ro followed them into a room three corridors away that faced a busy street, where they secured the door from within.

The curtains to the floor-length windows were open, and Merja and Captain Red put their backs to either side.

"You see it coming?" Merja asked.

"We're a little ahead of schedule," Captain Red replied in a quiet voice. "That beast of a king lost his temper sooner than expected."

Ro wanted to ask so many questions, but she trusted Captain Red. If she had a plan, Ro would happily go along with it.

Then again—she cleared her throat and casually said, "Perhaps I ought to mention that the . . . mercenary who kidnapped me has permission from Madame LaChance to break my legs should I attempt escape."

Both women's heads whipped around, Merja's eyes wide, and Captain Red's furious.

Ro shrugged. "I'm not opposed to whatever you have planned. Just to being caught."

Merja tilted her head. "LaChance really said that?"

Captain Red's full lips thinned. "Sounds about right. She's all perfume and soft pink lace, but a serpent hides in wait."

She turned back to the window, her carefree manner gone, her jaw clenched.

Why don't you tell us what you really think of Madame LaChance, Ro couldn't help but think.

Footsteps rushed by the door.

Quieter, Merja said, "If the guards outside return too soon after the distraction . . ."

"They'll be here."

The three women waited, Ro sweating a bit, if she were being honest. She wondered if her legs would heal correctly, how he would do it, if she could kill him before he got the chance to maim her . . .

"There." Captain Red threw open the window and gave Ro a solemn look. "On my mark, jump with me, huntress. If you don't jump exactly right, I don't have to tell you what a fall from this height will do."

Ro peeked at the street three stories below. "No one would have to break my legs for me," she muttered, darkly.

They backed away from the window.

"Ready? Trois, deux, un, go!"

Then they were running toward the open window that was wide enough for all three, thank Dieu. And jumped off the balcony as one.

Weightlessness surrounded Ro for a split second before the ground sucked her toward it.

Ro copied Captain Red's motions on instinct, curling her body protectively right before crashing into a slow-moving cart below. Thankfully the cart was overflowing with hay. A sailcloth was thrown into place and secured, whoever had done so melting into the crowd. The cart never stopped in its plodding, rumbling journey.

Ro lay there, sprawled out and wedged partially under both Captain Red and Merja, every part of her aching where it had landed and been landed upon, but honestly, she was so thankful to be alive, she didn't mind one bit.

A laugh bubbled out of her in a squeak. Captain Red's eyes danced with laughter, but she held a finger to her lips. Ro nodded and clamped a hand over her mouth, but her smile couldn't be stopped.

Energy cycled through Ro until she vibrated with it, and it was all she could do to lie still and silent while her body urged her to throw off the cover and *fight*. Or flee with all haste. She forced herself to stay put.

They listened for pursuit while the wagon jounced its way through the crowded Londres streets in the slowest escape of Ro's life. She was certain at any moment they'd be caught and hauled before the king to be berated and sentenced, while flecks of fish spattered out of his mouth. Ro shuddered.

She never wanted to see him eat again for the rest of her life.

Soldiers came thundering past at some point, but no one stopped them, and no one followed.

After quite some time, after they'd buried themselves deeper in the hay and nothing could be heard but the light patter of rain on sailcloth, Ro relaxed for the first time since she'd been taken. She was safe now.

Adrenaline fled her system, allowing weariness to catch up with her in what felt like a flood.

And . . . much to her embarrassment . . . she fell fast asleep.

17

Ro woke to rain splattering her face as the covering was yanked away. Each taking an arm, Merja and Captain Red hustled her out of the wagon and into a waiting carriage, amid a sea of similar black carriages.

Groggy from deep but too little sleep, Ro stumbled into the dark interior and pulled the lap blanket all the way up to her chin. She'd forgotten how cold and rainy Londres was.

Merja rapped the roof, and the carriage lurched into motion as Captain Red drew the shades.

As Ro rubbed grit from her eyes, joy at their narrow escape flooded her. She blamed it entirely on being half asleep, but she laughed aloud and attacked both women with hugs, which they tolerated and Merja even returned. "You came! I can't believe you came! And so quickly."

Captain Red crossed her arms, as if to ward off any more hugs, and smirked. "I said I would, didn't I?"

Merja just grinned, her nearly perfect teeth standing out against her light-brown skin.

Ro said, "But how are you here? Already? The Caribbean is at least three months away."

Rose Red and Merja exchanged amused looks, but

Captain Red answered. "Ah, well, fate has a way of making sure I'm where I need ta be."

Ro looked to Merja for an explanation.

"We were already in port picking up supplies," the captain's first mate said.

Ro sat back and grinned, thoroughly pleased at thwarting Madame LaChance. Without having anything broken.

Though she'd been hoping to wake Snow White, if for no other reason than to restore her to the sister sitting across from her.

Her smile dimmed, and Ro instantly sobered. "You shouldn't have."

Captain Red's eyebrows climbed her forehead and nearly disappeared off her face. "And that's the thanks I get? Merja, tell the huntress she's an ungrateful brat."

"Yer an ungrateful brat," Merja rejoined cheerfully.

But Ro was already shaking her head. "I mean it. What Madame LaChance is asking me to do . . ."

"Huntress."

Ro met the captain's eyes.

"You're doing that thing again, where you take on guilt that isn't yours. I know what she's asking you to do, and 'tisn't your fault. It's hers."

Ro chose her words carefully. "But she deliberately asked me to do something that will cause you a great deal of pain, and she forced me to contact you so you can watch it up close. And then she destroyed your compass."

Captain Red's ruddy face drained of color. Merja shifted, just a little, till her arm pressed against the captain's. The captain nodded at Ro. "Go on," she whispered, allowing the contact with her first mate, to Ro's surprise. She wasn't the touchy-feely type. "Tell me everything."

Ro swallowed and did. Captain Red cursed and ran her fingers through her hair, getting them caught in her tightly bound braid.

Tears filled Ro's eyes. "I am so sorry. I can't tell you how sorry I am. If there's any way—if there's anything I *can* do . . ."

Captain Red held up her hand, and when their gazes clashed, Ro flinched at the level of pain in the captain's eyes. "Can you do it?"

Ro blinked, startled out of coherent words. "Can I—?"

"Yes. Can you do it? Can you wake my sister from death? Don't lie to me."

Ro blew out a breath and tugged at her own braided hair. "From death? I don't know. I don't think so. From a magical poison, possibly fey made?"

The captain made a sound of disgust. Merja sat still and silent through it all, a stalwart support for her captain.

Ro licked her lips, treading carefully. "Madame LaChance seems to think it's possible. And the way the queen is preserved . . . it makes me wonder."

Captain Rose Red barked a laugh that wasn't. "I examined her myself, one of the times I broke into the palace to try to take her body home for burial. She's dead, huntress. Dead. If you bring her back after all this time—she won't be herself." She leaned forward a little, to emphasize her words. "You won't know what you're bringing back."

Cold fear slithered down Ro's spine. "What do you want me to do? Madame LaChance . . ."

"Bah!" Captain Red flung her hands up and slouched back, crossing her arms as the carriage rattled its occupants over the cobblestones. "You dare not cross her again, huntress."

"I know," Ro said simply. She'd never felt such a level of magic before, and she'd met many magic users. Not to mention the woman had some kind of hold over Ro, one she didn't understand.

And that didn't begin to address Ro's missing memories.

Grandmère had said something about Ro learning to

protect her memories, to keep more from being taken. Ro needed to look into that, but somehow, she never remembered to do so. And it scared her.

No matter which way Ro looked at it, she stood on shaky ground.

The carriage covered some distance while the passengers were lost in their own thoughts, Captain Red staring at the covered window with tight eyes and clenched jaw.

Merja leaned over to say something to the captain, but she slashed a hand through the air and said, "Let me think."

Ro felt like an utter fool. She *knew* how much this subject hurt Captain Red, how much she didn't want her sister kept in some unnatural preserved state instead of laid to rest, and Ro had dragged it all up anyway.

One more thing to be thankful to Madame LaChance for.

Abruptly, Captain Red pinned Ro with a fierce stare. "I need your professional opinion. Your gut instinct. Can it be done? If there's even the smallest hope, tell me now. I know you. If anyone can do it, it's you."

Ro faltered. If that didn't add even more pressure.

She spread her hands. "According to Madame LaChance, I have to, since it's the only way to fulfill my bargain for your ship, your crew, and the lost combs, but nothing I saw or did led me to believe that I *could*. Dieu, I wish I had a better answer. You know I do. But if I can figure out a way, I'll do it in a heartbeat."

She quickly explained what was happening in her forest, recounting her grandmère's death and the passing on of Darya's mantle.

Captain Red didn't respond, and Ro wondered if she were even listening. Or still reeling from the reason Madame LaChance had dragged Ro here.

"Je suis désolé. I am sorry," she whispered at the end.

"All right," Captain Red said. "Leave this to me. I'll meet with Madame LaChance, work something out with her."

Merja spoke up, her gentle voice filling the carriage. "You barely escaped her last time. She won't be forgiving when you go back to her, not after what we've done."

"What you've done—?" Ro began. Was there more?

Captain Red cut in. "Stole her ship. Ran away and hid in the Caribbean. Left a gap in her mercenary base and a power struggle behind. Beyond that, you don't need to know."

Ro snapped her mouth closed.

Captain Red nodded once, decided. "I will send her a missive, hinting at an offer to come back and work for her in exchange for forgiving the huntress's debts."

Merja touched her arm. "Rose, no! You know what she'll do to you . . ."

Captain Red shot her first mate a look that silenced her. Then she turned her gaze to Ro. "Maybe she'll forget this whole debacle and let you return to your duties."

Ro frowned, mind whirling. She needed to get back, oui, but this wasn't an acceptable option either. Captain Red had fought so hard to get away.

Besides, if Captain Red's sacrifice wasn't enough, Madame LaChance would simply send another bounty hunter, and Ro might not survive the next one.

"Non," Ro said firmly. "Merja's right. We'll find another way."

Captain Red smirked. "And there's the huntress we all know and love, determined to save all and sundry by doing things her own way."

A warm glow filled Ro, the words a vast improvement over Madame LaChance's cutting remarks.

"All right," Captain Red said decisively. "I'll take suggestions from the crew. Give them a chance to voice their objections. But then I'm doing what I think is best."

Ro nodded, but Merja frowned and appeared disgruntled. With both of them.

"How did you find me?" Ro asked.

Captain Red and Merja exchanged glances. Captain Red said, "Didn't you call me with the compass?"

Ro closed her eyes briefly. "Madame LaChance made me use it. Right before she destroyed it." Her eyes popped open. "But I used it there, at Madame LaChance's, a week ago, and you found me at the palace."

Captain Red nodded. "There were rumors that Madame LaChance had a bounty on your head. We figured sooner or later you'd end up in Angleterre, so we had errand girls watching."

"Glad to see you had such faith in me," Ro grumbled.

The pirate captain smirked. "You're here, aren't you? Besides, Madame LaChance has a way of getting what she wants."

Merja snatched up Red's hand and squeezed. "I *won't* let her have you."

Captain Red gave her a kind if somewhat condescending smile, before taking her hand back and patting Merja's knee in a "there, there" gesture.

Ro raised an eyebrow. Not the reaction she'd been expecting from the fiercely independent pirate captain. She'd expected more knives or swords or "don't touch me" moments to their interaction.

And maybe for Merja to punch her back or something.

Captain Red took a deep breath and faced Ro. "You know how I feel about this, but Madame LaChance wouldn't have demanded such a thing if she didn't think you could accomplish it. If you think of anything—anything at all—that you can do to wake her, I want to know immediately."

As if realizing belatedly that she sounded rattled, Captain Red sat back, arms crossed, foot tapping, back pressed into the seat.

"I give you my word, Captain." Ro nodded solemnly. "But as I told the king, it would go so much better if I could see what the queen mère used to poison her, her potion books, or where she made her concoctions."

Captain Red dipped her chin. "I had the same thought, years ago. However, when Wilhelm found out what she'd done, after he'd had her killed, he emptied her rooms and burned everything. Her clothes, her books, her furniture, everything."

"Well," Merja said with a grin, "except the jewels."

With a flicker of a smile, the captain said, "Aye. Except for the jewels. 'Tis funded many an adventure."

Ro's shoulders slumped. Well there went that lead.

"Did someone train her? In her use of fey magic?" If that was even what this was. It felt so foreign to Ro, she wasn't sure.

Merja shook her head. "All leads died with her. Believe me, we tried."

Ro grunted, thoroughly disgusted. Of course the king would've been the one to block their efforts, even while demanding results.

Then again, Ro would've burned such things too, though perhaps not to the same extent. The deceased queen mother had been a master of poisons. Even her garden had been over-flowing with deadly plants, which she'd used on anyone who disagreed with her. Only others who'd died at her hand hadn't ended up perfectly preserved like Snow White.

Merja cleared her throat and asked what Captain Red couldn't. "Did she look . . . well?"

Reorienting herself to the conversation, Ro briefly, gently described the queen, what was being done for her, the book-cases stuffed full of research, and the two tongueless servants who cared for her.

Merja glanced at Captain Red at that part, and although she appeared disinterested, now staring at her boots, Ro could tell from every tense muscle that she was listening . . . intently.

"Although I'm glad to be free, you have no idea how glad,

I do wish I'd had more time to see if anyone else had gotten close to figuring out what kind of magic caused it. I was—"

Ro paused and eyed Captain Red. She didn't want to bore her, but she also didn't want to leave out something that could give her hope.

Neither woman stopped her, so she continued. "I'd been training with my grandmère, who was teaching me how to recognize fey magic and which species it came from. I wish I could've learned more before, well, you know."

"I am sorry, huntress," Merja whispered. She made a motion like she wanted to take Ro's hand too, but she pulled back, either not wanting to reach across the carriage space or unsure how Ro would react.

Blinking back tears, Ro nodded, cleared her throat, and continued. "She was teaching me to unravel curses. I *should* be able to do this. But it didn't feel anything like a sleeping curse, and no life force was being drawn from her, suppressed, or changed. Once it settled, it was just . . . empty. I don't know how else to describe it. I'm sorry for that too."

Captain Red lifted her chin in acknowledgment, and the carriage slowed.

Ro flicked a glance at the door and spoke rapidly. "I was taken from the Black Forest at the worst possible time, right in the middle of an attack. I have to get back—"

Captain Red waved her hand. "We'll discuss it on my ship."

Merja peeked out the window and tapped the roof twice. The carriage came to an abrupt halt, then it swayed as the driver jumped down to open the door.

Before he could do so, all three women piled out into a misty fog swarming with seagull cries, briny air, and the lap of water against docks.

Ro took a deep breath and smiled.

It felt like coming home.

18

Moving as one, Captain Red and Merja shielded Ro by throwing a drab brown cloak around her shoulders and pulling its dingy hood up to cover most of her face. All three wore nondescript brown cloaks, Ro's red cape balled up and hidden in the lap blanket they'd swiped from the carriage like the pirates they were.

If Ro's nose hadn't already told her, the moment her foot hit the damp boardwalk confirmed where she was.

They hustled Ro down the docks, through misty rain, and Ro went with them gladly. Salty air, the cries of gulls, and creaking docks drenched Ro's senses, and she soaked it in.

Perhaps Captain Red could ferry her down the river Thames and back across the Channel to France. Surely they could work out some kind of arrangement.

Water lapped, and even though she couldn't see an arm's length ahead of her in the dense fog, soon a shape pierced the mist.

Captain Red's glorious British galleon loomed over them, and Ro blinked back a fine sheen of tears. The *Siren Hunter*. She hadn't thought she'd ever see it again.

The fog cleared just enough to take in all its glory. This

galleon would easily house a crew of three hundred, but fifty could run it in a pinch, which was about the size of the crew Captain Red had left with. Had she picked up more in the Caribbean? Excitement coursed through Ro. She would soon find out. Each deck was now striped an alternating red and black instead of the yellow and black of before.

Before Captain Red had stolen it from Madame LaChance.

Siren Hunter was emblazoned proudly in gold letters on its sides, all kinds of swirls sprouting from the letters that still made the name clear as day and big enough for any approaching ship to know to run if they valued their lives.

If possible, it was even more gorgeous than it had been before.

Ro breathed out. "My, but it's good to see her again."

"Aye," agreed Captain Red, a tone to her voice that said something had been soothed deep in her soul.

Merja didn't move ahead as Ro expected her to.

Ro grinned over at the captain. "Permission to come aboard, ma capitaine?"

"Huntresses first." Captain Red swept her hand to the side with an elaborate bow. The only thing missing was the broad-band feathered hat she liked to wear.

Which would most likely be atop her head the moment she was back on deck. Along with her blazing red frock coat, tall leather boots, and comfortable breeches.

Ro sincerely hoped the captain had something for her to wear as well. As kind as servants had been to provide her with a dress to sleep in, she was about done wearing the same clothes she'd been kidnapped in day in and day out. Besides, she needed a disguise for when the time came to escape from or fight off Grant.

Which she wouldn't have to do alone now. Because she had help.

Ro smiled and moved up the gangplank.

Eight decks later, the raised boards on the plank and handrails allowing her to make the near-vertical climb — a vast improvement over the rope ladders she'd climbed before — Ro paused to savor the feel of stepping aboard.

Also, she was slightly breathless. Not from the exertion, non, but because eight decks was rather higher than she was strictly comfortable with.

But she was safe. Finally.

She smiled and climbed onboard.

It wasn't until she stepped fully over the gunwale, helped by two of the crew, that she felt the barrier snap closed behind her.

Ro gasped and spun around, but Captain Red and Merja were already aboard behind her, eyeing her warily and blocking the plank. Worse, they were crouched and ready to fight.

Ro immediately tried to dart between them, but they were ready for her and shoved her back. More pirates came up behind her, keeping their distance but hemming her in all the same.

"Won't you come to my ready room, huntress?" Captain Red asked without asking. "We'll talk."

"What have you done?" Ro cried, more hurt than she cared to admit.

Captain Red flinched. Just the slightest bit, but it was there. So she'd done it on purpose? Ro thought Captain Red was her friend.

Yet she was a pirate. Ro had trusted a *pirate*. She should've known better.

Ro tried very hard not to stare at the captain with betrayal in her eyes, but she doubted she was succeeding. She didn't have all the information here. It could be protection only. She was a wanted woman, after all. They all were. The whole crew.

She simply needed to find out what the captain meant by this.

But her mantra didn't calm her racing heart.

Captain Red raised placating hands. "Steady on, huntress, I can explain. But I need you to be calm so I can do that. You can be calm for me, can't you? If you'll just follow me—"

"I'm not going *anywhere* with you until you explain this!"

At no reply from the captain, Ro shoved past her—Merja and Red kept her away from the plank but let her go to the railing. Ro pressed both hands over the rail, and they stopped midair, flat, as if a solid wall extended straight up from the gunwale.

She looked to the captain for an explanation.

Captain Red gazed steadily back, still ready to fight if need be. "It's the only way I can keep Madame LaChance from finding us, and in turn, you."

Ro glanced at the mist creeping through the docks like a living thing. It wasn't as thick up here. On the bustling docks, everyone had their heads down and were moving cautiously. As if the fog was much thicker below.

"The fog, too?"

"Aye. I don't have to tell you how dangerous it is for me to be back in Angleterre, especially Londres."

Ro tried to reason through it. Captain Red had stolen Madame LaChance's ship, hidden halfway across the world, and sworn never to set foot on English soil again, not while the mad king kept his wife and her sister in a glass coffin.

Which he still did.

Pacing like a caged animal, Ro tried to see the situation from Captain Red's point of view. She not only had to keep herself safe, but her crew too. And she'd come to rescue Ro, after all.

She took several deep breaths, trying to calm herself enough to have a rational conversation instead of throwing herself at the blockade. At least it didn't zap her with painful magic like Odette's barrier had.

Ro turned to the captain. "I understand," she said stiffly.

Some of the pirates exchanged surprised glances, and Ro took that as encouragement to keep going. With a calm, rational voice.

"But as I was telling you, I was taken during a wolf attack. Not . . . normal wolves. Loups-garous. They somehow tore into the Black Forest through a veil between worlds, and now they're taking over. Killing people. I—they shouldn't even exist."

She took a step closer to Captain Red. "If I don't get back, if I don't stop it *now*, more will come through, and once they're done with the Black Forest, they'll spread to other kingdoms. Other peoples. Who knows? Maybe even here. I can't let that happen."

Merja frowned. "I haven't heard of such creatures . . ."

"Sad as that may be, huntress," Captain Red cut in, "I can't risk my people either. I'm sorry, but I cannot allow you off this ship."

As she spoke, more of the crew hurried over to the plank and lowered it with ropes, effectively cutting off Ro's escape.

Ro couldn't put her head over the rail more than a handsbreadth, not with that barrier, so she pressed her face against it sideways and watched the plank being dismantled and stored along the dock and hidden among crates for future use.

Apparently it was more important to keep it in a place Ro couldn't access it. Not that Ro would know the first thing about lowering such a long, heavy, complicated walkway.

But what if there was an emergency and they needed to get off the ship quickly?

That feeling of being trapped threatened to drown her, and Ro had to fight for every breath until her heart rate slowed. Surely they still had rope ladders.

Not that she could see any at the moment.

Pirates still surrounded her, waiting on her next move.

Once she was certain she could speak without raising her voice or throwing herself overboard, Ro lifted her chin. "I'm sorry, ma capitaine, but I cannot stay here. You know this."

"But stay you must." As soon as the opening in the rail swung shut, Captain Red relaxed—Ro assumed she now had no way off the ship—and nodded at several of her crew. "You remember Mary, Sheba, and Oksana?"

Ro didn't, but then again, she was terrible with names, and they did look familiar. Possibly.

"They will see to your needs." The captain started to walk away.

Ro called after her, "Why imprison me here instead of leaving me where I was? At least then I would be working toward waking your sister and gaining my freedom. How does this help anything? I—"

Captain Red spun on her so quickly, Ro shuffled back half a step, but then Rose Red was right in her face. She hissed, "*Never* speak of my sister again, huntress. What I told you was spoken in confidence, and not to be discussed in front of my crew."

Ro opened her mouth to apologize, but the captain spoke right over her, raising her voice. "Need I remind you who is captain of this ship? While you are aboard my vessel, my word is law, and you will do as I say."

Ro ground her teeth. "Spoken just like Captain Montrose. Remember him? He liked to boss me around too. Thought women huntresses were worthless. Almost cost me peace talks with the sirènes due to his stubbornness. It didn't work out so well for him, did it?"

Captain Red stepped closer, her eyes flinty. "Are you threatening me, huntress? In front of my crew?" She showed teeth, but it wasn't a smile. "Because I promise *that* won't go well for you."

"Non," Ro said, "but I *am* saying I refuse to be held prisoner. My people need me, just as yours need you. I must be allowed to leave. You know this." Tears clogged her voice, but she refused to cry in front of the captain. Once was enough.

"And I wish I could give that to you, huntress, truly, but I cannot. I suggest you make yourself useful. Once supplies are loaded, we'll be casting off."

Ro's mouth fell open. "You don't mean—that you're taking me to the Caribbean with you? Away from my home? My family?" *Away from Olt.* "Just leaving those creatures to take over my world?"

Ro was nearly blinded by the wave of panic beating in her chest, strangling her throat.

Captain Red gave her a tight smile and moved away, nodding at her crew as she went. Her first mate followed in her footsteps. Ro tried to go after her and Merja, but the other three crewmembers blocked her bodily.

"Why don't you take a moment and breathe, huntress."

"I can show you to your bunk, if you want."

"Yeah, yer duties don't start till tomorrow."

Ro raised her hands and stepped back, needing space. "I just, I need to think. I need a moment. To myself. Alone."

They eyed her, then each other, eventually nodding and moving away. But not far.

Ro stumbled over to the rail and gripped it, able to get her hands around it, but her knuckles pressed against the barrier.

Trapped again. Always, forever, frustratingly trapped.

Trapped in the château with the beast.

Trapped on a ship with the king's men.

Trapped in the Caribbean.

Trapped with Odette and her swans.

Trapped by Madame LaChance.

Trapped by King Wilhelm.

And now trapped by Captain Rose Red herself, who *knew* Ro's story, knew how much Ro hated to be held against her will, knew what staying would cost her. Cost everyone, eventually.

Though she was certain Captain Red didn't understand the severity of the situation, or she wouldn't make Ro stay. She knew how important it was to Ro to keep those she loved safe.

And if Ro didn't get out in time, she'd be pressed into service and taken all the way to the Caribbean. Who knew what would be left of the Black Forest by the time she found a way back? How far the loups-garous would've spread?

And not at all important in the scope of lives lost, but important to her all the same: Would Olt have moved on? To someone who *was* willing to marry him?

Her chest tightened, and she took several deep breaths to calm her wildly beating heart. It felt like losing Olt all over again.

Non, she needed to get out. Now.

In full view of the entire crew, Ro pressed her hands against the barrier and began testing it. Placing her hands as high as she could reach, then below the rail to the openings in the gunwale, she moved toward the prow of the ship, step by step, examining every inch within reach.

Surprisingly, they let her. Although they followed her, watched her every move, where she placed her hands and how long she lingered in each spot, her three watchers didn't stop her. Probably because they knew how trapped she was and that there was nothing she could do about it.

Still, Ro made her way around the entire ship, crawling over crates and around barrels, climbing on anything strapped down, and placing her hands as high as she could reach.

She eyed the masts, three on this big of a ship, but one of the three pirates—Mary, was it?—stepped in front of her and shook her head, so Ro moved away from the shrouds used for accessing the crow's nests.

If she were being honest, she was grateful. She hated high

places after the last mast she'd climbed had fallen out from under her, but she still needed to revisit this part of the ship later. Make sure she wasn't missing anything.

While she worked, the crew scurried all over the deck and the riggings and in and out of the ship's hold, carting supplies away and tying ropes and doing whatever needed doing on a working ship.

Ro returned to where she'd started and took in the deck.

The crew had swelled since the last time she was aboard.

Captain Red's crew had always been entirely female, so the sirens wouldn't bother them, but some of the new faces looked like they'd been picked up in the Caribbean, with dark or bronzed skin, healthy from working in the sun and from the captain's insistence on paying and feeding them well. Exactly as Ro would expect.

But theirs weren't the only new faces.

Many girls were much younger than Ro was used to seeing as part of Red's crew. Most of them pale and sickly. Some with sores, some malnourished, some wounded or with curled or damaged or missing limbs.

One girl's cheek was half melted off her face, her hairless eyebrow drooping into her eye, her skin waxy.

Ro's chest grew cold. Captain Red's crew had always been robust, healthy. Varied in nationality, oui, as she gave a chance at a new life to anyone who wanted it, but this was different. Wrong. Something was so very wrong.

She took a step toward the girl with the wounded face, and one of her three shadows stepped in front of her with a small bow.

"I am Oksana. I will take you to your bunk now, huntress. Your duties start early and last late. I suggest you rest while you can." Her voice was clipped, her diction perfect.

Tiredness that had her falling asleep in the wagon came flooding back, and all Ro could think of was how good a bunk or a hammock would feel right about now.

Was it bad that rest felt more important than escaping?

Brooking no argument, the three crewmembers escorted Ro belowdecks to a tiny private room in which a hammock and a water bucket had been placed. As before, a small desk was bolted to the floor, and Ro wondered if she could get some research material while she was here. She'd ask the captain at her next opportunity.

She turned to her guardians. "Am I being locked in, too?"

Sheba smirked. "Now why would we do that, huntress? You are the good captain's guest."

And with that, they left. Ro waited till their footsteps faded to peek, and sure enough, Sheba eyed her from her position alongside the bulkhead.

So not locked in, but not allowed to wander free, either.

Ro slammed the door, then, after a second, slammed the side of a fist against the bulkhead, which didn't exactly feel good or make her feel any better. She cursed Madame LaChance for making her ask for Captain Red's help.

Though she'd had no idea things would turn out like this.

Surely something else was going on here. Something she couldn't see, didn't know. A plan Captain Red had. But would the captain tell her what it was?

She clung to that hope like one of the barnacles on the hull.

But more importantly: How long would Captain Red hold her captive on her ship? A ship that had been renamed after Ro herself?

Right now, at this moment, the name felt like a mockery, as did Captain Red's supposed friendship, and Ro wanted to scream.

So she wrapped herself in her hammock to sulk and was startled when, what felt like seconds later, a pounding at her door roused her to attend to her new duties . . . early the next morning.

PART III

"Snow White and Rose Red"
Blanche Neige et Rose Rouge
—Jacob Grimm and Wilhelm Grimm—

The two children were so fond of one another that they always held each other by the hand when they went out together, and when Snow White said: "We will not leave each other," Rose Red answered: "Never so long as we live."

Les deux enfants s'aimaient tellement qu'ils se tenaient toujours par la main lorsqu'ils sortaient ensemble, et lorsque Blanche Neige disait : « Nous ne nous quitterons pas, » Rose Rouge répondait : « Jamais tant que nous vivrons. »

Laura Hollingsworth

19

"The captain has asked to see you in her ready room, huntress."

About time. Ro had only been demanding to see her for three days. But oh no. Captain Red was far too busy with more important things than to bother with the unhappy captive.

Ro stretched out her back, amazed at how sore she was after only a few days on a working ship, and surreptitiously eyed the pirate to see if she could remember her name.

The pirate hooked a thumb at herself. "Aisling."

Ro flushed. "Of course."

Had she met Aisling before? She couldn't remember.

The younger pirate grinned. "'Tisn't a problem, to be sure. Now hustle it, huntress. The captain don't like ta be kept waiting."

Ro set the tool she'd been using to scrape buildup off planks on a barrel and hurried after the young, freckled, and redheaded pirate.

At least Ro wasn't one of the swimmers sent to scrape barnacles off the hull, though she would've gladly used such an opportunity to escape. She had to wonder if the water was deep enough to jump, should she find an opportunity.

Before hunting the sirens, when she'd been on Captain Montrose's ship, which was half the size of this one, they had to anchor away from the wharf and row in for supplies, since there weren't enough docks for large ships to make berth. Each ship had to take turns.

While the docks had been extended since her last visit, the Port of London was even busier than before. Ships still had to take turns or else weigh anchor and row in for supplies while they waited for an open spot, and there were traffic jams all up and down the river Thames as the activity had more than doubled.

Yet, just like last time, Captain Red somehow had access to a mooring she was not required to move away from nor to make room for another ship. And since the *Siren Hunter* was such a massive vessel, Ro could only think that meant this water was deep enough to jump, should she find a way to do so. She hoped.

And if she got that far, was there a way past the barrier in the water? Or did the barrier end at the railing?

All things she wouldn't know until she tested them.

As soon as they reached the captain's ready room, the girl knocked and called out, "Huntress ta see ya, Cap'ain."

"Merci, Aisling. Show her in."

Aisling swung open the door with a grin, touched her forehead then flicked her fingers toward the captain in a salute, and pulled the door closed behind Ro. Leaving Ro facing Captain Red and her first mate, Merja.

Ro crossed her arms and lifted her chin. "You called?"

Captain Red sighed. "That's how it's going to be between us, is it?"

"Unless you're planning to escort me off this bloody ship, then oui. That's how it's going to be." Ro clenched her teeth. Blast it all. Her voice had trembled on that last bit.

Merja and the captain exchanged glances, then Captain Red held out her hand to the chair across from her massive desk, which was bolted to the floor to keep it from sliding in storms or rough water.

"S'il vous plaît, sit."

"Why should I?" Ro demanded, voice sure and strong. Thank heavens. "I'm treated as a prisoner, not a guest."

"Because, huntress," Captain Red said, folding her hands on the desk's surface, "I need more information before I make a decision. You can give me that, can't you?"

Ro's jaw tightened at her patronizing tone.

"It is my sister, after all, that Madama LaChance has commanded you to aid. I would like to know why."

Ro winced, then tilted her head. "Then why won't you let me at least try to help? Your interests align with hers."

Now it was Captain Red's jaw that clenched. "I assure you, our interests never *align*. Well, unless there are chests of gold to be had, but oui, huntress. I would very much like to know why the woman who used to own me is so interested all of a sudden in bringing back a queen who has been dead for *years*."

Ro was almost too stunned to reply. "Dead? Non, the more I think about it, the more convinced I am that she isn't dead—not exactly. Yet she's not sleeping either. Like I said, it's somewhere in between. Like an . . . absence. Of everything."

Lost in thought, she tugged at the hair that was now long enough to put back in a braid. She needed to cut it again, but for now, a lumpy and lopsided braid it was.

If only Cosette were here to help her make it into a piece of art.

Or better yet, if only Ro were *there* with her sister instead of tangled in this mess.

Home with Olt.

Wrenching her mind away from that painful subject, Ro

struggled to put her thoughts about Queen Snow White into words. "I don't know how to explain it. It's not that the queen has been preserved, such as by an embalming method"—she frowned—"non, wait, that's exactly it." She glanced up in sudden excitement. "Whatever has been done to her keeps her in pristine condition, maybe because they knew she could one day be awakened?" She snapped her fingers. "That's it! The preservation is completely different than the poison used to try to kill her. Someone is giving us a chance to bring her back."

Ro hummed with energy. Now all she wanted to do was march in there, bring back the queen, and ride off to her duties in the Black Forest.

If only it were that easy.

And if only she could figure out *how.*

Captain Red stared back, not a change to her expression, but Merja, leaning on the bulkhead at her captain's side, shot her captain a concerned look.

"That very well may be, huntress," said Rose Red, "but it means nothing if you've not found a way to bring her back. And you still haven't explained *why* Madame LaChance wishes you to do so."

Ro threw her hands out in frustration. "How am I supposed to know? Other than her promise to the king, she didn't tell me why—only that I had to, or there would be consequences. Dire ones."

"Perhaps there was something else she said, some other clue to her motives . . ." the captain mused.

"I told you everything she said, I promise you," Ro vowed.

The captain nodded, accepting her words, though it was clear she wasn't happy about it.

Ro ran her fingers through her hair, further dislodging strands from her braid, and began to pace. "As long as I'm here—which won't be much longer," she said, shooting Captain Red a fierce look, to which one side of the captain's face rose in a smirk, "then why don't I keep working toward that goal? Give me something to research, to study. Since you have so many crew now to work your ship, you certainly don't need me for such tasks."

At that, she spun to face the captain, shoving her hands on her hips. "That reminds me. How do you have so many new crewmembers? Where did they all come from? And why are so many"—her mind spun for the right word—"wounded? Sickly?" She frowned. "Disabled?"

Captain Red gave her a tight smile. "I think that's enough for one day. Merja? See the huntress back to her room, s'il vous plaît."

Ro threw her hands wide. "It's the middle of the day! Don't tell me you're going to keep me locked up like Captain Montrose did. Besides, I was scraping the deck of buildup." Gross, nasty, smelly work. Her nails would likely never be free of grime. "Unless you're letting me look further into Queen Snow—"

"Enough!" Captain Red shot to her feet. "Merja. Take her to her quarters. *Now.*"

Merja was already on Ro, twisting one arm behind her back and marching her straight to her cabin, not letting her go, nor letting her offer any resistance, though surprisingly not causing much pain. As if she knew exactly how much pressure to apply and no more.

Ro spun around the moment she was shoved into her room. "Are you *kidding* me? After all we've been through, you're just going to let her—"

Merja hissed. "Do *not*, huntress. Do not finish that sentence. There is much going on here that you do not understand, much that I cannot tell you. That *we* cannot tell you. For your own safety and protection."

Ro spread her hands, trying so hard to be reasonable. "Then help me understand. Madame LaChance threatened to break my *legs*, Merja. She did something to me where I couldn't move, couldn't speak. It felt like I was being strangled, and she wasn't even touching me."

Startled, Merja stepped back.

Ro waved her hands around, something she did when she got worked up or words came pouring out without her permission. "And she said it was because of something I'd eaten—"

"Stop!" Merja had both hands up, panicked, eyes wide. "Just—you—stay here. Don't leave this room. I mean it!"

And with that, Merja swung the door closed and took off, her footsteps pounding away down the corridor.

Ro frowned. Hadn't she told them that part? She could've sworn she had . . .

Still standing, she sank back against the hammock stretched across her room, till it reached its limit and held her weight, and crossed her arms. Great. Now she had even more questions.

And zero answers in sight.

20

After that day, Ro was kept so busy she hardly had time to think. She moved delivered cargo into the hold, scrubbed and scraped everything in sight, repaired nets and sharpened harpoons, and both the captain and Merja stayed far away from her. Almost as if they were avoiding her. Which stung far more than Ro cared to admit.

She didn't make friends well or often, and losing these so-called friendships crushed her soul in a way that hurt to her very core. Because if she consistently lost friendships, had a difficult time forming those friendships in the first place, something had to be wrong with her, wasn't there?

It hurt too much to think about, so she threw herself into her work on deck—which she was oddly escorted to and from multiple times each day. From the sounds of things, she was hustled to her room whenever they got another delivery of cargo.

So she watched, and she waited. And she planned.

It seemed the only time she might escape was when the barrier was lowered and cargo was brought onboard. Yet she was well-guarded at all times.

That meant she'd have a fight on her hands. If only she

189

could be above when cargo was loaded to see what she was up against . . .

But non. She was only allowed abovedeck once there was a new pile of goods to take deep into the belly of the ship. If it hadn't already been lowered into the hold with ropes and their pulley system attached to the ship's spars, that was. Even then, they still had to secure it belowdecks for the long journey across the seas.

The mist hiding the ship stayed strong at all times, fluctuating slightly with the sun. As if whoever created it fought to keep the sun's rays from burning it off.

Captain Red had once mentioned her crew had special abilities, which was why she'd chosen them. Ro had assumed that meant they were good at their jobs, but watching that mist, she had to wonder . . . what else was going on here?

A shout interrupted Ro's thoughts. "Cap'ain! Here she be."

Ro turned from her task as a scrawny, filthy young girl in a cap and trousers was shoved to her knees in front of Captain Red. Strands of dull brown hair straggled out from under her cap.

Malnourished as the child was, even Ro could tell she was a girl blooming into womanhood. She wouldn't last long on the streets.

"What's your name, girl?" the captain asked.

Her hands were bound behind her, and although she seemed scared out of her mind, she lifted her chin and gave the captain a defiant flare of her nostrils. "Siobhan."

Captain Red smirked.

Ro's blood started to thrum louder in her veins. What were they doing with that poor girl?

One of the pirates dumped a small pile of gold and silver coins, coin pouches, and pocket watches on the boards in front of her. "And here's the stuff she stole. Some of it mine."

She shot the street urchin a dirty look, though Ro thought

it looked false. As if she'd set up the girl to steal from her and now had to act upset.

"I ain't stole nothin'," the girl insisted. "It's all mine, fair and square." She had a Welsh lilt to her voice.

"Is it now?" Captain Red raised an eyebrow.

The girl nodded once and stuck out her chin.

The captain slapped her. The girl gasped, her defiance slipping away. As Ro stepped forward, a pirate moved into her path.

Captain Red grasped the girl's face and held a ruby dagger to her throat. "Don't ever lie to me again."

The girl nodded repeatedly, chest heaving, eyes swimming with tears.

Ro instantly felt sorry for her, then hesitated. Considering her hard life on the streets, could they also be false?

Didn't matter. Ro tried to get to the girl, but the other pirate pushed her back to the rail, clamping a filthy hand over her mouth when Ro started to demand Captain Red stop.

"Let the cap'ain handle it, huntress. She knows what she be doing."

Well Ro didn't care for how she was handling it.

Captain Red nodded once and stepped back, putting the dagger away. "Bon. She'll do. Now brand her."

The girl screamed, fought, struggled, tried to get away but couldn't, while two muscular pirates dragged her toward the galley, where Ro had seen branding implements hanging on the wall.

The encircled R.R. for Rose Red.

Ro once again tried to go after the girl, but the pirate held her in place. It was like she wasn't even fighting. How strong were these women the pirate captain recruited?

The moment the girl disappeared into the hold, Captain Red quelled Ro with a look. "Not a word, huntress. You don't get to object on my ship without consequences."

The muscular pirate that held her released a hand and

touched her belt, and Ro's eyes went to the lash coiled there. Stunned, she looked up at the captain. Surely she wouldn't have Ro whipped.

Captain Red just gazed back at Ro.

Oui, she would.

"Do you yield?"

Ro thought about fighting the pirate off for about three seconds before sagging in her hold.

"Say it," Captain Red practically snarled.

"I yield," Ro said, more weary than she'd been in a long, long time.

But as she stood slumped there, fury built in Ro's chest until she vibrated with it. How *dare* she? How dare they all?

She lifted furious eyes to the captain's.

Captain Red snapped her fingers. "My ready room. Now."

Ro started to object.

"It's either that or the brig, huntress. Your choice."

Yet without giving her that choice, Captain Red turned on her heel and marched away. Another pirate flanked Ro's other side, and even though they didn't drag her, they made sure she kept up with Captain Red's long strides.

The girl started screaming as Ro was hustled into the captain's ready room.

The moment the door closed, Ro shouted, "You can't brand her! She's just a child! If you think I'm going to stand by while you . . ."

"Don't." Captain Red hadn't lost her rock-hard look. "Huntress, you will obey me instantly and without question while aboard my vessel. I'll not have a mutiny on my hands because you disagree with my methods."

"Methods? You're branding a *child*."

Captain Red slapped the desk. Ro jumped, and the captain

leaned over the desk, hands splayed on its surface, eyes on fire. "I'm *protecting* her."

Ro froze. "What?"

"Do you know what Madame LaChance would do with someone of her talents? She's fey-born. Other street gangs may use her now for petty thefts, but once her powers show themselves, Madame LaChance will take her."

Ro's mind spun with all the things she hadn't known about Madame LaChance. About either of them, really. "And that makes it acceptable to snatch her off the streets and use her instead?"

"My brand protects her, huntress. From everyone, including LaChance. It'll give her a chance to be more than a pawn."

Ro let that soak in a moment before her jaw hardened. "Don't you think the knife to her throat was a bit much?"

Captain Red didn't flinch. "It's what would work for *her*. And I'll only have to do it the once."

Ro's mouth fell open. "So you're conscripting her? Forcing her to work on your ship against her will?"

"Huntress, I don't answer to you. I've made powerful enemies here by leaving, to help *you*, I might add, and I need to fill this ship."

Ro gasped. "You plan on kidnapping, what, two hundred girls?"

If she estimated correctly, the *Siren Hunter* already had between one hundred and one fifty—the captain had been busy—but there was still room for so many more.

Captain Red softened her voice. "I take good care of my girls. Don't make them do things others might. She'll be safe here. They all will be. Well," she amended, "safer."

Ro most definitely remembered battles and storms upon the open seas.

"I take the lost, the abandoned, the helpless. Those who have no one. Those this world is not kind to. I teach them how to fight, then I give them a better life. Oui, it may not be their choice at first, but it will be. After they serve their time in my crew, it will be."

Ro couldn't let herself be happy with that. The captain had threatened a girl she'd snatched off the street. Branded her. And was planning on doing it again and again. She'd known Captain Red was a pirate, that she did . . . things . . . Ro hadn't had to worry about on their last encounter, but she couldn't stand by and watch this happen.

Ro lifted her chin. "And if she wants to leave?"

Captain Red took a deep breath. "She can't. Not once I brand her. She's . . . mine. Bound to serve me."

The words crashed into Ro like a physical blow. "I cannot be on this ship."

She turned and blindly tried to make her way out, just wanting to get away from this vile creature she'd thought was her friend.

In a move that must've had her leaping over her desk, Captain Red slammed her hand on the door before Ro could exit. "It's not safe for you out there. Madame LaChance—"

Ro smacked her palms against Captain Red's chest and pushed her back a step. "Non, it's not safe for *you* if I stay on this ship."

Angry tears welled in her eyes, and the captain flinched.

Ro growled, "And believe you me, you are not kidnapping two hundred girls with special talents, or so help me Dieu, I will burn this ship to nothing."

Captain Red's eyes went hard. "I'm afraid that's not how this works, huntress."

"What's that supposed to mean?" Ro asked, hotly.

"It means," Captain Red said, pushing into her personal space, "that you are a guest on my ship, and until we push out of this harbor, guesting rules apply."

Ro blew out a breath. "No harm."

Which meant the threat of being whipped was a ruse meant for the other girls.

"That's right. No harm. Which means I cannot allow you to leave, or harm shall come to us both, as well as to those who are mine. You're not going anywhere."

Ro stared at the captain, stunned. She really meant that, didn't she? According to guesting laws, one couldn't be held against their will either, but Captain Red had circumnavigated it by adding that bit about Ro's leaving causing them both harm.

She would have to give that careful thought.

"Now, shall you return to your duties on deck? Or would you care to become better acquainted with my brig?"

Ro winced. She'd only been locked in the one time, long ago, but it wasn't an experience she cared to repeat. Nor did she think she could go out on deck and pretend all was well. Because it wasn't.

With all the dignity she could muster, Ro lifted her chin. "I prefer to return to my cabin, s'il vous plaît."

"Very well." The captain stepped aside. "I'll have those books you requested delivered."

Shallow consolation, and it did nothing to ease the ache inside.

Ro would've loved to sweep past her, leaving disdain behind like a lingering presence to keep Captain Red company, but she was too drained, too heartsore to make a worthy exit. So she trudged past the captain and to her room with heavy steps, wondering how she was going to get herself out of yet another mess.

And to think, she'd been excited to be on the *Siren Hunter*'s decks once more.

21

$\mathcal{R}$o saw her opportunity and took it.

Her current watcher's back was turned, just for a moment, and Ro seized her bucket, emptied it on the deck, and ran straight for the railing.

Toward the space that gaped slightly wider than other areas.

The pirate guarding that area of the boat turned, saw her coming, and raised her hands. "Now there, huntress . . ."

Ro slammed the bucket into the side of her head.

It bounced off with a clack, and the pirate went down, hard.

In one fluid motion, Ro jumped over the rail, praying with all her soul that it was deep enough where they were docked. She hadn't been able to tell while dropping small objects in earlier.

Ro twisted her body to fit, the barrier firm at her back, and slid down.

And stopped. Her hips stuck fast between the lip of the hull and the barrier.

Shouting, the crew were already abandoning their stations and swarming toward her.

196

Ro's eyes widened, and she started wriggling, trying to get loose with all her might.

Nope. It was definitely wider here, just not wide enough.

Merja reached her first. And grabbed her.

Eyes furious, she stared between Ro and the water beneath her feet.

Eight decks beneath her feet.

"Huntress!" Hauling Ro up by the back of her tunic, Merja lifted her bodily up and over the rail, and they both went sprawling on deck.

Ro had never been so humiliated in all her life. Her face burned with the inferno of a thousand suns. Now that the excitement was over, snickers all over the deck started to evolve into full belly laughs.

Two crewmembers grabbed Ro's arms and lifted her straight off Merja, pulling her away from the pirate who'd aborted Ro's escape attempt.

Although, to be fair, Ro's hips had done the bulk of the work.

Merja was on her feet in an instant and in Ro's face. "What were you thinking? Do you know the depth here? Grant wouldn't have to break your legs—you'd do it for him! How would you be able to escape if he came after you?"

Fine, she'd probably rescued Ro, too. Maybe saved her life?

"I can answer that. You wouldn't!" Merja was shouting now.

If Ro thought she'd reached her maximum level of embarrassment, she'd been wrong. It was almost painful how hot her face burned.

"At ease, Merja."

Captain Red's quiet voice intruded on one of the most humiliating moments of Ro's life, and Merja's face shuttered as she stepped back.

"So the huntress tried to escape, did she?" Captain Red

eyed Ro, not trying too hard to keep an infuriating smirk off her face.

Ro ducked her head, even as Merja said "Aye" with enough acidity to burn Ro's cheeks a few degrees hotter.

Remembering belatedly that she wasn't sorry for what she'd done, Ro lifted her chin and stared back at the captain, though judging by Captain Red's twinkling eyes, her glare wasn't having the desired effect.

"Well, then," the captain said. "Perhaps some time in the brig to show that such attempts will not go unpunished?"

She said this loud enough that the girls hovering close and watching the proceedings with shining eyes and a smidgeon of hope didn't miss a syllable.

"And those who attempt such," she continued, "will always be caught and punished."

Before Ro could think of a pithy response, she was being marched belowdecks and locked in. The clang of the metal bars closing and the lock sliding home sent a shiver down her spine. Great. She'd be watched even closer now.

And not only that, she didn't have a savvy comeback fast enough.

That would probably haunt her for the rest of the night.

But at least she'd learned one thing: Jumping into the water was out of the question. What should she try next, then?

The next time Ro was allowed above, she meandered about the deck as she worked, trying not to be obvious as she circled closer to the girls who looked like they didn't belong on *any* working ship. She tamped down her temper.

There would be time for action later. For now, information.

She chose one she'd been keeping an eye on and approached.

Hair black as moonless midnight, skin as pale as fresh cream, and eyes so startlingly blue, they almost seemed to shine of their own volition—the crew called her "black Irish." Ro hadn't heard that term before, not in conjunction with the Irish, so she wasn't sure if she should use it.

Perhaps because her hair was so raven-wing dark? Or a nickname? Best not to use it in case it was derogatory.

But that was the least of Ro's concerns. She looked so young. And one arm was curled and held tight against her chest. Which seemed to make her all the fiercer. It may have been foolish, but Ro felt a kinship with her. They were both fighters in a horrible situation.

How could Captain Red willingly conscript someone that young? And wounded? What did the captain have in mind for her? Rage boiled at the thought that they might have taken her simply because she couldn't have fought back as well.

No matter. Ro wasn't about to stand around and let some girl's life be wasted, stolen to fill a ship for its return voyage to the Caribbean.

She waited until the girl's captor moved away a few paces, keeping an eye on the other girls forced to work. Approaching the girl, Ro moved her bucket to where it wouldn't be obvious to onlookers that they were speaking and kept scrubbing the boards she'd been assigned to. Well, close to where she'd been assigned.

Still, the girl's head came up, and she moved so her back wasn't to Ro.

Ro leaned over her task, scrubbing away, and spoke low. "I'm sorry about what happened."

"Yeah? Wot's it to ya?"

Ro met her eyes briefly. "No one should be taken against their will and held captive."

She looked away before drawing attention to their conversation.

The girl snorted and went back to her task. "Nosy do-gooder."

Waiting for someone to pass, for the overseer to observe the girl's work and move on, Ro debated what to say.

She gritted her teeth. Captain Red *knew* how she felt about impressment. She *knew* how the sirens had only agreed to sign a peace treaty and to stop sinking ships if the humans stopped selling and trading and conscripting each other upon their seas. And she was willing to throw all that away, for what? A full crew?

Ro spoke quickly and in a low voice. "I can cause a disturbance. While the barrier is down. Get you and the other girls free. We'll need to work together—"

The girl snorted. "Like that worked out so well for you last time?" She propped her healthy hand on her hip, clutching the mop in her other elbow. "No, thank ye."

Ro's eyes went wide. "Why in heaven's name not?"

"Not only do I have no reason to trust ye, but Madame LaChance takes girls for precious few reasons. For her houses, to steal for her, or to sail with her mercenaries. If I hafta be in one of those lots? I choose ta be a mercenary."

"But, then, you are fine being held here? Against your will?" Ro couldn't wrap her mind around it.

The girl smirked in a self-deprecating way. "Ye ever hear the saying 'like a dog returning to its vomit'?"

Ro frowned and hesitantly nodded. They also liked to roll around in dead animal carcasses. Or excrement. At least, her hometown leader's hunting dogs had.

The girl shrugged again. "Lots of girls here would go right back to squalor or bad situations they came from. Including me."

"But, but *why*?"

The girl gave her a pitying glance. "Ah, huntress. Even

though we know we'd have a better life here, despite the dangers, there's a pull to go back to what's familiar." She gestured at the barrier. "I don't mind a little friendly persuasion to stay put."

Mouth parted, Ro just stared at her. Did the other girls feel this way?

"Might as well move along. You won't be getting any help from me." The girl went back to slinging her mop across the deck.

Ro tried so hard to think of something that would sway her.

"Back to work, black Irish! And you, huntress. Leave the girl be."

Ro startled as the burly pirate took them by surprise.

All right, just her. The woman only took Ro by surprise.

The thickly muscled woman stood over them with a whip, nostrils flaring as she clutched the instrument she'd so far only used on the deck to scare the girls.

Still, Ro hated it, hated everything about it, with a passion.

"Black Irish?" Ro dared to voice.

"Cause my hair 'tisn't orange as brass as Aisling's over there, even though we come from the same land." She jerked her chin to where Aisling lounged against the rail, chatting with several young Mesdemoiselles she was supposed to be watching, and from the looks of it, making fast friends of them all. The dark-haired girl's Irish brogue thickened as she mock-glared at the overseer. "Though that ain't no reason ta be flinging such terms about, ta be sure."

The overseer rolled her eyes and moved on, much more good-naturedly than Ro was expecting.

The girl smirked and went back to swabbing, preparing the ship to set sail. Whenever the hold was bursting with cargo and Captain Red had tired of kidnapping innocent girls off the streets.

Fortunately or unfortunately for Ro, it took several weeks

to fully load a ship of this size, especially with their trying to sneak cargo onboard.

That and making girls disappear without word getting out. Hence why numbers blossomed overnight. They got them aboard as quickly and as quietly as possible and then began training them in their duties before they set sail.

Ro spun on her heel and marched toward the crew quarters belowdecks. She was going to find someone willing to talk to her. If Captain Red wasn't going to tell her anything, maybe the other girls would. The stairs were busy with female sailors loading stores in the many holds, especially those that couldn't be reached by the pulley system.

She fumed as she went. Just wait till she laid eyes on that lying, deceptive, despicable—

A booted foot came down on a crate in Ro's path, just as she was about to go around it, blocking her.

"I'm afraid I can't allow that, huntress. No fraternizing with the crew allowed, you know that."

Ro's furious eyes met Captain Red's calm ones as the pirate cupped her cheroot and took a long drag, her broad hat shielding her face from the sun.

"And I want off this ship. Right now."

Captain Red's eyes were troubled, something she rarely let Ro see. "And what'll you be doing once you let LaChance's men capture you again? Tell 'em where my boat and girls and dock be? I don't think so. I can smell the compulsion wafting off ya from ten paces."

Compulsion? What on earth? "That doesn't even make sense. Another excuse to justify your behavior?"

Whether she put it out of her mind or it drifted away on its own, Ro wasn't thinking about it for long, and Captain Red didn't bother with a rebuttal.

Ro growled. "I didn't want to believe it, but this isn't the first time you've done this. It was you, wasn't it? You took all those girls for Madame LaChance. I didn't want to believe

Olt's dislike of you was due to anything more than your unwanted attention, but it was more than that. Wasn't it?"

Captain Red's face went still, unreadable, like a mask had been draped over it. "If you've got something to say, huntress, out with it."

Ro gritted her teeth and poked the pirate captain in the chest. "You did her dirty work. Girls who couldn't pay her outrageous boarding school fees, families who fell into her debt, you tore them apart and condemned them to a life of terror. For what? Gold? Notoriety? Fame?"

"Aye. I did all those things and more besides."

Ro didn't back down, even though they now had an audience. "So you decided to come back and do more of the same? Inflict the same life of horrors you fled from on others? Did you think hiding in the Caribbean would redeem you? Why didn't you *stay* there?"

A muscle jumped in the captain's jaw, and her eyes went flat. "Merja, take the huntress belowdecks and secure her in irons. When she's remembered her place, well, maybe we'll let her out, maybe we won't."

Ro readied herself to fight, but Merja placed a hand on her shoulder, and the fight drained out of her like she'd sprung a leak.

Ro's voice was thick when she spoke. "Why? Just tell me *why*. How could you do such things?"

"Ah, we never like when our idols fall, now do we?" Captain Red gave her a hint of a smile. "I may allow you to question me in private, but I don't tolerate my authority being questioned in front of my crew, and I especially don't tolerate subterfuge and the start of an attempted mutiny."

"That wasn't—I didn't mean—" Ro's heart dropped right past her toes. The punishment for an unsuccessful mutiny was instant death, and although that wasn't Ro's intention, that's exactly where her attempt to get the girls on her side would lead.

The captain was taking it easy on her.

"Use your time in my brig wisely, huntress, and when you can be civil, I'll gladly discuss what I may with you over a glass of port. Until then." She nodded at her first mate.

Ro didn't resist as Merja led her below and locked her in once more, but she couldn't say why.

Though some of the fight trickled back in once Merja left.

22

Once Ro was released from the brig, she spent several precious hours each night, when all she wanted to do was fall into the hammock exhausted, teaching herself to silently and carefully unlock her door.

Which was hard to do with the heightened vigilance of her guards.

It wasn't a skill she was good at, which is why she worked all the harder at it, due to some people's tendency to lock her up the moment she didn't do what they wanted.

Though she never would've put Captain Red in that category before now.

Ro also wasn't good at thievery, but she'd taken advantage of breaking up a fight on deck by swiping one of the girls' hairpins. Of course, because her skills were hunting and fighting, not sleight of hand, she'd accidentally yanked the girl's hair, so the girls had both piled on her with yells and kicks and punches.

But she'd curled into a ball and kept hold of the pin with all her might. She wasn't about to fight some girls who were frightened and just as frustrated at their situation as she.

She'd made it to her room with the pin, so that was all that mattered.

From what she could tell from listening and watching through a crack in her door, her guards—one next to the door, one at the end of the hall, right before the stairs leading to the deck—changed once per night, and twice during the day.

But all she cared about was the next time a shift change aligned with a delivery of goods. Then the guards would be distracted.

Guesting laws may have stated she couldn't bring harm to the captain and her crew, but Ro was certain that didn't give Captain Red the right to hold her here, no matter how she twisted it.

So when another shipment arrived, Ro was taken belowdecks, and her guards were lulled into distraction by the bustle one deck above, she seized her opportunity.

When their backs were turned, she carefully unlocked her door and slipped from her room to another close by.

Hardly daring to breathe, she did it once more, then waited for a call for help to momentarily move the second guard up the short flight of wooden steps.

Ro bolted.

Up the steps, on deck, in full view of the crew. Whose eyes were above on the crates and barrels in a giant net being directed into place, dangling from ropes.

Perfect.

She scrambled up stacked barrels—ones she'd be carting belowdecks had she waited any longer—and took a running leap onto the dangling crates, sending them back the way they'd come.

They swung wildly, which was exactly what she wanted, because they headed right for the edge of the ship. Her weight served to tip the floating cargo back toward the dock, much slower than if she'd flung herself off the side.

She just might make it.

The girls working on deck started whispering and pointing, quickly followed by shouts as soon as the pirates saw her.

"The huntress!" One of the pirates groaned. "Not again."

Ro grinned as the crates swung out over the edge. Her smile died as she looked eight decks straight down to the dock. Blood rushed away from her head.

Maybe she hadn't thought this through exactly . . .

The girls cheered her on. Well, then. She couldn't give up now, could she?

Come on, come on, she chanted inside her head as the crates took their sweet time oozing toward the docks.

Other pirates ran to join the one struggling to hold her, and they grabbed the rope and started swinging the heavy load with Ro on it up and back the other way, toward the ship's deck.

The others holding stabilizing ropes on the docks below worked hard to keep the load steady, even as they called up to find out what was happening.

Looking around wildly, Ro wrapped her hands around a loose rope, prepared to slide down it as far as she could go and then leap, when Sheba came running out on deck and raised her hands.

Ro could *feel* the pressure change as the shield sprang into place.

It smacked into the barrels from below, cutting them in half, spilling wooden crates and barrels and their contents all over the water and dock, while the other half fell inside the barrier. It was swept onto the deck by the barrier snapping back to the rails, shoving the cargo violently in its wake.

Girls and pirates scattered as oil, food, rum, clothing, and wood shards scattered all over the deck, making a humongous mess and showering anyone too close with debris.

Ro timed her jump, yet the rope tethering the load to the ground was also sliced in two pieces. She plunged for only a moment before the barrier also swept her along and batted her back onto the deck along with the spoiled cargo.

She landed on the mess with a squelch and just lay there, gulping breaths.

Ro hastily checked herself. Nothing missing. Nothing cut in half. She wasn't dead, thank Dieu.

The girls who'd been cheering her moments ago were hustled back to work, snickering as they went.

A shadow fell over her, and Ro knew it could be none other than Captain Red. She didn't dare open her eyes.

After a prolonged moment, "Well, now, huntress. This is a surprise. Though I suppose it shouldn't be. And it has cost me quite a bit of coin and time to boot. Who will be cleaning this up, I wonder?"

Ro sighed and struggled up to her elbows, gazing up at the captain sheepishly. "I suppose I will."

Captain Red nodded once, the feather in her wide-brimmed hat bobbing in the breeze. "Aye, that you will. And who'll be paying for it?"

Ro closed her eyes and fell back, so relieved over not dying that she felt weak. "Not I," she grumbled. "This wouldn't have happened if you hadn't kept me locked up . . ."

"That's right, you will," the captain said without missing a beat. "And locked up? You haven't seen locked up yet, huntress."

Ro peeked as the captain waved over several of her crew, who'd been standing back and staying out of their way.

"You three, watch her. The rest of you, get down below and clean up her mess. We can't afford to draw attention to this particular dock."

The crew scurried to obey, casting Ro sullen looks. Which she of course pretended not to notice. But Ro also couldn't help but notice the girls, the ones who shouldn't be here, were watching her with . . . what. Admiration? Hope?

Whatever it was, their eyes were shining and they kept covering their mouths, whispering among each other.

Then again, they could simply be laughing at her.

But Ro didn't think so. Not with the way Captain Red was frowning as she glanced over the girls herself.

"Get up," Captain Red said quietly.

Ro climbed to her feet, shaky. Gunk caked her, and she tried to breathe shallowly, then through her mouth, as the smell of rum and strong oil mixed with flour and other food-stuffs meant to survive a long journey. It was not pleasant.

"Let me guess," she said sourly. "To the brig?"

Captain Red grinned, her teeth a flash of white in the shadow of her hat. "Naw. We have additional methods of punishment when the brig fails to work. Besides. After you clean this up by your lonesome, you'll be too tired to attempt anything else this night." She looked Ro up and down. "And by the looks of things, too sore to try anything for a few nights yet."

Didn't Ro know it.

The captain nodded at her crew and walked away, guarding the opening herself that Sheba made in the shield so a handful of crew could climb down rope ladders and start cleaning up the docks and fishing detritus out of the water.

Ro stared at the rope ladders.

Of course! That was how she'd climbed aboard before. If she could stash one, wrap her hands, and slide down it . . .

Captain Red saw her looking and shook her head once. Ro simply grinned back.

Oui, she'd be trying that, and soon. First chance she got. Though she'd likely try to sneak this time. Maybe use a disguise? At night?

Captain Red sighed and looked put out, but a challenge rose in her eyes, one that dared Ro to try. She would just take that dare.

One of the pirates shoved a mop in Ro's midsection and

dropped a pail and hand spade at her feet, making her *oomph* and step back.

Oh, yeah. There were definitely bruises already.

Although the pirates crossed their arms and refused to help, several of the girls came close and picked up around the edges, dumping bucketfuls in an empty barrel for disposal, a few scrubbing oil off the deck after the detritus was mostly gone.

After looking to the captain, the pirates let them, but Ro didn't miss the way Captain Red watched the girls helping her.

Or the way her brow puckered like she was seeing something she didn't quite care for.

23

Ro made herself useful, doing what needed to be done, staying out of Captain Red's way. Not that the captain wasn't equally avoiding her as well.

For her next escape attempt, she would be swift, sneaky, and silent. And she'd be using rope ladders, even if they did keep them under lock and key. They'd start to relax, and they wouldn't see her coming.

Because she would be a model guest until her moment of escape.

Then she would get out of Londres and back to the Black Forest, as fast as her horse could take her. Forget Madame LaChance. Forget Grant the bounty hunter. Forget Captain Red. Ro had more important things to worry about.

If she had to hire protection until she could deal with them, so be it.

She moved into the hold, rounded a stack of crates that needed to be sorted, and came face to face with the thief they'd brought on board and branded, who was struggling to pick up a heavy crate.

Dull brown hair, skin so thin and papery it was almost translucent, and a wisp-thin frame that had Ro wanting to feed her, for some reason, she couldn't have been more than twelve years of age.

She gave Ro a hard look.

Ro wiped away whatever expression was on her face, not meaning to pity the girl. Hefting the crate into her arms, she moved past Ro.

"Here, let me help you."

The girl jerked away from Ro with another glare.

Ro swallowed and amended her words. "May I help you?"

After a moment, she heaved a sigh and spoke in a whisper-thin voice. "I suppose."

Ro grabbed one side and kept her head down as they navigated the many stairs into the hold, currently being filled from the deepest levels up. If Ro guessed right, the ship was about half full, her escape attempt barely putting a dent in the amount of cargo being squirreled away. Her time was running short.

But that was a worry for later. Right now, she couldn't miss this opportunity.

Ro struggled to find the right words. She didn't want to offend the girl, make it so she refused to speak to Ro, but she needed to find a way to stop this. To stop other girls from being taken. Captain Red . . .

Non, she wasn't thinking about Captain Red right now, much less speaking to her.

"I'm . . . sorry about what happened. That you were taken. And branded."

The girl paused, shoulders hunched, then nodded once.

Ro licked her lips and tried again. "If there's anything I can do—"

The girl mumbled something Ro didn't catch.

"Je suis désolé, I didn't hear you. What did you say?"

The girl paused at the bottom of the steps and met Ro's gaze. "My family is coming for me."

Too stunned to know what to say, Ro didn't notice Captain

Red materialize from the shadows until she was nearly upon them. She knew the captain kept a close eye on her ship, but this was uncanny.

"I think you can manage the crate yourself, Siobhan. Huntress? Go back for another, s'il vous plaît."

Ro glared at the captain, but the girl dutifully nodded, grabbed the other side from Ro, and moved away, nearly bent in two under its weight.

Just as Ro was opening her mouth, Siobhan paused and met the captain's eyes. Though frightened, she raised her chin. "My family will come for me."

Ro's heart began to pound. "You took this girl from her *family*?"

Captain Red's eyes flashed. "She means the street gang she was raised in."

She turned to the girl. "I don't think you understand your situation, young Mademoiselle. We may have found you on the streets, but you were being enrolled in Madame LaChance's . . . secondary education. No one is coming for you. No one. They sold you out quicker than gold could exchange hands."

Ro made a noise of protest. The look Captain Red turned on her was fiery. Although she kept her gaze on Ro, she spoke to the girl. "Best get that in your head. Now *go*."

The girl raised her chin defiantly. "They *will* come for me."

Ro swallowed hard, wrangling her frothing emotions under control. "For your sake, I truly hope so, Mademoiselle. With all my heart."

Then the girl was moving down the next flight of stairs, and Ro's head whipped around to find the captain walking away.

Ro followed hot on Captain Red's heels. "How could you say such things to the poor girl? Why would you take her from her family, even if it's one she made for herself? Where does Madame LaChance come into this—"

Captain Red spun so suddenly, Ro nearly fell headlong into her. "Do you truly not know? Truly? Or are you really that stupid?"

Ro stumbled back, eyes wide. First of all, the captain was just so intimidating. Second, she hated being called stupid. More than anything.

Her fists clenched. "I am *not* bête."

"Then I'll spell it out for you. Slowly." Captain Red gritted her teeth, as though she had difficulty saying the words. "Mesdemoiselles who cannot afford Madame LaChance's boarding school, who, say, find themselves in an agreement with her and cannot pay, have no family to fall back on, go to a very . . . different . . . kind of boarding school." Her gaze slammed into Ro's.

Ro stared at her, waiting.

"Oh for the love, do I have to spell it out for you? Madame LaChance runs a brothel, huntress. Quite a few of them, actually. She keeps herself, her reputation, distanced from them, of course, but those who do not know her as an upstanding businesswoman know her in quite a different manner. Many girls have disappeared who could not pay, only to be found abandoned with child or dying in a poorhouse after a brief, painful existence working the houses. Her houses. Which are poorly run and full of disease. All she cares about is the coin used to further her enterprises."

The captain's voice took on a low growl. "I detest her."

Ro's eyes had grown progressively wider with each syllable, and Captain Red continued. "Do you know who took those girls to her? Me. Do you know who started as one of those girls?"

Captain Red snapped her mouth closed, as though she hadn't meant to say that last bit, and like a mask, her sardonic grin slipped back over her face.

"Well, perhaps detest is too mild a word. Branding a girl to *my* service, under *my* protection, saves her from a worse fate than the one awaiting her at Madame LaChance's hands. And that, huntress, is why you should listen to all the people telling you not to trust her. Sometimes others know more than even you do."

The words painted a fuller picture of what these girls were up against, filling in gaps she'd missed completely, and the rage that had started as a slow burn exploded all at once.

Ro shouted curses in French and paced the narrow space, feeling completely helpless, stuck on a ship in the middle of the labyrinth that was the Port of London.

Madame LaChance's other business was a *brothel*? And girls who couldn't pay the exorbitant boarding school prices disappeared to . . . there?

She would've sent Cosette into that! Had Cosette listened to Ro and gone to the boarding school all those years ago . . . Had the payments to Madame LaChance stopped when Ro was trapped with the beast . . .

Oh, if she were free to come and go as she pleased right now, she'd march right into Madame LaChance's office and — well, she didn't know what, but furniture would be thrown. At the very least. And then her houses of ill repute would be no more.

Ro cursed some more, called brimstone and hellfire down upon the Madame's head, then spun to Captain Red as something she'd said dropped in her stomach with the force of a cannonball. "*You* were one of those girls?"

Captain Red had leaned against the bulkhead at some point during Ro's tirade and with a penknife was trimming her nails, which she kept clean, short, and in good repair. "Does it matter if I was?"

Ro's heart splintered. No wonder this woman had worked so hard to get away and make a life for herself—on her own terms.

No wonder she fought to get other girls out of the life she'd been raised in.

"Non. It does not change our—friendship—but it will most certainly change my conversation with Madame LaChance when I see her next."

Captain Red gave her a true smile, a sad one. "Be careful, huntress. You may not be able to come back from such a confrontation."

Ro lifted her chin. "Someone needs to stop her."

"And that would be you?"

"Oui. Someone has to. What do I do? To stop her?"

Captain Red threw back her head and laughed. Then she eyed Ro with an amused look. "I'm afraid that's for me to know. Not you."

She slipped away the knife and turned to move away, but Ro stopped her with one hand to her arm. "Tell me. Please."

Several moments passed, and the curiosity in the captain's eyes won out. "Why?"

Ro released her hold. "I would know the kind of woman I'm dealing with. The kind of woman I've made a bargain with." She dropped her voice. "I would know how to set those girls free and make sure another will not, *cannot*, join their ranks."

Captain Red's eyes misted, and she blinked away the moisture. Though it could've been a trick of the light down here. "Leave the girls to me, huntress. And Madame LaChance. She and I have unfinished business. You see what you can do about waking my sister and then return to your forest where you belong."

The words were gently said, but they hurt nonetheless.

Ro opened her mouth to argue, but Captain Red moved swiftly away.

Wait. Did that mean the captain was going to let her go? Maybe drop her off at a port in France before sailing for the Caribbean?

If Ro had learned anything from her last disastrous voyage, it was not safe to sail across the ocean during hurricane season or in winter, and most captains would wait for spring.

But not Captain Red. Non, she'd deemed it important to come back to Londres when she had, and now she was determined to return to the Caribbean while hurricanes were currently swirling the ocean into whirlpools.

Ro hoped she was successful. As long as Ro didn't have to go with her.

The gentle lap of water against the hull and the distant cries of seagulls and the creak of the ship moving with the waves kept Ro company as her mind spun with all Captain Red had revealed of Madame LaChance.

What demon was this woman Ro had admired for so long from afar? And would she ever answer for her crimes? And Olt's dislike for them both . . .

Ro ran a hand down her face. Oh, merciful heavens. What if Ro had sent Cosette to a monster? Worse than any other Ro had fought.

And Père Guise had urged her to send her sister there, to get her out of the curse's clutches, though he'd pretended to be reluctant to share information about Madame LaChance's boarding school.

Ro didn't care if Madame LaChance made most of her profit from such a venture. She was finding every. single. one. and shutting them all down.

Permanently.

Although Captain Red thought she was saving the girls — all right, even though she *was* saving them, in her own way — Ro wasn't happy with the kidnapping and conscription part. She'd have to do something about that, too.

Then she was having a discussion with her sister about leaving their chapel in the clutches of Père Guise.

And what she could do to extricate such a cancer from his hold in the palace.

24

Screaming woke Ro. She bolted from her hammock, taking a moment to pick the lock, and slammed open the door, only to find her current guardian coming toward her, hands raised.

"Now, huntress, 'tis a matter that don't concern you none . . ."

And that was as far as she got.

In a move she'd learned from Liam, Ro dropped low and used her center mass—and her legs—to catch the pirate right under the ribs, hoisting her up and slamming her into the bulkhead.

Her skull cracked against the wooden wall, and she went straight down, unconscious.

Ro took a precious second to stare at the pirate. That had actually worked? She'd have to thank Liam the next time she saw him. *If* she ever saw him again.

Non, she refused to think like that. She was getting free, and not even Captain Red would stop her.

She sprinted past the pirate toward the stairs, where the screams were coming from. Ro popped up on deck to a mass brawl, shouts of "Hold her!" and "Don't let her get away!" and "If you don't knock her out, I will!" surrounding her.

But her eyes riveted on the opening in the rail, the extended plank, the barrier down as girls were brought aboard.

For a moment, she was torn. Use the distraction to escape?

Or help the new batch of girls currently being tackled by the crew and chained?

Her eyes went wide. *Chained?*

Brief disappointment that she would not be escaping this night swept her before she was in motion.

She entered the brawl, flinging pirates away from the younger, scrappier, and malnourished girls they were mishandling. The girls were no match for the healthier pirates who'd been working with Captain Red for quite some time.

How dare they. How *dare* they do this to these girls!

Captain Red had gone too far. What was she thinking? There was no explanation she could give that would make this acceptable. Especially after what she'd said about Madame LaChance.

Ro let her anger fuel her as she fought for the girls, wresting them from pirates, yanking chains away to drop them over the edge between the railing and the barrier, not pausing to listen to the splash below.

"The huntress! She's loose!"

Against her better judgment, Ro jerked toward the voice, and someone tackled her to the planks. Then a mass of pirates piled upon her, turning their attention to the bigger threat.

Ro fought, but she was no match for them without the element of surprise and with the sheer number of muscular bodies holding her down.

"What is the meaning of this?" thundered a familiar voice.

"Cap'ain on deck!"

A flurry of activity followed those words, and it took

seconds for the girls to be wrestled under control and the barrier closed. Ro's face remained plastered to the deck, so her view was of boots and bare feet and precious little else.

The captain marched down the line of girls, pausing at Ro with a sigh, then continued until she reached the end and headed back.

Panting breaths, the gently creaking ship, and water slapping against the hull were the only accompaniments to the captain's steady march.

She stopped next to Ro again, and although Ro tried to move her head, the pirate smashing her face to the planks kept her there.

Then the captain spoke two words that struck Ro's heart like an arrow.

"Brand them."

The girls squealed and sobbed and begged, but one by one they were held down, branded, and released from their bonds only to be escorted belowdecks, possibly to the rows of empty hammocks waiting for new girls in the hold.

And Ro's face was held immobile to watch as each one was shoved to the planks and into her line of sight, even if that wasn't the intent of the pirate who held her.

One girl in particular went wild when it was her turn.

Fire-bright hair, skin as pale as fresh cream, and a spattering of freckles across her nose, she not only looked fierce, but the pirates were having a time of it holding her down.

More pirates converged on the girl fighting for her life, flipping her over and splaying her on the deck until her cheek pressed to the wood. Much like Ro's.

"Quickly, now! She bucks like an eel."

This was met with a round of laughter.

"You saying you can't hold a wee mite of a girl, Mary?"

"What I'm *saying*," Mary growled, "is to do yer job before the mite does herself an injury."

The woman who'd been heating the brand came over then,

still chuckling, and the pirates holding the girl bared her shoulder.

Mary was right. The girl bucked and thrashed, and the pirates, who'd had no problem holding the other girls, used most of their body weight and were still moved by the girl's efforts.

Ro could only watch in horror.

The pirate with the brand grunted. "Best listen ta Mary, girl, and hold still. You're getting marked either way, and I'd prefer it clean and neat instead of too deep or causing oozing and an infection."

The girl stilled long enough, as if shocked at the words, that the pirate struck like a snake and landed her brand just right on the shoulder blade to a sizzle of flesh.

The girl screamed and arched her back, and Ro fought harder, but unlike the wee mite of a girl, as the others had called her, Ro couldn't get her captors to budge.

Some huntress she was. She might as well hand in her red cape right now.

Then it was over, and the girl curled into herself, sobbing quietly.

The iron was placed back into the contained fire—no one wanted a ship to go up in flames in the middle of the water—until it glowed bright red again.

"What do ya want done with the huntress?" asked one of the pirates holding her.

Ro couldn't help but hold her breath while she waited for Captain Red's response.

The captain hesitated a beat too long. "Brand her too. It's time."

Ro bucked and cried out, but she was well and truly stuck fast.

And then the pirate with the brand was coming for her.

Unable to do anything else, Ro closed her eyes and prayed

as she'd never done before. *Please get me out of this. Please, please, please.*

She didn't need to see the glowing R.R. in a circle; it was seared into her memory from the first time she'd been aboard Captain Red's ship. She just didn't want it on *her* body. Or anyone else's. Against their will.

Her tunic was yanked low over her shoulder blade, and she tensed all of her muscles at once. She wasn't going to give them the satisfaction of crying out.

And then a scream tore from her as agony such as she'd never felt before shredded throughout her entire body, as the veil on all her suppressed memories was ripped away, as her mind was flooded with crystal-clear images of things she hadn't even known she'd forgotten.

Of Madame LaChance compelling her to steal the Siren Queen's coral crown.

Of the Fairy Queen's kiss on her forehead, sealing her protective nature of Cosette. Sealing a bargain Ro had been too young to make but had made anyway with a fierceness that hid her fear.

She'd do it again in a heartbeat. She just wouldn't have accepted some of the terms.

Of a man with a blue beard, long, long ago, sewing his magic into her skin, then meeting justice as his head was separated from his body by his own axe at Ro's hand.

Also, she now knew why she'd lost three years to the Caribbean. Or more accurately, to an island she and Olt had been stranded on. But that was a story to dwell on another time.

Olt. Suddenly, part of her hesitation became crystal clear. They needed to talk. She couldn't marry him, even if she wanted to. Not until she told him the truth.

Memory after memory burst to life inside of Ro, in such startling clarity, a part of her wondered if she'd ever be able to forget them.

Some were painful. Some she wouldn't mind suppressing again. But most were of things done to her by someone else, someone who wanted to use Ro's abilities for their own gain. Positioning Ro like a pawn on their chessboard. Clearing Ro's mind for their own use.

Someone like Madame LaChance.

And the Queen of the Fairies.

She still didn't know *how* the memories had been suppressed, just that they had.

A chain she didn't even know was linking her to Madame LaChance snapped, and although she shouldn't have been able to, she sensed someone cry out from the backlash.

Someone far away, holding the chain, the woman who'd forged it without Ro's knowledge or consent.

Ro smiled. She was no longer bound to Madame LaChance in any way.

The deck came into focus, and Ro raised her head. At no resistance, she climbed to her feet and stood there, fists clenched, vibrating with rage that anyone would dare use her, dare manipulate her in their game.

"Ah, there she is. I was hoping that would work!"

Ro's head whipped around to focus on Captain Red's grinning face. She snarled at the captain, but the woman with piles of gleaming red curls about her shoulders just laughed.

"Welcome back, huntress. It is a pleasure to finally meet the real you. Shall we talk in my ready room?"

Ro studied her for half a heartbeat. This Captain Red appeared delighted to see Ro, no longer the unsmiling woman who'd kept Ro under lock and key and chained up a time or two. Like the Captain Red she'd first met, long ago.

She reached out slowly with her senses, and a warm glow radiated from the brand, one that stretched to Captain Red. She tugged on it, just slightly, and it gave, allowing her movement, freedom. It wasn't a chain, it wasn't bondage, but it was still a tether.

"I would love nothing more," Ro said in a low, dangerous voice.

"Right this way, huntress my huntress." With a flourish and a bow, Captain Red swept away, a spring to her step that hadn't been there before.

Now that she had her memories back, Ro knew Captain Red had always been straight with her about who she was and what she did, and Ro knew, deep in her bones, that whatever the captain was doing here, Ro needed to hear her out.

The fire in her shoulder dulled to a smoldering reminder that Madame LaChance was everything the rumors said and more—not one to be trusted.

And there would be a reckoning.

25

"*E*xplain the brand. Now. Am I bound to you? Must I do as you say?"

Captain Red laughed as she rounded her desk. "Nothing like that, chère. The brand simply marks you as mine and places you under my protection." She grinned, still looking delighted with herself. Or with Ro. Or both. "No other magic can penetrate or place you under its spell."

Another inarticulate growl ripped from Ro's throat. She paced as the captain settled behind her desk, propped up her feet, and lit another cheroot that was her near-constant companion.

Ro remembered her grandmère placing her hands near Ro's head and saying many of her memories had been repressed, but she couldn't do anything about it without dire consequences. Perhaps even erasing all of Ro's memories.

Ro stopped suddenly. "And if the brand is removed? Melted down or destroyed?" She couldn't even begin to imagine *that* level of pain. "Will it fail then?"

Captain Red frowned. "Well, now. I'll admit a few of my girls have had my brand removed over the years, some by choice, some not, and although they're no longer under my

225

protection, per se, they tend to still have incredibly good luck."

Captain Red grinned in unabashed pride, and Ro couldn't help but offer the tiniest of smiles back.

She squashed the expression flat. Non. She couldn't trust Captain Red, remember? It didn't help that the captain was just so darn likeable.

Captain Red dropped her feet off the desk, snuffed out her cheroot, and leaned forward with an intensity that commandeered Ro's attention.

"Now that you're no longer under Madame LaChance's thrall and her compulsion has been broken, what shall we do about your bargain with her? Now that you're under my protection, there will be consequences should she try to force you, but the bargain must be fulfilled, and the bounty hunter is still a real threat."

Ro rubbed her forehead. "I think I'd like to—"

She stopped abruptly and eyed the captain. Should she trust the captain, really?

Captain Red waved a hand through the smoke drifting in lazy curls. "Speak plainly, s'il vous plaît."

Ro's voice dropped to a whisper. "I'd like to wake her."

Captain Red closed her eyes as a muscle ticked in her jaw.

Ro waited, concerned she'd offended—or worse, hurt—the captain, but she needed to be honest. She *had* made a bargain with Madame LaChance. She *hadn't* kept her side. And she wanted it abundantly clear that she and Madame LaChance were *done* after this.

Whether she was no longer under a compulsion or not, her mind no longer a playground for any fey who wished to lead her along as they pleased, it was a fact that her huntress and protectress powers would unravel if she didn't keep her word.

She'd seen as much with the sirens, their broken promises turning to poison in their blood.

She couldn't afford to be the next raving lunatic hunting

for her own pleasure or causing pain instead of defending those she'd sworn to protect.

"I was afraid you were going to say that," the captain finally said. She looked up at Ro and smirked. "Oh, I may not like it, huntress, as it will be particularly painful for me, but I understand fey bargains better than most. And Madame LaChance may not technically be fey, not that I can figure out, anyway, but she wields powerful fey magic, and the bargain she struck with you is ironclad. Besides, if the situation in the Black Forest is as dire as you say, you'll want to get back sooner rather than later."

Ro threw her hands out to the sides. "That's what I've been trying to say! Wait." She eyed the captain suspiciously. "I thought you were going to press me into service in the Caribbean?"

Captain Red gave a full-throated laugh. "Oh, that I could! You would be a boon to my crew, and make no mistake. But *non*, you are needed here, my sweet. Much as I'd prefer it otherwise. I needed Madame LaChance to believe you were being conscripted, if she could reach your mind through the barrier. She's been scrambling like mad with your disappearance, and the king is none too pleased, I'm sure I don't have to tell you."

Ro was too stunned to reply. She'd been terrified she'd soon be sailing far away from Olt, Cosette, Allura, and any semblance of a life she'd been fighting to build for herself.

But having Madame LaChance rooting around in her mind was worse. Much worse.

As if Ro had spoken aloud, Captain Red winked. "I couldn't be telling you that beforehand, now could I? You so closely bound to the Madame and all. Who knows what would've happened had you managed to escape?"

"Then why didn't you do it earlier?" Ro asked. She'd been here for weeks.

A flash of unease spread across the captain's face. "Ah,

well, there was the slightest chance it wouldn't work right, considering how many others have tried to claim you, and what with your other abilities. And it was difficult to get information without letting it out that we had you."

Ro sighed. Sounded about right. "Where shall I start? I'd like to go back in there with knowledge of how to wake your sister, not guesses."

Captain Red winced, then held up a hand when Ro would have apologized. "I'll just have to get used to it. Leave it be, huntress."

Ro nodded and waited.

"You have more books in your quarters, ones I couldn't give you before, including my own research. Not that it'll do much good." Speaking slowly, as if working it out while the words were forming, Captain Red said, "But I have this feeling, huntress, that now you are more yourself, you'll discover what to do. Sleep on it?"

Ro nodded and turned away, not waiting to be dismissed. Then she paused and peeked over her shoulder. "I'm not being locked in tonight, am I?"

Captain Red waved a hand. "Naw. Seems a bit uncouth now that we're friends again, I should say."

Ro's blooming smile was chased away by a frown. "Those girls you press into service . . ."

With a sigh, Captain Red said, "Thought that might come up. You see, huntress, everything I said about Madame LaChance is fact, I'm afraid. And as the one who used to do her dirty work, I should know.

"Those girls—they would be pressed into work at her poorhouses, in her brothels, as her mercenaries. They are the forgotten, the lost, and they have no one left to look after, nor to look after them. I aim to give them a better life.

"After their service to me is over, they are free. And with skills that will allow them to thrive."

Ro frowned. "But . . . if you are in the Caribbean, where will they go?"

Captain Red waved a hand. "Most stay on with me. Some establish new families and plant themselves at one of our stops. Some move to the Americas. And some return here, but to a better life, captains of their own fates." She grinned. "All things not possible before this ship became my own. Does that answer meet your satisfaction?"

"For now." Ro gave her a halfhearted smile. "I—don't know how I feel about it. It still seems wrong. But I can, perhaps, see where you're coming from."

The captain doffed her hat, eyes twinkling. "Happy to oblige."

Knowing Captain Red was laughing at her, Ro shook her head and made straight for her bunk. She doubted she'd sleep tonight.

But the moment she was in her hammock, book of research open and waves gently rocking the ship, Ro was out like an extinguished candle, and she slept better than she had in an age.

And she dreamed.

🐌

"It will work?" Ro asked dream-Grandmère.

The old woman huffed. "It's a sight better'n what you were trying to do without any results, ain't it?"

Ro slanted her grandmère a look and went back to studying the glowing ball of light hovering in front of her.

It was the curse Snow White was under.

She wasn't sleeping. Non, someone had tried to murder her, something else had frozen the magic mid-assault, but the poison was still reaching for her. The moment whatever was stopping it ceased to work, the attack would finish its job.

All efforts so far, everything she'd read in the queen's

tower, even what Rose Red had tried to do so many years ago, were all wrong. If any of them had succeeded in waking Snow White, she'd be dead right now.

"Will I remember this when I wake up?" Ro asked.

Darya grunted. "Now that's a question, ain't it?"

Was it just Ro, or was her grandmère grumpier than normal? Ro's head came up, and she studied Darya. "What is it?"

"I'm just glad your memories were restored, is all."

That wasn't exactly right. "But you weren't the one to do it."

"Aye. But I wasn't the one to do it," she whispered.

Ro nodded and returned her gaze to the orb, trying to absorb as much as her brain could handle. Everything was clear here, including the knowledge that things wouldn't be so outside of her dreams.

"I don't blame you, you know," Ro said as she glanced up again. "For leaving or for being unable to help. But I do miss you."

Tears flooded her grandmère's eyes. "That's . . . good. That's . . . I thank ye."

Ro nodded and went back to her task. After another moment, she stepped back. "I have what I need."

And without another word, Grandmère sent Ro back to the waking world with knowledge she couldn't have gotten any other way.

Ro opened her eyes. Sat up. And went to find Captain Red.

26

Merja, Oksana, Sheba, Aisling, and Mary all surrounded Captain Red's desk, along with the captain and Ro, staring down at a rough-sketched map of the palace.

Mary scratched her head. She was of indeterminant age, though she appeared older than many of the crew, and her extremely pale skin and mouse-brown hair and bland features nearly made her blend into the bulkhead when she wasn't asserting herself. "So yous saying we need to break back into the palace. After we went to all that trouble to break yous out?"

"Oui," Ro said simply.

They exchanged glances, one that said they thought Ro might be unhinged.

Captain Red just watched the proceedings with a delighted grin.

"They will have stepped up security," Oksana said in a strong, quiet voice, her diction clear and precise, hardly an accent from her native Japan at all.

"And what shall we do about the vault itself?" Sheba asked.

Sheba's husky voice sounded as if she smoked Captain Red's cheroots, though the captain put them out in the Ethiopian woman's presence, out of respect for the woman's intense dislike of them. Her accent was thick and exotic, her hair cropped close to her scalp, and her posture that which made Ro straighten in subtle imitation.

Ro could have listened to her all day.

"The vault?" Ro repeated. "I know how to get in. I need someone to guard the opening so I can get back out." She bit her lip. "It's a complicated process, unlocking the queen's chamber. I can do it, but if that fails, I'll need someone to pick the locks. I'm not as good at locks as I'd like to be . . ."

Merja waved her hand dismissively. "We've got someone who can see to the locks, huntress, if need be."

"Good. Then I'll just need someone to hold off the soldiers while I wake the queen."

Aisling whistled, her wild orange hair and freckled nose and tapping foot vibrating with energy. "That be throwing the whole kit and kaboodle straight into the fire, and make no mistake. How're we ta keep the guards held off fer as long as all that?"

Her Irish accent was so strong, Ro had to pause a few seconds after each time she spoke to work out what she'd said.

After a precious few seconds, Ro looked to Captain Red. It would be her crew thrown straight into the fire, as it were. She'd have to agree to it.

Captain Red grinned. "Since when has our crew balked at a little hardship?"

"Hardship is one thing," Merja put in, her light-brown skin gleaming in the candlelight, her accent slipping into pure aristocratic English when she was tense, "but going into an impossible situation without a plan is quite another."

"Aye." Captain Red nodded. "You know those suits of armor I promised you?"

Merja's eyes lit up. "We have armor?"

"We have armor. Palace ceremonial armor. Hard-boiled leather armor. And weapons." Captain Red's grin stretched even wider, if that were possible.

Merja made a sound that was disturbingly like a purr, and Ro blinked at her, just a mite unsettled, if she were being honest.

"Well that changes everything, now don't it?" Mary chortled with glee and rubbed her hands together in a miserly fashion.

"Only so long as they remain unaware of our presence," Sheba pointed out.

"Not ta mention," Aisling said, "the guard tasked with watchin' the queen be especially trained. They be nearly impossible ta fight."

"All right," Ro said, then processed Aisling's words. "Trained how so?"

Mary answered, thank goodness. "They be knights of the first order. Swordsmanship, hand-to-hand combat, the best of the best in tourneys and jousting. Strong, golden, manly men."

Several of the women sighed or growled at that, leaving Ro blinking and Captain Red laughing at Ro's reaction.

Ro was *not* used to women openly stating their appreciation for men. Usually it was the other way around. It was . . . awkward. And slightly embarrassing.

But thinking of Olt, she could understand it.

Her heart gave a pang. Surely he thought she was never coming back by now—and even when she did, her returned memories reminded her that it would be a painful conversation where she likely lost him anyway.

She focused with all her might on the task at hand.

"Is this a mission you're willing to take on? Getting me into the palace?" Ro asked.

"Well now"—Mary crossed her arms—"we don't work for free. Wot's in it fer us?"

Ro sneaked a glance at Captain Red, who kept her head

down, studying the map carefully and not looking at any of her crew.

Merja about broke Mary's ribs elbowing her in the side and nodding at Captain Red, to which the older pirate cleared her throat.

"Not that we wouldn't help fer the sake of waking the good queen, o'course, but should we be caught or not able to wake her, there's a branded 'P' on the forehead in it fer us, what then a noose at the hangman's first opportunity. And we all remember how it went down last time."

Several of them made grunts or other noises, but Aisling's head came up. "I t'wasn't part of the crew yet. What happened?"

"It went poorly," Sheba said. "We were caught. And would've been hanged if not for Madame LaChance."

Merja shrugged. "At least Madame LaChance chose to claim us then." She looked to Captain Red. "She won't this time."

Captain Red sobered at that. And still left the decision up to her crew.

Yet Merja watched the captain like a raptor, and Ro remembered Rose Red's words about returning to work for Madame LaChance. Ro had to make sure that didn't happen.

Ro swallowed convulsively a few times before she could speak. While she was no longer poor, thanks to many hunting jobs and several well-funded investments, she also didn't have ready funds at her disposal. "While I cannot speak for the captain, I'm sure we can come to an arrangement that would be satisfactory . . . for all parties."

Mary grunted. "Cut the fancy talk. How much?"

And so the haggling began, and at the end of it, Ro would be overseeing a rather large mound of her stashed-away gold transferred to the pirates' safekeeping.

Now to survive long enough to see it happen.

A fête in honor of the queen's birthday was the perfect excuse to invade the palace. Also, it was the perfect trap. For them.

Which was why Ro found herself trussed up in striped leggings, ankle boots, a many-petticoated skirt that came to her knees, and a sleeveless corseted vest with a ridiculous number of ribbons and bows.

Her red cloak had been ingeniously wrapped and flounced into a layer of petticoats, peeking out from under her vibrant skirt, in case she had to escape in this costume. Ro had no idea how it was even possible her cloak had been turned into a petticoat, and she'd watched the pirate in charge of their costumes do it.

A bag with a change of clothes and provisions had been placed among their equipment for her to grab before she fled the country.

She was counting down the seconds.

Her hair had been pulled back in tiny loops and twists behind her head, almost as if a ball of yarn had exploded, secured in a multitude of ribbons by a crewmember who could make hair designs bend to her will, unlike Ro.

Her face had been painted white with talcum powder and egg whites, which meant she couldn't move a muscle in her face without cracking paint. Grease had been used to draw mime-like diamonds under her eyes and a beauty-mark heart over her upper lip. Making Ro unrecognizable.

Some of the others had cracked their paint on purpose, giving them a slightly unhinged look, but it fit their performance personas perfectly.

Ro was amazed at how talented the crew were.

Once inside the palace, several dangled from the ceiling on lengths of silk that swept the floor. Another rotated in a slow spin on a hoop secured to the ceiling.

Just outside the open doors into the garden, one blew fire,

and still others juggled or played the accordion with a tiny monkey in a matching costume, moving through the crowd to entertain the pleased guests.

Although most pirates wore breeches that ended below the knee, and similar corsets to Ro's without an underblouse, they flashed bare arms and calves, hosiery noticeably absent. Instead of being scandalized, the king and courtiers oohed and aahed and clapped their hands, thoroughly enjoying the spectacle.

Ro couldn't help but note that these were the very same courtiers who'd been scandalized by her hunting gear, which covered her from head to toe, who now clapped and cheered and watched half-clad performers with delight.

There was nothing indecent about the costumes, truly, but Ro was amazed at how much the crowd would accept, simply because they were being entertained.

Glancing at the pirate juggling flaming clubs, Ro tipped her head to the side. Would her reception have been different all those years ago had she come in juggling?

Probably. In fact, she should keep this in mind. The performance aspect, not necessarily tossing around flaming weapons. It would likely help her not care quite so much what others thought of her, if she treated each introduction to those who looked down upon her as a performance.

As Ro watched the pirates make a spectacle of themselves, infiltrating the palace in plain sight, Ro had to admit even she was impressed. She'd be gleaming with sweat if she had every eye upon her such as they.

She was a part of the floor team, easily interchanged with other girls so the seven of them tasked with freeing the queen could slip away when ready.

When Captain Red gave the signal, Ro's pulse jumped. The other pirates lit up fireworks outside as well as fire-crackers on long sticks, drawing designs in the air and guaranteeing no one would be paying attention to the few pirates slipping away.

Six pirates and one huntress faded into the crowd and past servants scurrying with platters and pitchers raised high to instantly replenish any part of the diminishing feast. Ro followed the pirates into a secluded room deep in the palace's underbelly to exchange their vibrant clothes for palace armor. Aisling helped her wash off face paint.

And then they marched smartly to where the queen was laid to rest.

Entering the large chamber, they halted before two soldiers guarding the queen, and Captain Red said in a deep, no-nonsense voice, "The king demands an update on his queen for the partygoers."

The elite guards exchanged a glance. "There is nothing to report. No one is in the chamber except—"

"I do not question my lord's commands," Captain Red said, cutting him off. "He asked for a report. I am here to give him one."

The other guard sighed. "Tell his drunken lordship that she rests peacefully and will join the spectators later. That should appease him."

Captain Red didn't budge, staring them down.

Without another word, the first soldier began opening the many boxes that held keys to undo the chains on the door. It apparently wasn't the first time the king had drunkenly demanded such a thing.

"I'm just saying we don't actually have to open it," the other protested.

Captain Red leveled a stare worthy of her fearsome reputation and kept her voice low and growly, the scarring on her vocal cords from the cheroots coming in handy just then. "I obey my king's orders. And you should hesitate the next time you care to speculate on your lord's state of being, ere it be your last thought upon this green earth."

The elite guard stiffened, and he didn't say another word as his companion continued the arduous task of unlocking the queen's chambers.

Ro watched their every move for the exact moment she would need to jump in and seamlessly take over. If it came to that.

She was already glistening with sweat from the march to the chamber in heavy ornamental armor, but with the elite guard glaring at Captain Red and the good captain staring stonily back, as if she were in the right and this soldier scum under her boot, Ro started to sweat in earnest.

The others had to feel the pressure of just standing here, waiting to be granted entrance, oui?

But no one twitched, no one gave away their unease, and Ro had to stand there and roast in her helm. Would the blasted doors open already?

And then, as the first guard was nearly halfway unlocking the chains, a faint clanking sound intruded on the standoff.

The guard unlocking the chains paused, and they all turned as one toward the doors as they were pushed open. A surprised guard stared back. "Who are you? The king sent us for an update on the queen. For her birthday."

Just as Ro was getting ready to hurl herself at the closest elite guard, the captain waved her hand dismissively. "He must've forgotten he sent us already. As you were."

The guard dipped his head and started to move back, closing the doors as he went, before he stopped and frowned. "But I do not recognize —"

And that was as far as he got. Pirates exploded into motion all at once, and Ro went straight for the guard unlocking the chains.

She flipped off his helm and slammed her gauntleted fist into his temple, and he dropped like a stone. She would need her hands for this. Ro ripped off her leather gloves and the open metal demi-gauntlets covering them and tossed them aside.

She immediately took over from where he'd left off, studiously unlocking the chains one by one.

Was she remembering this correctly? She clenched her jaw and kept going. That girl needed to be here in case the locks had to be picked. She was supposed to follow in servant's garb, since she was far too petite to be taken seriously in armor.

Of course, the girl might use the opportunity to escape and try to find her family.

Ro pushed her worry aside and focused wholly on her task.

Thanks to the good captain's brand, Ro's mind remained clear, and she remembered each step of what she'd seen earlier, something that hadn't happened in a very long time but that she used to be quite good at.

She could get used to this kind of mental clarity. She never wanted to be held in someone's thrall ever again.

Metal clashed and swords clanged as pirates battled guards, Captain Red going after the still-standing elite guard while the rest went after the contingent sent for the king's amusement.

Soon the sounds of their fighting drew running feet and more clanking armor.

"Get those doors closed and barricaded!" Captain Red bellowed, trading blows with the elite guard, who was holding his own. "Where is that girl?" she muttered.

"We're trying!" Mary called back, frustration in her voice. "And I ain't seen her!"

Guards went down all over room, the king's other elite fighters losing to the brilliant captain and her swordplay, and Ro was partway done with the chains.

"Well, well, well. I have to say I'm almost disappointed

you came back, huntress. Though I knew you would. Couldn't stay away. Like a moth to a flame, eh?"

Ro's heart dropped right past her toes.

Several women in the room froze, staring at the man standing along the wall opposite the door, as if he'd appeared out of nowhere. His arms were crossed, sword dangling from his fingertips, as he watched the fight in apparent amusement.

Ro gritted her teeth and kept on with her task. "I can't stop," she ground out to anyone listening. "Else the locks will reset and we'll be bolted out for the next twenty-four hours."

Captain Red hissed as the remaining soldier slashed at a vulnerable spot in her armor, and getting an "I'm done toying with you" look in her eyes, she stepped past his defenses and punched him right under the jaw, knocking him out cold.

She turned to the man watching them and grinned. "So you're the bounty hunter Lady Luck sent after my friend. It will be a pleasure to end your life."

Ro jolted at hearing Madame LaChance called Lady Luck, an English version of her name she'd never before considered, but Ro put her head down and kept on with her steady, relentless work.

As Ro hurried back and forth between the small chests filled with keys and the chains she was unlocking, she caught the action in the room in small vignettes, keeping an eye on her surroundings so she wouldn't be caught by surprise should she be attacked past the pirates' defense.

Grant whipped his heavy sword out and up, in a fencer's salute, though the heavy broadsword was nothing like the fencing saber he was pretending to emulate. "The pleasure will be mine, I assure you."

The other pirates had effectively knocked out—or killed, but Ro couldn't think about that—the other soldiers in the room, and they spread out, watching the single man warily.

"This is between you and me"—the man pointed his sword

at Captain Red, then moved it slightly past her—"huntress, and I suggest you face me for your comeuppance."

Ro stiffened, but she kept going, unlocking the chains exactly as she'd seen them done before. She couldn't lose her composure and duel this man, no matter how much she wanted to. Break her legs, indeed. She'd like to break *his* legs.

She took a deep, steadying breath. Almost there.

Captain Red barked a laugh. "Any problem you have with her, you can resolve with me."

At that moment, Mary opened the crack in the door she was peering through wider, and a small, wisplike form darted into the room, heading straight for Ro. Grant's sword lashed out like a striking snake, spearing the girl and sending her sprawling only to land curled up in a ball at Ro's feet.

Red slowly blossomed over the girl's middle, and her face scrunched up in pain even as she gasped for breath.

Cries rang out all over the room, Aisling's the loudest.

Ro stared down at the girl, eyes wide, her hands frozen on the locks. She couldn't stop. She couldn't! Or their time here was for naught.

But she also couldn't stand by and watch this wee one bleed out.

Just as she started to move away from the locks, Aisling took the choice from her. Skidding up next to the girl, she pulled the half-fey child into her arms and pressed on her wound, attempting to staunch the bleeding.

She lifted eyes full of fire and swimming with tears to Ro. "You have to keep going. For Siobhan."

Ro nodded once and turned back to her task, blinking away tears, praying for the girl's recovery, trying with all her might to remember what came next.

But her hesitation cost her. The steady ticking that announced when each key should be inserted abruptly halted, and Ro's heart plummeted from crow's-nest heights between that chilling sound and the next, when all the locks would engage at once.

But the ringing cacophony did not come.

She looked down to find Siobhan holding her hand toward the door, keeping the locks from engaging.

"Keep . . . going . . ." she said in her whisper-thin voice.

Ro faced the door and turned the correct key, just in time. The door allowed it, and the young girl kept her hand raised, even as sweat beaded on her forehead.

Feeling Grant's poisonous stare, Ro risked one brief glance behind her to find the bounty hunter staring at the girl with a small smile on his face. "Well, well. Hiding something important from Madame LaChance, are we?"

Captain Red bared her teeth at the bounty hunter. "You just made the last mistake of your life. She's *mine*."

"And yet she's about to become mine. For Madame LaChance, of course." He eyed the captain. "Shall we duel? Just you and me? For my right to the girl?"

"Forget that. Mesdemoiselles, show him what it means to be one of my crew."

With feral grins, the rest of the pirates surrounded him and lunged as one. All but Aisling, who held Siobhan in her arms and kept an eye on the soldiers sprawled out in the room. Which must mean they weren't all dead.

Working steadily, Ro angled herself just enough to keep as much of the fighting in her periphery as she could.

Scrambling to stay on top of the multi-pronged attack, the bounty hunter took a moment to find his stride, but then he was taking on all six pirates at once, delivering efficient jabs and slices to each. Too much red bloomed on the pirates.

But very little on the bounty hunter himself.

The captain fought harder, taking the brunt of his attacks, and soon the other pirates were simply supporting her, using their weapons as distractions so Captain Red had every advantage.

"I'm in!" Ro called, dropping the last chain and heaving the metal bars aside so she could swing open the heavy door.

"Bon." Captain Red flashed her a grin. "Now go wake my sister."

Ro nodded and, helping Aisling pull the now-unconscious Siobhan into the queen's chamber, left the battle to the pirates. Hopefully they could take him. And if not, hopefully waking the queen would be worth the price of their lives.

The two serving women stood on either side of the casket, alarm evident in their wide eyes.

Ro made a calming gesture. "I'm here to wake her. I think I may have . . . found a way. I mean you and yours no harm. Her sister, Captain Rose Red, is here."

Because she had no doubt these two seemingly harmless women were a final defense for the queen, should all else fail.

They glanced at each other, then nodded and stepped aside.

Ro breathed a sigh of relief and rushed to the casket. "Can you lift the lid, s'il vous plaît?"

They retrieved their keys, then unlocked and raised the clear glass. After that, they hurried over to bind Siobhan's wounds and help Aisling fight for the girl's life.

Wood splintered in the other room, armored feet pounded into the outer chamber, and the sounds of fighting grew more desperate.

More soldiers had arrived, and Ro was out of time.

At a sudden noise at her back, Ro spun, and Captain Red was there, grin fierce, teeth bloody, a gash over her eye. She kept her eyes carefully away from the coffin. "Godspeed, huntress."

And with those words, she swung the heavy door closed, and all the locks engaged at once.

*N*on. Non! Ro stared at the closed door, heart pounding. They were trapped. If the pirates were overrun and Ro wasn't able to wake the queen, they would be dead when the door could once again be unlocked.

Ro turned toward the queen's coffin with determined steps. Then it was time she woke the queen, wasn't it?

"Stay with me!" Aisling demanded of the feyling, Siobhan.

Ro's heart squeezed. It was her fault the girl was here. Ro had requested she be present, and Ro would make it right. But she couldn't be distracted right now.

So she blocked the fight for Siobhan's life and the battle outside the chamber as she focused solely on the queen.

And reached for the magic and the poison at the same time, as she'd discussed with Grandmère in her dream. Yet something was wrong. She couldn't quite reach it. Something was missing. Something else she needed.

Just then, a sound caught her attention, and she paused, senses alert. Like a blazing comet, a light hurtled toward her, flying with abandon. As if with barely contained excitement.

Ro was reminded of a puppy, its entire body wriggling

with happiness to see its owner, right before she reached out and caught it.

She opened her hand to a pulsing red star glowing within her grasp. After a few more heartbeats of light, it dimmed enough for her to see what it was.

Ro stared at the ring, pulsing, glowing. She should've been surprised that it had shown up here on its own, but somehow she wasn't.

"Well, hello there," she said, picking it up and examining it. It winked happily at her, as if saying hello back. "What are you doing here, I wonder?"

On a hunch, she walked closer to Snow White's body, and the ring grew brighter until it was blazing, almost painful to look at. "Got you."

Ro slipped on the ring, her ring, the one Olt had so lovingly picked out for her and that someone had surely tricked him into buying for her—she would need to look into that—and her body flooded with ruby light.

The wavelike motion within Snow White's body came alive and writhed madly, trying to get away, trying to drive Snow White's spark away, trying to flood her body with poison, but Ro reached out and took hold of it.

Whatever it was, it had been comfortable, and whatever its original purpose, it now wanted everything to remain the exact same.

Non, that wasn't quite right. Ro examined it, even as she fought to keep it within her grasp.

Whoever had poisoned the queen had done this as well, preserved the queen at the moment of her death to cause the most pain possible to those who loved her. It was given with ill intent, not to keep the queen in a state she could be awakened from, but to give hope where there was none.

Yet it had taken hold a moment too soon, and there was still a spark of life, deep within Queen Snow White. A spark Ro was letting go nowhere.

Frowning, Ro tried to ignore the faint sounds of slaughter coming from the next room. She hoped with all her heart the pirate crew were prevailing, but she once again had to push it from her mind.

The magic fought her, but she held on with all her might, knowing if she let go for even a second, this creature would take Snow White with it and there would be nothing left. Of either of them.

Not sure how any of it worked, only knowing she had to do it, Ro strangled whatever the creature was, compressing it until it began to shrink.

It didn't make sense, but Ro was done trying to figure it out. If her instincts said to do it this way, that's what she was going to do.

She was done doubting herself and questioning herself and tying herself in knots. It was time she learned how she worked without berating herself at every step.

At the same time, Ro coaxed the poison back to where it came from and, as soon as it was gone from Snow White's body, sealed it into the object that had poisoned her.

Because the moment this being lost its hold on the queen, she would no longer be preserved, and the poison would be free to kill her.

The fey creature shrank until it fit into the palms of both hands, and it screamed in pain and terror. Ro gritted her teeth and kept going. Fey creatures used human compassion against them, and if the person stopped fighting, the creature would bounce back and eat them in one gulp.

Ro wasn't about to be taken in.

All of a sudden, the creature winked out of existence, and its ethereal remains wafted away in a puff of white smoke.

The queen bolted upright in her coffin. Ro screamed.

Aisling echoed her scream. The servants clasped each other, unable to make a sound, but their mouths opened as if they were screaming, too.

The queen didn't make a sound, but she was holding her throat, grasping it, tugging at it, desperate.

A memory flooded Ro. One where Cosette had run in from the apple orchard, clutching her throat. Face turning purple. Unable to make a sound.

How the old cook had whipped the little girl over her knee and pounded on her back until an apple piece came flying out. How she then made sure the girls knew how to save each other from choking.

Ro lunged at the queen, wrapped her arms around her middle, and heaved, over and over, the only thing she could think to do.

A piece of apple flew out of the queen's mouth, hit the far wall, and fell to the stone floor, smoking and leaving an acid burn on both the wall and the floor. Then Snow White vomited all over her pristine white dress and Ro's arms.

Great. Just great.

Sobbing, Snow White reached out to her two serving women, and they rushed over and immediately began fussing over her and wiping up the mess she'd made.

The apple piece along the far wall hissed and steamed and started eating a hole in the solid stone beneath it.

Ro shuddered as she took off her splattered vambraces and tossed them aside. It was a miracle the poison hadn't eaten straight through the queen's throat. Powerful magic protected her.

Ro could only wonder where it had come from.

Making her way to the water basin, Ro took off the armor on her shoulders and upper arms and washed her arms. Meanwhile, the servants helped Snow White out of the coffin and wiped her down and changed her clothing.

Snow White clung to her maidservants and sobbed and babbled on about her awful mother-in-law who'd forced her to eat the poisoned apple or watch her son die.

That sobered Ro right up, and she removed the rest of her

armor. Thank goodness the pirates had rigged it to be easier to get off.

How had the queen mother made an apple poisonous? Was there an apple tree in her poison garden? Or did she somehow taint it herself?

Although she was glad the old witch's books had been burned, Ro sincerely wished she had access to the queen mother's garden and chambers, if only to learn how to more effectively defend against such a thing in the future.

The moment her last piece of armor came free, her ring glimmered happily and went to sleep, its inner glow winking out and returning to its gorgeous work-of-art state. She smiled at it. Just wait till she told Olt.

Her shoulders sagged, and her smile died. Oh, right. She could no longer share every important moment with him first thing.

Her jaw tightened. But she was going to change that. Apologize. Tell him her secret, do whatever it took to make it right.

Which reminded her of Aisling, still fighting for Siobhan's life. Another thing she needed to make right. Which meant she needed to get them out of here.

She moved to the door and examined every inch for a way to open it from the inside, to bypass the timed locks. Surely now that she'd awakened the queen, they would stop fighting and the king would pardon the pirates, oui?

Then again, things rarely worked out so well in Ro's experience.

But non, the room was locked up tight. The sounds of battle had faded, and it was all Ro could do not to claw through the door to find out what had happened.

With a sigh, Ro turned and screamed right in the queen's face.

The queen didn't even flinch.

Ro grabbed her chest and sagged against the metal door,

heart pounding. "Oh! Votre Majesté. You gave me such a fright."

Still without reacting, Snow White stood uncomfortably close and watched her with an intensity that was distinctly uncomfortable.

Gone were the tears, the distress, the emotional queen; in their place was a coldly distant woman. Freshly bathed and in a new dress, nowhere near as elaborate as the ones she'd worn in her coffin, the queen watched Ro with a detachment that chilled Ro's skin, as if she were a rare and newly discovered specimen.

"My ladies-in-waiting tell me I have you to thank for removing the poison and waking me."

Ro swallowed. "Oh, um, oui."

She glanced past the queen to the two beaming women, tear tracks on their faces, unable to take their eyes off the queen they'd watched slumber for years.

"How can I ever repay you?" Snow White continued.

As if a hunting horn had pealed in the forest and she were prey caught in a predator's sights, Ro felt the words down to her toes. This way lay danger.

She gestured to the girls on the side of the room, Aisling clutching a still Siobhan to her and watching the queen with wide eyes. "Please, the young Mademoiselle."

The queen turned emotionless eyes on the fey-born child curled up in the corner. Her skin appeared even more translucent, and — Ro's eyes widened — was she . . . fading?

"She was wounded helping me free you. Might you . . . do you think you can help her?" Ro bit her lip. She knew how dangerous bargains with the fey were.

Well, she knew that *now*.

And if she guessed correctly, this creature before her was not human. May have been once. But most definitely was not anymore.

"You wish to strike a bargain with me?" the queen asked, eyes still on the girl.

"Oh non. Absolutely not." Ro shook her head fiercely as the queen's head whipped around to study her with a perplexed gaze. "I'm only asking you to see what you can do. In honor of what she did for you. I believe you owe her a life debt?" At the queen's sharp look, Ro changed tactics. "She's one of yours, after all."

Queen Snow White considered this for three heartbeats before turning toward the girl. "I shall see what I can do."

The queen knelt beside the girl, ran her hands over Siobhan's frame without touching her, and then laid one snow-white hand on the girl's middle. After a moment, the girl relaxed, releasing the stomach she'd been clutching, and her skin returned to its normal color.

As if a great weight had been lifted from her, Ro sighed in relief and looked up to find the two Mesdemoiselles-in-waiting with smiles so wide, their faces had to ache.

"How can we ever thank you?"

"You have done the impossible."

"Brought back that which was lost."

"And we shall be forever grateful."

"How shall we repay such kindness?"

Ro's neck almost got whiplash from trying to keep up with the volley of gratitude being flung her way. Apparently both women somehow had their tongues back.

Snow White was most definitely more than a human queen.

Ro rubbed the back of her neck. "Ah, oui, yes. That." Uncomfortable with any thanks or praise, she quickly added, "The queen's sister brought me here. You should thank her instead. Or Madame LaChance. She hired me to wake the queen."

Suddenly, Snow White was standing at her elbow, either

moving silently or simply appearing there, and Ro jumped a kilomètre.

Snow White tilted her head, a quick, birdlike motion that set Ro's teeth on edge. "Did she? My, yes, I'll have to thank her." She flicked a glance past Ro. "Will you let me out?"

"Ah . . ." Ro bit her lip, wondering how best to explain this. "I can't seem to, I mean, we're kind of locked in. Till tomorrow."

"You locked us in here?"

"Non!" Ro raised both hands. The question sounded dangerous coming from this pristine creature with hazel eyes that seemed to glow from within. "The king—it was for your protection. While you were sleeping. I tried . . . there was a battle . . . I'm not sure how to get out . . ."

"Very well." Snow White waved Ro aside, and she gladly fled to stand next to the two servants who couldn't take their shining eyes and blazing smiles off their queen.

Snow White raised both hands, felt along the door without touching it, and frowned. Then she stepped back and *pulled* the wall toward her with one hand and *pushed* the door with the other.

The wall exploded toward the queen, though the stone broke apart before it touched her, while the heavy door fell outward. Ro had barely enough time to pull the two women under the coffin, which toppled upside down over them, shielding them from the blast.

Coughing as stone and dust and other debris rained down all around them, Ro heaved the padded coffin off the three of them in time to watch the queen calmly step through the gaping hole she'd made in the stone wall.

After casting a quick glance to the side to make sure Aisling and Siobhan had survived the blast without injury— they had—Ro scrambled after the queen to find soldiers picking themselves up after being blasted with debris and stones. Everyone was coated in a fine gray powder.

Apparently the outer stone wall had exploded outward as well.

Grant lay panting against the wall, propped up, uselessly holding a cut in his thigh that ran crimson with blood. He wouldn't survive that much blood loss much longer.

His eyes went to Captain Red.

Captain Red, in chains and held between two guards, bared her teeth at him. "A life for a life."

"Touché," he said, right before his head slumped.

Someone rushed over and bound his leg, but Ro had a feeling they'd be too late.

And then the captain looked up, eyes skipping over Ro and landing on her sister. Her face drained of its natural ruddy color, and cautious hope filled her eyes.

The pirates had been seized and were raising a ruckus, and although Ro could see Captain Red through the mass of soldiers, it appeared Queen Snow White could not. She rubbed her temples as if she were in pain.

"Quiet," the queen commanded, and the entire room fell silent. "Where is my sister?"

A shuffle, then chains clanked as Captain Red was hastily brought forward. Blood poured down her temple and from her split lip, but she stared at her sister as if soaking in the sun itself.

Snow White reached for her, then pulled back with a hiss when she got close to the iron clamped around Rose Red's wrists.

"Release her," the queen said with a dangerous quality to her voice.

"But, Your Majesty," said a soldier, "she is a pirate. A traitor to the crown. She has attacked the royal household and as such—"

With a twisting motion of her hand, Snow White snapped the guard's neck without touching him, and the guard fell dead at her feet. "Someone else release her."

Several guards scrambled to obey.

After Rose Red was released, chains hastened out of the room, Snow took her into her arms and whispered, "I've missed you, sister."

Captain Red put her head on Snow White's shoulder and wept, her shoulders shaking as she made a low keening sound.

Ro started to back away, but then Snow's head came up, and she looked right at her. Ro stood rooted to the spot. Something in her gaze . . . wasn't right.

The queen patted her sister's back, and as Captain Red tried to do away with all evidence of her tears, Snow beckoned Ro close.

"Huntress. I have much to thank you for."

Ro's eyes darted to Captain Red and back. "I assure you, it was a group effort. Madame LaChance got me here, your husband gave me access, and your sister made it possible for me to wake you."

At the mention of Madame LaChance, Captain Red joined the conversation, her face expressionless as if to make up for losing her carefully constructed composure.

"So you see," Ro continued, "your sister is the one who came for you, and she should be thanked, not I." Ro didn't want any part of fey gratitude.

The queen's eyes sought Captain Red's. "I'm so glad you did. That you both did. All of you." She waved a hand, encompassing the pirates still held by soldiers. Then her eyes were back on Ro. "Yet I still thank you for your part."

One fair with dark hair and hazel eyes, the other ruddy with fire-bright hair and warm chocolate eyes, the sisters both nodded at Ro, who nodded back, but Ro's heart pounded with fear.

When she'd met a siren for the first time, the creature had been flawless, beautiful, wearing a human form. But the perfect replica had been soulless, inhuman. No matter how close to a human it appeared, it was something other.

Just like Snow White.

"Please, my crew," Captain Red said, unable to take her welling eyes off her sister for long. "They need to be released. To be given letters of marque, to become privateers in the queen's navy, no longer hunted as pirates."

Ro blinked, perplexed that the captain was insisting on this now, but Snow White nodded and commanded an elite guard to carry out the order. Captain Red gave him a fierce grin—he was the one who'd antagonized her earlier.

At that exact moment, the king burst into the room, wheezing, his face already turning purple. "Wot's the meaning of this? Filthy pirates! Off with their heads! Off with their hea—"

In the middle of his tirade, his eyes landed on Snow White, and he faltered.

Courtiers and party guests crowded in behind him, eagerly taking in the tableau.

The king made a strangled noise, and Snow White turned to him. She took him in from head to toe, his large girth, his ruddy complexion, his pockmarked skin. He came up to her, whining, tilting his head as if seeking her approval.

"My love?" With a low moan, he knelt before her and placed his head on her stomach. "Is this a dream? Are you real?"

Snow rubbed the king's head as one would a pet. "Oh my darling, big, handsome bear. My time away has not been kind to you, has it?"

The king leaned into her touch and closed his eyes.

Ro felt distinctly uncomfortable, like an intruder. Watching something she shouldn't.

She looked away to find others staring in fascination or slight disgust or also glancing away in embarrassment. At least she wasn't the only one who felt that way.

The queen continued to stroke her fingers through his greasy hair. Yet the queen was pausing at different places—

his temples, the crown of his head, the back of his neck—placing her fingers firmly there before moving on to another spot.

"Oh my love, you have not been kind to our people, have you?"

The king didn't answer, just leaned into his wife's touch, as if he'd been reduced to a mindless animal.

"But where is our son?" She searched a moment more before she let out a sigh of relief. "Oh, I see. You hid him away. He is safe. I thank you for that."

At that, he seemed to rally. "Help me up!"

He snapped his fingers a bunch of times, and several servants hurried over and heaved him up. Ro looked away as it took far longer than was comfortable to gain his feet.

Once he was settled, King Wilhelm placed his arm around his wife and stared at her with tears in his eyes and rolling into his beard.

"Huntress," he said, choked up, "I cannot thank you enough for what you've done. Bringing my wife back to me."

He looked so suddenly at Captain Red, she flinched.

"And you!" His loud voice boomed in the chamber. "You knew she was still alive. You never gave up." Keeping his wife firmly in his grasp, he bowed, pulling her with him, fist over his heart. "You have my deepest gratitude."

Warily, Captain Red said, "I could do no less for my sister, Majesty."

The king's eyes were back on his wife, though he spoke to the room at large. "Give them whatever they want. All the gold, all the jewels—empty my coffers for all I care."

Captain Red's eyes lit up. Someone else in the room spluttered, quite possibly his accountant, judging by how the room had filled with the king's courtiers.

"And letters of marque," Captain Red insisted. Again. "We want to be privateers in the queen's armada, not pirates."

The pirates in the room grinned in delight, and the soldiers holding them glared down at them in disgust. A few of the pirates held their breaths, as if afraid to hope for such a thing. And Captain Red, of course, grinned directly at the elite guard who was now, apparently, her mortal enemy.

"Yes, yes, fine. My wife and I are going to retire to my seaside palace. I don't want to be bothered with affairs of state for a whole month. No, three months!"

"But Your Majesty!"

So many of the king's cabinet objected, Ro couldn't tell who had spoken.

But that wasn't what had punched her in the gut. Held her rooted to the floor.

Her grandmère had said her prince, the prince she'd left the sea to marry, the one who'd married someone else instead —leaving Darya to give birth to his child alone—had a seaside palace.

Surely many royals around the world had seaside palaces. She couldn't be related to this monstrosity before her. Although as much as she balked, the words struck a chord within her she couldn't deny.

Yet he wasn't old enough . . . perhaps his père was Ro's grandpère?

That would make the king, what? Her uncle? And Snow White her aunt.

Her eyes flicked to Captain Rose Red, currently haggling for vast amounts of gold for her and her crew, as well as pardons to be granted immediately.

She liked the captain. They'd always gotten along well.

Well, when she wasn't kidnapping Ro or threatening to take her to the Caribbean. Or branding her or other girls against their will. But still.

The fey were all about bonds, connections. Not to mention it made her work as a huntress so much easier to know people who could help when Ro came racing through, chasing the next predator eating people or draining their souls.

Even though they'd only be related via marriage, how would a familial bond affect her and Captain Red's relationship? How much more willing would Captain Red be to help her in the future?

Something in Ro soured at the thought of using someone, even with the best of intentions, for her own gain.

So she took a deep breath . . . and let it go. Her grandmère had wished his identity to remain secret, and she would respect her wishes.

It was enough that the mystery had been solved.

"Come, let us away." King Wilhelm took hold of his wife's hand and tried to lead her from the room.

Queen Snow White stood firm. "Hold. Our kingdom's affairs have yet to be settled, and you have yet to answer for your crimes against my people."

The king's face went purple, but at one touch from his wife's hand on his forearm, skin on skin, he settled.

"I thought you would do better, be better." Snow White let out a long-suffering sigh. "It appears I was wrong."

"But there're so many of them, and they all want something from me," he whined.

"No matter," the queen soothed. "I will take care of it for you. And then I will bring our son back from the convent and train him to take my place, once I have set this kingdom to rights, of course."

He mumbled a halfhearted protest, then fell silent, head bowed. With one hand, she swirled her fingers as she maintained contact with her other hand. A swirling mist of—snowflakes?—that matched her movements rose out of the ground and consumed him.

Ro stepped forward to do . . . something. But how could she fight against a swirl of snow?

Mere seconds later, the cloud dropped suddenly to the ground, a pile of snowflakes at their feet, and a . . . *bear* . . . sat on his haunches in the king's place. Still being petted, rubbing its head against the queen's hand, sitting before her and soaking up her attention.

His fur was ruddy, as the king's hair had been, and even sitting, he was nearly the height of the queen. His girth hadn't changed much, but standing, he would easily tower over anyone else in the room. He was massive.

Ro made a strangled noise and stepped back, reaching for a crossbow that wasn't there, but Captain Red held up a hand. Not just to her, but to all the pirates who'd gone for their weapons. Fingers on empty air where her favorite weapon should be, Ro missed her crossbow fiercely and wondered what to do next.

"Bring me my collar," the queen demanded.

One of her maidservants ran into the room the queen had been laid to rest in and soon returned with a diamond-studded collar and a leash resting on a red velvet cushion. The leash looked like it had been woven from pure silver.

The queen clipped it around the creature's neck one-handed, and as soon as it was secure, only then did she remove her hand from the bear's fur.

He dropped to all fours, panting and grunting in a guttural tone, tongue lolling out of his open mouth.

Snow White then turned to Rose Red and held out her hand. "Have you my compass?"

Captain Red dug deep in her pocket and held out the compass, the silver one with the snowflake engraved on its cover. The captain's matching golden one with the engraved rose was the one Madame LaChance had destroyed.

Snow smiled, yet the expression didn't look right to Ro. Oh, it was perfect, and so beautiful Ro could have watched the queen smile all day, but it was too perfect. Too beautiful. And her eyes remained cold and lifeless.

"I see you kept my compass in perfect repair, sister."

She carefully inspected both sides, then opened it, peering closely within as well. Then she withdrew a thin silver chain from her dress's pocket. She slid the chain through the end of the compass and looped it around her neck.

She caught the wistful smile on Captain Red's face and crooked an eyebrow. "But where is yours?"

The captain shoved her hands deep in her trouser pockets. "Ah, well, it got destroyed. You know how hard I am on . . . everything."

Red grinned, but even Ro could tell losing her compass stung.

But before Ro could feel even more guilty, Snow said, "That will never do."

Handing off the bear's chain to one of her ladies-in-waiting, she swirled her fingers over her other hand, and Captain Red's compass materialized. But it was transparent and wavered like a mirage. Snow frowned, concentrating harder. It burst apart in a shower of sparks, and Snow looked at her sister with wide eyes.

"The anchor has been broken."

The captain rocked up on her toes and then back on her heels, and said as nonchalantly as possible, "It appears so."

"But who would do such a thing? Who would be so brazen to—"

"Madame LaChance." Every eye in the room swung to Ro, and she swallowed against the sudden pressure of so much attention. "She broke it. She . . . stabbed it with a ruby-hilted dagger, and it shattered."

Captain Red winced and shook her head at Ro, as Snow's expression grew even more remote and cold. "If it is as you say, I shall have a talk with her." She turned back to her sister. "Though I can't imagine why *she* of all people—"

"Me neither," Captain Red said brightly. "You should probably ask her. Right away. Well, as soon as possible. After you put your kingdom back together and announce your return, of course. So many things to do!"

Ro frowned at her. Why was she acting so odd?

But it didn't matter. She needed to leave.

"Votre Majesté."

Silence swept the room as everyone turned to Ro. She startled at the force of their attention. She'd unknowingly put the smallest amount of power behind her words, as her grand-mère had taught her.

She couldn't help but shiver under Snow White's inhuman gaze. It reminded her of the Siren Queen's gaze . . . of the Swan Queen's gaze . . .

Ro's breath stalled in her chest. Something about that . . .

"Yes?" the queen asked, somewhat impatiently.

Ro would have to think about that later.

"An urgent matter calls me away. I wish only to be on my way. May I take my leave?"

Snow White's voice filled the room, commanding more power than Ro's had. "That is *all* you wish, huntress?"

Ro didn't miss Captain Red's sidelong glance at her sister. From the looks of it, she still wasn't convinced that something else hadn't either come back with her sister or taken her place, a concern she'd expressed more than once aboard the *Siren Hunter*. Ro didn't blame her.

Still, a small smile touched Ro's mouth. "I may call on you, should I ever need aid, but I must return to my duties. Imme-diately, s'il vous plaît."

Snow White inclined her head. "Then may God speed you on your way."

Ro bowed and backed away, casting one last glance at Captain Red, who raised her hand in a "wait just a moment" gesture. Ro paused.

Taking back the silver chain, Snow White turned to her husband—who was a *bear*—and said, "Come, my pet. I shall not banish you, although I should, but I'm afraid you will live out the rest of your days as this dumb beast, as you should have done from the first." She sighed. "I suppose I should see what you've left me of this great kingdom of ours."

She tugged on the leash, and the bear followed, docile as any pet. When Captain Red didn't follow, Snow White paused and looked back. "Sister, are you coming?"

The captain gave Ro a small, fierce smile. "I must needs speak with the huntress first. I'll join you shortly."

After a slight hesitation, the queen gave a regal nod. She and her entourage spilled out of the room, a healthy amount of space around the bear on his thin silver chain.

Ro stuck her hands in her trouser pockets. What could Captain Red possibly want to say to her? They'd been butting heads since she'd kidnapped Ro.

"So. You saved my sister."

Ro nodded, staring after the queen and the *bear* who'd once been King Wilhelm.

"Your mouth is still hanging open," Captain Red said in a deeply amused voice.

Ro snapped her mouth closed. "What? Who? *How?*"

The captain chuckled. "Oh, the bear? Yeah, he's really a bear."

Ro sent her a dirty look. All she knew was that her head hurt. Abominably.

"Well, I suppose he wasn't *always* a bear, but he was when we first met him."

"I thought you said you were children together? Played together?"

"Oh, we were. Yet one harsh winter we took in a wounded bear. Snow was forever bringing wounded wild creatures into our home, but I thought even Maman would object to a bear. She didn't. And once winter was over, we found the dwarf who'd cursed him so he could take his treasure. Imagine our surprise when Snow unraveled the spell while I got the gold back, and we found our childhood playmate, now a handsome prince that Snow fell for immediately. I tried to warn her off —his father was abominable and hated women—but she would have none of it. They returned to his kingdom, were married at his family's seaside palace, and she became queen of Angleterre."

The words hit Ro like a slap, just as when the king had mentioned the same.

Seaside palace. King Wilhelm was possibly related to her. To her grandmère. Once again, she was tempted. Did she want to pursue the matter?

Non. Non, she did not.

That was one family connection that could remain consigned to the dusty halls of mystery and time lost.

A soldier who'd been hovering nearby was called away by his superior, and before Ro knew what was happening, Captain Red stepped close and dropped her voice, mouth smiling but eyes intense. There were still plenty of soldiers and members of her crew in the room, but none were close enough to overhear a private conversation.

Captain Red spoke in a low urgent voice. "Pay attention. Pay close attention."

Ro blinked.

"My anchor has been broken, so I can tell you this. I will never be anything more or less than what I am right now."

The urgency in her voice, in her eyes, was incongruent with the wide smile on her face, and Ro was having a hard time not being distracted by that. Besides, her words didn't make any sense.

"I don't know what you mean," Ro said in a low voice.

The captain went on as if she had much to say and little time to say it. "Don't eat what they offer you. Don't agree to their bargains. Listen, but keep your own counsel. Promise nothing. My mark will protect you, but you must be on guard at all times."

Frustration built as the words remained decidedly unclear. Ro hated intrigue. "I don't . . ."

"Listen," the captain nearly growled. Unnerving with that smile. "Pay attention to the queens. To those in power. To the anchors they possess. Find out what *she's* planning. And whatever you do, don't let *her* succeed."

"Who?" Ro asked. "LaChance, Snow . . . someone else?"

Then with a complete change to her demeanor, the brazen captain in place once more, Captain Rose Red stepped back and swept an imaginary hat wide. "As always, it is a pleasure to be near you, huntress. I look forward to our next rendezvous."

A few of her most trusted pirates had moved closer, perhaps drawn by her odd behavior and whispered words. They glanced between Ro and the captain, concerned or wary looks on their faces.

Popping into their midst, Siobhan handed Ro the bag she'd stashed with getaway clothes. Then she turned to Captain Red. "There. I did as you asked. Now return me to my family."

The captain jerked her chin, and Siobhan darted away. The captain turned to Oksana next. "Watch her. And when they double-cross her, make sure she has a way back to the ship, if she wants it."

Oksana bowed and padded out of the room on silent feet. That reminded Ro.

"One more thing." Ro faced Captain Red and squared her shoulders.

The captain groaned. "I had an inkling we'd be having words about this before you left."

But her eyes twinkled with merriment, so Ro didn't think she was too upset. Probably.

"The girls. The rest of them." Ro pressed on adamantly. "They *must* be given a choice whether they set sail with you or not."

The pirates came over the rest of the way, openly listening now, expressions carefully blank. To support her? Probably not. Ready to back their captain, more likely.

This could go either way.

"And who knows?" Ro shrugged. "Maybe they'll spread the word that someone's willing to take them out of a life of misery and give them a chance at a better existence. You might have girls flocking to your ship."

Captain Red's teeth were clenched. "Or I could simply hand Madame LaChance the location of my ship and my base of operations and invite her to come take it by force."

"Or you can make the change you want to, honestly, with willing participants, and set sail the moment you have a willing crew. You seem to be hiding well enough," Ro persisted.

"All it takes is one slipup," Captain Red insisted. "I may have letters of marque—well, will have them soon, anyway—but Madame LaChance is still a problem. I cannot risk it."

Ro lifted her chin. "Or it takes one person to do the right thing and make these girls feel like they matter, that they have a choice, that not every decision in life is taken away from them, even by someone with good intentions."

Captain Red pursed her lips and appeared to be giving the matter some thought.

When Captain Red made her decision, Ro's heart squeezed painfully in her chest. Ro could see that she was about to be brushed off. Again.

Just as Ro was scrambling with what to say to convince her, Aisling pushed forward and propped her hands on her hips. "I like it. To be sure, had we not forced Siobhan onto our crew, she wouldn'ta almost died today."

"We also wouldn't have gotten in the vault," Ro muttered, even as Aisling gave her a "Who's side are you on?" look.

Ro raised both palms in surrender. She hadn't meant to say it aloud.

Merja's quiet voice came next. "We could train them while we finish stocking the ship. Let them know they'll have a choice to go or stay when we set sail."

Sheba nodded. "Then use our network to put out one final call before we shove off."

Ro glanced between them. "Wait. You're still planning on going back? Isn't everything different? Now that your sister —the queen—um, Snow White is awake?"

Captain Red slid her a mildly disgruntled look. "Plans don't change until we know . . . how this is gonna go."

Ro could understand that.

"Besides, we have a supply run ta finish," Mary said offhandedly.

After giving Mary a "shut your trap" look, to which the pirate snapped her mouth closed, Captain Red reached up to push back a hat that wasn't there. "So we're agreed that this is the best course? Continue to stock the ship, give the lasses *a choice*"—she slid Ro a begrudging look—"stuff and nonsense," she muttered, "and put out one final call afore we set sail?"

"Aye, Cap'ain" rang out in hearty agreement.

She gave Ro a smile that was all teeth. Gritted teeth. That she spoke through. "Happy?"

Ro smirked. "Incandescently."

"Cheer up, Cap'ain," said Aisling, now all smiles. "We'll whip 'em into shape in no time, show 'em what they'll miss out on, not being upon the open seas with our fine vessel. We'll convince 'em to stay."

Ro couldn't help a full smile. "I do like the sound of that."

"What'd'ya say, Cap'ain? Willing to give her all you've got?" Aisling grinned.

Captain Red gave the optimistic pirate a sidelong glance. "I said I would, didn't I?"

"Nothing to worry about a'tall, then. Leave the younger girls to me." And Aisling was off and whistling, her confident stride a fair bit on the cocky side.

Ro and Captain Red glanced at each other, then chuckled.

The other pirates nodded at Ro or clapped her shoulder

before ambling off as well, giving their previous captors smug grins that spoke to no sense of self-preservation whatsoever.

Then again, their captain was the queen's sister, and she'd gotten verbal agreement the entire crew would be given letters of marque. And piles of gold. And made privateers instead of pirates. They had a right to be feeling rather self-confident.

"The girls." Ro paused. "In the brothels . . ."

Captain Red's grin was fierce. "Where do you think we've gotten half our crew?"

Ro remembered to shut her gaping mouth. Then said, "And the rest . . ."

The captain's entire demeanor changed. "You leave them to me, huntress. We have a plan, and I don't want Madame LaChance catching wind of it." Her cheeks dimpled. "I can tell you my sister happens to be a part of it, though she doesn't know it yet."

"But you will tell me if you need help? I'll come."

"Aye. I'll send for ye if need be."

Ro's shoulders relaxed. Captain Red was more motivated than most to get those girls out.

The captain took a giant step back, swept her hand out in a swirling pattern, and gave Ro a deep bow. "As always, it has been a pleasure, huntress. Thought a bit frustrating and confusing at times as well."

Ro couldn't restrain her smile. "I appreciate it, Captain. Truly. I'm so pleased you're willing to treat these girls well. Merci."

Captain Red grumbled a little as she straightened. "I *always* treat my girls well."

Ro touched her arm. "But you're giving them a choice. Even if they make a poor one, it means the world."

Looking slightly mollified, the pirate captain nodded once and ambled away, inspecting the soldiers as she went and staring down any who dared meet her gaze.

Ah oui. The good captain would be milking her pardon for all it was worth.

And then Captain Rose Red swept from the room with a swagger that Ro would give her best hunting knife to emulate with any confidence whatsoever.

But the smile slipped from her face the moment the captain was out of sight. Something still wasn't right. Snow White wasn't herself.

Not that she knew what the queen had been like before her years-long sleep, of course, but she was all wrong. Like Marie, the sorceress called Magic, and the Siren Queen and the Swan Queen and the Nightingale Empress—something was taking the core personality of each queen and suppressing it into something dead and flat and inhumane.

Something fey.

Ro wanted to fix it. She started to go after them, to talk to Captain Red about her fears, but stopped. Laughed at herself. What could she say that the captain didn't already know?

Captain Red was aware something was wrong. And had tried to warn Ro in her own way. She'd be watching.

Ro changed her trajectory. She needed to talk to Madame LaChance. Make sure her debts were paid in full and there wouldn't be a dozen bounty hunters on her heels while she raced back to the Black Forest.

Surely waking the English queen had sealed their bargain. Surely she wouldn't keep Ro from her task. Surely the rift had already burst open like rotten fruit and sprayed fey creatures all over the woods.

Hopefully the loups-garous hadn't destroyed everything.

28

Ro ran all the way to Madame LaChance's office and burst into the room. "Call him off."

Madame LaChance glanced up from her desk, a pair of pince-nez perched on her nose, an assistant holding out several papers for her to sign. "I beg your pardon?"

Just then, Grant surged into the room, his nose bloody and his eyes furious. He was still pale from blood loss, and when his body had been removed, Ro had assumed they were hauling out his corpse.

Not so. His bleeding had been tied off and patched up in time, it wasn't as dire as it appeared—in other words, not the femoral artery—and he'd gone after Ro at his first opportunity.

He'd popped out from between two dilapidated buildings and tried to grab her, and she'd punched him right in the nose out of reflex. And then he'd chased her the full way to Madame LaChance's office. His wound was the only reason she'd outrun him.

Ro gasped for breath and made sure her back wasn't to either of them. "Call off your dog, LaChance. I woke the queen and fulfilled our bargain. I need to go home *right now*

268

and stop those loups-garous from destroying the world. I don't have time for your stupid games!"

Madame LaChance appeared just as startled by Ro's outburst as Ro herself, but she didn't have time for the woman to argue. Ro needed to get back, to finish off those wolves, and to find out what had happened to Gustave.

Her unsettling eyes landed on Grant. "Is it as she says?"

A muscle ticked in his jaw, but as if compelled to answer, he gave a swift, jerky nod. "Aye. The queen is awake."

"I see." Madame LaChance inclined her head to Ro. "Very well. Your bargain has been fulfilled. You may go."

Ro felt the words as a physical release, and something eased deep in her chest.

"One more thing." Ro marched to the desk and leaned over it, bringing her face close to Madame LaChance's. "Get out of the business of taking girls, or I will make you."

Madame LaChance's only response was a startled blink.

Without another word, Ro spun on her heel and left. She had to push past Grant to do so, but she didn't let that stop her.

"Watch your back, little huntress." His hot breath blasted the side of her face.

She didn't pause, didn't glance aside. She refused to fear this man any longer. If he came after her? She would defend herself, and he wouldn't like it.

And she was never working for Madame LaChance, not ever again. The woman would have to hire another huntress from this day forward.

One day Ro would be back. And if Madame LaChance didn't make the right choice, she would no longer be able to sell girls who didn't have anyone to protect them.

And whatever Captain Red wasn't able to clean up, Ro would do so herself.

❧

Ro bolted out of Madame LaChance's boarding school feeling as if she'd been freed of prison, and ran straight into the last person she'd expected to see. "Olt? What are you doing here?"

He grabbed her with his one hand, steadying her. "Ro! Praise Dieu. We came just as soon as we heard—"

He didn't get any further, because Ro grabbed his frock coat's lapels and pulled him in for a rough kiss, all her desperation and longing and hopelessness at never seeing him again pouring out.

After a frozen moment, he wrapped his arm around her and pulled her as close to him as she could get, returning her kiss just as desperately.

All of a sudden, Ro yanked back, keeping a firm grip on his coat. He looked dazed. "I'm sorry. For leaving. For running. You were right. I was scared. So scared. My grand-mère needed help, true . . ."

She faltered, the memory of how she'd found Darya derailing her.

His arm tightened around her. "Gustave told us what happened. I'm sorry for your loss, Ro. So very sorry."

Ro nearly collapsed from relief. That meant Gustave was still alive. Her tightly held emotions threatened to crack, so she took a deep breath and let it out slowly. She could fall to pieces later. Once she was out of Angleterre.

"Merci, Olt. Still, it wasn't fair to you. I wasn't fair to you." She straightened and lifted her chin. "I'm ready. When-ever you want to get married—*if* you still want to get married —I'll do it."

"Oh, Ro." He cupped her face. "You don't have to force yourself to marry me, don't you see? I *do* want to marry you, I *do* want to make a family with you, and I *do* want you to be mine forever, but you do not ever have to force yourself to do something you're not ready for. I just want to be with you, however that looks. I can wait for you. I just need to know that's what you want, too."

Ro melted at his words. And found herself staring at his mouth. Still, there was more she needed to say, wasn't there? Oh, right. "Listen, I have to tell you something."

"Whatever it is, yes," he said, just as distracted taking in her features.

She was leaning in to kiss him again when a disgusted grunt interrupted her.

"It's like the rest of us don't even exist," said a familiar voice.

"Yeah. She's all 'Oh, Olt, thank you for rescuing me!'" another familiar voice said in a falsetto. Then in his normal tone, "Like we didn't tear pell-mell across half the world to come watch her rescue herself."

Ro blinked at her brothers. Then rubbed her eyes and blinked again. But nope. It wasn't a mirage. There they stood, arms crossed, giving her disgruntled, relieved, and exasperated looks.

Although Pascal's teasing was slightly unsure. They still hadn't made up after their last fight, moving carefully around each other at each interaction, not quite back to their normal, easy banter. It was time Ro changed that.

With a cry, she hugged them both at once. "Claude! Pascal! What are you doing here?"

"Rescuing you. Obviously." Claude rolled his eyes.

"Not that you need rescuing."

"But please don't thank us. Save all your thanks for Olt." Claude made a retching sound. "I will gladly do this for no payment whatsoever."

Speaking of payment . . . Ro glanced behind her. They were in full view of Madame LaChance's residence and anyone she had watching Ro. It wouldn't be that hard for the woman to change her mind and attempt to take Ro back.

"Are you not listening to us?" Claude demanded. "I feel like she's not listening to us."

Pascal snorted. "Rude."

Ro made a shushing sound and slashed her hand through the air. "Not here. We need to get out of sight before . . ."

She was already in motion, but she pulled up short when she found Liam standing by a row of horses, burly arms crossed, watching them with his stoic face on.

The one he reserved for when he *looked* displeased but wasn't *actually* displeased.

"You came too?" she blurted.

A smirk barely touched one side of his face. "Don't act so surprised."

"We heard about the bounty on your head . . ." Olt started to say.

"And we weren't about to leave you to the wolves, as it were," Liam said in a gruff voice. He had no idea how accurate his words were.

On impulse, giddy from relief, and leaving half her senses behind, she hugged him tight and said, "Merci beaucoup."

He stiffened for half a heartbeat before setting her away from him. "We should be off." His tone was curt, and he immediately pulled one of the horses forward, placing it between himself and Ro. "For you."

She squashed a grin and glanced over her shoulder at Olt. He gave her an encouraging smile, knowing how fiercely she and Liam had argued, fought, and then refused to speak to each other, though not about what.

And if Ro had her way, he would never know.

She turned back and took the reins. "Merci, Liam."

He crossed his arms again, almost as if shielding himself, and asked, "What happened?"

Olt pushed his way forward. "Yeah. Gustave said you were both knocked out, and when he woke, you were gone."

And that brought everything back in painful, sharp relief.

She sent them an apologetic look. "Not here, I beg of you. We have to get back to the Black Forest. I'll explain on the way." She flicked another glance behind her, but she couldn't tell if anyone was watching through the curtains. "And I may have a very angry bounty collector with a grudge after me."

No matter that Madame LaChance had agreed their bargain was fulfilled, no way would Grant let her go after she'd humiliated him. Especially not after that threat.

Liam brightened and turned to look at the mansion as well, as if he'd just been offered a gift. Something in Ro relaxed. She might have a shot at escape with these men by her side. All good men. Men she could trust.

"But please, we must hurry," she insisted.

"Saddle up." And then Liam was on his horse's back and leading the party away before anyone could possibly follow.

It was likely the most of an apology she'd get from the surly huntsman. Not that she didn't owe him one herself. She needed to learn to control her temper.

All of that aside, it was good to have everyone she loved in one place. Well, almost everyone. She couldn't wait to see Cosette again.

Olt pulled her up onto his horse behind him, even though Liam had brought her a horse. "Fairweather is fit to be tied that you left him behind."

Ro winced. That meant he was going to try to bite her, first thing. Oh joy. "It wasn't on purpose, I assure you."

They took off after Liam as Claude and Pascal scrambled to catch up.

"What happened?" Liam asked calmly the moment they caught up. "Tell me about this debt collector."

Which meant he was planning the bounty hunter's precise death in a myriad of interesting ways—ways she didn't want to know—if he dared to follow her or harm her in any way.

Ro quickly explained, cramming in as much information

as possible as they made their way to the docks for the crossing back to France.

Olt, even though he was deftly handling the reins with one hand, kept squeezing Ro's arms around his waist, and Ro hugged him to her. They needed to talk, oui, but she never wanted to let him go.

He was her home. He was her safety.

And although she could spend the rest of her days on her own, she didn't want to. She wanted to spend her life with this man who, at a moment's notice, could put their squabble aside and run headlong into danger for her.

"I love you," she whispered and kissed his back. His horse pranced as he mishandled the reins a bit so he could draw her hand to his lips and kiss it in return.

"I love you, too," he whispered, sounding choked up. He paused at the ring, fingering it. "My ring! I mean, your ring. How did you get it back? I thought I'd lost it."

Ro smiled. "Funny story about that . . ."

He wasn't overly thrilled with how the ring had found its way back to her, but when he tried to convince her to have a new ring made, she refused. She wanted this one.

And him.

It had come to her for a reason, and she was going to figure out why that was. Besides, it didn't *seem* evil.

Ro held Olt close all the way to the docks, then he returned the favor for the English Channel crossing, while they planned how to take down the wolves before they spread to other kingdoms. If they hadn't already done so.

It felt good to be her own master again, setting out to right the world of its wrongs.

Well, to greatly reduce its wolf population, anyway.

Black Forest, here I come.

PART IV

"The True History of Little Golden Hood"
La Véritable Histoire du Petit Chaperon d'Or
—Charles Marelles—

It was the little fire-colored hood that had burnt (the wolf's) tongue right down his throat. The little hood, you see, was one of those magic caps that they used to have in former times, in the stories, for making oneself invisible or invulnerable.

C'était le petit chaperon couleur de feu qui lui avait brûlé la langue (du loup) jusqu'au fond du gosier. Le petit chaperon, vous voyez, était un de ces bonnets magiques comme on en avait au temps passé, dans les contes, pour se rendre invisible ou invulnérable.

29

They reached the Black Forest one week later, each second ticking away as if it held an eternity. The forest had exploded with color while she'd been away. Before, a few yellow leaves were interspersed among all the green. Now vibrant red, orange, and yellow decorated every tree that wasn't an evergreen, the colors nearly violent in their display.

They entered the clearing where her grandmère had lived, and Ro had to deliberately turn away from where her grandmère had died.

"All right," Ro announced, riding her own horse now. "We split up and ride for reinforcements."

And Fairweather, whom she'd left stabled at Gustave's.

Liam said, "Shouldn't we stick together?"

Ro gave him a tight smile. "Go in pairs, oui, but get to your destinations before nightfall. Don't be caught out in the open."

She couldn't help her glance at the cabin she and Gustave had been rebuilding. Still completely destroyed, no more progress had been made since Ro had been forced to leave. Which would make sense if Gustave had been wounded.

She just hoped the brownies weren't too upset with her for

being unable to set out treats, even if it hadn't been on purpose.

Ro forced herself to focus on the matter at hand. "Olt, your brothers and sister are directly east. You and Liam should ride there immediately, get there before the sun goes down. We'll meet you there in a day or two."

He reached for her hand. "What about you?"

She gave him a half-smile and squeezed his hand in return. "I ride north for Gustave's cabin. He's close, and I'll pair up with him if he's able to fight."

She looked to Claude and Pascal next. "Go southwest. To the border of the forest. You'll find a series of villages. Stay overnight in each, make our case. See if you can get anyone to join our cause. Tell them they can stop the creatures from reaching their homes, that they can stop the nightly attacks from happening ever again. And then gather whoever will join you at the palace."

"And what about me?" came a familiar voice.

Ro's mouth fell open as a group of women rode out of the forest, to the northwest where Ro's group had just come from, decked out in fighting leathers and brandishing cutlasses in an impressive display of pirate might. Their horses were lathered as if they'd been riding hard.

"What are you doing here?" Ro demanded.

Captain Red gave her a fierce grin. "You didn't think we'd let you run off all by your lonesome to fight impossible-to-kill wolves, did you? Besides, you had a pest on your tail I simply had to get rid of." She sent Liam an appreciative look. "Though had I known you'd have such fine-looking muscle at your side, I'd've come all the sooner."

Olt bristled—apparently telling him the captain wasn't working for Madame LaChance any longer hadn't made a dent in his dislike—but a small smile touched Liam's mouth, and he sent an appreciative look right back as he took in the flamboyant captain from head to toe.

She glowed under his perusal.

While they twinkled at each other, Ro rolled her eyes and turned away. "Then let's get to it. The loups-garous wait for no one."

&

Olt, Liam, Captain Red, and half of the pirate crew rode straight for Olt's brothers at the Prussian palace. Claude and Pascal and the other half of the crew set off to gather villagers. And Ro headed to Gustave's to get an update on the loups-garous and to trade out her horse for Fairweather.

And to make sure Gustave was alive and well, of course.

Olt didn't want to leave her, but he did, and that made Ro love him all the more.

Because if that man still wanted to marry her—and it seemed he did—he'd have to be content with exactly what they were doing right now: working in their strengths to accomplish the right tasks for them, whether together or apart for a time.

Besides, she half-wondered if it was wise to send Olt and Captain Red together, and which would survive the inevitable clash. Oh well. They needed to work out whatever issue was between them.

Liam, of course, had no problem teaming up with Captain Red. Once things went back to normal—if they ever did—Ro was curious if anything would come of it.

Of course, there was the little problem of Captain Red returning to the Caribbean—or roaming the seas as a privateer doing the exact same things a pirate did, just under the queen's banner—but Ro was distracting herself.

Loups-garous first, then she could amuse herself with whatever romance might come of her friends meeting each other. Besides, romance and gossip and matchmaking were better suited for Cosette anyway.

Foliage blazed with gold, umber, and rouge as she rode up to the cabin.

She found a surly Gustave hobbling around inside. "About time you came back," he groused at her first thing.

Ro smiled. "I'm glad to see you, too. Are you well?"

"As well as can be expected with this old thing." He tapped his homemade crutch against his leg, near the wound the bounty hunter had given him. "Those young men of yours find you yet?"

Ro nodded. "Just as I had fulfilled my bargain to Madame LaChance and was leaving Angleterre. It was fortuitous timing."

He grunted and settled himself in his chair. "Got any more debts or bounties upon yer head I should know about?"

"Not that I'm aware of. My debt to Madame LaChance is paid in full, yet I should caution you: the debt collector who came after me isn't too pleased with me. I might have trouble from him outside of any bounties." At his sharp glance, she amended, "Not that I know of any bounties or debts against me. I always pay what I owe. At least, I try to."

Which was why being trussed up and hauled before Madame LaChance had particularly stung. She prided herself on not only paying her debts, but not amassing them in the first place.

"Well if he comes back, I'll give him as good as he gave, bum leg or no," he said with an obstinate look on his face, squinting at the door as if he'd love to tear into the man who'd given him the wound.

She smiled a bit indulgently at him, then wiped away the expression before he could see. "Of course you will. Though I highly suspect Liam may get to him before he gets to me."

Gustave grunted once more. "I knew I liked that lad. Sure you want to marry the other one?"

Ro rolled her eyes and changed the subject. "What is the latest update on the loups-garous? We haven't seen any, but I used the paths Grandmère showed me so we didn't have to camp overnight in the forest. Are they still attacking? Have they gotten outside the forest yet?"

His bushy eyebrows furrowed into one, reminding Ro of a caterpillar. "Attacks have gotten worse. They're ambushing inhabitants, tearing down homesteads, destroying crops, and devouring cattle. I don't know how the villagers in their fortresses are faring, but I can't imagine well. All rebuilding of the palace and surrounding town has come to a halt as soldiers are run ragged trying to get the innocent to safety. Which for now means getting them out of the Black Forest."

He shook his head. "Haven't heard from anyone outside the forest, but as far as I know, the loups-garous are held to the boundaries of the Black Forest. Specifically the area Darya oversaw, as that's where the rift originates. It's possible they thought attacking her would lower the barrier. I don't know what she did, but they can't escape, and for that I'm glad. But it won't be long until they get out."

His eyes homed in on Ro. "People are dying, *Fräulein*. Homes are being destroyed. The forest is weakening. It needs a protectress, someone to strengthen the borders, to hold back the creatures. All those that mean harm, anyway. This realm needs someone to not only take up the axe, but to *choose* to protect it."

It was as Ro feared. She'd been gone too long.

Ro's palms turned clammy, and she wiped them on her trousers. "The axe. I lost it when Grant knocked me out. I don't know where . . ."

Her voice ground to a halt at the grin that blazed forth on Gustave's face, surprising on one so grouchy. Without a word, he heaved himself out of the chair and hobbled past Ro.

At the front door, he started to reach for a pair of axes hung crossed above it, then winced and pulled back. "Care to grab our axes, huntress?"

Ro eagerly took them down, handing Gustave his and

cradling the one that had belonged to her grandmère. "I thought they were lost. How did you come by them?"

He grunted, settled back in his chair, and laid his axe across his knees. "The trees protected them for us. When I woke up after that old badger knocked me out cold, the tree roots gave them to me and told me to keep yours safe. As you can see."

"Merci," she said quietly, blinking away moisture in her eyes. "It means more than I can say to have her axe back."

"Well." He cleared his throat. "How can you rid this forest of wolves without it?"

"How indeed." She gave him a gentle smile.

His eyes slid past her. He jerked his chin toward the door. "Those boys coming back anytime soon?"

"They're gathering reinforcements as we speak. We'll need to stay here overnight, but we can join them at the palace in a day or two. If you're up for traveling, that is."

She went over to the window and peeked past the curtains that matched the ones in her grandmère's cabin. If he'd helped her build it, perhaps she'd helped make his more homey.

It was such a little thing, but Ro felt her grandmère's loss all over again.

Dusk would soon sweep over the land, and a few wolves howled. Ro shivered, even though she was certain these were real wolves, not loups-garous. It was still eerie.

"*Nein, nein, nein,*" Gustave insisted, pulling her from her thoughts. "We cannot wait for reinforcements. I don't know how long the protections will hold. You have to accept your *Großmutter*'s mantle *now*. We have to go after the loups-garous *now*. Bah! Those young men should've come with you instead of running off to all corners of the Black Forest for reinforcements that will do us no good."

Ro looked from the window to the grizzled old man. "But dusk is falling. Wolves are out, and isn't it better to fight loups-garous in daylight? We should wait till tomorrow."

"We can't afford to. Gather your axe, girl. You gotta tell the trees you'll take good care of them so they'll accept you." He heaved himself to his feet and struggled his way to the door.

Ro stood there, heart pounding. If she followed him out that door, chose to become the protectress and wear the mantle her grandmère had handed her, her life would never be the same.

Non, she'd had weeks to deliberate. It was time for action.

Resolved, she followed him into the forest.

A riot of color surrounded her, glorious even in the fading light, leaves giving off a blaze of glory before the trees would shuck them off and slumber the winter away.

He led her to the same tree, the maple that had helped them, then stood back, panting for breath. "Go on. Place your axe against the tree and speak the words."

Ro wanted to ask what words, but she did as he said and gently placed the axe against the trunk, careful not to harm it with the wicked-sharp blade.

After seeing the tree pummel loups-garous out of existence, she didn't want the thing to feel threatened. Or to ask for its help after accidentally wounding it.

The giant maple stretched as if coming awake. Leaves fell to the forest floor in a gentle rushing sound. *Ah, huntress,* it said inside her head. *Are you ready? Have you come to claim your birthright?*

"I have," she said solemnly, not wanting to say the wrong thing. Or babble on.

Because with this swirl of emotions inside her, she feared if she said too much, she'd blather on incoherently for hours. She already had to press down a bubble of hysterical laughter she did *not* want to let loose.

The tree let out a deep, contented sigh. *We have waited long for this moment. Let me ask my sisters if they shall accept you.*

A breeze swept through the trees, one Ro couldn't feel but that sounded like whispering.

She stepped back and waited, and the whisper that went out came back again. Sweat beaded on her forehead. This was taking much longer than she'd expected.

Come, it finally said. *Receive your mantle.*

Ro reached for the tree, and a blue swirl lit up on the trunk's bark, the size of her hand. A matching swirl etched itself into her palm.

Once again, memories flooded her.

This was how she'd returned that pixie to its home. She'd placed her hand upon the tree, and a portal to the fey realm had opened, allowing the trapped pixie to dart through.

She briefly wondered how the pixie was doing, and if she'd get stuck to this tree as she had to the other, then placed her hand on the bark.

And the trunk split down the middle and opened wide.

Ro blinked rapidly, trying to take it in, as the tree waited patiently for her.

Easily removing her hand, thank Dieu, she stepped inside, and the trunk sealed shut behind her.

Ro tried very hard not to gasp and claw her way out, but it was a near thing.

Expecting it to be pitch-dark, she was shocked when she found she stood in a cavernous space, warm, friendly, and dripping in golden sap within a dark-brown circular room of some sort. Light-brown motes danced through the air, gently lighting the space.

A woman-shaped being coalesced from the light motes, swaying gently as the small spheres drifted within her frame.

You are strong. You have been through much. And your trials have fortified you. My sisters have accepted you, huntress. Rise as our protectress, and take your place in our forest.

"Merci beaucoup," Ro whispered, touched that these ancient beings trusted *her* of all people. She only hoped she lived up to the faith they had in her. The faith her grandmère had in her, by passing on her mantle.

Ro cleared her throat. "And how exactly should I do that?"

The being smiled. *You are within my heart, protectress. You must join my heart to yours, and then the mantle will rest upon you.*

Ro's eyes widened. "I—I accept."

With a nod, the woman made of light motes withdrew a wooden yet human-looking heart from her own chest and held it out to Ro.

She couldn't help it. Ro drew back slightly. "I—will not harm you, will I? By taking this from you?"

Her response was gentle and caring. And resonated within Ro's bones, unlike the rustling whisper Ro had heard outside the tree. *You are kind to think of me. And you reinforce my faith in you with your words. No, protectress. This shall not harm me. But it will ensure you can listen to this forest, that you are bound to us, that you can protect us as you should.*

Still, Ro couldn't make herself take it. Grandmère had done this? Willingly? And it was safe?

Only you can make this choice, Daughter of Darya.

With a deep breath, Ro reached out and took the heart from the spirit of the tree. It was heavy, weighty. As in the manner of a difficult decision.

Ro looked up at the tree. "What do I do now?"

She made a gentle shooing motion, as if her movements were leaves dancing in the wind, slow yet elegant. *Place it upon, within, and around your own heart. Box it within.*

Understanding dawned. Just as Darya had said. The heart, the box, the forest. This was what she'd been talking about.

If Ro thought about it, she wouldn't be able to do it. So she took the heart and placed it within her own chest, her hand plunging straight through as if she too were made of spirit.

Ro cried out in surprise, but the moment the tree's heart touched her own, the motes enveloped her heart, sank within, and circled around it, enveloping it completely—as if protecting her.

The heart of the forest was boxing *hers* in, keeping it safe. In exchange for Ro keeping them safe.

And Ro could see it all. She could feel every tree within the Black Forest. She could feel every animal, every bird, every insect.

She knew where they were, what they were doing, and where they were in their life cycle, whether coming into this world or going out.

She could tell which trees were getting ready to slumber the winter away, and which were grumbling about the loups-garous invading their home and the danger of falling asleep while they were overrun.

She knew where the rivers, the valleys, the settlements were. Who was taking care of the forest, replanting what they took to live, and who was stripping it, with no care for the generations to come.

She could feel footsteps of those passing through. Where the secret paths were—her grandmère had only shown her a few. She could traverse from one side of the forest to the other in just a few steps, if need be.

Giant quarries of stone stretched deep underground into elaborate cave systems, and she could feel the life within those as well.

Glowing fey portals dotted the Black Forest, each combined with a specific tree, all entrances the fey used to enter the human realm. She could tell which were robust and healthy, and which were sickly and closing.

She would need to reinforce the healthy ones and close the sickly ones as part of her duties.

And then there were ruptures within the skin-like veil that separated the two realms, tainted with a stench and a rusty-brown color, where loups-garous had torn through again and again. The veil was having trouble healing.

Although she couldn't control the loups-garous, she could smooth away where they'd torn through so they couldn't use that entry again, herding them to the one rip she wanted them to use. She could decide where they broke through next.

And then make sure they never came back.

Yet the same rules she could use to influence the loups-garous didn't apply to the giant creature wreaking havoc on her forest, stomping through it, crushing undergrowth, breaking limbs, and then rushing away to wherever he went, leaving his own gashes the loups-garous could use at any time.

His footprints dotted the forest in a mad pattern, as if he were frantically searching every inch, then tearing down trees in anger when he didn't find what he was looking for.

The trees were afraid of him, shivering in fear after he passed, motionless when he was nearby to escape his notice, and hopefully, his wrath.

And although Grandmère had said she only protected a small part of the forest, the part with the portals to the fey realm, Ro could feel the entire forest, and the paths crossing it from end to end. She could access any part.

It was all hers. Hers to protect.

The scope of it was staggering.

Coming to herself in mere seconds, Ro looked to the tree spirit.

The spirit inclined her head the moment their eyes connected. *Go. Rid our forest of this plague.*

"Gladly." Ro nodded and withdrew. The trunk closed behind her, and the maple settled into a tree once more, the swirl on its bark winking out.

The moment she reached Gustave, he demanded, "What happened? What did she say?"

Gustave reached for her but immediately dropped his hands, and Ro nearly laughed aloud as the image came unbidden of him jumping forward and shaking her for answers.

"Well?" he said. "Did they accept you or didn't they?"

She grinned. "They accepted me." She stared past him. "I have work to do."

The ripped and bloody veil called to her to smooth away its hurt. She wanted it done before the next attack.

Gustave, his eyes glowing with fierce glee, balanced his crutch in one hand and the axe in the other. "What are we waiting for? Let's go take out those loups-garous for good."

Ro took him in. He seemed so frail all of a sudden. "You need to wait for reinforcements, Gustave. I beg of you."

Although Ro couldn't feel footsteps outside of the forest, where the villagers were that Claude and Pascal had set off to recruit, movement scurried all around the Prussian palace, within the forest itself.

Olt and Liam had been successful. They were preparing for battle, many soldiers rallying to their cause. She would join them when she could.

"We dare not wait," Gustave insisted. "You have to send the big one back so the rest can't keep coming through. Come."

Hurrying back to the cabin—well, as much as Gustave was able to, anyway—they gathered provisions and prepared to set out. It wasn't long until Gustave was sweating and leaning heavily on his single crutch, keeping his weight off his wounded leg as much as possible. He would not survive if he tried to fight in his current condition.

As he attempted to hobble down the steps of the cabin, Ro turned to him. "Stay."

His bushy eyebrows raised. "I beg your pardon, *Fräulein*?"

"Stay, please," she repeated. "You are wounded."

Gustave bristled. "That doesn't make me useless in a fight."

"I know." Ro nodded solemnly. "But your time would be

better served riding to the palace, letting them know to meet me in the forest instead of waiting for me there. But tomorrow, when it's daylight. And if you cannot ride, wait for me here. S'il vous plaît."

Gustave blustered and swore and put up a fuss, but Ro didn't budge, and she didn't say another word until he started making his way back inside the cabin.

"I feel so darn useless," he grumbled.

"On the contrary," Ro said firmly. "We wouldn't have had a chance of defeating them if not for you. You have been nothing but useful."

He muttered something along the lines of "Well, isn't that a load of poppycock," but his back straightened, his step lightened, and he returned to his safe and secure cabin without further argument.

Ro smiled and faced the trees.

Now to secure the forest and to find the one and only Wolf King.

*R*o's steps were silent as she delved into the dark wood, following footpaths the new map in her head showed her. The trails let her pass without getting lost, moved debris out from under her feet, and sped her on her way.

Since accepting her role as protectress, she could step in any direction and find one immediately instead of having to search. She had a feeling she could open new paths as well, once she figured out how this worked.

Maybe living in the Black Forest wouldn't be all bad. As long as Olt chose this life with her.

Listening to her senses, she sought the wrongness that followed the loups-garous, the stench they left on the veil, the weak points where they'd torn their way through. And she repaired each tear, working from the edges of the Black Forest to its center.

The loups-garous would come through where she chose, or not at all.

If she closed them all, the Wolf King would simply rip open another entrance, allowing them to follow wherever he led. Not an option.

She took another step, and suddenly, Ro was surrounded by wolves.

Not loups-garous, the grinning, hairless, crouching things that could run on two feet. Non, these were the gray wolves of the Black Forest, and there were so *many* of them.

Moonlight filtered through the trees, dappling coats that blended in perfectly with the surrounding woods.

They'd been lying in wait for her, and the forest teemed with so much vibrant life, she'd missed them completely.

She needed to get better at this and fast.

Ro reached for her axe, wondering how she could possibly defeat or outrun them all.

"Stay your hand, protectress. I would speak with you," said the largest, most muscular wolf with scars across his face.

She stared at the wolf in disbelief. Had it just spoken to her?

"Yes, and the matter I wish to discuss is urgent. Please, stay your hand. My family will not harm you."

Ro relaxed her hands. "I can hear you," she said in a normal voice, even though the wolf's voice had been internal. "Why do you seek me?"

The alpha wolf sat, and as if taking their cue from him, their pack leader—though Ro had never seen a pack this large—the rest sat as well. Perhaps many packs had joined together?

"We were informed you were the one to seek regarding returning our forest to its rightful state."

Ro blinked. "Pardon?"

"You are the one who can rid our forest, our home, of these creatures. So to you we bring our request to do so."

She took in the other wolves, but they sat there, statue still, watching her. It was unnerving. "That is my intent. To rid the forest of these loups-garous in such a way that they can never return."

For just a moment, the wolf panted a doggie grin, ears

perking up, and he wagged his tail, twice, before it lay still. "That is good to hear."

"Why can I hear you?" Ro couldn't help but ask.

"You are our new guardian. That allows you to communicate with us. Yet the tainted wolf's poison flowed through your veins when they bit you. That allows you to track *them*."

Ro gasped as the memory blazed forth. How the loup-garou sank its teeth into her shoulder. How much it hurt. How she'd acted like an animal until the wolf's poison left her system, burned off by moonlight.

She reeled under the remembered pain. She was grateful to have her memories back, oui, but she wished she could tone down how vibrantly each flared to life, as if she were reliving them.

"We have come to pledge ourselves to fight at your side, and to lead you to the great one's den."

A few more tails wagged, then went still.

"Wait, you know where he is?" Ro searched the map that appeared to have taken up residence in her head, but she couldn't sense the Wolf King. At all.

"Certainly. His den stinks of rot and filth and decay, and every time he enters, our home floods with his stench. We want him gone. He slumbers as we speak, gathering strength for his next attack."

That would certainly save Ro time. "Why are you helping me? You must know what I am. Who I am." She swallowed. "I used to . . . hunt your kind. To stop them from hurting my people. During the curse."

Several ears went back at that, but the alpha stared at her, steadily. "Those were the starving times. We did what we had to do to survive, as did you. You were not cruel. You protected your pups, which we can understand. Besides, we asked who could send back the ugly wolves, and we were told it was you."

Huh. Had he asked the Queen of the Fairies? Gustave? The Creator?

Mind whirling, Ro reached up and rubbed her forehead. Several wolves whined or laid their ears back, so she dropped her hand. "My apologies. I did not mean to cause distress."

The lead wolf cocked its head.

"I would love your help," Ro said, "both to find the den and to hunt the loups-garous. But may I have your word that you will not harm any humans? I will have reinforcements soon . . . I hope . . ."

She flicked a glance behind her. She'd known it wouldn't be immediate, but she could use their help. Yet they milled at the palace, making camp, settling down, preparing to set out once Ro joined them. So Gustave hadn't reached them yet.

Not that she doubted him, but she sincerely hoped he'd be able to make the ride and get her message to the palace to bring the fight to the forest.

"He said you would say that. Very well, human. If your kind doesn't hurt mine, we shall not harm yours. Nor allow harm to come to yours, if it is within our power to prevent it."

Ro smiled. "Bon. Merci."

And now she needed to find a way to tell her friends about their newest allies.

She glanced up at the trees, then placed her hand on the nearest one. "Will you tell him? Will you tell Gustave the wolves will aid us in our fight against the loups-garous?"

We will tell him, huntress, the tree whispered.

"Merci."

A breeze rustled away through the branches, and Ro removed her hand and returned her focus to the wolves.

"So will you do it? Will you send the false wolves back?" the wolf leader asked her.

"Absolutely. Believe me, I want nothing more."

The wolf barked some commands, ones Ro couldn't

understand, and wolves scattered, disappearing into the forest as if they'd never been.

At her questioning glance, the alpha explained. "They will drive the loups-garous toward us, then join the fight."

Ro nodded. She was glad to have these vicious attack wolves at her side.

A motley group of about ten wolves joined the alpha, varying in sizes and pelt colors. "Come, human," he said. "I will show you your quarry."

Ro started forward, then once more glanced behind her.

"There is not time to wait for the others, slayer of wolves. We must strike now, when we are least expected. And before he wakes."

Ro winced at the title. She wondered how many other creatures, if they could talk, would have such names for her. She needed to think about that. After this hunt.

Using her new ability, she eyed the few slashes in the veil she hadn't been able to repair. It left the loups-garous more options of where to attack next, but if she didn't stop the Wolf King from bursting through wherever he liked, creating weak points they could rip through, all the repairs in the world would mean nothing.

So she followed the wolves into the trees, hoping Gustave got her message to the soldiers in time.

The loups-garous came out of nowhere.

One moment Ro and the wolves were racing through the trees, intent on their destination, and the next, a pulling, stretching, broiling feeling came from nearby, and then creatures were spilling through the veil like pus from a boil.

The wolves went for throats while Ro swung her axe. While she focused on wounding instead of killing, wolves crushed windpipes and tore out throats, leaving carnage in their wake. Yet somehow the loups-garous did not regenerate when wolves killed them. Lucky wolves.

Ro struggled with how pointless it felt to fight without being able to end the loups-garous, trying not to be envious that the wolves could.

Until she slammed a loup-garou into a tree. And it stuck fast. Just as it had happened right before she'd been kidnapped.

Suddenly, it all made sense.

The moment the loup-garou hit the tree, sap covered the wolf in an oozing cocoon that Ro had mere moments to utilize before it tore itself free.

She reached out and gathered up a handful of the invisible veil. It was smooth and soft and silky, but the moment she started to pull, to stretch it, it turned skin-like and clearish opaque in her hands.

She wanted to drop it and jerk away—the change in texture made her own skin crawl—but somehow she knew she couldn't do that. So she held on, stretched it beyond what skin should, and wrapped it securely around the not-wolf.

Once it covered the entire creature, the loup-garou was violently ripped from the tree and sucked into the veil with a squelch that reminded Ro of maggots and carcasses and being sucked into a bog, of all things.

It was a good thing she wasn't more squeamish. Because it was all she could do not to heave her last meal all over the ground.

"Drive them against the trees!" she called out to the wolves. They did, and soon loups-garous were stuck and struggling against their sticky bonds.

She immediately went to work on the next loup-garou. But when she tried to stretch the veil as she had before, it wouldn't budge. Hard, thick, firm—she had to move to another section that was pliable.

She only tore the skin-like veil once, just the smallest bit, and something she couldn't even describe stared back at her. Ro couldn't decide if the creature with black eyes was hungry or merely curious, but she let the veil go with a snap, and it sealed itself.

The next loup-garou writhed to get away, so she gathered up another section of the veil and carefully stretched it over the unnatural wolf, careful not to tear it.

All things Ro somehow knew from impressions she got while touching it, but she couldn't have explained it to anyone if asked. Yet she leaned into her instincts and reveled at how naturally it came to her.

So the pack of wolves fought at her back to wipe out creatures while she got rid of loups-garous one by one in such a way that they could not come back and bring more.

Amazing how everything she did just created more questions.

But for the first time, she was excited to discover how her powers worked and leaned into it with all her might.

They were doing so well, working together, when the hair on Ro's nape stood on end, and a waft of the vilest scent swept past her.

Little Red Hood, won't you come face me? I would have words with you.

Ro turned toward the whisper-soft voice that felt like it had teeth.

Blast. That meant the creature was awake.

Instantly, the wolf pack leader was at her side. "Go. We will remain here and fight at your back. Keep them from following you."

Still, she hesitated. There were so many loups-garous.

"You let us worry about the unnatural wolves. You worry about that . . . that *foul beast*." He growled the words, and Ro had a feeling that if he could've sunk his teeth in the Wolf King's throat right then and there, he would have.

"D'accord. I will." She looked from him to his pack and back. "Watch yourselves."

And without another word, she took off after the voice, hoping she wasn't making a terrible decision.

❧

The voice taunted her as it led her deeper into the woods.

Little Red Hood, Little Red Hood. This way, Little Red Hood.

Talk about creepy. Ro's flesh crawled as the voice echoed all around her, ever leading her on, meandering toward where it wanted her to go. Or perhaps trying to get her lost.

Every time it tried to misdirect her, she felt a fiery tug in her bloodstream, telling her the right way to go. Also there was the stench. The stronger it wafted toward her, the more certain she was that she was going in the right direction.

Each time she could not be turned from her path, the eerie voice growled before it started whispering once more.

Suddenly, Ro stopped. Something told her if she took one more step, there was no going back. She would face the wolf.

And if she faced him, she would end him or die trying.

There was no alternative to how her story would play out.

Taking a deep breath, she pressed forward, and there he was.

The wolf was gigantic. Hulking. Corded with muscle. Crouched, but still looking down at her from above.

Although he was hidden in shadow, her eyesight blazed and lit up the surrounding wood as if he sat in a patch of daylight.

Its eyes glowed golden, and Ro couldn't help swallowing as she tightened her grip on the axe. The thrill of the hunt raced through her. A chill chased on the heels of adrenaline, and she valiantly attempted not to shiver. The last thing she wanted to show this beast was any hint of weakness.

Its muscles were coiled taut, ready to spring. Ro had to time her counterattack perfectly. She couldn't miss.

But instead of springing at her, the wolf started to circle her, eyeing her from all sides. As she faced off with the wolf, Ro matched his prowling steps, not allowing the creature any closer and *especially* not letting him circle around to her back.

She didn't dare lower her axe. It could be upon her before she'd even blinked, and she'd already seen what it had done to her grandmère.

"Clever huntress," the wolf purred. "Able to find me when I do not wish to be found. However did you manage that?"

"Because I know who you are," Ro said.

A laugh rumbled out of his chest and shook her bones. "Who, pray tell, do you think I am? Name me if you dare."

"You are the Wolf King."

"The Wolf King?" The giant creature wheezed out a laugh. "I haven't heard that name in an age. Here's a name perhaps you will recognize: some call me the Beast of Gévaudan."

Ro blinked. "They killed you."

The wolf snarled its grin. "That's what they like to think, isn't it? Non, they killed a wolf, but it wasn't me." He sniffed. "Although he hunted beside me, a lesser creature could not compare to one such as I."

She tried not to give away how terrifying that thought was, but something must've changed—the creature scented the air as if savoring her fear—because her nonreaction pleased the great wolf immensely.

And why shouldn't it? La Bête du Gévaudan had killed over one hundred peasants over the span of three years, making it the single most dangerous wolf in all of France. It was directly because of this creature that Gautier had hired huntsmen to deal with France's wolf problem, created by the curse and the starvation it brought.

At some point, the wolf had picked up a friend, a second wolf, and they'd both killed with abandon and in the most gruesome way possible.

If this creature was who he said he was . . . well. Ro didn't stand a chance.

She shook out her shoulders. Of course, many fairy-tale monsters had told her the same throughout her time as a huntress. They hadn't a say in her story's end, either. Nor would this monster.

"You could say I'm the reason you exist," the creature continued. "There was no need for so many hunters before me."

Oh no. Ro was *not* letting this creature claim her skill as his design. "How dare you. You—you killed over one hundred people!"

"More like five hundred. You mortals are such tasty morsels, after all. More of an appetizer, really."

Fear struck Ro's heart. So she compensated by glaring even more fiercely at the monster.

"And if you've heard of me, then you've heard of my wife, Jade."

Ro's mind scrambled, and it settled upon a fairy tale she'd read once upon a time. The Wolf King's wife, Jade, had been snatched from his side after he'd been placed under an enchanted sleep. Thousands of years ago.

And he'd been searching for her ever since.

"Now I will ask you this, puny huntress, and you will answer me. *Where is my wife?*"

"I don't know!" she shouted back. "I've never met her, never heard of her outside of fairy tales. As far as I know, she isn't here. You're looking in the wrong place. Besides, that doesn't excuse *murder*."

He studied her as he paced, his eyes roiling with fury, until a cool mask slid over his massive wolfish face. "If you will not help me, I have no choice."

"There is always a choice," Ro said. "Leave my realm, take your loups-garous with you, and leave us be."

His chuckle rumbled away into the forest, a physical thing. "So be it. Now, Little Red Hood," the beast said, rising from its crouch to tower overhead on its hind legs. The tips of its ears reached the top of the trees. "It's time I gobble you all up."

Ro strangled the handle of her axe and sent him a LeFèvre-worthy scowl. "I don't think so."

He laughed, the sound delighted. "A worthy foe, huntress. How long has it been since I've met with such a one? Perhaps you shall be a challenge. Time will tell, won't it?"

And he opened his monstrous mouth, jagged teeth gleaming and dripping with saliva, and lunged at her.

Ro spun, grasped the veil, and swung her axe, almost in the same movement. The veil parted for the enchanted axe as if trying to get away, and she pulled with all her might.

The giant black wolf tried to reverse, but it was airborne and couldn't change direction, and Ro had timed it perfectly. Even as she wrapped part of the veil around her body, protecting herself from its outstretched claws, he went sailing right past her, his momentum carrying him through the veil.

Before she stepped through after the Wolf King, Ro glanced behind her. Should she wait? For the others? She had to admit she'd love to have pirates, villagers, and Olt's family's soldiers at her back.

You do not have time to wait on your companions, huntress, the closest tree urged. *You must go after him. Quickly. Before he escapes and returns with an army of his creatures. One too innumerable to defeat.*

Ro nodded decisively and faced the torn veil. Taking a deep breath, she stepped through and let the veil seal itself behind her.

It was time to slay this wolf.

Ro stepped into a realm she'd only dreamed of. Well, generally when she was reading books, and specifically when she was reading fairy tales.

There was no sun, but a golden glow lit everything, somewhat similar to sunlight yet coming from all angles, with no discernible source.

Colors were vibrant, and the way the forest shifted slightly around her, yet not when she was looking directly at the trees or bushes or scrub, reminded her of a child's finger painting.

It also made her think something was watching her, something other than the beast she hunted. That and the prickling over her skin and at the back of her neck.

Yet she somehow knew that she was not in the Realm of the Fey, but that the beast had led her to another place altogether.

It almost felt like it half resembled her realm and half resembled the fey realm—not that she'd ever been to the fey realm, not to her knowledge—which made her think she was at an in-between state somewhere.

She kept an eye on the shifting shadows that stilled when

she gazed directly at them, yet moved the moment she looked away, as she searched for the wolf's trail.

There wasn't one. Not a crushed blade of grass, which was more turquoise than green, not a bent leaf, which was the golden yellow and vibrant pink of sunset, not a snapped twig, which was a metallic sheen of gold or silver or copper.

Almost as if he'd never passed through at all.

"Please," she whispered, hoping someone who might be able to help would hear her. "He means harm to my realm as well as yours. I must find him."

A chittering rushed through the wood, a breeze scraping metal branches against each other, and although Ro could only hear it if she tricked herself into not paying attention, it sounded very much like an argument.

Suddenly, a ball of light burst from the trees, and Ro staggered back a few steps.

The glowing object came to a stop directly in front of her face, and as Ro squinted against the light, a form became visible.

About the length of her forearm, wearing mid-calf-length trousers made of turquoise grass and a golden-yellow vest made of leaves, a male pixie revealed itself to her, grinning madly.

Ro blinked rapidly as a jolt of recognition swept her. She'd met this fey before . . .

Her expression must've revealed her thoughts, for the pixie made a high-pitched squeak and a firecracker-bursting motion, as if to say, "Ta-da!"

"I know you, don't I?" Ro kept her voice low. One, out of respect for the quiet wood, and two, in case the wolf was nearby. She smiled. "I'm glad you're home and doing well."

The pixie flew around her head in a dizzying swirl, and Ro sincerely hoped the afterimage wouldn't keep her from seeing the wolf if it chose to attack right then.

"Will you lead me to him?" she asked quietly. "I'm afraid I cannot let him go, not if I want to protect my people."

He squeaked, nodded furiously, and took off into the forest with a blaze of light that resembled a shooting star.

Ro hurried after him, ignoring the shifting shadows that followed them both, keeping her eyes on that light, though it shouldn't have been possible with how fast the fey traveled.

The pixie led her right up to a clearing, flung his arms around her neck in a brief squeeze, then was gone.

A waft of death and decay hit her full in the face, and Ro covered her nose and tried not to gag. It was as if she'd stumbled upon a burial site, only the bodies were exposed and at just the right level of ripeness to bring her to her knees.

Nothing grew past the clearing, but a mound of dirt and a yawning opening in the base of the hill spoke to a cavern underneath. Trees and scrub and bushes grew on the other side, but not anywhere near the cavern.

Once again, Ro wondered if the trees had died, been cleared, or had taken a giant step back.

It was from this opening that the stench of decay wafted.

Every instinct screamed, "Do not go in there!" but this was where her quarry lay. If she wanted to stop the Wolf King from killing, she had no other option.

The Black Forest wolves fought the loups-garous on the other side of the veil. Any reinforcements would be on the other side as well.

No one was coming to help her here. She was on her own.

A prayer in her heart, fingers clutching her axe, Ro steeled herself and stepped into the clearing.

At the entrance to the cave, Ro had to rip a length off her tunic and tie it around her nose to breathe past the stench that was so thick in the air, it felt like a physical fog.

Bones littered the cavern floor, many still with rotting meat on them. Unsurprising that it smelled so bad, but very surprising that so much meat was wasted. Normal wolves stripped the bones clean and sometimes ate out the marrow.

They also didn't build a den atop the carcasses. Yet this beast had made a place to sleep right in the midst of the filth and rot. No wonder he smelled so horrible.

But unlike normal wolf dens, where skeletons of small woodland animals were left outside for ravens and crows, these skeletons belonged to creatures Ro had never seen before. She could only assume they were fey, or from those other realms the wolf had spoken of.

But worst of all? Human remains were scattered among the other carcasses, most with clothing or flesh still attached, all with screaming faces as if they'd died a slow, horrible, painful death.

Ro strangled the handle of her axe as she fought her fury. If she let anger overtake her, she'd make mistakes. And that could leave an opening for the wolf to add her to its gruesome collection.

She would not let that happen.

Staying along the perimeter, where the bones were fewer in number, Ro kept her back to the cavern wall and skirted deeper inside, hunting the wolf. He would not take her by surprise, and he would not be leaving this realm to hurt others, not ever again.

"Ah, Little Red Hood. You have chased me all the way to my den. How fortuitous for us both."

His voice echoed so that Ro could not tell from where it came. She remained silent.

"I smell you, Little Hood. Try as you might, you cannot pretend your presence away."

That was not Ro's intent, but nor would she speak and give the wolf her exact location. She was in his territory, and she needed every advantage.

"Very well. You remain stubborn and silent. You must know I only meant to find her. That I never meant any harm. Not to any who do not deserve it, that is. But when I am on the hunt, I am not always . . . myself."

Ro wanted to snort. Didn't mean any harm? Could he then explain the deaths that followed in his wake? The innocent people—and possibly, creatures—that filled this cave of horrors with grimaces on their faces?

She rounded an outcropping of stone, where the bones next to her nearly came to her waist. Farther in, they would cover her head. And the cave went deeper still.

She couldn't fathom the sheer number of creatures he'd killed. So why hadn't her grandmère's remains been placed among them? Was that why the wolf had returned, yet it hadn't seen them because Ro had spread her mère's cape over them both?

Ro's heart filled with thanks to her mère, grandmère, and Creator that the cape worked as intended.

It must be the reason the wolf hadn't found her yet.

She carefully made her way among the bones, back to the wall, completely silent, her huntress skills enhanced nearly tenfold in this realm that heightened fey magic. Steps light, she was able to skirt bones at the edges without their shifting, without their announcing her presence. As if she weighed nothing.

She could get used to this.

"Little Hood, Little Hood, won't you come out and play?"

Although the voice still sent chills down her spine, a note of despair urged her to pay attention. She rounded yet another jagged outcropping and came upon him.

Only, it wasn't the wolf. A man stood there, his back glistening with sweat, his torn, filthy, threadbare breeches speaking of better days, his feet bare and covered with the filth surrounding him. Over his arms lay a wolf pelt, shaggy, filthy, and enormous.

Ro froze and steadied her breathing.

Where was the wolf? Who was this man?

"I feel you watching me, Little Red Hood," came the voice. "Shall you come out and play? A delightful morsel such as yourself will make a perfect, bite-size meal. And your bones, oh, your bones. A glorious trophy to add to my collection."

Ro stiffened. She was not going to be this monster's *meal*. Or a part of his bone collection.

If only one of them left this cave alive, it would not be him.

His head came up, and he sniffed, swiveling his neck from side to side. "Little Red Hood . . ."

Oh, yes. The man was definitely speaking, but in the creature's voice.

Ro's mind searched through the lore she'd gathered on the loups-garous. The lore she'd spoken of to Gustave. Unlike those fey beasties, this creature must wear the pelt to become a wolf, rare and powerful magic that had been lost to the annals of time. Ancient magic.

Which meant, if her lore was correct, that only one creature could wield such magic.

A fairy-tale creature stood before her, one she'd read about, supposedly thousands of years old. He carried many names: the Erlking, the Elf King, the Goblin King, the Wolf King, and now, apparently, the Beast of Gévaudan. And probably many more titles that had been lost to time.

If he put that pelt back on his shoulders . . . well. In this realm, Ro's magic was stronger, since she was closer to the source of her magic, but so was his.

To defeat him, she had to destroy that pelt.

As she readied herself to attack, a thought struck her. He had only to remove her cape to ensure she could never defeat him. So they both would be guarding their raiment while trying to get it away from the other. Magnifique.

Ro deliberately turned her mind to the hindrance of the bones. Here, near the perimeter, her steps were light, the bones not as deep. There, she would sink amid a shower of bone, not only announcing her presence but trapping her as well. How to get past them?

"Ask for my help, in return for services rendered," came a disembodied, whisper-thin voice.

"Um, can you help me?" Ro said under her breath.

The Beast of Gévaudan came alert at her voice.

As if in response to her query, her hands chilled. "My gift to you," the voice whispered as it echoed away.

The wolf-man's head came up, and he snarled, "You cannot interfere!"

The cave shook at his shouted words, and bones rattled and squished together, shifting where they lay. Ro put out one hand to steady herself, and a thin layer of ice spread over the cave wall and the bones closest to her.

She took a tentative step forward, the thin sheet held, and the bones underneath didn't shift.

Yet the shaking cavern had done what Ro couldn't do herself. The sounds of falling bone echoed and grew louder, creating even more chaos.

She shifted the axe to her other hand for the next step, and another sheet of ice formed under her foot. A gift from none other than the Fairy Queen, perhaps in repayment for Ro freeing her granddaughter and Cosette's daughter, Allura Aurore, from the sleeping curse.

Fey bargains were tricky. The way this one was worded, though, perhaps Ro wouldn't be indebted to the Queen of the Fairies when this was over?

Regardless, Ro would take it.

She made her way to the wolf on silent footsteps, even as he clutched his pelt and swiveled his head madly, trying to parse her scent from the stench billowing up from the settling bone piles.

Ro was one step away from snatching his wolf pelt from

his hands when he spun to face her. Golden eyes widened as she lunged for his pelt.

He whipped it away from her just in time and swirled it around his shoulders. The moment he pulled the wolf head over his own, he transformed to the crackling of his own bones into a giant wolf, one that filled the cave and towered over Ro.

She dove out of the way as his paw came crashing down. His sharp claws just barely missed snagging her red cloak and sweeping it from her shoulders.

Before she could gain her feet, he swept her aside as if she were a bug, and Ro crashed into the wall before tumbling into the bone pit. Bones buried her as she sank into their midst. The wolf came after her, digging just shy of where she'd fallen.

Ro lay there, gasping for breath, desperate for the air that had been driven from her lungs. After what felt like an eternity, her lungs filled, and she almost cried in relief.

Her face covering was gone, and the rot was overpowering. But she gathered the Fairy Queen's gift into her palms, then released it, blasting the wolf with a shower of icicle-covered bone.

He flew back, and Ro climbed out of the pit on frozen stairs that were somehow not slippery, thank Dieu. Must've been part of the Fairy Queen's gift.

Before he could pick himself up, Ro ran at him, axe held high and ready for the killing blow.

Well, to separate the wolf pelt from his shoulders. *Then* she could think about a killing blow.

She aimed for his shoulder and sank her axe deep into flesh, angling it so that she sliced fur from muscle.

With a roar, the monster swept out his arm, and although Ro dodged, he clipped her shoulder and sent her spinning away. She climbed to her feet with difficulty, bones shifting underfoot. She froze them in place.

She ran at the wolf and was deeply satisfied to see the pelt flapping at his shoulder, flesh peeking out from below. He tried to smooth it into place, but it wouldn't reattach.

She just needed to sever the other side. Then the man would be revealed once more and the pelt could be taken.

And make no mistake, Ro would take it.

The Wolf King hunched down on all fours, angling away to protect the exposed shoulder, readying himself to meet Ro's advance.

She swung her axe at his other shoulder.

He blocked her swing. Grabbed the axe. And tried to shake her off.

She held on, raised her feet, and kicked him in the chest.

Snapping his teeth, he bit into her cape and tried to tear it from her shoulders. With a gurgle and a hiss, a boiling sound came from the wolf, and he did three things at once: cried out, jerked his massive head back, and heaved Ro away from him.

As Ro fell back, smoke broiled out of the wolf's snout, and he pawed at his nose and tried to spit the jagged pieces of Ro's cape out of his mouth.

Great. She'd have to repair it again.

Jumping to her feet, she immediately flew at him.

Ro caught a glimpse of blistered skin on his muzzle and tongue right before she attacked.

She struck again and again, but he protected his shoulder and clawed at her, driving her back or batting her aside. Ro tried to use a sheet of ice on the wolf, but apparently part of not interfering included Ro not using the ice directly against the wolf. Just on the bones.

So she coated bones with it, everywhere, and where Ro had sure footing, the wolf slipped and slid and missed her more often than his giant paws connected.

But she couldn't get close enough to cut away the rest of the pelt.

At least he was flinching away from her cloak and no longer trying to tear it from her shoulders, so there was that.

Fire lashed across her leg as his giant claw caught her, but here, so close to the fey realm, the wound gaped for only a moment before sealing itself shut.

Ro grinned and bit into him with her axe, slicing at every opportunity.

He roared in frustration. "Where is she? I can smell her!"

His voice came out slightly garbled, but it only added to the terror of his deep voice.

"Who?" Ro asked, dodging another swipe.

"My wife!" he bellowed. "She passed through your realm. And in this century!"

Overcome with rage, he flung himself at Ro, and she rolled under his lunge just in time.

"I don't know what you're talking about," she shouted. "Who is she? Your wife. What does she look like? How do we find her? And how do I know she isn't running *from* you?"

At this, the great wolf let out a bellow that shook the cave and swiped claws at her that would've taken off her head if she hadn't tucked herself into a crevice just in time.

As it was, she had to wiggle out the other side—thank Dieu there was another side—since he'd collapsed the way she'd gotten in.

"You won't distract me! I will find her, and I will bring her home!"

There was no reasoning with this beast.

Whoever he was, whoever his wife was, Ro's obligation and loyalty was to her people. And he was killing them and eating them.

She had to bring him down.

To stop him from ever returning to her world.

Whatever kept him from hurting her people. Permanently.

As they exchanged blows, Ro was almost despairing of finding an opening when she struck out with her axe like lightning and the wolf jumped back and slammed into the cave wall.

The entire cavern rattled, and Ro's eyes caught and held on a stalactite overhead. Most were stunted, as if they'd been broken off by the giant wolf's passing, but this one in a circular opening far above was long, sharp, and jagged.

The Wolf King launched himself off the wall, aiming for her, and instead of rolling away, Ro stood firm.

Timing it so he would be directly below when the stalactite fell, she sent a blast of ice shards over both their heads.

Expecting it to strike him, the wolf flinched, then barked a laugh. "You missed."

Ro grinned in response.

He cocked his head, reminding her so much of the village dogs that ran wild, for a moment he almost wasn't an enemy.

But then the stalactite fell, the wolf's cry pierced the air, and Ro was standing over him, slicing into the pelt's other shoulder. The pelt separated from the creature's skin, a snarling wolf head appeared above the man's, and Ro threw it back, separating it from him.

Blood poured from a wound in the man's side, but his body had shrunk so much, his ribs had torn themselves free from the jagged shard pinning him to the ground.

Ro raised her axe for the killing blow.

"Wait." The wolf-man raised a feeble hand, chest heaving, gasping for breath, blood pooling around him and dripping down into the bones. His mouth was swollen and blistered, almost as if her cape had . . . burned him. And it wasn't healing. "You cannot kill me. I will only regenerate anew and return with even more fire in my heart. Your people will not survive."

And Dieu help her, she didn't bring the axe down upon his head.

Instead, she left herself wide open to a swipe of his wicked claws that still sprouted from his fingertips, even in this form, and gave in to her curiosity.

"Why shouldn't I?" she demanded.

"My wife," the wolf said weakly. "I'm just looking for my wife. Someone stole her. I think—I thought—she'd been taken to your realm. But for her scent, I can find no trace of her."

Ro sucked in a breath. That's right. In the story she'd read, the Wolf King's wife was stolen while he slept, and he roamed the worlds searching for her.

But could such a fairy tale be true?

"Why? Why should I show you mercy when you've shown no mercy yourself?" She leaned close and spit in his face with the force of her words. "When you killed my *grandmère*."

Non, she was a fool for listening to him. He didn't deserve to live. She reset her swing and started to bring her axe down, but he spoke again. And like a fool, she listened.

"You must banish me. For a thousand years." He took a gasping, wheezing breath every few words. "Only then will I have time to bank my rage and start my search anew, with a rational mind, instead of through a blaze of anger."

"Why are you telling me this?" Ro demanded. Was it a distraction? Was he readying himself to spill her entrails and stalling so she didn't see it coming?

Although the shaggy man before her still somewhat resembled a wolf, with long sideburns, a scruffy beard, and stringy, scraggly hair, he smiled in a self-deprecating way, canines sharp and pointed and much longer than his other teeth.

"Because, my dear huntress, you have bested me. I would hate to see your hard work go to waste."

"So you yield?"

"Aye. I yield."

Ro lowered her weapon and stepped back, giving herself plenty of room should he try anything, staying out of range of the wicked claws tipping his human-length fingers.

Well, if the human in question was a giant, hulking beast of a man who looked like one of the false gods of the ancients who had come to earth in human form.

He nodded to the pelt Ro had separated from his shoulders. "My rationale returns with the removal of the pelt. I am more myself. Though, not as much lately. And the rules of combat state that you have won. But I assure you, it will be no victory if you kill me in this realm only for me to return with my beast raging, in full control."

Dieu help her, Ro believed him. "I don't understand. Why would you tell me this? Where is the deception?"

He smiled. "Ah, huntress. You remind me of my Jade. All fierceness and determination. Though you wear yours quietly, and she blazes like the sun. Although you may believe otherwise, I truly wish to find her. I do not wish to be imprisoned for a thousand years, true, but it will give me a chance to find her." His slight smile disappeared. "Else I will burn all the worlds in my quest to free her from her captors."

Once again, Ro believed him. Wholeheartedly, with all her might, believed this creature before her would burn her world —every world—in his quest to find and free his wife.

He stared at her with hopeless, ancient eyes. "I will go, I will take my underlings with me, but do not banish me from the realm for good. Allow me to return one day, to search for my wife once more. Let me come back in a thousand years."

The thing that troubled her most about that was she wouldn't be here then if he decided once more to destroy huge swaths of forest and people.

Ro considered. "Only if you promise to do no harm. Well, to anyone not directly involved with capturing your wife, that is." She understood more than most how important it was to ensure that those who hurt others could no longer do so. "And to never bring your loups-garous with you when you return."

"I give you my word."

The words coalesced into a fey contract with a snap,

binding him to his promise, to her terms. Um, maybe she shouldn't have been quite so hasty? Or perhaps should've thought through her words a bit more?

It looked like she no longer had a choice. They had made a fey bargain, and it was ironclad.

Resigned, she gave him a swift, single nod. "All right. I will hold you to your word. How do I go about this? How do I bind you?"

He grinned, and now the action was sharp with a hint of cunning. "Ah, huntress. I'm afraid if I tell you that, it will not work."

"Let me guess. Because you'll give yourself a way to get free?"

"Aye." His grin turned fierce. "My altruism only runs so deep."

All right. She could do this. She simply needed to banish him . . . somewhere, preferably away from her realm. And the fey realm, since he could access hers through it. For a thousand years. Somehow.

Nothing in her training had prepared her for this.

Help. I need help, she prayed silently to the Creator.

Suddenly, a presence stood at her elbow. "You found him."

Ro jumped a kilomètre, spinning on the voice that had startled her. "Grandmère?"

The old woman—younger somehow, as if the old woman were an overlay covering a much younger, and spritelier, version of herself—snapped, "Keep your eye on him, girl!"

Ro spun back to the Wolf King and held out her axe, head reeling. What was her grandmère doing here? *How* was she here?

Ro said, "I don't understand. How—?"

"You asked for help from the Creator, didn't you?" the old-but-somehow-young woman demanded. "What, you think your prayers just fly up to the heavens and bounce off the clouds, never to be heard nor answered?"

That was exactly what Ro thought. But she didn't wish to voice that aloud.

Apparently she was still terrified of her grandmère.

Darya sniffed. "Well. I see."

The Wolf King hadn't moved, but his attention had sharpened on the old woman, and he held perfectly still, very much looking like he was on the cusp of changing his mind about being banished.

"Why would He answer so swiftly? And send you, no less." At the look Darya shot her, Ro raised her hands and splayed her fingers, still holding the axe. "Not that I mind! I'm grateful. This simply hasn't been my experience."

"The creatures in this realm allow the Creator to work here, more so than others." She eyed Ro. "You do realize you are responsible for how much the Creator moves and works within your own realm, oui?"

Ro frowned. "I've never heard such a thing."

"It's true. He uses humans as His hands and feet, you know. Quite literally. Now, what are we doing with that one?" Darya jabbed a finger at the Wolf King, and he shrank back, just a twitch, from the old protectress glowering his way.

The one he'd brutally killed.

Ro blew out a huff of air. "I don't know. I was getting ready to land the killing blow, but he said it would be better to banish him."

Darya shot her a look. "And you believed him?"

Ro took a moment to answer. "I believe he wants to find his wife. I believe he is more rational without his wolf pelt. Oui, his words rang with truth. Was I wrong?"

Disgruntled, her grandmère blustered a moment. "Non, you weren't wrong." She sent her granddaughter a sharp look. "Yet you weren't about to trust him to tell you how to do it, were you?"

Ro spared a smirk for her grandmère. "Of course not. But nor did I know how to do as he asked."

Darya relaxed at that.

Although softer around the edges, truly, Grandmère was the same as Ro remembered, and it did much to put her at ease. Though she was still having trouble believing the Creator had answered so swiftly, and had used her grandmère, no less.

Her grandmère who was dead.

Dreams were one thing, but this . . . it boggled the mind.

Darya grunted and eyed the wolf. "It's been a long time since I've done a banishing."

Ro's eyes widened. "But you've done this before?"

"Aye. Only a handful in my time, but I imagine it's similar."

Ro quickly added details. "He said it needed to be a thousand years. He said something about being imprisoned. And he said something about doing it in such a way that he kept his mind instead of being a raging wolf and burning all the worlds."

Darya's eyebrows climbed her forehead higher with every word until they were nearly swallowed by her hairline. She looked at the wolf in disbelief. "You told her all that?"

He barely moved his mouth to reply, not daring to twitch in the protectress's presence. "Aye. I wish to find my wife. My Jade."

Darya sniffed. "Well, she isn't in *this* realm, nor the human realm, I can tell you that."

"I know." He dipped his head. "But I meant what I said. I only wish to find her. To punish her captors. I mean no harm to anyone innocent, but I can no longer control my wolf."

"Which is why I was trying to put you out of your misery, you old coot," Darya said. "It's far past time there was a new Wolf King. By thousands of years."

"I know," he said quietly. "But I will not give up my pursuit of her, nor my crown, until I find her. You must chain me. Only then will I learn to control my wolf again. Only then will I be free to search for her, one last time."

Ro was watching her grandmère carefully. Did Darya believe him? Did he speak truth?

After staring at him for the longest time, Darya nodded once, decisively. "Very well. I shall banish you, though you deserve your crown wrested from your head."

"I cannot disagree with you," he said quietly.

As if tasting something sour, Darya's face puckered, and she jerked her head at Ro. "Come. Learn how this is done. My banishing days are over, but yours have just begun."

Ro eased closer.

"And put away your axe. You won't need it for what we're about to do."

Ro highly disagreed, but she slid it away so both her hands were free.

"Now," said Darya, "this is how you create chains out of words."

32

The wolf hung between two pillars, completely wrapped in translucent, iridescent chains. No part of him touched the floor, ceiling, or the pillars themselves, which was only possible because he wasn't in his wolf form.

His pelt was wrapped in its own prison of chains, yet a portion just barely touched the Wolf King's foot.

Ro and her grandmère had argued long and hard over that. Ro argued that if they weren't touching, he wouldn't be able to control the beast when the chains disintegrated in a thousand years. Darya insisted he'd escape faster with access to his pelt.

In the end, the pelt touched the wolf, and the wolf was left hanging by himself in his den.

Grandmère also helped her bring down a layer of stone from the ceiling to cover the bones and bury them.

They backed out, speaking in tandem, webbing the entire place with impassable netting.

No one was getting in, and the wolf would have a harder time getting out once he was released. Which hopefully wouldn't be for a very long time.

They sealed the cavern with something that looked like

molten lava, and after their voices fell silent and the red glow of the molten rock had cooled, Ro stood there, staring pensively at the hidden cave.

"What is it?" Darya asked.

"I feel like I should do more," said Ro. "I hate this. I should've lifted his head from his shoulders. Ended this. Instead I left a problem for someone else well past my time. Created a problem I could've ended here and now."

Every part of her that had trained as a huntress rebelled against what she'd done. Why had she let him talk her into binding him? And why on earth had Ro listened? Not only listened, but insisted he was right?

Had she just made the worst mistake of her career as a huntress?

Darya patted her shoulder. "As long as you train up future generations right, they'll be ready."

Ro blinked. "Future generations? But I can't—"

"Hush now. All will be as it should be. In time." And with that, her grandmère turned and started to walk away.

"Wait. Where are you going?"

Darya smiled over her shoulder, and her age fell away, revealing how she looked now. Young, spritely, mischievous. "You'll see one day, my darling girl. Until that day, know I'm proud of you. Your mère is proud of you. And we both miss you very much."

Ro gasped and stepped forward. "Wait!"

But Darya was already gone. And the clearing seemed to dim without her grandmère's presence.

Although she wanted to stay, wanted to chase after Grandmère and demand answers, Ro turned and made her way back to her own forest—and the wolves who'd fought at her side.

Blinking back tears the whole way.

The helpful pixie once again darted out of the brush and led her to where she could enter her forest. He gave her another quick hug around her neck, painfully tight, before darting off to his friends, who yet again scolded him for helping a human.

Ro entered her woods to snarls, snapping teeth, and howls that filled her skin with ice. Ro stopped. What were they doing here? Shouldn't the loups-garous have been forced to leave once she bound their master?

Ro didn't have time to dwell on it. In the moment she'd stood there frozen, a wolf was flung against a tree and lay still at its base, even as a team of wolves brought down a loup-garou and tore out its throat.

"Arrête!" She infused power in the word, and the fighting stopped, all eyes on her. "Your master has been defeated. Leave! Now."

The loups-garous curled lips back from monstrous teeth and ran at her as one, forgetting entirely the wolves at their backs. Which the wolves most definitely took advantage of as they lessened their numbers.

Ro raised her axe and ran to meet the loups-garous.

She should've been exhausted, but every step within her woods renewed her and filled her with strength, readying her to keep fighting, well past what she should've endured.

She swung her axe, separating a loup-garou's head from its shoulders. It rolled, landed, and didn't disappear. It didn't melt back through the veil, and it didn't return to the Black Forest with more creatures at its side.

Hope filled her as she met the next attack and divested the loup-garou from its life. It also stayed dead.

The remaining wolves howled a victory and renewed their attack, teaming up to kill every loup-garou they fought.

The loups-garous saw this and faltered. Thrown off, they attacked with far less vigor, shying away and avoiding attacks from Ro and the few remaining wolves, until Ro had driven them to where she wanted them to go.

Even though they greatly outnumbered the Black Forest wolves, the loups-garous huddled in a circle, surrounded by Ro and snarling, snapping gray wolves. Once there were no more attacks, she spun, sliced open the veil, and pulled it wide.

Again filling her voice with power, she called, "This is your one chance. Go! Now. Return to your realm, and do not *ever* come back."

The creatures hesitated, unsure. As if they thought she was tricking them.

Ro gritted her teeth and sincerely hoped nothing else came through while she was trying to talk sense into these mindless beasts.

"If you stay, if you come back, if you harm one of mine ever again, I will find you and I will end you. You die here, you stay dead. You can no longer regenerate, not with the Wolf King unable to help you. And believe me, I will show no mercy."

They glanced at each other, and after some hesitation, the lead loup-garou made a low whine, answered by the others. Then they lowered their heads, hunched their shoulders, and moved forward.

Ro didn't like it.

Heads down, shying away from Ro and the wolves, the loups-garous submissively made their way toward the opening in the veil.

She frowned. They'd truly given up so easily? Unable to stop the relief that flooded her, her shoulders relaxed, and that was when she saw it.

One of the loups-garous glanced up with a quick fierce curl to his lip, and Ro didn't have time to call a warning.

The next moment the loups-garous sprang as one, crushed the wolves' throats in their teeth, and flung the bodies away. Yelps and then nothing. Silence.

Non.

The one that heaved itself at Ro bounced off the veil she tucked herself into as it flew at her, yet it still sliced five long claw marks down her arm and side.

With a snap, she let the veil go and sank her axe deep into its skull, pushing past her burning pain and the horror at the sudden deaths of all her allies at once.

She wanted to scream for her reinforcements, but they were nowhere nearby. No matter. She had to end this.

Besides, she had reinforcements she'd forgotten about entirely.

Blood dripped down her arm and onto the forest floor. A breeze trembled the leaves overhead.

"I warned you," she hissed at the creatures, who looked not even a little afraid. They pranced and grinned and prepared to attack.

Not taking her eyes off them, she placed one hand on the nearest tree and spoke.

"Wake, my friends. Hem them in, strike them down, bring them back to me. Do *not* let them escape."

Before the creatures had a chance to wonder at her words, the trees came alive.

Moving across the ground without taking any steps, roots churned up dirt in their path and patted it down solidly behind them, leaving trails of hard-packed dirt in the forest as they chased down loups-garous at inhuman speeds.

The loups-garous scattered, but trees stepped into their path, slammed them with their branches back to Ro, or trapped them with sticky sap and held them fast for their new protectress.

And Ro chased down each loup-garou and killed them all.

33

Ro stood in the midst of the carnage, axe dripping blood.

Her chest heaved, and she eyed the mass of still limbs, tumbled in a macabre dance that spread all around her.

The fey creatures would never harm the humans in this wood again.

Even now, not that long after the battle, the wounds on her arm and side were healing. Was it just her, or were her wounds closing even faster than normal?

A gray pelt caught her eye, and a pang lit up her heart. The wolves. They'd come to her aid, attacked the fey wolves tearing apart the forest.

And they'd paid a costly price.

Ro blinked back tears and went to see if there was anything she could do.

A whimper carried on the wind, and Ro spun toward it, axe ready. One of the brown-skinned corpses was moving.

Changing direction, she picked her way through the tangle of limbs, axe up and ready to swing. The creature, lying on its stomach, hunched its back like it was trying to rise.

Ro jumped forward and aimed for its head. She diverted the axe at the last moment.

A gray bundle of fur halfway under it was pushing at the corpse, pawing at it. A real wolf, then.

She hesitated, not quite able to abandon her wariness of all wolves. But the thing was so small. It pawed furiously, head and nose buried under the creature, whine high-pitched and thready.

Ro used the head of her axe to roll the fey wolf aside, and a wolf pup jumped back with a yelp. Then it darted forward again, nosing a bloody mass of fur and crying plaintively.

Ro's heart ached. It was a pup. And she assumed it was nosing its mère, smearing blood all over its light-gray and tan fur.

Ro reached for the she-wolf to check, just in case, but the body was already going rigid. The pup yipped and jumped back, then growled low in its throat and nipped at Ro's hand.

She jerked her hand back too late. Sharp puppy teeth stung her skin, and she sucked in a breath through her teeth. But the wolf pup was whining and nosing its mère again, making even more of a mess of itself.

Ro sighed. She couldn't just leave it here, in this carnage.

She checked for other living wolves but found none. She explored the area until she found a den the she-wolf had likely been protecting once the fighting got too close, Ro's new senses leading her right to the well-hidden spot. Ro crouched down and found it empty. No other pups, then.

She yelped as a cool, wet nose touched her fingers. The wolf pup nosed under her hand, shivering and leaning against her as if weary and losing strength.

After checking her newly enhanced senses to make sure no more pups hid nearby, Ro took off her red cape and wrapped it around the pup, lifting—it? She checked—him, into her arms and carrying him to the old woodsman's cabin.

Opening the cabin door, axe clutched in hand, Gustave

harrumphed as he took in her filthy, blood-smeared clothes and covered-in-dirt self. "Don't tell me it's over and I missed it. You couldn't have waited till the sun was up?"

Ro laughed and edged past him into the cabin, not waiting for an invitation. "Weren't you the one urging me to rush out and take care of it by myself?"

"I didn't expect you to do so in one night," he grumbled, then squinted at her. "The problem is taken care of, *ja, Fräulein*?"

"*Ja*," she said wearily. "The Wolf King and loups-garous will no longer trouble our forest." She frowned. "Though we may want to see if any wolf packs are willing to make their homes here."

He did a double take. "You *want* more wolves in our forest? Why?"

She moved her red cape enough so Gustave could see the wolf pup asleep in her arms and explained.

After cleaning the pup and bedding it down by the fire to get warm and dry, Gustave showed her how to care for him. When he offered to watch over the pup while she joined the others at the palace, Ro hesitated, then refused. She needed to take care of him. As a thank-you for what his pack had done for her.

She also refused his offer to clean up. She needed to get to Olt as quickly as possible.

"What'll you call him?" the old woodsman asked.

"Kip," Ro answered with a smile, gathering what she needed while Kip slept by the fire. At Gustave's questioning glance, she said, "After a character from a favorite childhood book of mine."

After waking and feeding Kip by dipping a clean sock in milk, and after the pup refused bits of meat, she saddled Fair-weather and carefully stowed a few jars of milk. She mounted, Gustave settled the pup in her arms—he curled up and started gently snoring right away—and she nodded goodbye to the old woodsman.

Shifting the reins to one hand, Ro held the pup close and rode straight for the German palace.

Once she reached Olt's family's palace, right as the sun had fully risen and welcomed the day with its blazing glory, she found a veritable army prepping for war.

Her blood-spattered face and clothing got a reaction, and soldiers she didn't know swarmed her and asked questions, not letting her pass.

She searched for Olt among the teeming masses but didn't see him.

As she was trying to explain who she was for the third time over the din of the soldiers and villagers gathering supplies and brandishing weapons and loading wagons, a familiar voice called out to her.

"Ro? Ro!" Olt pushed his way through the crowd, and Ro nudged Fairweather toward him with her knees.

She swung one leg over and slid from the horse's back, and Olt took her in with wide eyes. She gave him a weary but satisfied smile. "All this bustle for me, huh?"

"Ro, what happened? Why are you covered in blood?" His eyes were a bit wild as he reached for her. "Did wolves attack you on your way here—ouch!"

His yelp was accompanied by a sharper, high-pitched yelp, and the wolf pup went crazy wriggling and trying to nibble on the man who'd dared touch Ro.

Olt gave a hesitant smile. "And who's this fellow?"

"This is Kip. Um, he's a wolf pup."

He took one look at the squirming pup still trying to get to him and huffed a laugh. "Kip, huh? Where'd you find him?"

He held out his hand, keeping it out of biting range, and

Ro found the bits of meat Kip had only licked up to this point. She handed one to Olt, and suddenly the pup was more interested in licking Olt's fingers than biting them off.

"I, uh, found him in the woods. After the battle."

"What happened out there?" Olt asked.

Ro quickly explained, and Olt looked horrified that she'd gone off to fight the big bad wolf all by herself.

"I swear we were getting ready to leave the moment you got here"—he glanced around at the tumult rather helplessly—"but it takes a while to get an army moving."

He deflated a bit, and he looked so adorable, Ro couldn't help but laugh. All the stress and worry drained out of her.

"Not to worry. You stick with me, and you'll have to ride to my rescue at least once or twice." At Olt's sharp look, Ro bit her lip. "That is, if you want to? I know I'm not the easiest to get along with . . . and the way I left you in Paris . . . we haven't really talked about it yet . . ."

Casting a quick glance around at the milling soldiers, Olt pulled her aside, and then, when it was still too busy and loud, into nearby castle ruins where they could have a private conversation.

Or at least not be found for a little while.

The clanging noise hushed with the stone barrier and distance from the soldiers, and Ro instantly felt better. She wasn't one for crowds, even if they had gathered at her request.

Ro glanced behind her. "So should you tell them or should I that they can stop preparing for battle?"

She tried to say it in a jesting manner, but her throat was thick, and she nearly choked on the words. Olt's lack of response sent fear crashing through her heart.

Ro took a deep breath, steeled herself for the talk she knew they needed to have, and faced him. "If you don't want this anymore, just tell me. I'll understand. I treated you horribly, and I shouldn't have, but I was so scared . . ."

"Ro, that's not it. But if you're going to run off every time things get uncomfortable or difficult—you can't do that. We have to talk it out. Even if you need space—and I respect that!—you can't just leave when things get hard—"

"It's more than that, Olt."

Ro marched away, tugging at strands of her hair caked with muck from her battle as she balanced the pup in her other arm. She should've taken time to wash up, but she'd been focused on getting here as fast as she could.

Farther away from Olt, the wolf pup flopped over and hung there, limp, perfectly content to be carted around. Maybe she should find a length of rope so he could explore the ruins without being trampled by the milling horses nearby or lost in the woods . . .

"Ro, what is it? I'm sure we can work it out—"

Tension that had been building since her memories were returned reached a boiling point. Carefully chosen words exploded all at once, ruining Ro's plans of what to say.

She spun around. "I can't have children, Olt!"

"What?" He looked dazed, like she'd just sucker punched him.

"I know you want them, but I can't have them."

Neither of them said anything while he digested that. "How do you even, well, know such a thing?"

Ro shrugged, scratching the pup's ear. It leaned into her scratches with all its might, nearly falling from her arms. "It's part of the protectress powers from the Fairy Queen, for when I was watching over Cosette. So I wouldn't be *distracted*," she added bitterly.

Not that she had her heart set on children. But one day, perhaps.

"How on earth do you—"

"It's something I recently . . . remembered . . . that she'd said to me. Long ago." And then made her forget, but that was a whole other conversation she was having with the Queen of the Fairies. After thanking her for her help with the Wolf King.

Well, not that she should thank anyone from the Realm of the Fey.

"So . . . after . . ."

"Non, Olt!" Ro's chest heaved, and tears filled her eyes. She clenched her fingers buried deep in the pup's fur and glared—not at him, but at the whole situation. "The Fairy Queen will never allow me to leave her service. Don't you understand? As long as Cosette lives, I'm hers."

The pup wriggled in her arms at her agitation, and he was the perfect excuse not to look at Olt and see the heartbreak there. She flipped Kip over and rubbed his belly, and he yawned, relaxed, and splayed his large puppy feet so she could have better access.

Her mind spun with this new memory she'd been dreading sharing with Olt. She tried to act like it didn't bother her, but it did. What right did the Queen of the Fairies have to decide if Ro could or couldn't have children?

Not that she wanted any right now. But every once in a while, thoughts of making her own home, having her own family, whispered that she just might want those things one day. "Not yet" didn't mean "not ever."

Something she knew would be especially painful when Cosette teased about her and Olt settling down and having an Allura Aurore or two of their own.

Still not looking at Olt, Ro cradled the pup closer and said nervously, "It's not fair to you *not* to know such a thing before you make a lifelong commitment."

Olt was clearly struggling. "Perhaps you can ask her to reverse it . . ."

"Non, Olt," she said too sharply. She softened her voice. "Non. It's permanent. I—there's nothing I can do." She shrugged. "Whether it was something my body would've never been able to do or something the Fairy Queen made happen, she said it could never be reversed. I agreed, Olt. I might not have known what I was doing back then, but the fey bargain is ironclad."

He just stood there, a dazed look on his face, mouth agape, not moving.

She knew it. She *knew* this would be the end to their relationship, that he'd want to make a family with whatever woman he chose, and that woman could no longer be her.

She couldn't stand this. She couldn't stand here watching his heart break. Not again.

Ro spun to make her escape. Was almost to the edge of the ruins when Olt's shout stopped her in her tracks.

"You are enough!"

Footsteps, then a warm hand closed around her elbow and tugged her to face him. She stared wide-eyed into his gorgeous face, his eyes blazing.

"Did you hear me? You are enough." He grasped her shoulder, every word urgent. "I don't care that you can't have children. I don't care. You are who I want. You. Only ever you."

"But—children—you said—"

"What I said be hanged! What about the lad down by the wharf whose *Mutter* beats him and is always trying to get someone to take him? What about the little match girl who watches families with such longing it breaks your heart? If we need a family, we can build one, find those who are lost and broken and hurting. But I want *you*. Not for what you can do for me. Not for the children you can or cannot have. You."

After a shocked moment, tears filled her eyes and spilled down her cheeks. "You don't mean it. Sure, you may say that now, but one day you'll hold it against me."

Olt barked an exasperated, somewhat wild laugh. "Hold it against you? For what? Something you have no control over? Do you know how many children live on the streets? How many are orphaned?" He shook her a little. "We can make our own family, Ro. We can make it whatever we want it to be. If it needs to be just you and me for a while, fine. When we're ready to open our hearts, our arms, our home to anyone who needs it, then we'll do that. I don't *care* that you can't have children."

Ro's tears had a mind of their own, and they were now falling so fast she could hardly see. "But you said . . ."

"You know me. I'm always saying the wrong thing, most of the time to get a laugh. Besides, I didn't have all the information before. Now I do, and I can decide what I want. I'll take you however you're willing to be with me, my Mademoiselle, and I'll never regret it. *Never.*"

He moved close to her, too close, and she shut her eyes and took a deep, shuddering breath to steady herself. Olt's scent enveloped her and tore away a smidgeon of her resolve.

She tried to back up a step, but he went with her.

"Ro."

It was said so quietly, with such feeling, her eyes were drawn to his as metal shavings to a magnet.

He took her hands in his. "Don't push me away."

"But you're just going to leave." Ro's voice cracked, and she bit her lip. "It's better if I do it first."

Where on earth was this coming from? Everything she'd planned to say was coming out all twisted up and inside out and *wrong*. Her deepest fears spilling forth without her permission.

"I'm not. I wish you'd believe me."

"I'd like to," she whispered. "I'd really, really like to."

"I'm still here. I don't know how else to prove myself to you, but tell me what to do, and I'll do it. But, Ro, you have to decide *you* want this. You have to decide to trust me. Because I want you, and I'm not afraid to show you that."

Ro's mouth went dry, and it took a moment to put her thoughts in order. "I—I do, Olt. I do want you. I want to give us a chance, not base every decision on fear." He deserved her honesty. "I want to marry you. I want to be your best friend. Your confidante. I want to show you a smidgeon of the same trust you've always placed in me."

Olt's eyes widened.

Ro looked down. "But I don't know how to do that. I don't know if I'll ride off again the next time something scares me. I don't want to, but I might. It's how I solve a lot of my problems, moving on to the next hunt. But I don't want to be that way. I—don't expect you to forgive me for everything I've put you through. I don't even know if you can. But I want to give us a chance. If that's possible."

She still couldn't look up.

Gently, oh so gently, Olt lifted her chin, gazed deep into her eyes. "Are you sure? You've been running as long as I've known you. If this isn't what you want, what you really want, please, tell me now. I don't want to pressure you, but, Ro, I can't handle watching you ride off again after telling me to take back my ring—"

"I'm sure," she whispered. She swallowed and spoke louder. "Scared, but sure. Olt, I know I'm not the easiest person to get along with. I keep making dumb mistakes and decisions based on fear. But if you can forgive me and are willing to give us another chance, I would love to spend the rest of my life with you."

She jolted when his lips covered hers.

Everything within her screamed at her to flee, that they couldn't possibly make it work, but she held her ground. If she wanted this, she would have to fight for it. Even if she was only fighting herself and the lies she'd believed for so long.

His large hand cupped her face in the gentlest of touches, and his mouth moved against hers, gentle, caressing, urgent.

Just as she was starting to relax—to lean into him and kiss him back—the wolf pup yipped and squirmed like crazy, and Olt pulled away, breathing heavily, his lips parted. Desire curled from her belly and streamed throughout her entire body—the same desire she read in his eyes.

He leaned his forehead against hers and closed his eyes. His voice left him in the faintest of whispers. "I'm sure too. I want *you*. Just you."

Her breath was ripped away from her as she realized: He meant it. For the first time in her life, she stood before a man who actually meant what he said, and she could choose to believe him—or not. It was up to her.

She pulled back and stared at him. "You really mean that, don't you?"

His grin rivaled the sun and moon and all the stars. "Of course I do."

"Why on earth would you want me? I'm a hunter. A woman hunter, at that. I travel constantly. And now I'm tied to the Black Forest in ways I can't even begin to comprehend."

His roguish grin did not-unpleasant things to her insides. "Do you have time for me to tell you? Because I will. Gladly."

She groaned and dropped her face against his chest, leaving room for the pup between them. "This is awful."

He gripped her shoulder roughly. "Why? Because you think you don't deserve this? That you aren't worthy of love? That you can't have a normal life?"

She eyed him. "Define normal."

Her insides danced and sang and soared at his way-too-beautiful-for-anyone's-good smile. "Hunting magical beasts with your husband."

She almost gave into a full-fledged smile. Her raging emotions needed to calm themselves. She mock-scowled instead. "Really. You'd let me do that still. Not cook and clean and darn your smelly socks."

He threw back his head and laughed. His sparkling eyes caught and held hers. "Oh, you'd do that for me, would you?"

She doused her smile into a smirk. "Hardly."

"I'd expect no less from you, my love."

Her heart panged. That's what her père had called her mère. Before. Before he'd retreated so deeply inside himself, he'd never returned.

"And when you tire of me?" she demanded.

His grin dampened. Sadness lingered in his eyes. He cupped her cheek once more. "Never," he whispered.

Tears glistened on her eyelashes without permission. "That's what my père told my mère, too."

His mouth opened, but no words came out.

Then, gently, he said, "Oh, Ro. How I wish I could heal all the hurts this world has inflicted upon you. But I can't. There's only one who can do that if you'll take your burdens to Him and let them go. And I promise I'll be here for you. That's all I can do. Keep showing up every day, keep showing you how much I care, keep showing you that I can be trusted with your heart. Won't you let me prove myself to you?"

His hand drifted down to play with the pup and his sharp little teeth as he stared into her eyes. Ro couldn't look away.

A future she couldn't control didn't matter. What mattered was the very real person right here in front of her.

Something crumbled inside of her, a wall she'd been fiercely protecting. Tears slipped down Ro's face, and she smiled and nodded. "All right. Oui. I choose to trust you."

"Ro, I want nothing more in this world." With a heated look, Olt leaned his forehead against hers while the pup busily chewed on his fingers.

Suddenly Ro couldn't get close enough. She threw an arm around his neck, pulled his head down to hers, and kissed him, moving as close as she could get with a mass of wriggling pup between them.

She pulled back to give Kip space. "I love you, Olt. Let's get married. Right away."

Olt's expression turned concerned. "Are you sure? I mean, are you ready? Because I can wait. As long as I know we're on the same path, that we're willing to take this journey together, I can wait as long as you need me to."

She kissed him softly, gently. "I'm sure. And I'm ready to be yours. For the rest of our days together."

His smile was magnificent. "Then I would love to marry you, my Mademoiselle."

Ro launched herself at him, and Olt laughed, the sound so full of joy it brought tears to her eyes.

Praise Dieu, she hadn't ruined everything. Somehow.

He took the pup from her arms and set him down, then picked her up and spun her around, once, and Ro was so happy she didn't even mind. The wolf pup barked wildly, whether in concern or sharing their excitement, Ro didn't know or care.

The moment her toes touched the earth, Olt was kissing her like he couldn't get enough, like he could never get enough, like she was his air and warmth and life itself, and Ro forgot everything else.

Come what may, he was hers, and Dieu willing, they would have an entire lifetime together.

❧

When Ro pulled away, she started babbling, her relief was so acute. "Oh, Olt. I was so scared to tell you. So scared you'd walk away, and it would be completely understandable. When the Fairy Queen told me—"

Olt frowned. "By the way, when exactly did she tell you this?"

The pup chose that moment to wander off and explore the castle ruins, so Ro kept a close eye on him. "It was part of the agreement when I became Cosette's protectress, long ago. I couldn't, uh, remember it until recently."

Olt folded his one arm across his body in a believable

approximation of crossing his arms. "Oh, really? I think I need to hear this story."

With a sigh, Ro told him how her memories had been altered—and how Captain Red had branded her to get them back.

By the end of her explanation, Olt looked like he was ready to march off and fight a duel with the pirate captain.

Ro placed a hand on his arm. "She saved me, Olt. Captain Red undid whatever had been done to me, and memories are coming back I didn't even know I'd lost. *And* she said I wouldn't be able to be influenced again as long as I have her brand. I owe Captain Red . . . a great deal."

"I still don't like it. I hate that it was done to you, and I hate that Captain Red . . ." He drew his hand down his face and blew out a breath. "I'm grateful she helped you, of course I am, but I don't want you beholden to her either."

"I understand. But, well, couldn't you try to get along with her? For me? I, uh, she might be . . . somewhat . . . related to me. By marriage. Maybe." Ro bit her lip.

Olt looked thunderstruck. "What?"

"I didn't verify it, because Grandmère wouldn't have wanted that, but I'm almost certain she might be."

Olt shook his head. "I . . . am going to have to get used to that."

Ro wrapped an arm around his waist. "She doesn't need to know, but if it ever comes up, well, I wanted to give you warning. Because even if you don't like Captain Red, I do. Very much."

Olt rested his chin on her head. "I'll try, for your sake. But the things that woman has done . . ."

"And does no longer," she said immediately.

"Probably."

Ro hesitated. "Probably."

Olt pulled back to look at her. "You believe me, right? We'll be our own family, Ro. Just you and me."

"Are you sure?" She frowned. "Because I distinctly remember you saying you wanted a big family."

"Oh, I don't know. Peace and quiet and getting to know each other, just the two of us—I could get used to that."

Ro nestled closer. "Just you and me sounds good. And Kip, of course."

"And Kip," Olt said with a smile in his voice.

After a moment of staring down at her, he leaned forward. She stretched up to meet him in a fiery kiss. They couldn't get enough of each other. Ro could've kissed him all day.

Until she was interrupted by her brothers.

"Ugh. How does every hunt we go on begin with Ro kissing Olt?" Claude said in disgust.

"Don't forget it ends that way too," Pascal said with a smirk.

Ro was too happy to care about their teasing, but she pulled back and blushed to the roots of her hair anyway. She tried to hide her embarrassment by retrieving the pup just as he was scampering out of the ruins.

He wriggled in protest, but she ran her fingers through his wiry fur, and he decided he could put off his escape until after his massage and settled into her arms.

"Do you need any help from the rest of us lowly supplicants, Majesté? Or shall we continue with important tasks such as readying ourselves to hunt these loups-garous of yours." Claude crossed his arms and leaned against the crumbling wall. He didn't look like he was readying to go anywhere or hunt anything, the lazy cad.

"Looks like she already did all the hunting herself," said Pascal, taking in her disheveled and filthy clothing. "Anything you'd like to tell us, sister of mine?"

"Yeah, or would you prefer to go back to kissing your paramour and leave the rest of us in the dark?" Claude added unhelpfully.

Though her face burned as if it had been set on fire by the

sun, Ro explained her fight with the Wolf King and how she'd taken out the last of the loups-garous.

Claude whistled. "It's a wonder we come along with you on these little excursions at all. Once again, you run off and take care of everything yourself, leaving the rest of us to sit here and twiddle our thumbs."

"Oh, and that's such a hardship for you, is it?" Ro demanded in mock-outrage.

Claude stretched and yawned. "Nah. It's how I prefer it, actually."

Ro shook her head with a smile.

Pascal's eyes danced with mirth and pride. "Well done, Ro."

Now she blushed for an entirely different reason—the pleasure of a job well done. "Merci, Pas."

Olt moved to her side and wrapped his arm around her shoulders. "Anyone up for an impromptu wedding as soon as I can find us a priest?"

Now Pascal whistled. "Oh, Ro. Is Cosette going to kill you."

Didn't she know it. "Pas, you know she's going to make a big production of it. Reserve the biggest cathedral in Paris, stuff me in a monstrous gown, invite the entire realm . . ."

She felt queasy just thinking of it.

Her brother shook his head, even as Claude stayed uncharacteristically quiet, for once. "As long as you get a priest to bless your union, I suppose I can't object to your getting married."

Pascal turned an unsettling gaze on Olt, and Ro couldn't help but remember the argument they'd had so long ago. Over Olt. Over whether he was a good man or just wanted to use her.

She was far too mature to shove her finger under Pascal's nose and say, "Ha! See? I was right!" but she dearly wanted to.

Of course, time would tell.

"As long as you take good care of her, provide for her, and make sure she isn't unhappy a day in her life," Pascal continued.

Ro almost stepped away from the blistering glare Pascal was leveling on Olt, and then Claude stepped close to his brother's side, crossed his arms, and leveled a nearly identical glare on Olt.

Olt may have started to sweat. Ro wished she could squeeze his hand, but hers were currently full of wriggling pup.

"I give you my word that no bride shall be happier," he said earnestly.

Ro rolled her eyes. Again. It happened quite often around her brothers. "As if he could promise such a thing," she tried to object. "It's up to both of us."

Her brothers were having none of it. Apparently if Olt wanted her, they would have to be satisfied. Ro sighed and let them have their fun. She was satisfied, and that was all that mattered.

Thankfully, a familiar voice interrupted just then. "Huntress LeFèvre, what on earth are you doing here, looking like you took on a battalion all by your lonesome? Don't tell me the excitement is over and I missed it."

Ro smiled at Captain Red. "Ah, well, it seems the loups-garous shall no longer be a problem in this part of the forest." She frowned. "Well, *any* part of the forest, hopefully."

The pirates at the captain's back all groaned and made disgusted noises or spit on the ground.

Ro almost chuckled, but their disappointment was likely real. These pirates would be happy to join any fight, wouldn't they? "What are you even doing here, by the way? Weren't you stuffing your ship full for the return voyage?"

Captain Red grinned. "Ah, I couldn't tell you I was planning on following you, now could I? Not with Madame

LaChance's spies everywhere, and that despicable Grant pulling through and deciding to chase you down, life-threatening wounds or no."

"Is he, um . . ." Ro wasn't sure how to finish.

The captain flicked her fingers. "He won't trouble you again. Nothing ta worry about, huntress."

Ro wasn't sure if she should ask for more details or not.

"Aye, we greatly inconvenienced ourselves to aid you." The captain spread her hands wide. "But in typical Ro fashion, you have the whole mess cleaned up neat as a pin before we could help." She took in Ro's bloody clothing. "Well, perhaps not neat as a pin."

Ro shook her head with a smile. "What about your sister? How was she willing to spare you so soon?"

The captain shrugged. "She knew I had business elsewhere."

Ro wasn't buying it. "Still, she'll probably want to spend time with you now that the threat is gone —"

But another thought intruded and threw their conversation right out of her head. She spun on Olt, not giving the captain a chance to answer.

"Do you trust me?"

He blinked at her. "Of course I do. But regarding what, exactly, this time?"

She whirled back to the captain. "Marry us. Um, s'il vous plaît."

After a startled silence from everyone in the clearing, Captain Red burst into laughter. "Red looks good on you, huntress, but I'm not sure smeared blood is the best look. You sure you don't want to clean up first?"

Olt leaned close and said in an aside, "Didn't we just agree your sister's going to kill us both if she's not part of the ceremony?"

She turned on Olt. "I don't care. I want to marry you now. I almost died so many times, Olt, and I never knew if I'd see you again, or be conscripted to the Caribbean for the rest of my life, or my legs broken, or thrown into a shallow grave by that beastly bounty hunter, or torn apart by wolves. I finally know what I want, and it's you."

Olt was staring at her with enough warmth to melt her insides, a look Ro felt right down to her toes. A deep blush rose on her face as she couldn't tear her gaze away.

"All right. Yes. Let's get married. Right now." He grinned. "I just pray your sister likes me enough to forgive us once we tell her."

Captain Red rolled her eyes and divested Ro of the wolf pup. "I'll marry you both, but I draw the line at letting you do so covered in blood and guts and filth. You'll thank me one day, I promise you."

Captain Red handed off the pup to Sheba, latched on to Ro's arm, and pulled the huntress after her.

Ro twisted around to make sure Kip was all right with the arrangement.

Sheba held the pup at arm's length with a disgruntled look on her face as it wriggled madly, but Aisling immediately took Kip from her, holding him close and letting him lick her face and fingers while crooning that she'd take good care of him and who needed boy kisses when there were such things as pup kisses?

Relieved that Kip was in good hands, Ro allowed herself to be led away.

34

Ro found herself hauled away, scrubbed clean, and placed into a frilly red dress Captain Red happened to have with her. Some kind of plunder Ro didn't want to know the story of. Not only did it have Spanish origins, it kept slipping down one shoulder, no matter how often Ro yanked it back up.

Captain Red laughed at her. "It's meant to be worn that way, huntress."

So she let it be, enjoying the scandalous thrill of wearing something lovely and simple and elegant yet unlike anything she'd worn before.

When she came back, the clearing had been hastily emptied of soldiers and horses and wagons, and her entourage of pirates guided her to a quiet field of wildflowers on the other side of the castle ruins.

Ro married Olt under a canopy of early stars as dusk settled over the landscape. Someone had taken her rose ring to Olt while she dressed, and he gave it back under Captain Red's direction, kissing her deeply after.

An impromptu feast was thrown together at the palace and brought down to the field with long tables set out, roaring

342

bonfires easing the chill of the autumn air. Soldiers, villagers, and pirates were their guests.

Ro loved every minute of it.

After an evening of feasting and dancing and laughing, she and Olt rode back to her grandmère's cabin to camp out under the stars.

❧

Olt eyed the splintered cabin as they rode into the clearing and dismounted, Kip clutched in his arm. "Are you sure this is a good idea? I mean, my brothers have a few hunting cabins throughout these woods—if they're still there, that is. Shouldn't be too hard to clean one out. And then there's always Odette's old homestead, though she may be living there now. I'm not sure about that, actually."

Stopping his nervous words with a kiss, Ro smiled up at her new husband. "Trust me?"

His eyes danced as he gave her a searing look. "Of course I do."

It was the same thing he'd said when he'd agreed to allow Captain Red to marry them. Even if he'd tried not to glare at the captain the whole time, keeping his eyes on Ro so he wouldn't ruin the ceremony for her.

Just as she was leaning in to kiss him again, stomping and muttering came their way through the forest. Ro jerked her head back, and there came Gustave, tromping through the woods on his injured leg.

Amazing how the nearly silent woodsman could make such a racket. Ro had a feeling he did it on purpose.

"Gustave!" She rushed to meet him. "I told you we would come get it from you. We don't mind."

He handed her the reins to the pack horse she'd left in his stable. It was loaded down with canvas tent material, fire starter, and supplies for a few days spent outdoors. The horse whickered a greeting to Fairweather, who returned it and came over to nose the horse he'd spent time with in Gustave's stable.

"Thank you so much for the supplies," Ro said. She nodded at the destroyed cabin. "I'm so sorry. All your hard work . . ."

He waved off her words. "Eh, the loups-garous are gone. We can rebuild without fear of another attack." He gave her a searching look. "That is, if you're planning to stay."

Ro looked to Olt, and he gave her a wide smile. "We're planning to stay," she said.

Kip wriggled and yipped in agreement.

Then she couldn't look away, and it seemed like she and Olt were the only two people in the entirety of the Black Forest, Kip's antics fading into the background.

Gustave cleared his throat. "I'd best be getting back, then."

Ro tore her gaze from Olt's with effort. "Won't you rest before you head back? Eat a meal with us? Or at least take the horse to ride?"

"*Nein*. Might as well start your own stable." He fondly patted Olt's Black Forest horse, the one with a yellow-tan coat and a blond mane and tail, who wasn't interested in the other two horses at the moment, munching away at a nice patch of grass he'd discovered. "Besides, I need to keep this old leg of mine moving to heal properly."

Ro didn't think that was how injuries worked, but she nodded and thanked the old woodsman again.

He hobbled over and divested Olt of the wolf pup. "I'll just look after this *Welpe* for you for a few days, shall I?"

Ro wanted to object, but Olt smiled and handed him over. "That would be great, *Danke*."

Ro nearly pouted at that. She'd had to rescue the wolf pup from Aisling, who'd tried to whisk him away and back to the ship, and Ro wasn't certain she wanted to be parted from him.

Then Olt's gaze drew her like a magnet, and they were once again the only two in the forest. Ro smiled and kissed him. Kip would be safe enough with the old woodsman.

Gustave stumped off to his cabin, still moving slowly, muttering about young fools in love. Then he called over his shoulder, "Make sure you leave food out tonight!"

That's when Ro noticed rolled blueprints sticking out of one of the saddlebags.

Olt turned to her with a confused look. "Food?"

Ro grinned and kissed him again before answering. "You'll see." Then she held up a stern finger. "But you can't ask me any questions. Promise me."

"Not even one?" He kissed her cheeks and the tip of her nose.

"Not even one."

He sighed, as if very put out. "If you insist."

Ro smiled and leaned against him, tucking her head into his shoulder. "I insist."

Then they set up camp and spent a night under the stars, just the two of them.

And Ro took a moment when Olt wasn't looking to not only leave some food out, but to ask the trees to fill Gustave with strength to heal quickly, as they'd done for her.

She'd tell Olt someday what she could do, but first she needed to figure out what that was exactly.

❧

The next morning, Ro woke as the sun gently lightened the day, and stretched lazily. She smiled as she remembered last night. Now she knew why so many people got married. It all made perfect sense.

Cosette had been right after all. Not that Ro would ever admit such a thing to her sister.

She rolled over to find her new husband's place next to her

empty. She raised her head and found him standing barefoot, loose shirt untucked from his breeches, staring at the newly built cabin with his mouth hanging open.

Built out of gleaming blond wood with some kind of clear, shiny coating instead of paint, it was similar to her grand-mère's cabin, in that it reminded Ro of a quaint German building, but this one was even more distinct, with an old-world feel, as if the builders were from an age long, long ago.

Which they were, of course.

But even Ro hadn't expected the entire thing to be built in one night. And without a sound, too. Perhaps Gustave had mentioned it was a wedding present when he'd drawn the blueprints?

But the look on Olt's face . . .

She snickered to herself and moved to join him, pulling her cloak tight against the chill in the air. She stood next to him and propped her chin in her hand, taking it in.

"Hmm. I see Gustave added the loft I asked for."

He jumped a kilomètre and stared between her and the cabin, mouth working like he wanted to say something but couldn't quite figure out what.

She shook a finger at him playfully. "Not a single question, remember?"

"Oh, come on!" he cried. He pointed at the cabin with the brush for his teeth, his tooth powder canister also clutched in his fingers. "Seriously? You can't do this to me."

She wrapped her arms around his waist and made a contented sound deep in her throat. "I'm truly sorry, my love." She kissed his jaw. "Shall we tour our new house and see if we want to spend tonight indoors?"

"Um . . ." His gaze went back to the cabin, as if he couldn't tear it away. Also as if he were afraid of it, just a little bit.

Ro couldn't blame him. She had almost lost her mind the first time she'd seen lumber practically sprout from felled trees overnight.

Leaving him standing there, still gaping, Ro sashayed across the clearing, climbed the steps, and opened the front door. She leaned against the doorjamb and crossed her arms. "You coming?"

He stumbled toward her and trailed her throughout the interior, eyes wide. The cabin held her grandmère's giant cookstove, still dented from the great wolf's attack, though it had been hammered out quite nicely. A new table and chairs built out of the same sealed blond wood sat before the stove, two gleaming rocking chairs waited in front of a fireplace, and a single bed meant for two rested along one wall, close to the fire but furthest from the kitchen. A ladder led up to an open loft with a railing, a wall dividing it neatly in half for storage on one side and a single bed on the other, for a guest.

Or a child, but Ro wasn't thinking about that. Not today.

She couldn't help but marvel at the homey touches: the curtains, the warm blankets, and the new furniture. This cabin was more spacious than her grandmère's, which was incredible since they shared the same footprint.

This was so much more than she'd been expecting. Then again, she'd been too distracted to do more than glance at the plans Gustave included in their supplies.

She'd been certain to leave out several bottles of wine, loaves of freshly baked bread, and a bucket of fresh milk from Gustave, saving the other food items from her and Olt's impromptu wedding feast. Items had been packed into their saddlebags before they'd been sent off with good-natured cheers and brotherly ribbing.

Okay, the pirates had jumped all over the wedding night teasing, too, until Ro had urged Fairweather out of there even faster, to the delighted guffaws of their guests.

The new cabin was a marvel. And the speed with which they'd built it was just as astonishing. Hopefully it lasted her and Olt for a lifetime.

And all the while, Olt seemed about to burst.

Ro took pity on her new husband and looped her arm through his, leaning her head against his shoulder. "I have a book for you to read. We'll have to get it from Gustave's cabin."

Olt set his brush and powder on the table and ran his fingers through his hair, over and over, his tell when he was agitated. It dislodged her hold on him, but Ro didn't mind. She knew exactly how he felt.

"I don't know what a book has to do with anything," he said, "but I also don't know how much longer I'll be able to keep from asking questions."

"Once we get this book," Ro said smugly, "you won't have to."

Olt's eyes widened, and he did an about-face and headed for the door. "Then what are we waiting for? Let's go get this book!"

Ro barked a laugh. "Don't you want to get dressed first, sailor? I think you'll scandalize half the Black Forest going out like that."

He looked down at his disheveled state in surprise, as if he'd forgotten he was only half-dressed.

Without a backward glance, he tore down to their little encampment, found hosiery, shoes, and a vest, and hastily tucked his loosely flowing shirt into his breeches. "You coming?" he called without looking up—or slowing down from throwing on just enough clothing to be considered decent for company.

Ro laughed and joined him in getting ready, and soon they were racing their horses for Gustave's cabin.

She couldn't wait to see Olt's face when he found out who'd built their new cabin.

Ro greeted a surprised Gustave, falling to her knees to gush all over Kip, which she hadn't meant to do. Thankfully Kip was just as happy to see her, jumping around and yipping and licking her face. After she'd regained her feet—and her composure—she requested the book he'd shown her, the one she'd written in when she feared losing more of her memories.

He got it without argument, then invited them to stay for café and a quick meal.

"You leave an offering out last night?" he asked casually.

Ro smiled. "I did. They were very grateful."

He grunted. "Thought they might be."

Olt looked like he would burst, so Ro turned to the page he needed and handed him the book. He stood in the middle of the cabin and devoured the section on brownies, then threw back his head and laughed.

Then he came over and kissed her, right there in front of Gustave, who looked away quickly, a faint tinge of red on his weathered cheeks. "Ro, you astound me," Olt said. "One thing's for sure. Life with you will never be boring."

She grinned. "Will you help me remember to put something out every night?"

"Help you remember? I'll bake it myself so they'll have the best bread in all the Black Forest!"

He started to kiss her again, but Ro pulled back, conscious of how uncomfortable they were making the old woodsman. And herself. She gave Olt a look. "Take the warning to heart. They're deadly serious about not being spoken to or about."

He gave her a scorching look, staring a bit too keenly at her lips. Then he drew an X over his heart with his thumb. "Cross my heart," he said in a low, husky voice.

Wondering how soon they could return to their cabin and make it their own—not to mention so she could kiss Olt to oblivion—Ro sat at the table, taking up the baked apples covered with streusel and shoveling in a bite. "This is delightful, Gustave."

Once again, he grunted. "Yer sister-in-law, Odile, gave me enough food to feed an army for a month of Sundays."

Ro smiled. "Us too."

"You need anything? You know, to make the cabin more homely?" Gustave asked, shifting uncomfortably. He enjoyed small talk about as much as Ro.

"Plenty of firewood, plenty of food, and plenty of warm blankets. We have all we need, merci."

He nodded. "You let me know when you need something more. I'll introduce you to the merchants of the closest trading town, for the things you can't make or grow yourself."

Thank goodness. Ro would not be making much on her own. Not if she wanted it to turn out well.

Olt was shoveling in the streusel as if he hadn't tasted better. Or perhaps because he wanted to return to the cabin as fast as humanly possible. "This is great. Where did you get the apples?"

Gustave leaned back, sipped his coffee, and told them of the closest grove of apple trees, the best place to fish, and where to gather mushrooms and truffles.

Then he had mercy on them and shooed them off, giving Olt a wink Ro wished she hadn't seen with how much her face burned. This time, Ro took Kip with them.

Then they were on their way back to the home that was theirs alone for as long as they had time on this earth to spend together.

And they enjoyed every minute of getting to know each other as husband and wife.

35

Ro bit the end of her featherless quill—Trêve's favorite writing instrument had become her own, for the sole reason that she could chew on it to her heart's content without getting a mouthful of feather—and realized she was procrastinating. Again.

But the right words wouldn't come.

She knew she needed to write Cosette a letter. She knew Claude and Pascal had delayed their return so they could personally deliver it to the queen. She knew she was running out of time.

But the very thought of Cosette reading this, of her reaction—Ro had never experienced such a potent dose of writer's block.

And she penned fairy tales in her spare time.

In fact, she had another, this one called *Little Red Riding Hood*, that hadn't been half as difficult as this one page alone. Well, except for the ending. That she was still working on.

Olt kissed her neck, making her jump. "Still writing it, hmm?"

She gave him a sheepish look. "I'm on draft eight thousand."

"That many, huh?" His eyes danced with merriment as he sat at the table beside her.

Huffing a sigh, Ro glanced at the scattered crumpled paper halfway between her and the massive brick fireplace. Kip had worn himself out chasing them about the room and now lay next to the warm fire, sound asleep.

Still, there was plenty of evidence that she was wasting far too much paper.

He massaged her shoulder, and she closed her eyes and relaxed into his touch. She didn't normally like being touched, but Olt was somehow the one person who could sail past many of the idiosyncrasies she'd picked up in her lifetime.

"Why don't you just start? Don't think about it, write the first thing that comes to mind, and then send it. Without thinking about any of it. Just do it."

Shooting him a dirty look, Ro growled a little. "Don't you think I've tried that?"

Olt gave her the smallest of smiles, as if he just knew she'd gotten stuck in her own head and was agonizing unnecessarily over every word, and she got distracted by his mouth.

Without thinking about it, because she could do these things now, she leaned forward to kiss him.

And was rudely stopped with a hand to her face.

"Hold it, Mademoiselle."

Ro peeked between his fingers and gaped at her new husband.

"Pascal and Claude have already delayed their journey twice, and this is the fastest way Cosette will hear from you. And she needs to hear it from *you*, not from the gossip surely heading her way this very minute. Your time for such things is swiftly running out. No canoodling until that letter is written."

Ro made a frustrated noise. "What a singularly horrific word. *Canoodling.*"

He grinned but, unlike her, wasn't easily distracted. "I

promise I'll make it worth your while if you finish that thing and get it to your brothers."

Ro growled again, but she went back to her letter. "That just makes it worse," she moaned. "Even more pressure."

He stood and kissed her temple. "I have faith in you, my Mademoiselle."

And then he left, probably to go get Claude and Pascal and seat them at the table with her to add even more agony. Ro sighed and retrieved a fresh sheet of parchment.

&

Dearest Cosette,

I pray you will not be angry with me, but I have exciting news! (At least, I hope you will find it exciting.)

Olt and I are . . . married.

Are you surprised? Did you faint? Please don't be angry.

Before you rail against me for not letting you plan the wedding of . . . someone else's dreams, please know that this was the perfect wedding for me. We were married under a canopy of stars, Pascal and Claude and Liam and Olt's brothers were witnesses only because they were already there, and Olt and I have returned to Grandmère's cabin —well, I guess it's ours now, isn't it?—to enjoy marital bliss. Gustave (did Grandmère tell you about him?) has helped us settle in and learn what we need to know to make a life here.

I don't know when we'll come to visit, but I do promise we will.

Now, Olt is standing over my shoulder, urging me to finish writing this and to send it right away—something about how I'll put off telling you until the last possible moment, which we both know is ridiculous, ha!—so I guess I will, just to prove him wrong.

Cosette, I love being married. I had no idea how very much I would love being married. Merci. Merci for wanting this happiness for me. Merci for urging me to choose my heart's desire. Merci for throwing that fête in my honor and not letting me hide from Olt.

I don't think this day would've come about without you—we both know how dismal I am with such things—and I just want to say merci from the bottom of my heart.

See you soon in Paris! I love you.
Rosette

Cosette wiped tears from her cheeks and blinked rapidly to clear her vision so she could read the letter again.

Warm, strong arms wrapped around her waist, and Trêve pulled her back against him and kissed her cheek. "Do you think they are happy?" he asked in a low rumble.

"Oh, undoubtedly," she said, her voice thick with tears, her smile unstoppable. "It was almost painful watching Ro try so hard not to let him too close. I had to do *something*."

Trêve chuckled, and she could feel it in his chest against her back. "Of course you did, my love. Now, come to bed?"

Cosette sighed and regretfully pulled away. "I cannot, dearest. My mère has asked me to attend her right away—you know I can only spare evenings for her, and she demands more and more of my time—"

Her husband pulled her back into his arms. "Surely she can wait half an hour more?"

Cosette sighed and snuggled deeper, giving him a silky and half-lidded smile. "I suppose . . ."

That was all the concession Trêve needed, and he swept a giggling Cosette up into his arms and carried her into their bedroom.

She briefly thought how delighted she was that Rosette was as happy as she, before Trêve drove such thoughts out of her mind altogether.

PART V

"The White Wolf"
Le Loup Blanc
—Unknown—

And at these words the white wolfskin slipped from his back,
and the princess saw that he was not a wolf at all, but a
beautiful prince, tall and stately; and he gave her his hand,
and led her up the castle stairs.

Et à ces mots, la peau blanche du loup se détacha de son dos,
et la princesse vit qu'il n'était pas du tout un loup, mais un
beau prince, grand et majestueux ; il lui donna la main, et la
conduisit dans les escaliers du château.

36

Several weeks later, Ro came back after a day of hunting in her forest for things that shouldn't be there—as well as taking on small tasks for residents—to find Olt hard at work making something exquisite and edible.

Kip lay nearby, ears perked and eyes riveted on the food in Olt's hand.

She had no doubt he'd been tossing scraps in the wolf pup's direction, which was likely the reason Kip hadn't gone with her today.

The kitchen was a beehive of activity, brownies mixing batter, another kneading dough, yet another tending the fire in the stove, and several others scurrying around in whatever homemaking tasks Olt or they deemed important.

She should've been used to it by now, but to see the brownies during the day, so openly doing tasks they normally reserved for late at night, when no one else was around, was a sight to behold.

Yet she took a deep breath, turned her eyes to Olt, and ignored everything else in the room. She set a basket of traded goods for her services on the table.

"Making something scrumptious for us to eat?" Ro's

mouth watered just thinking about it. And from the glorious smells wafting from the kitchen.

His head came up, and his blazing smile melted her heart. "Ro! You're just in time. Taste this."

Kip leaped to his feet and wedged himself between them, staring at the spoon Olt raised to Ro's lips.

She eagerly obliged, happy standing next to her husband, but no matter how many times he shared something new with her, flavors exploded on her tongue and surprised her every time.

"Oh, Olt. That is exquisite. What is it?"

As he explained his new recipe in great detail, she held out the spoon for Kip to lick. Then a brownie snatched up the spoon and immediately washed, dried, and returned it to the table for Olt's use.

As Ro exclaimed over the delectable bite, the brownies paused, savored her praise, and moved on with self-satisfied smiles.

It was a delicate dance with the small fey creatures, every day.

Olt had charmed them, just as he did every new person or creature he met, and now they considered him one of their own, eager to help him at any time, with anything.

Ro wasn't even a little surprised. Olt had a way with people. And brownies, apparently. And although Ro couldn't acknowledge them in any way, they broke their own rules for Olt. She'd almost be jealous if she wasn't so proud of him.

Then again, she'd declared loudly and clearly that they would make an enemy of her for life if they dared trick Olt into walking any fairy paths or taking him into the Realm of the Fey—without looking at them or speaking directly to them, of course.

And then she'd followed it up by inking a small fey knot under the skin on his shoulder so that he would be unable to pass through fey portals, just in case. She needed all fey to know he was off-limits. So far it seemed to be working.

Olt was rather proud of the new mark on his shoulder, claiming him as hers.

She dare not mention that Captain Red had given her the idea.

He went back to his food preparations. "You find anything? Anything out of place or that shouldn't be there? Or is all well?"

"All good," Ro said. "Helped one family rebuild a fence the loups-garous had torn down, got a kitten out of a well, and then assisted an older woman and her young grandson in harvesting some apples for her canning and baking day." Ro nodded at her basket. "Got some preserves, apples, and a ten-pound bag of ground flour for my trouble."

Olt looked thrilled with her plunder. "That's great, Ro. Anything else?"

"The trees are getting ready for a long winter rest. Many have already started shedding their leaves."

He smiled and kept working. "Early snow this year?"

"I'm not sure. There's some chatter that it will be a mild winter, but we'll see." Ro happily stole another bite.

She was so grateful she didn't have to cook for herself anymore. They ate incredibly well now that Olt was in charge of such things, thank goodness.

And the brownies, of course. While they still preferred bread and milk, and the occasional wine for special celebrations, they adored making gourmet food at Olt's direction, and Ro adored eating it.

"Oh! I almost forgot." Olt wiped his hand on his apron and scrounged around in the pocket. He came up with a folded bit of paper. "This came from Cosette."

Ro cringed and took it from him. "Another summons to present our married selves at the palace?"

He grinned as she unfolded the letter. "That's my assumption, though I didn't open it as this one's addressed to you alone."

Ro scanned its contents and laughingly showed her new husband. "We are to acquit ourselves from our seclusion at once and present ourselves to Her Royal Majesté to receive the blessing this marriage needs, or Cosette will travel here to see it done herself."

His eyes twinkled. "I figured as much. Since her last letter was much the same."

Ro had written her sister several letters, but it didn't seem to matter. Cosette wanted to see them in person *at once*.

The first letter Ro had sent with Claude and Pascal. One, because she was a coward and wanted to give Cosette time to get used to the idea that Ro was already married, and two, so there would be plenty of time for Cosette to decide on whatever monstrous thing she wanted to do to celebrate Ro's nuptials—without Ro having to be a part of it.

In all honesty, she wouldn't have minded staying at the cabin with her new husband for the entirety of winter—she absolutely adored being married, as well as living far away from civilization—but she also didn't want to do that to Cosette.

Too much longer, and Cosette would do as promised and come looking for her, and wouldn't that turn their quiet lives completely upside down?

Ro glanced at the windows. Although it was broad daylight, each curtain was pulled shut so no one could peek inside and see the creatures who weren't supposed to be out during the day. "The messenger still here?"

Olt nodded. "I sent him on to the nearest village. He'll wait there till tomorrow, though I think you can still catch him today and be back before dusk."

"And you'd think the first few letters I sent her would've been good enough." She rolled her eyes as he laughed. She took her cape down from its hook by the front door. "Will those cookies be done by the time I get back?"

"Most definitely." He winked. "Dinner too." He abandoned his workstation and came over to kiss her deeply, and for a very long time. Eventually, after Ro was quite satisfied yet rethinking leaving, he pulled back. "Oh! Bring me some supplies? Wait. If we're leaving right away"—at Ro's heated look, he amended—"soonish, then we should get a few things for the nine-day journey."

He hurried off and soon came back with a list. His handwriting was still wobbly as he learned to write with his offhand, but it had much improved since he'd lost his arm.

He and Gustave had had way too much fun outfitting the cabin with small inventions to make Olt's life easier. He already had one-handed straps for his saddlebags, and now the cabin sported additional updates just for Olt.

Which he only got to use when the brownies weren't leaping to fulfill his every whim, of course.

Ro scanned the list and was so thankful Olt thought of these things. She kissed him again and waved the paper in farewell. "I'll be back soon. Set out tomorrow?"

He grinned. "First thing." At her look, he amended, "Well, maybe a *little* after breakfast."

Smiling more than she ever had in her life, or so it seemed, she resaddled Fairweather and took off for the nearest village. How long of a visit would Cosette expect anyway?

She already couldn't wait to be back in their own private cabin, just the two of them, and they hadn't even left yet.

※

The wolf pup was an excellent travel companion. For all his energy, for all the times she had to stop to feed him, to play off some of his energy, and to let him take care of business, Ro was seriously attached to the little guy.

Though her regard paled in comparison to Olt's. They frolicked together in a way reserved for children and pups, only one of whom was actually in the correct age category.

Not that Ro minded one bit. This pup was a godsend. It distracted her from the upcoming confrontation with Cosette.

Had someone told her years ago, when she'd first become a huntress due to a wolf trying to kill her sister, that she'd one day nourish a wolf, care for one, feel something other than hatred for one, she would've scoffed.

Now as the kilomètres fell away, she cradled the small body close and let him soothe the angst, the concern, the anxiousness.

The wolf pup seemed to sense her need, seemed to need her himself, what with losing his entire clan, and let her hold him as much as she needed to.

They bonded quickly.

But as she neared Paris, her heart beat faster. Would Cosette be mad? Scratch that. How mad exactly would Cosette be? Yet Ro had done what she needed to do, put her and Olt's needs first—and she was perfectly happy with her decision.

Until she got closer to Paris.

The pup wriggled and squirmed more than usual, and Ro had to force herself not to squeeze too tightly. He was done with their journey, and so was she.

But as the distance fell away, her stress increased in proportion to how close they got to the city.

She and Olt stopped at an inn for the last stretch of the journey, leaving the pup in the stable with their horses, paying extra to make sure he was fed well and watched over just as well. She scratched behind his ears and promised they'd be back soon.

The pup whined as they left to find their own meal, and she felt like she was betraying him in the worst way.

A quick meal and hiring a boy to take a message to

Cosette later, and Ro was back in the stable, checking on Kip. He was curled up in the hay, belly full, tummy gently rising and falling in deep sleep.

Olt found her there, on her knees, hovering protectively over the wolf pup.

"Ro?"

Her head jerked up, and the pup yawned and flopped over onto his other side.

"Olt! You surprised me." She smiled up at him and went back to watching the pup sleep.

Olt pulled her to stand and wrapped one arm around her waist, resting his cheek on her temple. "See? He's just fine. Nothing to worry about."

"I know. Just as you said. Still, I'd feel better if he slept in our room tonight."

Olt laughed. "Concerned he's going to run off? Or a stable hand's going to have a new pup come morning?" He sobered right up. "Actually, that's a valid point."

Ro shook her head, embarrassed at the level of her concern. But still. She couldn't put it aside. "Wolves terrorized France throughout the curse, preying on the weak and helpless, overrunning the city, coming close to where people lived, attacking."

She looked up at Olt. "Wolves are not well-loved in France. I should've left him with Gustave, but I didn't want to. Besides, his training is going so well, and I didn't want to mess that up. And I wanted him with me. And—"

Olt chuckled. "You trying to convince me or yourself?"

"Both." She gave him a pleading look. This particular inn matron was most vocal about keeping the pup in the stables with the horses. "Distract the owners? Please? I'll sneak him up in my cloak."

He gave her an indulgent smile, like he thought she was cute.

Ro scowled at him. "I'm serious."

"I know you are, my love."

He kissed her nose, so Ro pulled back and crossed her arms.

"All right, all right!" He raised his hand and backed away, laughing. "I'm just saying, what about when he gets vocal? Or needs to go out in the middle of the night? We've only camped outside until now. What if he hates the room and decides to howl all night?"

Ro chewed on her lip and watched the pup sleep. Any of those things meant she'd likely be up all night with him. "Maybe I should just sleep out here."

"Oh, non, non, non. We're nearing the city, dearest huntress, and that means vagabonds, thieves, and altogether untrustworthy people on the road."

"But I'll be in the stable."

He sighed and rubbed his forehead. "We're not going to bed until we figure this out, are we?"

She shook her head.

Olt groaned. "But there's a real bed upstairs! After eight nights on the road. Please don't do this to me."

With a laugh, Ro leaned forward and kissed him. Her eyes danced. "Then help me sneak Kip upstairs."

After a restless night of keeping Kip quiet, tiptoeing him out twice to take care of business, and nearly falling asleep in the stable waiting for the coast to be clear to sneak back inside, Ro was more than ready to get back on the road.

Olt, of course, slept through it all.

So he was bright and cheery and whistling as Ro drank four cups of café before she was willing to speak a single word. To anyone.

She was more than ready to be shown to her room in the palace for a nap.

Until they crested the slight rise to the northwest of Paris.

The beautiful city came into view, and Ro soaked it in. Trêve and Cosette had been busy. Even more wooden buildings were being replaced by stone, and at an astonishing rate, completely changing the face of the city.

The king and queen were truly making France a better place. Food was growing, people had work, and the city that had fallen into disrepair was being rebuilt.

Ro was so proud of them both.

And the people of France, of course, for doing so well for themselves after the curse. They'd worked hard to build better lives.

After they entered Paris, Olt tugged her to a side street. "Ro, wait. I want to show you something."

She raised an eyebrow. "Taking our lives into your hands already, are we? You know Cosette won't stand for us being in the city and not heading for the palace first thing."

Olt grinned with a confidence that said he knew he could get away with anything. It was a youngest-child thing he and Cosette shared, much to their happiness and everyone else's annoyance.

Well, to Ro's, anyway. She could never get away with such things.

He winked. "Trust me. It'll be quick, I promise."

With a sigh, Ro turned her horse after him, wondering what she could tell Cosette that wouldn't make guilt swarm her even more than it already was. Hopefully the note she'd sent yesterday to tell her they would arrive sometime today, but they didn't know when, would help?

She followed him to a small apartment on the rim of Paris, built in the manner of a château, but unlike the other buildings nearby, it was walled off on all sides and not connected to any of the buildings around it. Ro lifted an eyebrow at Olt.

"It's the new German embassy," he explained. "And my headquarters while I'm in Paris. Well, it was going to be, anyway, before Olov agreed to take over my ambassadorial duties. It's not entirely ready yet."

Ro brightened. "Olov is here?"

All six of Olt's brothers had been stoic at their wedding, with the only warmth coming from Oberon, the eldest, and his wife, Odile—the current rulers of Prussia. Whether it was their nature, they were still recovering from the horror they'd been through with the Nightingale Empress, or they didn't think she should be with their brother, Ro was determined to win them over.

Starting with Olov, if he were here.

Olt's ready grin was back in a flash. "I imagine he's at the palace, awaiting our arrival." He shrugged. "I sent a note telling him to meet us there, anyway."

Ro laughed. "Now why on earth would you do that?"

"To show you our rooms at the embassy, my Mademoiselle."

At Ro's sharp look, he gave her a tender smile. "Olov will be taking over my role here, true, and I will be returning with you to the Black Forest, but while we're here, if we ever want to get away and not be disturbed, the rooms at the back of the house are quite nice. And far enough away from the front not to hear the bell." He shifted nervously. "And, well, I wanted to show you. Before Olov moves in."

Ro leaned over to kiss him. "Then I cannot wait to see them. Lead the way, husband mine."

Olt gave her a brief tour, she saw to the pup's needs, then they had a merry fire going in the kitchen's hearth as the pup napped before its blazing warmth and Ro and Olt prepared café.

"It should be live-in ready in a few weeks," Olt said casually. "If you want to stay here whenever we visit the city."

He didn't look up from stirring his tea. Was that what he'd been so nervous to talk to her about? Ro leaned over the countertop and kissed him.

A log popping in the fireplace reminded her they were here to do more than kiss.

Er, less. To talk. Nothing more.

Because Cosette was waiting for them.

Ro cleared her throat and moved back. Olt let her go, but reluctantly. "What about my grandmère's mantle, my need to be close to the Black Forest?"

"Before you left"—Ro winced, but Olt squeezed her hand and kept going—"I was getting it ready for you. In case you wanted to live near your family. Now that Olov has taken over as diplomat, he'll make his home here, turn it into a consulate."

He looked up at her. "I understand you took up your grandmère's mantle. I understand you need to stay in the Black Forest. I understand we have a newly rebuilt home we both love. But I wanted to give you this option. If you want it."

Ro could only stare at him.

He shrugged. "We can just use it when we visit, of course. If we don't want to stay in the palace, though I'm fine staying there too. But Olov knew I'd been getting it ready for you, and he won't move in if you want it."

She couldn't make her thoughts line up with her mouth. How had she been lucky enough to marry someone so kind and thoughtful?

"But what about it being a consulate?" Ro finally managed to say. "I know Trêve is excited to start zoning off areas for foreign dignitaries and diplomats, and I'd hate to get in the way of that."

Olt smiled and kissed her. "And that's another thing I love about you. How you're always thinking of others. Believe me, this is a zero-pressure question. Just tell me what you want. If you want a home in Paris, it's yours. It was built with you in mind."

"You had this *built*?"

"If you want to stay with your sister when we visit Paris and—in the future—stay at my family's palace when we visit them, I'm happy to. If you want to keep this, Cosette says it's ours in return for services rendered."

He rubbed the back of his neck. "She kept me rather . . . busy . . . while we were waiting to hear from you. Otherwise I wouldn't have still been here when we got word of the bounty on your head."

And Ro felt guilty all over again.

"Don't." Olt reached across the table to take her hand. "I didn't tell you that to make you feel worse. I only say it so you can make an informed decision."

"About that . . . Trêve offered me le Château des Roses Noires, in exchange for keeping the grounds and seeing that any nearby are employed."

At Olt's wide eyes, she sent him a sharp look. "He didn't tell you?"

He shook his head, as if in awe of the king's offer. Exactly how Ro felt.

She sighed. "I suppose that's my fault. Not only for running off, but for asking to tell you myself." She quickly outlined the offer. "Honestly, I wasn't going to accept, not after my promise to Grandmère. But I do want your input."

The pup slept through it all, the log burned away, and Olt was quiet.

"Olt, I willingly took up her axe without talking to you first." She fiddled with her cup and met his eyes, letting her apology bleed through. "I'm so sorry. But that means I can't be away long. I don't think having another home is a good idea, whether the château or the embassy, especially since we may not be able to travel much. And Grandmère did offer the cabin before you proposed. I just never got the chance to tell you."

She nodded around them at the beautiful home he'd planned just for them. "I think it should be used for its intended purpose. I think Olov should have it, with free rein to make it his own. And I think we should let the château go to someone who can live there, oversee its upkeep, and work the grounds." She bit her lip. "You don't hate me for that, do you?"

He gave her a melting look. "Of course not, Ro. I could never hate you. But are you sure? That you don't want a home nearer your sister? Whether three days or a mere half-hour?"

"I think the bigger question is, are you willing to live out in the middle of nowhere for the rest of your life? I've given my word, and I'm only now beginning to understand the extent of my duties. But I know you, Olt. You love being around people. You're the life of the party. I think one of my biggest fears now is if you can handle being away from people for so long."

Instead of answering, instead of denying her words instantly, Olt thought about it, and Ro's heart dropped.

"There's another option, of course." She had to take a deep breath to say the rest. "Do you want to live here? Without me? You could always retain your diplomatic duties with Olov, come here for half the year or something."

"Do you want me to live here? Without you?" Olt asked in shock.

"Of course not!" burst out of Ro's mouth.

He sagged in immediate relief.

"I'm not going to lie: I'm still scared, Olt. I still have to choose every day to trust you, to believe you won't grow tired of living in the middle of nowhere, that you won't grow tired of, well, *me*. I still have to fight myself, fight my doubts, to trust you'll still want to be with me as you get to know me better. Of course I want you with me, but I have to fight to believe that every single day."

He frowned. "But when you left before . . . because of your grandmère . . ."

"I still would've run, Olt." It hurt to admit, but it was true.

Olt looked down and gripped his cup tighter.

"I wasn't ready then. I am now. I made my choice. But the question applies to you too. Where do you want to live? You didn't ask for this. You didn't ask for me to get stuck in the Black Forest, unable to leave except for short visits."

Ro traced the intricate carvings along the kitchen's waist-high table, massive enough for preparing elaborate meals. The embassy was most definitely large enough for a full staff, as well as hosting banquets for other heads of state. She preferred her cozy cabin.

She both wanted Olt to hurry and answer and she wanted to flee as fast as her horse could take her.

An impulse she could no longer give in to when it came to him.

"Then I guess the only question is . . ."

Ro raised her eyes to meet his, holding her breath.

"How soon shall we return to our cabin in the Black Forest?" He smiled, and it was like sunshine and happiness and every good thing, and in that instant, everything went right with her world.

Ro jumped up and threw her arms around him with a cry. "Oh, Olt, really?"

"Really." He kissed her. "Wherever you are, my home is, Ro."

"You won't mind returning to the forest? Living in seclusion?"

As relief broke inside of her like a dam flooding her entire system, tears overflowed on her cheeks. So many tears. She was worse than her sisters right now. Ro wiped her face.

"I would prefer it."

Ro pulled back, staring at him with wide eyes, surprised right out of her tears.

"I tried to fit in here because you were here, Ro. So you could be near your sister. I love being around people, you know I do, but I'm not cut out to be a diplomat." He grinned. "I apparently make too many jokes."

Ro laughed outright, and Olt kissed her.

"We have a good life in the forest, Ro. I'm happy to live there for the rest of my life with you. Besides, we're near my family." His eyes shone. "You know my sister-in-law won't let us go too long without inviting us to family dinners."

Ro sniffled and allowed the smile he was trying to draw from her out.

Olt extracted a handkerchief and handed it to her.

She laughed and wiped her eyes.

He stood and pulled her to her feet. "Now, let's go see your sister before she sends soldiers to round us up."

37

After spending far longer in the Prussian embassy than Ro had meant to, including cleaning off their travel grime and putting on fresh clothing, Ro and Olt set off for the palace.

They found Cosette calmly sitting and taking refreshments with her Mesdemoiselles-in-waiting.

After the servant announced them, she finished her sip of café before acknowledging them. "Rosette. How good of you to join us." She tilted her head. "Prince Odin. I see you finally persuaded my wayward sister to come home." She arched an eyebrow. "Or was it you who kept her away for so long?"

He grinned at her recklessly, not a hint of apology in his dancing eyes or spritely tone. "It is good to see you as well, Majesté."

Cosette's eyes fell on the pup, who was gnawing happily on the rope Olt had looped around his neck so he wouldn't get loose in the palace. "And who is this?"

"Kip," Ro volunteered. "We, uh, found him. And are taking care of him."

Cosette sniffed and turned to Ro. "Did you find all you needed at the new embassy? I almost thought you'd spend another two hours there. You know, since no one was waiting on pins and needles for your arrival or anything."

Ro laughed and shrugged off the formality of the room to hug her sister, who remained stiffly seated. "You can't have expected us to want to come so quickly, being newly married." Ro pulled up an empty chair, placed it at her sister's side, and sat, ignoring her miffed attitude entirely. "Wasn't it you who expounded upon the pleasures of marriage?"

Cosette's skin went a lovely rose color, and her Mesdemoiselles-in-waiting tittered behind their fans, which they raised at Ro's shocking words. Ro poured herself a cup of café with a smirk.

The moment she saw Ro's expression, Cosette rolled her eyes. "Oui, oui, you've had your fun. Satisfied?"

Ro smiled wide as she sipped her café. "Very."

With a huff, Cosette clapped her hands. "Out, all of you. I wish for a tête-à-tête with my sister."

The Mesdemoiselles left in a flurry, appearing to hurry but taking their sweet time evacuating the room. Cosette remained stoic through it all, as if bored.

"I shall visit Trêve, shall I?" Olt asked as the last few Mesdemoiselles left. "Where is he, anyway?"

Cosette waved a hand. "Where else? He spends all his time in his study, assigning this property or that, overseeing trade agreements, rebuilding our country. What else was he to do while waiting *months* for your arrival?"

Ro and Olt exchanged a lingering, sparkling look, and Olt bowed and quit the room without another word, the pup's claws scrabbling across the parquet floor as he rushed to catch up. Olt was most definitely hiding a smile. Cosette sipped her café while Ro seriously damaged the tray that held a wide range of pastries.

She was ravenous after their journey and their, er, slight detour along the way.

"At least you two are happy," Cosette muttered into her cup.

Ro let her sister stew. She'd talk when she was good and ready, and not before.

After a long pause, Cosette clinked down her porcelain cup on its base, sloshing café down the side, and turned on Ro suddenly. "You couldn't have hurried even a little bit? I've been waiting *months*."

Ro's resolve melted at the hurt in her sister's eyes. She reached out and took her hand. "Cosette. Did you honestly think I wanted a big wedding? That I would want to wait for however long such preparations take after I finally decided to marry him? That we would come visit you in the middle of our honeymoon?"

Cosette pouted. "Of course not. But I wanted to be a part of it all anyway! Did you know I kept him here for *weeks* after you rejected him and ran off? I had him running errands, busy with any task I could think of, no matter how small, waiting for you to realize how perfect he was for you and come to your senses and get back here and take him?"

Cosette's voice rose, her cheeks flushed an even deeper shade, and the guilt Ro had worked hard to shed on the road came flooding back.

"I'd almost run out of ideas when we found out about that stupid bounty on your head. *Believe* me, the moment we learned you'd been taken, I sent a strongly worded letter to the king of Angleterre, demanding your immediate release.

"And then after you were kidnapped, you didn't consider for one moment I'd want to see you the second you'd finished your stupid huntress business in the Black Forest?"

Now Cosette was on her feet, not caring to keep her voice low, chest heaving, fists clenched, staring down at her with the fire of a thousand suns in her eyes.

Ro stared up at her sister, mouth open, words gone.

"Did you even think of me *once*?" Cosette demanded, then burst into tears.

Ro immediately dumped her small plate on the tray, nearly upsetting the whole thing, and stood, taking her sister into her arms.

"Oh, Cosette. Non, je suis désolé, I didn't. I was only horribly, selfishly thinking of myself and how I could get out of having a public display for a wedding. I am so sorry."

Cosette continued to sob and hiccup in her embrace, and Ro felt worse than terrible. What had seemed a good idea, a way to get out of something she knew she was going to detest, was now the worst idea in the world. What had she been thinking?

That was just it. She hadn't been.

Ro had married Olt in an overwhelming sweep of passion, wanting to be his so badly she could taste it, not wanting to waste another moment apart.

She pulled back and looked into her sister's eyes. Cosette sent her a resentful look, still pouting.

"To make it up to you, to show I'm truly sorry, why don't you throw me and Olt a celebratory fête to announce the union? I'll even let you tell people it was your idea to have a small family wedding."

"A wedding where I wasn't even present," Cosette grumbled.

Ro winced. "Pas said something about having a private ceremony with a priest, just for family." She waved a finger under Cosette's nose. "I mean it. Family only. Captain Red married us—"

Cosette gasped, tears forgotten. "A ship captain? And a *pirate*, no less? Not a priest?"

Ro allowed herself a small smile. "A privateer, actually, and yes, a naval captain can legally marry a couple in Prussia."

Captain Red had been thrilled to inform Ro of that fact.

Cosette immediately went into action, bustling around the room and gathering supplies: namely a large booklet of paper covered in lace and ribbons with a quill pen. "That simply will not do." She paused. "Wait. Have you consummated this, this *union* yet?"

Ro blushed to the roots of her hair and all the way down to her toenails. "Cosette, *really*."

Cosette sniffed, giving her sister a haughty look. "I can see by the guilty look on your face that you *have*. No matter. We shall have you married in the sight of Dieu and *our* government soon enough."

She opened the booklet that Ro could see was overflowing with plans for her nuptials—likely from when Olt had first proposed. Perhaps even before. "Now let's see, where were we? Ah, oui! The gown. Rosette—"

Ro snatched the book from Cosette's hands and held it overhead.

Cosette jumped to get it back, but Ro had her père's tall, willowy build, and Cosette had a short, delicate build, so no matter how high she jumped, she couldn't reach it.

With a huff, Cosette swiped a tendril of hair out of her eye and sent Ro a glare. "Don't make me resort to hair pulling, sister. I will win that fight and you know it."

Ro sent a calm look her sister's way and nodded at the book in her hand. "Save these plans for Allura."

"Allura *Aurore*," Cosette corrected instantly.

"Save these plans for your daughter, Cosette. I mean it. I won't be made a spectacle, and if you insist on one, I will simply return with my *husband* to our home and continue our already married life, priest or no."

Cosette crossed her arms and stopped trying to get the journal back, but she did not look happy.

Ro softened her voice for her sister's sake, but she made sure to remain firm so Cosette knew she was serious. "I do not want a wedding. I am happy to recite vows before a priest, you know I am"—a thought struck her—"as long as it is *not* Père Guise . . ."

Cosette glanced away. "As our parish priest, it would be an insult . . ."

A name came to Ro unbidden. "Père Jérôme or no one. I mean it, Cosette. He did me a favor once, and it is thanks to him that I was able to defeat the Wolf King at all."

The first hint of interest appeared in Cosette's expression. "The Wolf King? You'll have to tell me—never mind. Important things first. You will not budge?"

Ro handed the book back. "I will not budge. No spectacle, family only, a simple dress, a small gathering, and only that priest. You can do whatever else you like as long as those requirements are met."

She wasn't picky, she really wasn't, but she couldn't stand the thought of standing in front of people she didn't know and taking something special and sacred and private and making a public display of something precious to her.

On this she wouldn't be moved.

As Cosette could surely see in her eyes.

"Whatever else I like, hmm?" Cosette's expression brightened mere seconds before dimming again. She dropped her gaze and smoothed the frilly cover of the book. "I really am quite upset with you, you know."

Ro looped her sister's unwilling arm through her own. Cosette remained stiff, gaze firmly on the book. "I know. And I'm upset with myself for not handling it better. But please, please, please believe me, Cosette. We are quite different, you and I, and I will never fit into your mold. Please accept this is who I am."

Head coming up at that, Cosette's wide eyes met her own. "Oh, I never wanted you to be any different! I just, I don't know. I wanted to have fun, that's all. I wanted *you* to have fun. And I want you to celebrate your wedding, not let it pass by unknown and unseen."

Ro squeezed her sister's arm. "I believe you. And I'm happy to celebrate with you, I am. But let's celebrate just you and me, and leave the spectacle for someone else, oui?"

Thinking about it a moment, Cosette finally relented. "All right. Oui. We shall celebrate your way this time, not mine." But she copied Ro's earlier movement and shook her finger under Ro's nose. "But a priest is non-negotiable."

Good-naturedly, Ro shrugged. "I'm already married, so it doesn't bother me either way. As long as it's the priest I want, I don't mind one bit." Her expression darkened. "Or at the very least, just not Père Guise."

Cosette eyed her. "You've become quite bossy in your married state, sister."

Ro laughed. "And you haven't?"

Cosette huffed and tugged Ro out of the room. "Very well. I concede I have lost. But when you have a babe on the way, I shall not be deterred, mark my words. We shall celebrate your child as it is meant to be celebrated, with fanfare and parties and gifts. Lots of gifts."

Ro halted suddenly at the unexpected words, her heart dropping right through the floor. She'd known this moment was coming and that it would be painful, but she hadn't expected how very excruciating it would be. How very much like a punch to the gut.

"Rose, what is it?" Cosette was peering closely into her face. "Oh, Rosette, why didn't you tell me?"

She immediately reversed course and dragged Ro back into the sitting room so their conversation would remain their own. She shut the door behind them.

"Don't you worry, I know plenty of doctors, and this midwife has the perfect remedy for conceiving that has worked for every patient who has tried it, even me. And besides! Perhaps it's too early to tell. How did you find out? Did you lose a babe? Oh, dearest sister, I hope not! But don't you worry. I know just the thing—"

Head reeling with the flurry of words being flung her way, Ro clasped her sister's hands to stop the flow. "Cosette, stop. It cannot be reversed, this, this, barren state of mine. Besides, I just got married. I'm not ready. I can't handle too much change at once, you know . . ." She said it lightly, trying to relieve the somber mood.

Cosette shook her head. "We won't give up, you and I. A babe changes your life, and in the best possible way. When you're ready, you come to me, and I will ply you with every remedy I know."

"And if I choose not to? Try, that is."

Raising both eyebrows, Cosette was shocked into silence for a few heartbeats. "Then," she said slowly, "I will respect your wishes and not bring it up again."

It sounded like every word pained her.

Ro laughed and kissed her sister's cheek. "She can learn."

"Oh, stop it, you." Cosette playfully slapped Ro's arm, returned the kiss, and then once more hauled Ro from the chamber, clinging to her arm as if still offering unspoken support.

Ro tried to act like it didn't affect her, but she had to swallow past the burn in her throat. Every time she thought she couldn't love Cosette more, she would go and do something like this.

Which made Ro feel even worse about leaving her out of the wedding.

"Now, about this wedding of yours," Cosette said suddenly, as if reading her mind. "I can decorate to my heart's content, oui?"

"Of course," Ro said easily, relaxing into the easy banter between them.

"And order any food I like from the kitchens?"

"We all do like to eat," Ro said solemnly.

"And I can commission you a dress?"

"As long as it is simple and I do not feel like a frothy ball of lace, absolutely." Ro gave her sister a side-eye. "Though I'd much rather have a creation of your own making."

With a slight flush, Cosette gave Ro a pleased smile. "I can work with that. Although I do prefer to have a completed dress as a base layer for my creations. Gives me more to work with."

And Ro smiled while Cosette launched into an elaborate scheme for Ro's second wedding, hiding her sister's offer deep in her heart.

One day, she might be back to seek Cosette's help. Perhaps.

But only once she was certain she was ready for such thing as a babe disrupting their lives, and hopefully, as Cosette had said, in the best way possible.

38

s Cosette devolved into an absolute flurry of getting ready for the ceremony, Ro and Olt settled into life at the palace. Which, for some reason, Ro hadn't been expecting.

Knowing her sister as she did, she should have.

Winter was fast approaching, and concern started to swell in Ro about riding home in cold weather—or being stuck in Paris until winter passed. But there were celebration dinners and dances and operas and art displays and extravaganzas they simply could not miss.

Also, Cosette insisted Olov needed Olt's help settling into his new role as diplomat far more than Ro felt he did, and Ro began to strategize in earnest how best to escape. Er, travel home. In the middle of the night, hidden in dark-blue cloaks, and bribing the guard to the city gates started to look like their best option.

Whether a blessing was performed by a priest or not. Surely putting something small together couldn't possibly take this much time.

It was like an itch under her skin, a need to be home, the Black Forest calling to her in her dreams, asking her to return and watch over the trees as they entered their winter rest. Ro didn't know how much longer she could listen to their call without obeying the urgency within.

Yet Cosette seemed to be scheming, and Ro couldn't for the life of her figure out what she was up to.

Until the day before the ceremony, on their way to the family dîner celebration.

They were walking down the palace hallway together when Cosette looped her arm through Ro's. "So I've been meaning to tell you . . ."

Ro nudged her sister when Cosette's voice trailed off. They were almost to the dining hall, where their conversation wouldn't be their own again for several hours.

Cosette flashed Ro a bright smile. "Père will be joining us for dîner. He asked to see you . . ."

Ro immediately reversed direction and walked back the way she'd come.

Cosette hung on for dear life. "Rosette, wait. Just listen to me, please."

Ro rounded on her and snarled right in her face. "Non, *you* listen." Cosette's eyes flew wide. Ro kept going, though her vehemence surprised even herself. "I will not be in the same room as that man, and you know it. I can't believe you of all people would do this to me. The ball was bad enough!"

She shook off her sister's strong grip and stalked toward her room.

"Oh, Ro . . ." The heartbreak in her sister's words nearly broke the dam Ro had so carefully constructed, so Ro shored it up as she marched away. "Won't you even give him a chance to talk to you? Won't you ever forgive him?"

Ro didn't answer. But non, she most certainly would not.

Cosette let her go.

Thoughts pounded through Ro's head, and she didn't see the château she walked through, yet she somehow made it to her chambers.

The nerve! After all these years, refusing to acknowledge

her as his daughter, not allowing her into his home, pretending she didn't exist. She'd worked hard to make a name for herself, to provide for herself and her siblings in a world that tried to shame her for that very thing, and he'd put her in that position. Now he thought she'd welcome him with open arms?

Like diable.

She paced like a caged animal. The walls were closing in. Her chest felt tight and ready to explode. She couldn't breathe.

She was trapped.

Ro bolted out the door and sprinted to the stables and Fairweather.

It didn't matter that she was starving. Who cared if she missed a dîner in her honor? She'd pilfer something from the kitchen later.

Ro still didn't know what to do the next day.

Servants were rushing everywhere, preparing for the evening's wedding and following fête. Ro had less than an hour to get ready, and after the long ride yesterday, she hadn't left her room once except to peek at the progress and to stress over it.

Olt had come and gone, checking on her before he was shooed away so he wouldn't see Ro in her gown before the ceremony.

Then Margo, Chantie, and Arletta helped her dress, and Ro ran out of time to make a decision. She barely noticed as they helped her into her gown. It wouldn't be much of a party if she hauled off and hit her père—as he'd done to her so long ago.

And when she'd come back to make it right, he'd thrown her out of his house, denied her as his daughter. She'd had to fend for herself, learning to hunt wolves to provide for herself and the family he was too drunk to care for himself.

Cosette had seen it all. How could she insist Ro see him? *Forgive* him?

She paused, one hand to her waist and the nerves fluttering there.

Was Cosette right? Was it time to forgive and move on?

Ro hadn't even known she was that angry until her père had been mentioned. She hadn't known she still felt so strongly.

She took it back. Why work this out on her own if she kept endlessly spinning without a solution in sight? She'd give anything to talk to Olt, to soak up a measure of his calm, to listen to his wisdom. But Cosette had insisted they not see each other before the ceremony.

She could do it. She could be in the same room as her père.

But that didn't mean she had to talk to him or acknowledge him.

Curse Cosette for putting Ro in this position.

For inviting their père to Ro's wedding.

She had no right.

Ro hated to admit it, but she was barely tolerable to her père that evening.

He and his new wife—new to Ro, as he'd married her several years ago while Cosette was the only one still in his household—and their two stepdaughters presented themselves to the king and queen of France, then to Olt and Ro.

Ro's head spun with how quickly everything had come together at Cosette's behest. Well, at least once Cosette realized Ro would leave if something didn't happen soon.

As Père Jérôme read Scripture and impressed upon them

the importance of placing Dieu in the center of their relation-ship—which the good captain had certainly not done—the ceremony was somehow short enough for Ro yet long enough for Cosette.

After Ro and Olt said their vows, they greeted their few guests, then joined them for a small wedding feast. Trêve and Cosette presided, Olt's brother Olov came with his guest, a beautiful young Mademoiselle who was just lovely and seemed perfect for Olov, then Ro's sisters and brothers and their spouses filled the rest of the table.

It was lovely, it was perfect, and it was far too much family all at once.

Ro couldn't wait to escape.

Yet Ro and Olt mingled as much as possible, greeting their guests and making dreaded small talk. For Ro, anyway. Olt was in his element.

At one point, Olov stopped next to her, observing the room. "I see you are taking good care of my brother."

She smiled. "It's the exact opposite. He's the one taking good care of me."

He gave her an appraising look, then smiled, as if she'd passed some kind of test. "It goes both ways."

He nodded to her and then moved away, and Ro couldn't help but feel smug. Two brothers down, four to go.

It was good to see the priest again, who'd once helped Ro in her hunt of the great white wolf. He delighted in her tale of defeating the Wolf King, especially since she'd first heard of the creature from one of his books.

Her père remained courteous when he spoke to her and Olt, inviting Ro to come see him before she left Paris, where he and Madame Béatrice and her two unmarried girls had settled in a modest townhouse in the city.

He remained weak, shaking, and leaning heavily on his cane, as he'd been at their engagement ball, but now his skin had a waxy, yellowish sheen that was decidedly unhealthy. It may have made her monstrous, but she couldn't force herself to feel anything for him, not even the slightest concern.

Ro made a noncommittal answer and moved on to her next guest, but not before she saw Cosette and Madame Béatrice exchange glances.

Oui, Cosette was most definitely planning something, and it had to do with her père. Which meant Ro would insist she and Olt leave soon.

Her père may have been civil to her, he may have asked to speak with her, but she could not forget when he'd denounced her, hit her, thrown her from his home—her home—and told her never to return.

How she'd had to make her own way in curse-laden France, teaching herself to hunt wolves for their bounty, all because she refused to allow him to sell her to the beast.

Who, granted, had ended up being the king of France, but the betrayal still stung.

Non, she'd not be seeing him, no matter what Cosette and the stepmère who had replaced her precious mère had planned.

§

A few days later, Ro stepped into Cosette's private sitting room to find stacks of paper everywhere. Though that wasn't quite right. They looked like books that hadn't quite been finished yet: innards only, wrapped in an off-white paper binding, without gilt on their edges.

"What is all this?"

Cosette gave her a dimpled smile. "I'm afraid your propensity to pen fairy tales has taken off like wildfire. All the Mesdemoiselles of court are scrambling to pen the wildest tale, the most fashionable, the most shocking or heartbreaking, and submit it to local chapbooks for publication."

"Chapbooks?"

Cosette flapped a hand. "You know. When they bundle several stories together in order to publish a booklet, but they don't have quite enough pages to make a full-fledged book? And the binding is odd, too. They bind it in paper, instead of the leatherbound hardcovers on regular books. I don't see how such books will hold up against wear, but it's easier to print more of them, I suppose."

Ro could only stare with her lips parted at the piles on the side tables, as well as stacked on the floor. "They've been busy, that's for certain."

"They have. Though the publishers are most ardently searching for stories written by the original author, and willing to pay most handsomely for new full-length tales."

Cosette stared at Ro expectantly. As if she had no intention of budging until Ro handed her something she'd written. Ro rolled her eyes. And dug around in her satchel and produced the dashing pirate tale she'd penned on evenings before the fire with Olt—the one Cosette had requested she bring to this very sitting room. This story had romance, adventure, and a happily-ever-after.

Cosette squealed and jumped up and down on her tiptoes. "Ooh, I knew it!"

And without another word, her greedy sister snatched it up and ran from the room to get Ro's latest fairy tale published. Though perhaps adventure story was a more apt moniker, this time.

That would bring her published books to a grand total of five.

Six, if she could finish the *Red Riding Hood* tale before they left. It still lacked a proper ending.

Ro rubbed the back of her neck and wished she'd used her own name on the manuscripts, just to see her true name in print, then decided she was better off without the attention. Maybe one book—her very last, perhaps—could have her name on it?

Worries for another time. The piles of new tales surrounding her beckoned like a siren call.

Ro sank into the nearest plush chair, settling in to see what kinds of stories were being written by the noble Mesdemoiselles in her absence.

A trend she'd started. Without her knowledge.

Who knew?

✦

Cosette returned with a satisfied smile. She dusted off her hands and beamed. "Well, that's settled, then."

Sparing her sister a quick glance, Ro sipped her café and kept reading. She honestly had no idea how long Cosette had been gone. "Pleased with yourself for displaying my stories for the whole realm to read?"

"Immensely," her sister said with a smug tone.

Ro smiled to herself. She didn't write her stories for others to read. She wrote because she loved penning tales, yet Cosette saw them all published anyway. And now that she'd gotten used to it, Ro didn't hate it as much as before.

After a long moment, she said, "Some of these are . . . interesting?"

"Aren't they just?" Cosette replied with a bounce. "Not all can match your skill, true, but the publishers are quite pleased to have such enthusiastic and numerous writers."

Ro tried very hard not to say how little skill these Mesdemoiselles had. There were a few gems, but for the most part, these young ladies were penning the most ridiculous stories that didn't have plots, endings, or logical characters.

If she had to read about one more maiden fainting at how handsome her prince disguised as a shepherd boy was, she might scream. Or a maiden given to a king as a prize, married sight unseen, only for the king to decide to marry someone else while his queen was away on a quest chasing down the sun and moon and east wind to find her way back to the lying, cheating . . . ahem.

At least they were short. A blessing, really.

She flipped the book over to read the title printed in a plain font on its odd paper cover. *Contes de Fées Français.* These truly were selling well?

"Oh! I almost forgot." Cosette held out an envelope. "Payment for your illustrious stories, Madame."

Ro smiled and took it. Now that she was no longer hiring out for hunts, this would go a long way to ensure she and Olt could live comfortably. Especially after she'd paid Captain Red's pirates for helping her complete her bargain with Madame LaChance.

"I suppose Olt and I should be off, then." She tapped the envelope's edge against her palm and then pocketed it.

Cosette raised shocked eyes to hers. "You don't mean to leave so soon?"

Ro groaned. "Cosette, I don't want to impose, and we need to get back."

"What do you mean, impose? You could never impose! It is impossible for you to impose. You—you just can't leave yet, d'accord?" Cosette fluttered her hands in a panic.

"Cosette. I can't be away from my forest much longer." Ro took a deep breath. "Besides, with how upset you were during my last visit, don't you need . . . space?"

"Space? What on earth are you talking about?"

"With how upset you were in Trêve's office." Ro's throat closed, and she had to swallow to keep going. "If I did something to offend you . . ."

"Oh, chère!" Cosette reached out and clasped her hand. "That was a private matter between me and Trêve. It had nothing to do with you, I promise."

"Oh. I thought you were mad at me."

"Mad at you? Whatever for?"

"You were so out of sorts, I guess I assumed . . ." She shrugged helplessly, face burning.

Cosette sighed. "Oh, dearest Rosette. It was nothing more than a tiff between spouses. It is resolved now."

"I see." Ro felt incredibly foolish.

"I'm sorry it caused you distress, though."

Ro offered a quick smile. "I'm sorry I made it a personal issue when it wasn't."

Cosette started to respond, but a servant glided in to refresh their café. Her foot caught on the table, and with a crash, the entire tray toppled, shattering cups, spilling hot liquid, and destroying those glorious pastries.

Cosette shot to her feet. "Imbecile!"

She raised her hand to strike the servant, but Ro lunged at her before she could do so. "Cosette! It was an accident."

No recognition that Ro held her wrist was in her sister's eyes as her chest heaved. She directed another biting comment at the servant. "Clean it up and get out. *Now*. I should dismiss you for such clumsiness!"

Sniffling, trying to hold in sobs and not quite succeeding, the servant shoved everything back on the tray with shaking hands. Ro's instinct was to help her, but she was more concerned about her sister's outrageous behavior.

"Cosette, look at me."

Rage-filled eyes turned to hers, bereft of feeling, intelligence. Nothing but unmitigated anger. Ro's chest ached like it was being crushed. This wasn't like Cosette. Her sister was levelheaded, kind.

"Cosette, what's wrong?" she whispered.

She blinked rapidly, as if coming out of a trance. "Why, nothing at all, dearest. Why do you ask?"

Ro didn't have words to respond. She was having trouble breathing. Something more was wrong here than a tiff between spouses. But how would she even begin to uncover such a thing?

The servant fled with her tray of broken porcelain and crushed pastries, and with her absence, Cosette's face cleared. Breaking Ro's hold on her wrist without any effort at all, Cosette sat gracefully and fluffed her skirts, not a care in the world.

Ro sank to her seat, mind whirling. For something to do while she scrambled to understand what she'd just seen, to figure out a way to broach the subject with Cosette, who was clearly pretending nothing untoward had happened, Ro lifted her half-full cup to her lips, grateful the servant hadn't gotten near it.

A second servant bustled in just then and curtsied. "Madame Béatrice to see you, ma Reine."

The elegant woman swept into the room, and Cosette composed herself in a flash, a brilliant smile springing forth.

Ro, who'd just buried her face in her café cup, jolted and nearly spilled it down her front. Her porcelain cup rattled in its saucer as she barely managed to set it on the table. Her chapbook, forgotten in her lap, dropped to the floor as she shot to her feet.

Even though Cosette was technically host, Madame Béatrice graciously waved a hand to Ro's chair. "Please. Sit. Do not stand on my account."

Ro sat and gripped the wooden armrests, her back ramrod straight and her heart pounding. What was her stepmère doing here?

She slid a suspicious look to Cosette, who was ignoring her.

Cosette had stood at the same time as Ro, and she and Madame Béatrice exchanged air-kisses as Cosette beamed. "Well isn't this a surprise! Welcome, Stepmère."

Her sister turned that blazing smile on Ro, and she instantly knew: this was a setup.

"I'll leave you to it, shall I?" Cosette spun on her heel and flounced out of the room.

That evil, devious sister of hers.

Ro was going to kill her.

But as she left, Cosette touched the side of her neck and her forehead with the back of her hand, as if shaken and trying not to show it. Ro's ire softened into concern. Oui, they needed to talk.

Madame Béatrice settled into a chair as yet another servant bustled in with refreshments. She waved off assistance, then poured herself café with a spot of crème and sipped with all the sereneness in the world. Leaving Ro with none.

She was already on edge from Cosette's behavior, and now this?

No wonder Cosette had gone on about how much Père had improved. How little time he had left. Neither woman had accepted the fact that Ro refused to see her père. They were going to strong-arm her into a meeting anyway . . . through guilt.

Though she had to admit, Père had not been . . . terrible . . . at her and Olt's second and unnecessary wedding.

Ro eyed Madame Béatrice warily. "My père is . . . much improved. I hear I have you to thank?"

Not that she would be doing so unless forced.

Madame Béatrice allowed a small smile to touch her face. "I have taken your père in hand, true. He is worth it."

Ro snorted, then covered her mouth with a napkin as her skin heated. "Désolé."

The elegant woman tilted her head. "I wonder if you took the time to get to know your père, to spend time with him, if you might find the same to be true."

"Yeah, that's not happening." Ro crossed her arms.

"You can sulk all you want, chérie, but you owe him this much." She lightly touched Ro's knee. "Speak with him. He so wants to make it right."

Ro's nostrils flared, and she sat ramrod straight to make

sure she didn't appear to be sulking. "Speak to him? You have no idea what he did! What we went through. Because of *him*."

The Comtesse calmly sipped her café, a gentle smirk in place. "I have an inkling."

"Ah oui?" Ro crossed her arms again, then quickly uncrossed them and kept herself from slouching at the last minute. "Prove it. What could my père have possibly done to you to mirror what he's done to us?"

Ro reached for her café to have something to do with her hands, only to find she'd spilled most of it.

Madame Béatrice calmly got Ro another cup and poured the rich brown brew, plunking in sucre and adding a dollop of crème. "Your père gambled away my family home, moved us to a derelict château with no roof and no windows—while wolves were still a threat, mind you—and we lost our Cosette along the journey, which he didn't seem to notice or mind."

Ro's mouth had fallen open. She shut it with difficulty. "Oh."

"Oh," Madame repeated, softly. "Oui, Madame. Oh. My daughters still fear she blames them, no matter how often she assures them she does not."

After a moment of reflection, Madame shook herself, then handed Ro her café. She accepted numbly as the woman—her stepmère—kept talking.

"At night, we would barricade ourselves into one of the upper rooms, praying it wouldn't rain or a wolf wouldn't find its way to the roof. Other nights, we barricaded ourselves into a lower floor as the upper rooms filled with rainwater and as wolves scratched at the barricade and howled all night long."

She met Ro's wide-eyed stare.

"I had made my bed, chérie, and I wanted to enjoy lying in it." She shrugged, the movement graceful. "I freely admit I am pleased with the changes, and your père took to them with relish." She leveled a long look at her. "Once he knew someone believed he could change and wouldn't accept his excuses any longer."

Ro bristled. "And you think his *daughter* should have—"

"Non," Madame Béatrice said sharply. Then softer, "Non, I do not think that was your place. But he has made the effort now, chérie. None of us know when the next moment may be our last. Talk to him before you have something to regret."

Ro set her café down with shaking hands, the rattling uncomfortably loud. There went a second wasted cup. "What I would *regret* is giving him the ability to wound me once more."

And with that, Ro stood and swept from the room.

Although stomped was more like it. Also maybe fled.

Ugh. Now she appeared even *more* petulant to her step-mère. Non. Her père's wife. Not her stepmère. Not after what she'd done to Cosette. She and her awful stepdaughters.

Cosette may have forgiven them, but Ro had not.

She gasped and stumbled back as she nearly ran into her eldest sister, Bernadette, who was standing there in the corridor, fists clenched, chest heaving, and glaring at Ro as if she'd like to set her on fire.

"You aren't even going to speak with him?"

Ro lifted her chin and marched past, not dignifying that with a response. She had already said everything that needed to be said.

Her sister sneered. "Of course not. The spoiled brat couldn't possibly *not* get her own way."

Ro frowned and turned back. "What are you talking about?"

"I wish Père could've seen you like this when we were children." Bernadette's sneer became even more ugly. "'Why can't you be sweet like Cosette, Bernadette? Why can't you be eager to please like Rosette, Bernadette?' Oh, please. You make me sick."

Ro was dumbfounded. "Where on earth is this coming from?"

"Don't act so innocent," Bernadette spat. "You and Cosette were always Père's favorites. Mère's too, but she hid it better. The sweet, perfect, youngest sisters, 'little Rose' and 'little Beauty.' Could do no wrong, and the rest of us couldn't possibly live up to you."

Ro's frown stayed firmly planted on her face. "Bernadette, please, I have no idea what you're talking about. He was hard on *all* of us —"

Bernadette rolled her eyes. "Sure you don't." True hurt blossomed on her face. "And yet after all this time, Père practically throws himself at your feet, begging your forgiveness for how he treated you, and you snub him. Again and again. Well if you ask me, you're the monster here, not him."

Ro had never been more baffled in her life. "You were there! When he struck me. When he sold me to a beast —"

"Because he loved you! More than any of us! He wanted you to be safe, and he didn't care what happened to the rest of us."

Bernadette's chest heaved, and she pointed one shaking finger at Ro. "And yet you were so blinded by your perceived slight, you couldn't see how the rest of us suffered. How he thought turning you over to the beast would give you a better life. Letting his precious Rose have the fine castle and food and dresses and all the roses her selfish little heart could possibly desire. He would have insisted on your taking Cosette with you, you know he would have."

Tears slipped down Bernadette's furious face, and Ro couldn't utter one coherent word.

"And now he comes to you, begs you like you once begged him — you who are fought over by kings, you who has all you ever wanted and more, you who are the right-hand huntress of our king — and you turn him away. Your heart is cruel and unfeeling, sister. The only sister you claim is Cosette, your precious queen, and you pretend the rest of us don't exist. You shove us away, Rosette, again and again, as you do him, and I won't be silent any longer."

She came close, enunciating every word with blinding rage. "I despise you. I hope one of the beasts you hunt tears you to shreds, and I never have to look at that smug, self-righteous face ever again."

Not bothering to wipe away the tears tracking down her face, Bernadette swirled away in a shower of expensive burgundy taffeta skirts, sweeping down the hallway with her head held high and her fists clenched.

"You didn't do anything!" Ro shouted at her back. "You made us do all the work, you made us do as you said, and you made us take the brunt of Père's drunken losing streak. How could *you*?"

Bernadette had stumbled to a halt and spun around at Ro's first shouted word, and now she started shaking her head, backing away. "I don't have to take this."

"I was a child!" Ro objected. "How dare you lay the blame on my shoulders. Not only couldn't I cook, I shouldn't have had to! How dare you put that kind of pressure on a *child*?"

"So was I!" Bernadette yelled back. "Do you think I wanted to lose my mère and have an entire household, eight children, thrust upon my shoulders? I didn't know what I was doing!"

Ro studied her sister's face as her ample bosom heaved. "Oh," she said.

"Oh, what?" her sister snapped.

Ro took in her silvering dark hair, the faint lines on her face she tried to hide with face powder, and the weight she'd put on since Ro had last seen her. She'd been under such strain, and it was showing on her body, more so than it should have been.

And Ro hadn't even noticed. She'd never noticed.

Ro stepped toward her, and Bernadette jerked away, as if expecting Ro to hit her.

Instead, Ro slipped her arms around her sister and held her tight. "Désolé, Bernadette. I didn't know. I only saw it from my perspective, never yours."

Bernadette started to sniffle.

"Of course that shouldn't have been on you. Of course you were just a child. Of course you didn't want any of that. You lost your mère, too."

Bernadette choked, and Ro held her tighter. And the sister Ro thought hated her more than anything else in the world clung to her and sobbed.

The moment her tears subsided, Bernadette said, "About time, you little . . . pest." Ro stiffened, and Bernadette sighed. "Too soon?"

"Definitely too soon."

Warily, they stepped back from each other. Bernadette awkwardly tweaked Ro's nose. Ro somehow kept herself from slapping her sister's hand away.

"I look forward to the day I can tease you without sounding like . . . me." Bernadette made her way to the end of the hall, gave Ro one last wistful glance, and rounded the corner.

Ro sat on the closest bench and gripped its edge.

Who knew her eldest sister, the one most like Ro in temperament, was a human being? That she'd been as lost as Ro, only she hadn't held up well under the pressure either. Maybe a sister Ro wanted to get to know better. One day.

And if Ro had been wrong about Bernadette . . .

Non. Père wasn't getting out of this so easily.

But the least she could do was talk to him. Especially if he was actually dying. Though a hard part of Ro wondered if he was pretending to be sick to rake in pity. But even she couldn't make herself believe that.

Just thinking about her père had Ro up and pacing, a

whirlwind of anger roiling inside. And suddenly, she stopped. Right there in the hallway, stood stock still.

Why was she doing this to herself? She sighed and ran a hand down her face. She was so very *tired*. It just—it took too much energy to keep this up.

She didn't like being angry and frustrated and wounded all the time. The hurt had to heal at some point, non? And she had a new family to think of now, even if it was just her and Olt. Even if it was always going to be just her and Olt.

Without giving herself time to talk herself out of it, she marched back into the sitting room.

Madame Béatrice lifted calm eyes to hers, and Ro tried very hard not to worry that she'd likely heard every shouted word.

"Oui, I will see him. But I promise nothing."

The elegant woman smiled. "All it takes is the first step. Then the next. I am proud of you, chérie."

And Ro didn't mean to, but she flushed, the kind words touching a thirsty place deep inside. She gave a cool nod and left.

And although she'd never admit it to herself, her step was the tiniest bit lighter.

39

Ro cautiously entered the small home on the outskirts of Paris. The housekeeper announced her, then bobbed a curtsy and fled.

After staring at her in astonishment, café cup raised halfway to his lips and in danger of spilling onto his lap, her père set down the cup with a clank, snatched up his cane, and struggled to rise.

"S'il vous plaît, do not get up," Ro said quickly.

At the sound of her voice, he blinked back tears, nodded, and stayed where he was. Ro swiftly took the armchair across from him so he wouldn't feel the need to stand. He stared at her, hunger and wistfulness and hope swimming in his watery eyes.

If possible, he looked even worse than he had at the wedding reception.

Ro glanced around the room. Smaller than a dwelling she'd expected the Comtesse to be willing to reside in, but then neither of them had much money after her père had gambled away Madame Béatrice's wealth as well.

A flush of anger washed from her belly across her body,

399

and Ro yanked her mind away from such thoughts lest she surge to her feet and storm out.

"This is a . . . lovely home," she finally managed to say.

His smile wobbled. "The Comtesse is a fine homemaker, no matter where we place roots."

Ro had to take another deep breath to remain civil. That meant he'd lost several homes in his time married to his second wife. How had she stood being married to him?

The housekeeper bustled in with café for Ro, then set a plate of nibbles between them before hurrying out again.

Ro took a sip for something to do, and almost spat it back out. Thin, watery, barely sweetened—surely they could afford more than this with Père homebound and unable to gamble further.

She almost reached for a digestive until she saw they were dry, cracked, and quite possibly stale.

Fine. No more distractions. Best to get this over with.

She met her père's gaze, which hadn't once left her.

"You wanted to see me?" Ro asked through stiff lips.

He struggled a moment, and she waited, well, not patiently, but she waited.

"I am dying," he finally said.

The words hit Ro as if she'd been slammed into a wall.

Of course Madame Béatrice had told her, as had Cosette, but it wasn't real until he said it. As much as she told herself she didn't care, that it wouldn't matter to her if he were, she found that she cared, very much.

She cleared her throat. "Madame Béatrice told me. Is there nothing to be done?"

A small smile. "Ah, little Rose, I've lived my life. It didn't go quite as I'd hoped, and I made my mistakes—many, many mistakes—but I am ready. Well, I will be, once I've made things right with you."

Instantly, Ro stood. She couldn't be here for this.

Before she could flee, her père flicked his fingers, and the housekeeper rushed in with a small chest and placed it in his blanket-clad lap.

He carefully kept his eyes off her as he opened the lid, as if he knew how close he was to losing her. "I've already spoken to the rest of your siblings, told them my regrets, and given them a few tokens, but this, my dear Rosette, is all I have left of your mère." His eyes finally raised to meet hers. "And I want you to have it."

Ro stood there, trembling from head to foot, then slowly stepped forward and reached for the box. He held it out to her, let her take it, didn't try to touch her.

Almost without realizing she'd done so, Ro sank back into the armchair and stared down into the contents. A haircomb, a necklace he'd given her mère when they were not yet wealthy but deeply in love, a few trinkets from his travels around the globe as a merchant.

All worthless in monetary value—expensive trinkets he'd gambled away or sold to pay his debts—but rich in sentimental value.

And a few pieces of stiff paper at the bottom.

Ro drew them out and found sketches from her grandpère. She may not have remembered his person, but she most definitely remembered his art. Her mère was so proud of it, she'd displayed his rich oil paintings on her walls.

Until her père had sold those as well.

Her heart swelled, and it was all she could do not to burst into tears.

They were not the family portraits in gilded frames that now graced someone else's home, as both the portraits by a renowned artist and the golden frames had been worth quite a lot, but these sketches were done in charcoal and matched those Grandmère had kept in her cabin before it was destroyed.

That reminded her: She needed to ask Gustave for the trunk of her grandmère's belongings so she could retrieve the sketches of Cendre, their parents, and Grandmère when she was young and first married to Grandpère.

These sketches were not unlike those.

Bernadette laughing, her head thrown back, eyes dancing, a carefree youth who had no idea how hard her life was about to become.

Her other sisters, in different poses of gameplay or reading or running outside in their garden, as if they had no idea their indulgent grandpère was taking quick sketches of their laughing faces.

Two boys, her brothers, covered in mud and playing hard, taking every opportunity to annoy their older sisters.

And chubby toddlers Ro and Cosette, leaning on their mère's skirts, clinging to her, eyes solemn, as if they knew she'd soon be taken from them and were staying close for as long as they had her.

Or, more likely, they'd just woken from naps and wanted to be close to their mère as they woke up further.

And their mère: lovely, stunning in her beauty, elegant, happy, and at peace in a garden filled with her children.

Each sketch was quickly done, that was obvious, but so lifelike, Ro felt herself a part of every moment, even if she didn't remember them.

She would treasure these portraits for the rest of her life.

Holding the sketches close to her chest, she bowed her head and struggled to speak. Once she was certain she would not burst into tears, she whispered, "Merci, Père. These mean more to me than I can say."

He cleared his throat, yet his voice came out thin. "I thought you would. All my children mourned her, me most of all, and not in a way that was good to any of you, to my great shame. But her death hit you hardest. No child wants to lose her mère, but you worshipped her, Ro. Watched her every move. Tried to emulate her. Clung to her skirts long after the rest had gained independence, even Cosette."

Ro blinked rapidly. She would *not* cry.

Not here anyway. She'd be sobbing her eyes out the moment she found a place all to herself, far away from other people.

"I only wish I had more of her to give you. That I'd kept some of the portraits, the jewelry she wished me to pass on to her daughters . . ."

He halted and seemed unable to speak, and Ro tried very hard not to judge him. Not to harden her heart against his suffering.

She'd been angry at him her entire life, ever since her mère had left this world and her père had been unable to care for his children, forcing them to fend for themselves.

Yet they were grown now. The curse had ended. They could care for themselves, including and especially Ro.

She was only hurting herself by holding tight to such pain.

Ro took a deep breath, let it out, and listened.

When her père could speak again, he pulled a ring from his finger and held it out. "I want you to have my signet ring. Our family crest. To remind you I was not always this husk before you, that once I had well-deserved pride in my profession, a noble title that served me well, and I took good care of my family. That I loved your mère very much and kept her in comfort as long as she was alive."

Stunned, Ro took it from him woodenly. He wanted her to have something that reminded her of *him*? It was all she could do to forget the pain he'd caused.

The ring lay heavy in her hand, their family crest from when they were nobles, their wealth coming from a successful merchant business that her père took great pride in and had been rewarded for by the crown, a life Ro had been too young to remember. Only snatches, and those followed by pain.

Pure gold. Had to be.

Her head came up. "You did not sell it?"

A little color came to his withered cheeks. "It was my

dearest wish I could regain the honor stolen from me by my own actions, that one day the crown would restore my title."

Ro hefted the heavy piece of jewelry in her hands. The ring would've brought quite a sum, and in his drunken stupor, her père had sold anything and everything he could get his hands on, often scouring his children's possessions for items of value.

That man would've been unable to hold on to anything of value for sentimental reasons. Her mère's jewelry, worth a fortune—it had been her dying request that it would be distributed among her daughters so they could marry securely —was far more important than a family crest, and he hadn't spared a single golden ring or silver hairbrush.

Yet he'd kept *this*?

"I don't believe you," she said through tight lips. "I watched you. I watched you riffle through our belongings, take anything of value, let your children *starve* so you could get drunk or be allowed one more night at the gaming table. No way would you have had enough self-control to keep *this*."

She thrust the ring at him in disgust, lip curled.

He couldn't meet her eyes. "Oui, you are right. Only, I hid it when they stripped me of my title and repossessed our belongings to pay my debts, not willing to give up every aspect of my former life. When your stepmère and I returned to Paris to live near your sisters, to make things right, I went through the ruins of our old home here and found it." He offered her a weak smile, still not looking at her. "I only wish I had hidden more."

Ro couldn't be here a second longer. She had to get out.

She sprang to her feet and thrust the ring back at her père, clutching the chest of treasures from her mère tight to her side. "I do not want this. Take it back."

Tear-filled eyes met hers. "I beg your forgiveness, Rosette. If I could take it back, if I could take it all back, if I could do things differently, raise you all as your mère begged me, give up gambling and drinking as she begged me, I would. I would in a heartbeat. Please forgive me, little Rose. Please let me go to my grave in peace, knowing I have done all in my power to make it right."

Ro stood there, shaking, staring down at him, wanting nothing more than to throw the ring in his face.

But she couldn't.

She knew what it was to make mistakes, to wish she'd done things differently. Perhaps not to the same extent as her père, but still.

There was still much life to be lived. For her. Who knew how her story would turn out? Yet his was nearly over.

She could do this one thing for him.

Ro nodded once, decided. "Oui. All right. I forgive you."

Her père burst into tears. "Merci, little Rose! Merci!" He launched himself out of the armchair with considerable effort and knelt before her, sobbing and clutching her hand to his forehead. His skin was clammy. "I have prayed for this day. Begged for it. How you put my heart at ease, dearest daughter! How your mère and I loved you so."

Ro stood there, stiff, desperately wanting her hand back, and embarrassed deep in her soul by her père's complete loss of composure.

She may have said she'd forgiven him for his peace of mind, but she knew the anger and bitterness would rise every day she was reminded of him. She'd have to forgive him again and again—until her heart and her mind believed her.

As soon as she could without being overly cruel, she removed her hand, helped him back into his chair, and covered his lap with his blanket.

"Merci for seeing me, Ro. Merci. It means the world. I cannot express how much it means to me." Père continued to cry, though quieter now.

With a stiff bow, she turned and left.

As she marched resolutely away, mind whirling, she eventually crossed one of the many bridges across the Seine. The ring's heaviness came to her then, penetrating the haze, and she looked down at it.

The crest filled her with hatred.

Without giving herself time to think it over, she hurled the ring into the water.

Perhaps she'd regret it one day, but today she couldn't stand to look at it.

She continued to the palace.

If only her père had been more of a man, they could've had such a different life, even with the curse falling over all of France. To lose her mère, then their possessions and their home, then to move to a hovel where the children had to fend for themselves while their père wandered the countryside — she took a deep breath and let it out slowly.

Oui, if she wanted to forgive him in her heart, she'd have to do it every single day.

She was already exhausted just thinking about it.

Ro stopped suddenly. Someone was walking toward her. Not like others on the street, but intent, focused, on her and her alone.

Then her feet were moving, she was running, and she threw herself at Olt, wrapping her arms around him, burying her face in his chest.

And to her complete and utter humiliation, she burst into tears.

"It went that well, huh?" he said gently.

She couldn't even speak, she was crying so hard.

"I would've been more than happy to go with you."

She shook her head, even as she hiccuped. Non, she needed to face her père alone. Still, Olt had given her space, waited for her, and been there for her when she needed him most.

She didn't deserve him even a little bit.

Once she calmed, they found a bench in a nearby park,

and she told him everything. He listened, didn't judge, didn't tell her she should've done differently. Even after she'd told him about the ring. Because even if she'd been foolish, she couldn't make herself regret hurling it away.

And then they went through the sketches together, and Ro moved one step closer to healing.

❧

Her père slipped quietly and peacefully into his eternal rest not a week later.

Ro stood with her siblings in the family cemetery, and although it made her feel like a monster, all she could feel was overwhelming relief.

Later she confessed this to Olt, lying in the dark while he held her, and thankfully he didn't tell her she shouldn't feel that way, didn't add to her guilt.

Because as much as she couldn't make herself stop feeling relief that the man who'd wounded her would no longer be able to do so, she couldn't stop feeling guilty that she felt that way.

Cosette managed to keep them at the palace another week while the city was draped in black flags, in honor of the queen's père's death, and finally, without telling Cosette they were doing so, Ro and Olt packed their bags and prepared to set out for the Black Forest.

"I'll go say au revoir," Ro told Olt, somewhat nervous whether her sister would let them leave or not.

She'd been more weepy, more clingy lately, and Ro didn't know how to account for it. Cosette hadn't been close to their père either, though she'd always hoped he'd choose to be a better man.

Non, it was more than that, and Ro couldn't figure out what.

She lifted worried eyes to Olt. "Think she'll let us go?"

Olt laughed and came over to kiss her. "It's not like she's holding us hostage."

Ro frowned. "I know. But her requests are reasonable, and before I know it, our plans to leave have been delayed yet again. I've never had such trouble getting away before. It's like she's worried about our leaving or something."

Yet pressure was building inside of Ro to get back, and she didn't know how much longer she could ignore it. In fact, she couldn't. She could no longer ignore it. It was as simple as that.

Olt put his arm around her and held her close, packed bags momentarily forgotten. "We really must get back and relieve Gustave. Besides, winter is imminent, and we want to travel before snow hits. Perhaps she'll understand that?"

"I'll try." Ro bit her lip. "Though I highly suspect she'll talk us into wintering here."

Olt kissed her worry away. "I'll go saddle the horses. See you in the stables."

Ro gave him a look. "If I don't meet you within the hour, come look for me. I'll quite possibly be chained in the dungeon."

Olt laughed, grabbed their bags, and headed out after one more lingering kiss that helped Ro forget for a moment that she'd likely be held hostage by her sister's good intentions once more.

Unable to delay, no matter how much she wanted to, Ro went in search of Cosette. No matter what her sister said this time, Ro would not be swayed. She would—

All of a sudden, the hall grew hazy, as if snow were swirling *inside* the palace.

Dizzy, Ro reached for the wall, and with her next step, she was no longer in the French palace.

40

Ro staggered, senses reeling, as she tried to comprehend what she was seeing. Slowly, things came into focus a few at a time, as if that was all she could handle. She stood in a place that was nothing but white on white, yet each object was distinct from the other. The variations were soft, muted. White balls of—something—floated lazily in the air, drifting as if each one had all the time in the world. Everything looked as if it were covered in snow. But it wasn't the slightest bit cold.

Where am I? Ro wondered.

"Why, the Land of the Fey, of course," spoke a familiar voice. "Well, a realm very near it, anyway."

Ro turned slowly, her heartbeat ratcheting up by degrees.

Their eyes met, and the familiar obeisance oozed its way through Ro, and all she wanted to do was bow and obey anything this lovely creature said.

"You." The word was not said with obeisance or respect, however, and Ro put every ounce of her rage, her heartbreak, her confusion behind the word.

The Queen of the Fairies raised one pristine eyebrow, and time ticked uncertain for a moment before it righted itself.

"Yes, Mademoiselle Rosette Jacqueline LeFèvre Reynard, it is I."

Ro took three menacing steps forward, and suddenly, a chest-high barrier of white thorns stood between her and the queen.

"My sister." Ro pointed at the queen, hand trembling, as she shook off the queen's influence over her. "You stole my sister!"

Something like regret passed over the queen's face. "I am truly sorry, but she had passed on, and I had to hide my daughter. Surely you can understand."

Ro shook her head furiously, too many words flooding to get out at once, creating a block.

The queen sighed, sorrow in her lovely eyes. "Then you are not the person I thought you to be."

The dam broke, and her words flowed out in a rush. "She was still alive. My sister was still alive when you took her, and I never knew her!"

The queen's eyes widened, and her hand rested at her throat for a moment, a rare sign of discomfort from the Queen of the Fairies. "What? What did you say?"

Ro's throat clogged, and her voice came out thick and heavy. "My sister was alive that night. When you took her and traded her for Cosette. I met her on my voyage to defeat the sirènes, but I didn't know who she was."

"But—that's impossible. I saw her. I saw the child, chose her specifically for her good family and the life that had fled her. She had no aura. None. No sign of life whatsoever." Her voice dropped to an almost inaudible pitch. "A fairy knows these things."

"How?" Ro demanded. "How could you have not known that she lived? What did you do with her?"

"I—I—" Again her hand rested at her throat. "I placed her at the base of an enchanted tree. Gave the child a proper burial." She straightened, regaining her composure with the motion. "You see, huntress, a fairy is often present when a soul moves from this world to the next. The child's soul had already departed, yet those of your mortal family watching over her sickbed had not yet awakened and discovered it."

Ro couldn't respond. She remembered that night. She remembered the joy when Cosette made a full recovery, how no one questioned it.

Because no one remembered that a different babe had been in the cradle before their long night of vigil, Ro did not remember her fervent promise to the Fairy Queen to watch over her daughter always, and no one remembered that Grandmère had lived with them until that night, when she'd followed the fairy into the woods to where she'd placed the infant's body. Cendre's body. At the base of an enchanted tree.

The Fairy Queen said, "I would very much like to meet your sister. Apologize. Perhaps give her a gift for allowing my daughter to take her place?"

Ro's entire being ached that Cendre had not had this offer before she'd met the sirens. Something to take away the pain when her breathing trickled to almost nothing, perhaps?

Ro shook her head once. "She perished in my battle with the sirènes."

The fight drained from Ro, and it was all she could do to keep standing. Something warned her she shouldn't mention that Cendre was a siren now. Besides, the human girl Cendre was no more.

Ro dropped her head and took a weary breath. "I didn't even know who she was. Not until—after. I never had a chance to know her."

The barrier between her and the queen slipped away without Ro's notice, and then the queen was lifting Ro's chin with her finger.

"I am sorry for your loss, but do you regret life with my daughter so much? Is she not like a sister to you?"

Ro's tear-filled eyes met the queen's. "Of course she's my

sister. Of course I love her with all my heart and will always do so. But Cendre . . . Votre Majesté, you made me a protectress, and I could not protect my own sister. The sister of my blood, if not my heart."

The Fairy Queen smiled faintly, at once sympathetic and satisfied. "I told you it would not be easy, being my daughter's protectress. You accepted my bargain."

"Something I didn't know I'd done, because you took my memories. How could you do such a thing?"

She frowned. "Impossible." The Queen of the Fairies raised her hands on either side of Ro's head. "May I?"

Ro hesitated, not sure she wanted the Fairy Queen privy to her deepest thoughts.

"If you wish, I can look at things pertaining to your sisters only, and our bargain."

Ro's mind spun. "But you will not take them? My memories? I just got them back."

"I will not take them, nor any other memory. They should not have been taken from you in the first place. I need to see how such a thing could have happened. No one should be able to touch you, not as my daughter's protectress."

Hesitant, hopeful, Ro nodded. The Queen of the Fairies hadn't taken her memories? Then how had she lost them?

As the queen moved her hands closer, Ro jerked back once more. "And children?" Her throat burned, and she had to fight to get the rest out. "I am married, protectress of my grandmère's forest. Must I remain barren when my sister is surrounded by those who love her, protected by her husband and soldiers, now that I live in an entirely different kingdom?"

Sorrow and a hint of wariness entered the Fairy Queen's eyes. "My dear huntress. That part of our bargain cannot be undone, I'm afraid."

"But I was a child! You had no right to make such a bargain with someone too young to know better."

Now the queen's words turned sharp. "Would you have

done any differently? Would you have refused to protect my daughter had you known then the consequences of your actions? You could not have been the protectress she needed any other way."

Ro opened her mouth, then closed it.

Something cold and foreign entered the queen's eyes. "All of my paladins throughout history must accept the same bargain, huntress. It is how the magic works, and such a thing is not under my control. You protect your charge, not another. A child would only go against every instinct, as your very nature fought to protect your offspring above all else. You would either choose your child above my charge at the worst possible moment, unraveling your powers with a broken promise, or you would fight constantly with yourself, wavering, making you unfit. Either way, your mind would fracture under the strain."

She leaned forward, a queen terrible and mighty. "So I ask you again, would you still have accepted my bargain, knowing then what you know now?"

The knowledge sank in that the queen was being far more considerate than she had to be—she didn't have to explain a thing, and she'd borne Ro's fury with the patience of a patron saint.

Ro tried to temper her response, and with it, the realization of the truth was a balm to her heart. "Non, Majesté, you are right. I still would've accepted the bargain."

"Very well, then. Shall we continue?"

Her cold, inhuman eyes held Ro captive until she could manage a nod. The Queen of the Fairies closed her eyes. Ro followed suit. At once, they were in Ro's memories. Together.

Ro watched them with the Fairy Queen, every emotion fresh. They blew past recent events with Cosette, past Cosette's tears when Allura Aurore was under the sleeping curse, to when Ro returned from hunting the sirens.

Meeting Cendre for the first time. Together on the same

ship. Cendre, working near her. Cendre, casting furtive glances Ro's way, finding every opportunity to help the huntress. Yet Ro had seen her as a pest.

Something else struck Ro as she studied her sister's disguised-as-a-boy self.

She'd known. The whole time she was on the ship, she'd known Ro was her sister. And Ro had brushed her off.

Sickness claimed her gut, and it was all she could do not to vomit.

Then Olt, cradling Cendre close when they'd discovered her secret. And something Ro hadn't noticed then. He looked at Cendre the same way he did his sister, Odette.

When he turned his gaze upon Ro, however . . . Ro blushed to the roots of her hair. All the saints above, had he truly been that smitten with her? And she'd never even noticed? She consoled herself that he'd eventually won her, even if she was as blind as a bat and as dumb as a rock.

But then they were past the memory, leaving Ro reeling. She felt the queen's eyes upon her, but too much was pounding through her head at a relentless pace.

Then Ro was setting off to hunt the sirens, leaving Cosette to her new life as a married woman and the queen of France.

Each memory came to her, as crystal clear and poignant as the day each had happened, and Ro couldn't stop herself from experiencing them anew.

She winced when Cosette won Prince Trêve's heart right away and was able to help the prince break the curse of the beast Ro had been trying to break for three years.

Ro's eyes smarted with tears, the pain as fresh as the day it had happened.

The queen turned her gaze from the memories and studied Ro for a heartbeat, her ancient eyes seeing too much.

You know they were fated to be together, yes? From the moment of her birth, their lifelines were twined together by his mother and I. Your perceived loss of his affection had nothing to do with you, dear one.

Ro's mouth gaped a little, but then they continued flying through her memories, seeking, searching for the reason she'd lost them in the first place.

Ro becoming a huntress so she could provide for Cosette. Ro and Cosette growing up together. Cosette's sweetness. Ro's fierce protectiveness of her.

They went back, back, back in Ro's memories, to when she was a child, fervently promising the Queen of the Fairies to protect Cosette always, as if a part of her had known she hadn't been able to do that for her other sister, even if she couldn't remember.

"Non, non, non," the Fairy Queen muttered. "Your memories were crystal clear then."

"But I didn't know," Ro dared to interject. The queen slid a look her way, and Ro swallowed and continued. "Just like the rest of my family, I didn't know you'd switched my sister with your daughter. So my memories were altered then, and by your own hand."

The queen's jaw ticked. "What you fail to realize, my dear, is that any alteration was due to my daughter living in your household. You agreed, yes, but the exchange itself is what led your family to accept her. Not my directly affecting your memory." She frowned. "Well, not in the way you mean."

Ro sighed. She had a feeling they were splitting hairs, speaking of the same thing but using different words.

"Now be quiet," the queen continued, "so I can get on with this."

Ro did so. They flew so quickly through Ro's memories, it felt as though there should be wind on her face, in her hair, as they swept past the entirety of Ro's life.

Because everything Ro had done had been for her sister. So of course the Fairy Queen could see it. Of course the fey woman would find such a loophole.

Ro should've known better.

All bargains with the fey came with such danger.

"Ah! Here it is."

Ro's memories halted on a time, long ago, when she'd gone up against a monster called Bluebeard. Her first hunt in Gautier's employ. He'd sewn his magic into her skin, paralyzing her, with the intent of adding her to his collection of immobile-yet-barely-alive mannequins—his wives.

After she'd lifted his head from his shoulders with his axe and woken his wives, those who'd survived anyway, the experience had affected her so deeply, the torture she'd been through as a new huntress had nearly broken her.

She'd never experienced such evil before, someone who derived pleasure from causing pain, from murder.

Although she'd been asleep, she could see just as clearly as the Queen of the Fairies when the well-intentioned woman, his latest wife who had not yet succumbed to his killing spree, had rooted around in Ro's memories, making her burden easier to handle, making it that much easier for other fey to mess with Ro's mind.

Making it easier to fall into Madame LaChance's trap.

As if plunging into ice water, Ro's memories went blank.

She waited, but they remained snuffed out. Back in the pure-white room, Ro glanced to the queen, but her eyes were closed, fierce concentration upon her face.

Yet nothing more came to Ro.

The memories were still there, they were simply no longer shuffling through them like a deck of cards.

After another agonizing moment, the queen's eyes opened, and what Ro saw there chilled her to the bone. Void of any warmth, her eyes pierced Ro in a stare that spoke of mistrust. "You have cut me off from your memories. How?"

Oh. That was what happened. Wait, what?

"I—do not know, votre Majesté. I did not mean to." Ro held perfectly still. She hadn't deliberately kicked the Fairy Queen out, yet it had happened the moment she'd thought of Madame LaChance. Odd.

The Fairy Queen turned, made her way up a tower of steps, and sat on an elaborate throne upon a dais. It was made of what looked like spun sugar and translucent caramel decorations, all the same pure white with hidden lights within.

"That is all I can see, Rosette. Your memories begin to unravel when Madame de la Tour tried to ease your suffering."

"Yet had you not first influenced my memories of Cendre, would I have been so easily influenced by Bluebeard's wife?"

A frown flitted across the queen's face. "I will look into this matter personally, Rosette. I owe your family much, and I truly regret your ability was hampered in such a way. And I regret the loss of a life that had not yet lived. It is most peculiar indeed."

Ro took a deep breath, and with the exhale, much of her sorrow and anger trickled away. "Merci beaucoup, votre Majesté."

The Fairy Queen inclined her head slightly.

"Why have you called me here? Surely it wasn't just to root around in my memories." Ro frowned. "And where is here, exactly?"

"I have to limit my time in your realm, huntress. And I do not think you would fare well in mine. I have called you to an in-between place." The Queen of the Fairies glanced around her. "Though I am not at all certain what you see here."

Ro answered promptly. "I see a grand throne room and a great throne, white on white, with fairy lights dancing through the air and giving off an ice-white glow."

The Fairy Queen gave a small smile at that. "Ah. Cosette sees a garden glade with a brook and a tree swing."

Ro blinked. Cosette came here too? But why?

"The reason I have called you here," the Fairy Queen said, interrupting Ro's thoughts, "is because I keep catching glimpses of something traveling through your realm that should not be there, only I cannot find it, and I do not know what it is."

Ro frowned. "It wouldn't be the Wolf King, would it? Because I banished him —"

"No," the Fairy Queen said decisively. "The Erlking does not sneak. He bashes in and lets his presence be known, and his Wild Hunt takes him far and wide, across all the realms, always hunting, always searching, and his underlings are unlike any of my own. He is not the one I seek."

"Why did you let him in my realm?"

The Queen of the Fairies gave her a look that said she was trying to be patient. "I do not *let* him go anywhere. He does as he pleases. Only one of your ilk could revoke his passage into your realm." She smiled. "I'm amazed he allowed his banishment for so long a term. A thousand years," she mused. "Fascinating."

Ro clenched her jaw. "I shouldn't have let him come back at all."

With a tinkling laugh, the queen said, "Oh, huntress, you could not have stopped him a moment longer. He will never abandon the search for his mate, no matter how often I urge him to. Now, on to my business."

The Fairy Queen leaned forward, and Ro felt as though the room shrank as her full attention riveted on Ro. "Have you any news of such a creature? One who hides in the shadows, slinks through the land, remaining unseen yet tainting all it touches?"

Trying not to let her fear show, Ro shook her head. "I assure you I do not, Majesté, though I am happy to keep watch for such a creature."

The Queen of the Fairies sat back with a frown, and although Ro took a full breath as the pressure of her looming presence eased, the frown turned her insides to water. Had the Fairy Queen grown in size?

"See that you do." She waved a hand dismissively. "You'll

be richly rewarded when you bring me word. What the creature is, how it hunts, what it hunts, and how it remains hidden from me."

Hesitantly, Ro asked, "This wouldn't happen to be another bargain, would it, Majesté?"

A flash of something like appreciation crossed her face, before the expression cleared and she was the unflappable Fairy Queen once more. "Ah. Caught that, did you? Very well. Should you do this for me, I shall owe you a favor. Once, and only once, you may call upon me in an hour of direst need."

Ro didn't like the sound of that. Not one of her interactions with the fey had been fully positive, and she didn't know if she even *wanted* the Queen of the Fairies riding in on a chariot pulled by dragons to come to her rescue.

Or so she'd read that's how fairy queens liked to fly about, since they didn't have wings.

"That is . . . most kind. But what happens if I don't find anything?"

The Fairy Queen frowned and contemplated. "I cannot escape the feeling that should this creature get away from us, something horrible will befall the realm of humans that will then affect the Land of the Fey. But I cannot for the life of me figure out what that might be. It is hidden from those who can catch glimpses of the future, though they all agree a sense of . . . heaviness, of wrongness, trails this being."

Although she tried not to let dread burrow deep inside, the Fairy Queen's words made Ro's heart beat faster. What was this creature? Was it worse than the Wolf King? Er, Erlking?

The queen sighed. "Though they do not think the creature is the threat I perceive it to be, I know I am right. It must be eradicated."

Just when Ro thought she'd be able to take a break, spend time with Olt, enjoy their new life together, she was pulled right back into the fey realm's mess.

Could she not have peace for once?

The queen's eyes flew to Ro's and captured her gaze as if physically holding her there. "Tell Cosette. Warn her. I . . . cannot speak of it to her. Each time I try . . . I cannot."

Ro bowed. "It shall be done, Majesté."

"Bon. I need you to begin the hunt, right away. You'll set off the moment you're back in the human realm —"

"Non." She hadn't meant to say it so forcefully, but there it was, bursting from her mouth like ripe fruit exploding.

"I beg your pardon?" The queen's eyes were not friendly.

Ro spread her hands, trying to appeal to her softer side. "I'm newly married. I've been tasked with caring for the Black Forest. I'll keep my eyes open, watch for a creature such as you've described. But s'il vous plaît, I ask for a reprieve. Cosette is safe. She has her own family, and many who look after her. I only wish to get to know my new husband and to watch over my forest, nothing more." She paused. "If the creature comes to me, I'll hunt it. But I'm not chasing it down. Not yet."

Because the moment she caught it, the queen would have another task for her. And due to her bargain with the forest, she could no longer live the nomadic lifestyle she had as a huntress.

Ro couldn't read the queen's gaze, but it remained cold and lifeless, and she had a feeling nothing she'd said was making a difference.

So be it. Ro took a deep breath and steeled her spine. "I am not accepting another hunt right now, votre Majesté. I cannot."

The queen's eyes blazed, and Ro felt the heat, physically.

"I will keep an eye on my forest, listen for rumors, and warn Cosette, but I cannot abandon my forest so soon after taking on my mantle."

The Fairy Queen stood and took one step, just one, and she was standing so close they breathed the same air. Her voice dropped an octave. "Careful, girl. I'm the one who gave you your powers, and I can take them away just as easily."

Ro's mouth snapped closed. She couldn't move, couldn't respond—fear froze her to the floor as surely as if vines reached up and held her there.

"I have a new mantle now," she managed to whisper.

"Your promise to me supersedes that one."

Ro lifted her chin, her voice growing bolder. "Not since Cosette married, it doesn't."

The queen's jaw tightened. Aha. Ro thought so.

Emboldened, Ro continued. "I may have been under your power once, but not anymore. Not since I accepted my grand-mère's mantle."

"Yet you still wear mine." The Fairy Queen reached out and plucked at the edge of Ro's red cloak. "And if I unravel it right now?"

Fear crashed in her heart, and Ro's resolve crumpled. Once again, Ro couldn't move, scared the queen was about to rip her mère's cloak from her shoulders and tear it to shreds, then it would be no more. Her eyes begged the queen not to, but she was too terrified to say anything.

"That's what I thought." The Fairy Queen moved back to her throne, sitting upon it with the regalness of a queen used to getting her way. "Because if you do not do as I ask, huntress, not only shall I strip you of your power, there will be dire consequences not even you can imagine."

Ro swallowed and asked the question burning in her throat. "Why? What will happen?" She had to know.

"You will continue to wear my cloak?"

Nodding furiously, Ro would've promised almost anything to keep her mère's cloak. The Queen of the Fairies may have somehow woven her powers into the strands, but her mère had made it, had stitched it together lovingly with her hands, had given it to her, and every time Ro wore it, she felt her mère's arms around her. She couldn't lose it. She couldn't.

She'd figure out how to separate it from the Fairy Queen later.

It seemed like the queen wasn't going to answer, but then she paused and tilted her head, as if listening to something. With a heavy sigh, she said, "The veil between our words is aging."

"Aging? You mean, getting older? More brittle? Thinner, perhaps?" Ro snapped her mouth closed, realizing she was babbling, unnerved by the threat to her cloak, her mère's final gift to her.

"Non, it's getting too thick. As it ages, it solidifies." She frowned. "But this should not be. The veil is ageless. Yet it is thickening, hardening, starving those who pass from my side to yours. I cannot figure out what has gone wrong. Or how to fix it."

"And that's bad because . . ."

"Because, huntress, the veil is the only way my kind can survive in your world. If it solidifies, the fey can no longer enter your realm."

That didn't sound like such a bad thing. Most creatures that came through wanted to eat people, and if she couldn't get them to stop or send them back, she had to put them down.

Life would be so much easier if fey who fed on humans stayed in the fey realm.

Ro frowned. "I repaired the tears where the loups-garous pushed through. Perhaps I could—"

"Non, this is different," the Fairy Queen interrupted. "You repaired what is already there. I must heal its source so that it continues to regenerate. Yet it does not respond to my ministrations."

"What does this have to do with the creature you cannot find, Majesté?"

"Bah! Absolutely nothing. No more than I must find a way to heal the veil, and you are well suited to find the monster.

Since I cannot, you must. Both are urgent matters, and my attention must not be divided."

"And what happens if you cannot heal the veil?" Ro asked, remembering how when she'd stretched it over the loups-garous, to send them back to the fey realm, it had grown firm, unwieldy, unwilling to stretch and bend to her will.

She'd assumed she'd simply been doing it wrong, that she hadn't learned what she needed to know yet.

But non. The veil was weary, old, getting ready to close itself off for some reason.

"It is not your concern, huntress. The veil is mine, the beast is yours. Are you willing to accept responsibility if you refuse to hunt it and it kills those precious humans your heart bleeds to protect? If it kills *my* people? Believe you me, you will face my wrath if such a thing should come to pass."

Ro bit her lip. The queen knew exactly where to sink her blade, and Ro had handed it to her on a silver platter.

She'd never allow the creature in her memories again. If she could help it.

But the damage had already been done.

Ro chose every word carefully. "I will tell Cosette, as you have asked. I will ask her to send her huntsmen to search for it. And if they bring me word of the creature and proof of its danger to the human realm, I will hunt it. As my forest allows."

Cosette could mobilize Liam's huntsmen far better than Ro. They were some of the best trackers in the world.

The Queen of the Fairies stared back at her with such a cold, inhuman gaze, Ro had the sudden fear that the queen might not let her leave this realm. Her body would never be found.

And Olt would never know what happened to her, for surely this creature would hide her death from Cosette, as she wanted nothing more than for her daughter to think well of her.

Ro had to say something before fear clawed her throat shut. "That is all I can do, Majesté. Take it or leave it."

"You are a cruel and unfeeling human, huntress."

Pot, kettle. Minus the human part.

"Do you not believe me when I speak of danger? Of urgency? Do you not truly care for your fellow mortals as you portray?"

Ro swallowed. "I do. But there will always be another beast, and if my duties to the Black Forest slip, violent fey will flood my realm, and I'll have more than one beast to slay on my hands. Many more of my people will die."

She couldn't allow such a thing to happen again.

The queen's jaw tightened. She knew Ro was right.

Ro waited. It was up to the queen now to decide what she could accept. Ro no longer had to do exactly what she said.

"Very well." The Fairy Queen sighed. "Keep your eyes open, huntress. Be vigilant. I may call you to visit me here again. And please, call on me if you find something. Anything at all."

"But I don't know how to . . . oh."

Once again, the distance between them evaporated.

The queen held out a mirror, silver and of an ornate design, much like the one Ro had used to communicate with the beast, long ago, and a silver ring, much like the one the beast had used to transport her to Gautier's château and back.

She should've known both objects were of fey design.

She took them carefully from the queen. "Merci."

"You know how to use them, I trust?"

"Oui."

"Bon. Then I bid you adieu, Mademoiselle Rosette Jacqueline LeFèvre Reynard."

This time, Ro had the urge to correct her with her new married name, but she didn't want to spend a moment longer in this creature's presence.

Ro hoped it didn't look like she was fleeing as she turned to go.

"Huntress?"

Ro glanced back at the queen.

Her voice and demeanor gentled. "Do not be afraid of the love you have found. It is a rare and precious gift, and it tends to only survive those who feed it, choose it, and treat it well."

Heat rushed to her face, and Ro didn't know how to handle the change from snow queen to concerned, matronly figure. So she nodded and spun away. She couldn't get away from the queen fast enough. But then she realized she had no idea how to get back. She turned around slowly.

The queen returned to her throne and sat, suddenly appearing drawn and fatigued. She noticed Ro standing there. "Go, human. I've shielded my granddaughter these many months, and I am weary."

"I understand," Ro said quietly. "And I'm so pleased you were watching over Allura Aurore."

The Queen of the Fairies held her gaze for three heartbeats, then gave her a nod and swirled her fingers. A whorl of snow whipped around Ro in an upright circle, and then she was back in the Parisian palace.

Before Ro could even blink, she was staggering forward from the disorientation that came from traveling between realms.

And that made her wonder how many realms there were, for some reason.

She cried out and would've fallen, but before she could face-plant on the shining marble floor, a strong arm came around her, and Ro found herself plastered against a warm and familiar chest.

"Ro! Where did you go? We've been searching everywhere for you."

She looked up into Olt's concerned eyes, and her entire world homed in on him. He had followed her across oceans, across France, across the Black Forest, all the way to Angleterre and back, just because she needed him. Because he wanted to be with her.

And she'd almost thrown the goodness she'd found with him away because she was scared. Well she refused to live in fear any longer.

She would enjoy every day she had with him.

Now that he was all hers.

Ro didn't think about it, didn't second-guess herself, just launched herself at Olt and kissed him with all her might. He caught her up close, returning her kiss with a fervor she felt down to her toes.

She pulled away and looked straight into his eyes. "I love you. If I've never told you before, I love you, and I'm so glad you're not a swan anymore, and that you returned from the sirènes unharmed. I don't know what I would've done had you not come for me. I'm so glad I married you, Olt, truly. It was the best decision I ever made."

Before Ro could feel self-conscious, Olt gave her a look that erased every lingering doubt and gathered her close, kissing her like he was getting what he'd always wanted and thought he'd never have.

Ro melted against him, her arms wrapping around his neck of their own accord. She barely noticed the mirror and ring clutched in her fingers. He pulled her closer, and she moved deeper into his embrace, certain she could never be close enough.

"Not again," Claude grumbled. "There isn't enough soap in the world to cleanse my eyes."

Ro gasped mid-kiss and jerked back, but Olt stared at her with a look she'd only seen a few times but couldn't decipher. And he didn't release her. Not right away.

"Ugh, Ro, seriously? Couldn't you have waited till we'd

left or something?" Claude rubbed his eyes as if he wished he could scour them from his face. "I can't ever unsee that."

To her dismay, Ro found herself the center of a bewildered and uncomfortable audience.

Pascal was looking at the ceiling, obviously pretending he hadn't seen a thing.

Her eyes drifted toward Liam, and heat crept up her neck. He was steadily gazing at the ground, as if waiting for the awkward moment to be over.

Olt was still staring at her like she was his whole world while he kept his arm around her waist.

Ro's eyes settled on Cosette. "I just saw the Fairy Queen. We need to talk."

Cosette blinked at Ro, then swept away in a flurry of skirts, clearly expecting Ro to follow.

"Is there anything we can do, huntress?" Liam asked in a low voice.

She didn't know how to answer that. "Let me talk to Cosette first, but . . . oui. Be ready. Be vigilant."

"As if we need to be told that," Claude scoffed. "Goodnight, but I am never searching for you again when Olt is around." And with that he stalked off, calling over his shoulder, "Let us know when we can be useful. And when there's no more kissing. Blergh! That was awful."

He made gagging noises as he strode away. Pascal immediately followed, not quite fleeing, but it was a near thing. Liam strode after them silently.

Ro didn't think she'd ever blushed harder in her life.

She edged away, and Olt released her reluctantly.

"Ro . . ." His voice was deep, husky.

Before she could get distracted kissing him again, Ro squeezed his hand. "I'll tell you everything, I promise. After I talk to Cosette. Are our horses still ready?"

He shook his head. "I honestly don't know. When you didn't come, and Cosette said she hadn't seen you, well, I may have panicked and gotten everyone I could find to look for you." He gave her a sheepish grin. "I know I shouldn't have worried, but you'd been gone several hours, and, well, after last time . . ."

Ro stepped close. "I'm not going anywhere, Olt. And if I do, I'll always find my way back to you. Always. You're not getting rid of me, sailor."

And with that, Ro gave Olt another heartfelt kiss and hurried after her sister, his smile warming her through.

As Ro followed Cosette to her private sitting room, she slipped the ring on her middle finger opposite the hand her wedding ring was on and tucked the mirror into her belt. She entered a few steps behind her sister. Two soldiers took up positions at either side of the heavy gilded doors and swung them shut.

Before she could say anything, Ro turned to find Cosette's arms coming around her. "I'm so happy for you," she whispered. Cosette pulled back and cupped Ro's cheek in one hand. "I love how happy he makes you. You are glowing."

Ro flushed, and it was all she could do to hold her sister's gaze. "I love how happy he makes me too."

It took a monumental effort to say such words aloud. She wasn't used to allowing herself to be happy.

Cosette kissed her other cheek and stepped back, her demeanor changing in an instant. "Now, tell me everything my mère said."

THE END

Ro's story continues in

Stop the
Snow Queen

Book Five of the Beast Hunters.

Available Now from L2L2 Publishing.

THANK YOU!

Thank you for reading this book!
Did you enjoy *Slay the Wolf*?
Please leave a review!
It helps new readers find my books,
lets me know what you think,
and encourages me to keep going.
Thank you so much!

~Michele Israel Harper

ACKNOWLEDGMENTS

To my readers. I write these stories for you. Thank you for such lovely responses and excitement over my books! It keeps me writing.

To my alpha reader, Alicia. My goodness, I love that you are my first reader. You make my stories so much better! I love the way you think.

To my beta readers, Heidi, TJ, Stephany, and Cathrine. I cannot thank you enough for catching plot holes! Every time you mention something to fix, I squeal, because I love making the story tighter. And thank you for pointing out when I got something right!

To my editor, Jasmine. I love working with you so much. Thank you for making this story shine! Your comments are spot on, and I am *thrilled* with all the changes to make the story stronger.

To Jenelle. Oh my goodness, your ART! I stand in awe of the portraits you create, and I am beyond honored that you work with *me*. I can't wait to see what you come up with next.

To Sara. Your paperback covers are glorious! Thank you from the bottom of my heart for bringing my covers to life—I love working with you so very much. That wolf is so much scarier, thank you!

To Laura. Your character art! And your hardback covers! I am positively giddy every time you send me a new illustration. Thank you!

To my family. Thank you for your patience with me as I pen these tales. I love what I do, and I appreciate your support.

And to my Lord and Savior Jesus Christ. Thank you for the beautiful gift of writing. I hope I do it justice!

With all my heart,

~Michele Israel Harper

ABOUT THE AUTHOR

Michele Israel Harper spends her days as a freelance editor, her afternoons guzzling coffee, and her nights spinning her own tales. Sleep? Sometimes . . .

Not only does she have her master's degree in publishing, she is also slightly obsessed with all things French—including Jeanne d'Arc and *La Belle et la Bête*—and loves curling up with a good book more than just about anything else.

Her previous experience in the publishing world includes acquisitions editor, line and copy editor, and writing-group leader; she is currently the author of multiple published novels (with more on the way); and she is most giddy about winning six Excellence in Editing Awards for her work as an editor.

Michele prays her continued involvement in writing, editing, and publishing will create many enjoyable books in the years to come.

Visit MicheleIsraelHarper.com to drop her a note or to learn about future books!

Michele loves to hear from her readers! Follow her on social media, check out her website, or drop her a line to let her know what you thought of Slay the Wolf. *Happy reading!*

www.MicheleIsraelHarper.com
Facebook: @MicheleIsraelHarper
Twitter: @MicheleIHarper
Instagram: @Michele_Israel_Harper

Join her newsletter for bookish news and an ebook copy of
The Lost Slipper!
MicheleIsraelHarper.com/My-Newsletter

FRENCH AND GERMAN GUIDE

Below is a quick guide to the French and German words I used in this book. I tried to ensure they were self-explanatory, had a translation close to the word used, and were sparingly used.

But in case you have questions, the meaning should be explained here.

I adore absolutely everything French, and I hope my love for this exquisite language and beautiful country and lovely people came through a little. Bon voyage!

- Angleterre: England
- Arrête: Stop
- Bienvenue: Welcome
- Bon: Good
- Bonjour: Good morning / good day / hello
- Ça va?: You good? Are you all right?
- Ça va: I'm good or I'm fine
- Château: Castle
- D'accord: Okay (But since "okay" wasn't around in the 18th Century, it means "all right" here.)
- De rien: You're welcome or it is nothing

- Désolé / Je suis désolé: Sorry / I am sorry
- Dieu: God
- Enchantée: Nice to meet you
- Excuse-moi: Excuse me, familiar
- Excusez-moi: Excuse me, formal
- Frère: Brother
- Grandmère: Grandmother*
- Incroyable: Incredible
- Livre: French money
- Madame: Ma'am
- Mademoiselle / Mesdemoiselles: Miss / Misses
- Magnifique: Magnificent
- Ma Reine: My Queen
- Merci: Thank you
- Merci beaucoup: Thank you very much
- Mère / Maman: Mother / Mom
- Mon ami: My friend
- Mon amour: My love
- Mon Roi: My King
- Monsieur / Messieurs: Sir / sirs
- N'est-ce pas: Is it not? Isn't it so?
- Non: No
- Oui: Yes
- Pardon: Pardon me
- Parfait: Perfect
- Père / Papa: Father / Dad
- Regarde: Look
- Rien: Nothing
- S'il vous plaît: Please—literally, "if you please"
- Sirènes: Sirens or Mermaids
- Sœur: Sister
- Tante: Aunt
- Vos Majestés: Your Majesties
- Votre Majesté: Your Majesty

GERMAN:

- Bitte: You're welcome
- Danke: Thank you
- Fräulein: Miss
- Gott: God
- Ja: Yes
- Mein Freund: My friend
- Mutter: Mother
- Nein: No
- Vater: Father

*Note: Technically, it should be "grand-mère" in French, but in all honestly, I just don't like how it looks. Since English is closed construction, I took the liberty of using "grandmère" in this series. I hope you'll forgive my changing it to match my preference!

More from L2L2 Publishing

If you enjoyed this book, you may also enjoy:

Every day is the same torture for Cosette at the hands of her stepmère and stepsisters. Until an encounter with a fairy of the forest and an invitation to a fête in honor of Monsieur Gautier promises Cosette's life is about to become the beautiful fairy tale of her dreams. Or so the story should go. Except her fairy godmère demands a high price for her help. Her stepsisters are as afraid of their mère as Cosette is. And the handsome Monsieur Gautier hides a dreadful secret, one she's desperate to know—if only she can get close enough. Cosette is faced with a difficult choice: Should she feign ignorance and accept her happily ever after? Or dig deeper to find what may be lurking beneath?

More from L2L2 Publishing
Read the Whole Series so far!

French huntress Ro LeFèvre chases fairy tale creatures across France, Angleterre, Prussia, the Caribbean, and more, to protect those she loves. Join her as she's hired to kill beasts, hunt sirens, break curses, depose queens, and negotiate peace, all to end the fey's destruction across the human realm. The Beast Hunters series is sprinkled with many beloved fairy tales, full of frightful creatures, and complete at seven books. End the Fey and Restore the Realm coming soon!

WHERE WILL WE TAKE YOU NEXT?

Devour *Beast Hunter,*
Hunt with *Kill the Beast,*
Sink into *Silence the Siren,*
Reread *Quell the Nightingale,*
and Discover *Slay the Wolf.*

All at
micheleisraelharper.com/bookstore
or your local or online retailer.

Happy Reading!
~The L2L2 Publishing Team

www.ingramcontent.com/pod-product-compliance
Lightning Source LLC
Chambersburg PA
CBHW031734180726
48283CB00005B/1512